A LESSON IN THORNS

SIERRA SIMONE

Cover Design: Hang Le
Image: Iness Rychlik
Interior Layout: Caitlin Greer

Editing: Nancy Smay of Evident Ink, Erica Russikoff of Erica Edits
Proofing: Michele Ficht

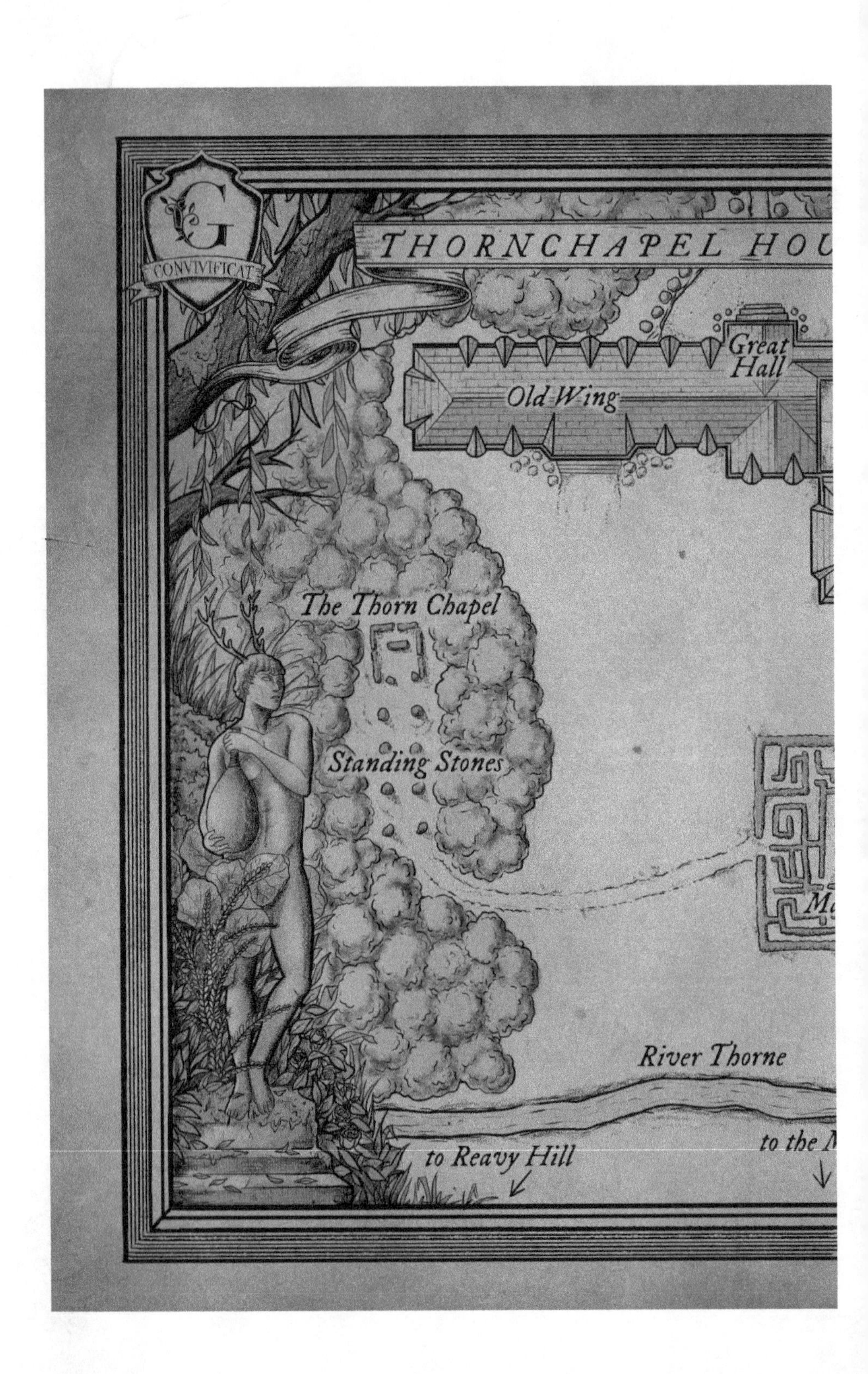
G
CONVIVIFICAT
THORNCHAPEL
Great Hall
Old Wing
The Thorn Chapel
Standing Stones
River Thorne
to Reavy Hill
to the

USE AND ENVIRONS
Library
Courtyard
South Wing
South Tower
Kitchen Garden
Walled Garden
aze
Moors
to Equinox Stones

In the faint moonlight, the grass is singing
Over the tumbled graves, about the chapel
There is the empty chapel, only the wind's home.
It has no windows, and the door swings,
Dry bones can harm no one.

T.S. Eliot, *The Waste Land*

Prologue

They found the roses right away.

The thorns took longer.

First, there was the escape, which wasn't an escape at all, really. The adults were busy with whatever it was that kept them cloistered and murmuring in the library, and the children were otherwise unsupervised since no one thought any harm could come to them this far into the countryside.

Then there was the maze—which only Auden could navigate with any confidence, this being his house after all—and it only took a single hour to find the center, and in the center, the roses twining around the base of the stone Adonis and Aphrodite, all their blooms white and fragrant and blown.

Fat bees blundered in a drunken crowd. A storm threatened overhead. And only an exploring child would have bothered to crawl under the small fountain at the statue's base to find the secret inside.

Today there were six exploring children.

And they found the secret inside.

Finally, after a dark and damp journey through the tunnel even Auden hadn't known about, they came to a gate with a latch rusted right through. St. Sebastian kicked it open.

Becket fretted, and Delphine yelled about the torn spiderweb and the spider that no longer had a home. Rebecca only rolled her eyes and helped St. Sebastian drag the thing open far enough that all six of them could squeeze through.

Proserpina was last because Proserpina was always last. Not because she was disliked or because she was timid, but because she was dreaming on her feet while everyone else was walking.

The gate led to a path so old that it had sunk into the earth. Trees branched and arced overhead, and to the sides were unbroken woods—oak, ash, birch, and beech. Rowan and elder. All leafy and lush and ivy-clad. Between them, blackthorn trees straggled at intervals, their thorns long and cruel, and their branches clumped with the dark pearls of early sloe.

Though it was only just past lunch, the heavy clouds darkened everything to twilight, and the wind tugged insistently on the leaves, making the entire path around them seem restless and alive.

"Auden, where does it go?" Rebecca asked. She and Delphine were both trying to be in the front, but neither of them really knew where they were going, and so their jostling was less violent than normal.

"I don't know," Auden said, bouncing a little.

He knew where everything went in *London*, where his family lived most of the time. Every road led to another road, every car and bus and train had a destination. Every day had a plan, and every plan had a goal, and every goal had a reason.

At Thornchapel, none of this was true.

At Thornchapel, time could slip by unmarked and you could walk places no one had walked in years. Maybe centuries.

This was the first day Auden began to see this, began to see the ways one of his homes was different than the other, even if he couldn't articulate it. He was old enough to feel it, to *feel* Thornchapel, even if he couldn't name what it was he felt, and he was old enough to love it, but not old enough to understand.

And maybe that's why later he would grow to hate it.

They walked for ten minutes more, maybe twenty, but so far away from the house and with nothing but trees whispering close, it felt much longer. It felt like they were brave, like they were having an adventure, with the bite of genuine fear that any real adventure is required to have. And then the trees opened up to a clearing.

Nearly knee-high grass waved against crooked standing stones, which were barely taller than the grass itself. They were arranged in a narrow row, and at the end—

"The thorn chapel," somebody murmured. It might have been Becket, but it didn't matter. They all realized it at the same time.

The chapel was really only recognizable by a remaining chunk of wall, on which a glassless window remained with its distinctive arch. The rest of the walls had crumbled into drifts of stone, barely visible over the layers of moss and grass and roots. Blackthorn trees—more like bushes—pushed up from the ancient rubble. Wild dog roses—just as thorny, just as sprawling—grew everywhere else in hues of almost-white and almost-pink.

It *was* a church. Only the walls had been replaced with thorns and the floor with grass, and where the altar should have been was a large grassy hummock instead. And everywhere flowers—not only the roses, but wood sorrel and foxglove and violets and meadowsweet in restrained riots of white and purple.

Delphine and Rebecca raced to the front while Becket approached the chapel from the side in awe. St. Sebastian found a stick and started whacking at the flowers to slice off their heads. Proserpina slipped into the stone row—the entrance of which was guarded by two tall menhirs—and began dreaming her way toward the chapel itself.

And Auden stood at the edge of the woods, unable to take a single step closer.

It's really here.

It wasn't a quaint name, chosen on a whim. It wasn't, as he'd once heard his grandfather say, a corruption of a Latin word referencing the thick forest canopy around the house.

There was a chapel.

It was covered in thorns.

Thornchapel.

And he had the strangest feeling that as he thought the name of this place, the place thought his own name back to him…

No one later remembered whose idea the wedding was, but it had probably started as a fight between Rebecca and Delphine, since that's how most of their ideas that summer had begun. But once the idea had been voiced, there'd been no doubt that it was a good idea, even to Becket who was really too old for these kinds of things. There was a chapel, after all, and something that looked like an altar, and weddings were something you did in chapels, in front of altars.

There was a brief fight about *who* should get married, because it seemed common sense that Auden, as the sort of lord of the manor, should be the groom, but Delphine and Rebecca both wanted to be the bride and their fight over it grew so heated that St. Sebastian observed, “You already fight like Auden’s parents, maybe you two should get married.”

This was not received well, by the girls or by Auden, and then Becket the peacemaker pointed out that Proserpina had already wandered down to the chapel proper and so it might as well be her. Rebecca and Delphine sullenly agreed to be bridesmaid and flower girl, respectively; Becket, as the oldest, appointed himself the priest; Auden turned to St. Sebastian and said, “Will you be the best man?”

St. Sebastian sniffed. “I’m already the best man.”

Auden rolled his eyes. He did that a lot with St. Sebastian.

“I’m going to sit in the back and interrupt the wedding,” St. Sebastian declared.

Auden sighed. “What?”

“You know, like in the movies. They say ‘speak now or forever hold your peace’ and then someone always speaks.”

“But that’s not real life.”

“And this is?”

He had a point, but Auden didn’t want to admit it. Something else he did rather a lot of with St. Sebastian.

No one really could remember the order of a wedding service, except that the flower girl came first. Becket and Auden waited by the uneven lump that had once been an altar while Delphine scattered hastily gathered rose petals down the center of the ruin. Then came

Rebecca, carrying a bouquet of foxgloves because they were tall and interesting compared with the retiring violets and sorrel. St. Sebastian sprawled in the back, lazily tossing pebbles into the air.

Auden felt strange so close to the altar, like the air around it was infused with an electric charge, or maybe that was merely the oncoming storm, or maybe it was that he was a boy playing a game he hadn't actually agreed to and he was bored. Whatever it was, he suddenly felt the fierce need to hurt something. Or to feel hurt himself. He couldn't figure out which, and the two needs tangled up into an untidy knot in his chest thornier than the chapel around them, and it felt like the knot was all he was, all he ever could be—

Proserpina entered the chapel with a crown of flowers on her head. The knot eased; it untangled some. And when St. Sebastian decided that Proserpina needed someone to walk her down the aisle and he hopped up to take her arm, Auden quite literally could not breathe for a second. He didn't know why—St. Sebastian irritated him, Proserpina fascinated him, but he wasn't entirely sure he liked her for having that effect on him—so why now, when the two of them approached the altar and approached him, did he think of the need to hurt and the need to *be* hurt and why did he want to grab them both and pull them into that need? Grab them and somehow shove them deep into his heart of thorns forever?

He couldn't speak as St. Sebastian escorted Proserpina right to Auden's feet and then gave her a puckish kiss on the cheek that had Proserpina laughing and Delphine scolding and Rebecca shushing Delphine's scolds and their resident barely-teenage priest tutting at the disruption of order.

"I thought you were going to interrupt the ceremony," Becket sighed as St. Sebastian took a seat on a nearby clump of grass.

"I can do both," St. Sebastian said in an *obviously* kind of tone.

Becket made a put-upon face, which was only slightly different than his normal pious expression, and then continued with as much as he remembered about wedding ceremonies.

There was a *dearly beloved* and then a story about Adam and Eve, and then he finally said the part St. Sebastian was waiting for, *speak now or forever hold your peace.*

They all looked over to the boy, who was currently grinning mischievously and was very busy *not* interrupting the wedding. Auden arched an eyebrow at him.

St. Sebastian arched one back, but still did nothing.

It seemed like the threat had passed, so Becket moved on to the vows. "Do you, Auden Guest take Proserpina Markham to be your lawfully wedded wife? You have to say *I do* here."

Auden, still afflicted with that disturbing and paradoxical need, answered in a distracted voice, "I d—"

"I do!" St. Sebastian jumped in, hopping up between them.

"Ugh, God," went Delphine.

"*Shh!*" went Rebecca.

"And DO YOU, PROSERPINA, TAKE AUDEN TO BE YOUR LAWFULLY WEDDED HUSBAND," shouted the young priest above the chaos, and smiling, Proserpina said, "I do," even as St. Sebastian once again interrupted her vows with his own emphatic, "I DO!" and yanked her flower crown onto his own head as if he were the bride.

Even Auden had trouble not smiling, although those thorns of hurt were everywhere in him now; he felt like he was going to break apart like one of the chapel walls or fall over like the altar; he felt like he was never going to fit inside his own skin unless he became someone else, some*thing* else, some*when* else.

But he didn't need to be some*where* else. He knew that, even if he didn't know how he knew that.

Thornchapel was right. Proserpina and St. Sebastian fighting over the flower crown in front of him felt right.

It was only him that felt wrong.

"This is *not how weddings work*," Becket accused. "St. Sebastian, stop it. Give back the flower crown."

"No," said St. Sebastian.

"You *have* to because three people can't kiss, only two can," Delphine said knowledgeably.

"There's going to be kissing?" Proserpina said, suddenly sounding very, very awake.

"That's stupid," Rebecca said back to Delphine. "Three people can kiss. All six of us could kiss if we wanted."

"Yes, there is kissing," Becket said to Proserpina, with the grave tones of one who knows these things.

"We don't have to kiss," Auden said quietly to his bride.

"Well, I want to," St. Sebastian declared, which surprised absolutely no one.

Becket pinched his nose, looking exactly like an exasperated grown-up. "No one asked you."

Delphine was still fighting with Rebecca, and she wrinkled her nose, which was one of those things that made her look even prettier than normal. "At the same time? It wouldn't work."

"You don't know *everything*, you know—"

Every moment of Auden's unmet destiny bit his skin and punctured his heart, and every second he stood still was a jagged clamp around his throat.

He had—he had to do—

Something—

Thornchapel—

Wounds and dying and fires burning against the night—

Sparks hissing as he was brought back to life—

He seized both Proserpina and St. Sebastian and pulled them both to his mouth just as lightning cracked across the sky.

A kiss.

A kiss that was almost a bruise, almost a bite, and how he wanted both, he wanted kissing and bruising and holding and biting—and he wanted to shelter them from the rain and force them to kneel in the mud too, and he didn't know what it meant or why it was happening or even why they were letting him yank them close.

It was awkward and bumping, and Proserpina had sucked in a stunned breath as St. Sebastian had shuddered, but yet when they stumbled apart to the deafening thunder and the shocked stares of the other three, Auden couldn't bring himself to be ashamed.

He could only feel like he wanted to do it again.

Rain began slicing down before any of the six could find the right words, and there was more lightning and more wind, and within fifteen seconds, it became evident that they'd have to run back to the house. Which they did, and after the long time it took, they were soaked to the bone and shivering, and then they were all roundly reprimanded by the parents, who were not impressed with their refusal to talk about what they'd been doing or where they'd been.

The rain continued for another week and well into the week after that, and by that point, the thorn chapel had become something like a myth or a shared dream and it slipped into the realm of reverence and dares and distance. They instead explored the house and the nearby village of Thorncombe and swam in the indoor pool and put on plays in the attic. Delphine and Rebecca fought, and Becket was an insufferable know-it-all, and St. Sebastian wandered in and out, and Proserpina dreamed.

And Auden was still everything inside of himself, unbearably everything, every single thing he'd been at the altar when he'd needed to kiss St. Sebastian and Proserpina and maybe bite them too.

Then the summer term ended.

Or rather, their parents left their strange house party to return to their real lives. Proserpina and Becket went back to America, and Delphine and Rebecca went back to London. St. Sebastian, whose mother hadn't been at the house but who lived in the village, and so he'd injected himself into their play, returned to life in a grimy semi with a tired parent and cupboards of expired food.

And Auden left too, even though Thornchapel was his. His parents whisked him back to the Chelsea townhouse, back to real life and boring parties and their fighting and their restlessness and their pain. He was not the same boy they'd brought to Devon, but they didn't notice, or if they did notice, they ascribed it to the usual pre-teen malcontent that often afflicts boys at that age. Soon enough, he was sent off to school, where he burned with all the things he didn't understand about himself. And though he was popular and well-liked, though he excelled in every imaginable way, he burned alone.

Thornchapel was alone too, though it had yet to burn.

There were a few scattered visits, but they were short, and never did Auden have the courage to return to the altar alone, although it haunted his thoughts constantly. Somehow, it became the place that he could blame for everything—for his parents' fractured marriage, for his father's treatment of him, for his needs and his uncertainty and his torment. And his blame shifted to hate, and the hate spread from the altar to the chapel to the grounds and the entire house itself. Until the house's thorns and his thorns became one and the same, and he knew if he could defeat one, then he could be free of the other.

And yet he still longed for it. He still dreamed of it as it was on the day of the wedding, and he still dreamed of his friends, of Rebecca and Delphine, whom he saw often in the waking world, but never in the same unfettered, near-wild environment they'd had that summer. He dreamed of Becket, too, clever and annoying, and St. Sebastian, whom he'd once kissed as torn flower petals and rain dropped onto their faces.

He dreamed of Proserpina the most often and the most vividly. They met at the altar in his dreams and they rambled around Thornchapel's forests and broken stone circles and hidden dolmens. They kissed too, and they held hands, and as he got older, the dreams grew both darker and richer, the place where he could be every bleak and tender thing he wanted to be. Sometimes it was him and St. Sebastian, sometimes it was him and Proserpina, and sometimes it was all six of them, doing things that made him blush the next time he'd see Delphine and Rebecca in real life.

He dreamed and he burned.

Thornchapel waited.

And in a clearing in the woods, in a church ruined by thorns and time, something stirred.

Something called all six of them by name.

I

Twelve years later

Everything is possible.

Thornchapel waits at the end of my journey, and everything is possible.

My cab wends west on an asphalt ribbon surrounded by stretches of snow-dusted moor. Granite tors frown down; the occasional clump of sheep gnaws on frostbitten grass. It's all white and brown and dead and cold, and it's so different from how I feel, from the things I normally crave—which are green and restless and alive—that I'm fascinated by it. I'm in love with it.

I already want more of it.

I look down at the paper I pulled from my coat pocket after the initial small talk with the driver faded away. The paper hasn't changed since it arrived in my apartment's mailbox last week—the day before

I accepted a job offer I would've never been able to refuse—but I can't stop staring at it. Like if only I look *hard enough*, it'll make sense.

But nothing has made sense for the last twelve years of my life. The world cracked open the day I married two boys at Thornchapel's altar...or maybe it cracked open before that, on the day my parents brought me to Thornchapel in the first place.

Certainly it was already cracked open by the time my mother disappeared from my life forever.

The envelope was postmarked December 21st—the date of my twenty-second birthday—and it was stamped by the Exeter Mail Centre, although the postcode was for Thornchapel, that ancient house tucked deep into a wooded Dartmoor valley. It had been gently battered from its trip over the sea, creased as the uncaring mailman shoved it in the narrow rectangle of my shared mailbox. Not that it mattered—the envelope only contained a single paper, and on that paper, a single word.

Convivificat.

It's Latin, and I don't speak Latin, but the benefit of being a librarian at a university is that I know many people who do. Within an hour of firing off an email, I had a translation.

It quickens.

It quickens.

I didn't know what that meant. I still don't.

I mean, I know what the word *quicken* conveys in the dictionary sense; I whispered its synonyms as I went about my business that evening, as if that would help me understand.

It stirs, it awakens, it comes to life...

But *what* was stirring? *What* was coming to life?

And that isn't even the real mystery of the note, that isn't even the real reason I said yes when Auden Guest's lawyer called the next day and offered me a job. No, the real reason I agreed to leave my career and friends and country was because of the composition of the note itself.

The handwriting—the sharp *C*, the narrow *v*s, the impatient but precise slice of every letter—it belongs to Adelina Kernstow Markham. A woman who's been missing for twelve years.

My mother.

Down a steep wind of road, the village of Thorncombe opens into a disordered but still postcard-worthy cluster of thatched houses, pubs, and the stone St. Brigid's-on-the-Moor with its massive bell tower at the front. There's a small grocery store, a few restaurants, and a public library, and then at the edge of the village, a clutch of tired-looking houses all in various stages of molting their render and growing weeds in their driveways. Something about those houses tugs at a long-discarded memory, but I can't dredge it up before we're past them and piercing through ever-thickening woods, heading deeper into the valley toward our destination.

And then we are over the narrow stone bridge and on the long, tree-pressed drive that leads to the house. When I came here as a child, arriving in the full flush of July green, the house was hidden by the leafy crowns of the trees, an edifice you could only take in entirely once you were standing right in front of it—or if you were at the back of the house, where the gardens seemed to stretch into infinity.

But today, the bare winter trees do nothing to hide the house. Not the crenellated teeth of its fortified heart, nor the uncountable windows glittering from the Jacobean extension to the west. I can see the entire imposing sprawl of it as we approach—clustered chimneys and disordered gables, and the castle-worthy front doors and smaller side doors, and the vast spread of dead rose bushes clinging everywhere to the house itself, promising blooms and bees in the summer.

This is Auden's house.

It's the thought I haven't let myself think, the dream I won't let myself dream. The job and the money and all the arrangements were done through his lawyer; I haven't spoken once to Auden himself. For all I know, I won't see him here at all. Not ever.

Which is good, that's a good thing. Because I don't care what he does or where he is, and he's not the reason I'm here.

My mother is.

Flushing with shame that my first thought was of Auden and not of my mother, I force myself to remember the strange note. The *convivificat* that she wrote, the *convivificat* that found its way to me.

This is what she would have seen, I think as we round the corner of the drive. The police knew from interviewing Thornchapel's caretaker that she'd been here on Halloween morning the year she left us; she'd been seen heading for the maze. The caretaker tried to follow her, found the maze empty, and then decided she must have struck out for one of the public footpaths on the edge of the property, because maze or not, people didn't just vanish.

Unless of course, she'd taken the hidden steps at the center of the maze and gone to the thorn chapel, but I suspected he didn't know about those. Or if he did, he considered them too secret even for the police. Even to save a woman's life.

Not that it mattered either way. The police found no trace of her here at all, not even after they tramped out to the silent ruins of the chapel.

I'm not foolish enough to think I'll find her here, or that I'll find her at all…except, what if I *could*? Or at least, what if I could find out *why?*

My father has always worried over my reckless hopefulness, my stubborn optimism, and he's gently encouraged me more than once to accept that she's dead…or at the very least, the kind of missing that doesn't want to be found. And it's not like I expect to succeed in finding her when so many police officers and the private detectives hired by my father have failed, but turning off the hope simply isn't possible, even after all these years.

Especially not after the *convivificat.*

Even if she wasn't the one to send it, even if someone else found it and then decided to mail it to me—it's still *something*. It's still worth building a little fire of hope under.

Anyway, this isn't how she would have seen the house on that last day, now that I think of it. She came on Halloween, when the trees would have been burning with autumn and the forest floor would have been carpeted with red and gold and orange. Leaves would have fluttered from the sky like rain, the climbing roses shedding ragged petals like tears.

No, she wouldn't have seen Thornchapel like I'm seeing it now—bare and barren. She wouldn't have seen it dead, only dying.

However, the house is actually anything but dead or dying—no matter how gloomy the bare rose canes and surrounding trees make it seem. This becomes very clear to me as we park, and I see several trucks and vans disgorging ladders and lumber and plastic pipes. Men in T-shirts, even in this cold, bustle in and out a side door with the industry of ants building an anthill.

"What a place," the cab driver says, opening my door before I can open it myself. "You really staying here?"

"For now," I answer as lightly as possible, secretly wondering what all this messy turmoil is. Auden's lawyer didn't mention anything about the house having work done—he only mentioned that I was welcome to live there while I worked for the Guest family. I accepted—it's unusual, of course, but it will save money, and anyway, Thorncombe didn't have any places available to rent. And if there had been a part of me that thought of Auden as I agreed, then I refused to admit it to myself at the time.

"Modernizing," the driver says wisely as we circle back to the trunk to get my bags. "Lots of these old places need it. Ah, it's warmed up enough to rain now."

It has, just a few soft spits here and there. I glance back at the trucks, the dumpster at the side of the house with odd bits of wall and plumbing sticking out of it.

The Thornchapel I remember had been modern enough—at least outside of the medieval rooms and the silent Long Gallery. There was running water and electricity, and televisions and an Xbox in Auden's room, so if there'd been hunter green carpet and floral wallpaper elsewhere, my ten-year-old self hadn't noticed enough to care.

"I think the owner died," I say in a tone of conversational speculation…though I know for a fact that Auden's father is dead because the family lawyer told me as much. "It's his son's now. Maybe he wants to put his mark on it?"

"Fixing it up to sell, more like." The trunk slams down and the cab driver rolls both suitcases closer to me. "These places are damned hard to maintain."

Funny how that's never occurred to me, that Thornchapel needs maintenance, that it needs roof repairs and masonry replacements and plumbing fixes and window sashes refitted. It's always seemed like a place apart to me, a place alive, like a temple in a myth or a castle in a fairy tale. It just *is*, it just exists outside any human intervention, a rambling stone sentinel surrounded by trees at the front and sumptuous gardens at the back. Even now, watching workers carry in supplies and hearing the faint but distinct noises of power tools and hammering, it's hard to believe this place is just a house and not the gorgeous, ancient gate to a mysterious chapel I only half remember.

I tip the driver extra for helping with my bags—and also for braving the hair-raising country roads—and after a quick *cheers*, he gives me a creased business card from his coat pocket with the cab company number on it.

"In case this place don't work for you," he says, giving me a small smile and then giving the house a doubtful look. Through his eyes, I can see how strange this all is. A chipper American girl about to live in a house that's not hers for a job she only accepted ten days ago. He can't know I've been dreaming of this place every night since I left, that in my mind this is the place that swallowed my mother whole. He can't know that I've spent almost every day of my life since she left trying to find a way back here.

"That's very kind," I say with an answering smile, which seems to reassure him. He gets in the car and leaves as I try to shove my wallet and things into my backpack, and after the car is swallowed by the trees and hedges on the way out, I pull out my phone and use the camera to make sure I don't have mascara smeared on my face or anything. I took a flight from Kansas City to Minneapolis, from Minneapolis to London, then I took a train to Newton Abbot and battled carsickness for nearly an hour on the twisting roads—and all of that sitting on a welted ass because I couldn't bear to face Thornchapel without one last kink scene with my ex-girlfriend.

I haven't properly slept in thirty-three hours, nor have I washed or changed my clothes, and the last thing I ate was a lukewarm sausage roll washed down with black coffee. I feel stale and strung-out, and I can't even imagine how I look. Certainly not fit to meet Mr. Cremer, the Guest family's lawyer.

The front camera on my phone is never flattering, but it's worse than usual today. My hair—dark, dark brown and falling past my breasts—needs a brush, and there is indeed mascara under my eyes from napping against my wadded-up cardigan. My complexion, which is the kind of translucent ivory-pink that shows every mark, bruise, and blush, betrays my exhaustion with bluish smudges under my eyes and cheeks splotchy from intermittent napping and the nipping wind. A glance down at my wrinkled dress confirms there's no part of me that looks professional.

I run a hand down the back of my thigh and suck in a breath as each welt and bruise sings a little song to me.

I'm awake and alive, those songs remind me. I'm awake and everything is possible.

Maybe I can slip in unnoticed and find a place to change.

If I recall correctly, there was a bathroom off the main hallway on the ground floor, and if I went in through the same door all the workers are using…

Mind made up, I slip my phone into my coat pocket, take hold of my suitcase handles, and start wheeling them through the side door—where I nearly run right into the firm chest of one of the workers.

His hands fly to my shoulders in an instinctive gesture to steady me, and the automatic apology spills out of my mouth before I even fully realize what's just happened. As a chronic daydreamer, I'm used to running into people...and doorways and light poles and walls...and so the hurried *sorry!* that spills out of me is one I've been practicing my entire life.

"No, no, it was my fault," the worker says in an accent that's almost American, and I glance up at him, surprised at the sudden pang of homesickness I feel hearing it. Especially because it's only been a day and a half since I left home.

He looks down at me with ink-black eyes. Longish sable hair frames his angular face, and dark eyebrows, long eyelashes, and high cheekbones give way to a stubbled jaw and an oh-so-slightly cleft chin. And when his mouth parts again, I catch the glint of a silver bead on his lower lip. A barbell. It pierces the middle of his lip, emphasizing the softness of his mouth, the lush but firm lines of it.

I shiver, even though I'm out of the wind.

"Are you okay?" he asks, searching my face to make sure, and it's as he's examining me that I realize I've seen him before, that I know him somehow. It only takes me a second, and in that second, two things happen. Firstly, a cloud shifts ever so slightly outside and allows a patch of meager sunshine into the doorway, which means that I can see his eyes are actually a dark, dark brown, as is his hair. His skin is tinted bronze but paler than it was when we were children, like he's known several rain-soaked years here in England since then.

The second thing that happens is that he says my name. "Proserpina?" he whispers, his eyebrows drawn together.

I bite my lip. "St. Sebastian?"

St. Sebastian nods, looking a little stunned.

"He goes by Saint now," comes a long, elegant drawl from behind me.

I shiver again because somehow I *know*, I just *know*, even though he wasn't supposed to be here, even though I thought I'd never see him again.

I turn, and I see the boy I've hated myself for loving for the last twelve years.

2

Auden Guest is tall, like I guessed he would be, and handsome, like I knew he was. There's the high cheeks and the square jaw hewn out of the promise of his boyhood prettiness, and a mouth that's still a bit too exquisite for a grown man. There's light brown hair that flops *just so* over his pale forehead, and hazel eyes that promise…well, that promise everything. Money and mystery and cruelty and all the pouty rich-boy things I've spent years armoring myself against.

And when he sees me, really sees me, he gives a wide, dimpled smile with white teeth and this fatally charming lift on one side of his upper lip—a human dash of asymmetry on an otherwise flawless face. Those hazel eyes make their lying promises under long eyelashes, and for a moment, I forget all my own promises, all the vows I made to myself back home before I came here.

After all, it's stupid enough that I never stopped thinking about the day we kissed, and it's stupid enough that I spent the early part of my teenage years convinced we were soul mates. It's stupid enough that my first stirring dreams and urges weren't about celebrities or even boys in my own school, but about Auden…and St. Sebastian. And Rebecca and Delphine and Becket. I must have been the only one of us six who missed that summer, who wished we were all together again. Who wished for something more than friendship. Something profane.

Anyway, I vowed to myself before I came here that I wouldn't compound my stupidity by falling in love for real.

Here's the thing: I finished high school at sixteen and crossed the stage for my bachelor's at twenty, crossed it again for my master's just this year. I have a mother who taught me every myth she knew, I have a father who loves me, I have friends who like me and colleagues who respect me. And I am hopeful and reckless and curious, but *I am not stupid.*

And I am not going to do something as stupid as fall in love with Auden Guest.

All at once, my defenses are back, and I'm able to return his smile with a steady one of my own, even if my heart won't slacken its frantic fluttering beat.

God, I'm so tired. It hits me suddenly, like a heavy sack thrown over my shoulders, bending my knees and making my head droop. "Auden," I say, the last syllable of his name breaking on a yawn.

"Proserpina," he says warmly. "You must be tired after your trip."

"Yes," I say, heroically fighting back another yawn. "And you can call me Poe."

"Poe," St. Sebastian repeats, as if to himself. As if to memorize it.

Auden's smile grows lazier and maybe more dangerous, even as he pointedly ignores St. Sebastian. "Poe then," he says, his eyes never leaving my face. "I'm surprised you recognized me."

There's no point in completely lying, because nothing matters with Auden and nothing ever will. So I settle for part of the truth. "I looked you up on Instagram before I came here," I inform him.

He makes a face. "Oh, that thing. I'm a little embarrassed."

"You shouldn't be," I say, and I mean it. It's the kind of sparsely updated account that speaks to a mostly unself-conscious life. A handful of selfies from his days at Cambridge, a few pictures of him with his rowing team. A picture of him smiling in his undergraduate graduation robes with his family and then a picture of a German shepherd puppy named Sir James Frazer. It hasn't been updated in the last year and a half, unlike Delphine's, which is updated almost daily—to say nothing of her stories.

And okay, yes, I looked at everyone's social media before I got on the plane, everyone except for St. Sebastian Martinez, who doesn't have a single social media account, who barely exists at all, according to the internet.

There was Auden of course, with his indifferent profiles displaying the slenderest peek of his charmed, rich-boy life, and then there was Becket Hess—or rather *Father* Becket Hess—who'd only just been ordained last year and been sent here to Dartmoor to shepherd an idyllic little parish. Then there was Rebecca Quartey, with her impeccably professional account showcasing her work in the last year as a landscape architect, and Delphine Dansey, who as far as I could tell didn't have a job, or if she did, it was simply to be pretty and happy in lots of different pretty and happy locations.

"Trust the librarian to do her research before she came," Auden says.

"I am a bit surprised to see you, though—Mr. Cremer made it sound as if he'd be the one to greet me...?"

"Oh that," Auden says, waving a hand. "I was here anyway, and besides, I was looking forward to meeting you again after all this time." He takes a step forward, and for a moment, I think he's reaching for me—maybe for my hand or to pull me into a hug—but he's only reaching for one of my suitcase handles. "Let's get you settled then, and show you around the place—"

"Oh, there you are!" comes a voice, and all three of us turn to see a beautiful, plus-sized blond woman and a tall sandy-haired man, both white, coming toward us.

Delphine and Father Becket—Delphine in a blouse, knee-length skirt and tights, and Father Becket in his priest collar—reach us in an explosion of chatter and greetings, and suddenly I'm pulled into hugs and given kisses, and then another voice comes from the far end of the hallway, and a slender black woman with braids coiled in a crown and an iPad tucked under her arm joins us too.

Rebecca.

And just like that, we're all together again, all six of us, and there's more hugging and exclaiming, except I still don't hug Auden and he still doesn't try, and St. Sebastian stands apart from it all, hovering in the doorway like a vampire cursed not to come inside.

I look at them all for a minute as they talk at me and then talk at each other and then argue about who's talking too much. How strange to think that we'd all been children together—for a summer at least—that we'd seen each other cry and fall out of trees and shout and laugh. Looking at them now is dizzying—like I'm seeing the past and the present at the same time.

"I can't believe you were just sneaking in without telling us,"

Rebecca says, giving me another warm squeeze, while Becket asks when I arrived.

"Oh, just now," I answer. "The cab just left."

"Auden, why didn't you send the car for her?" Delphine chides. "A cab for a friend, now *really*!"

"Well, Cremer *offered* the car, but she declined."

"*We* could have gotten her too, you know—"

"She probably wanted to nap," Rebecca tells Delphine. "Or work, and she wouldn't have been able to do either with you talking at her face for an hour."

"She's a *librarian*, she can't work in the car. What is she going to do, shelve books in the back seat?"

"All right, all right," Auden hushes them. "Poe is probably dying to rest for a minute—"

"*Poe*?" Delphine demands. "What kind of name is that?"

"What kind of name is Delphine?" Rebecca counters, and Delphine scowls.

"I like it," Becket tells me in a warm voice. "It suits you. Very literary."

"And easier to spell," I explain, which earns me a little laugh. I relax the tiniest bit, which makes me realize how nervous I was to be around them, how nervous I still am. They seem so glamorous right now, even chattering and squabbling in a muddy hallway. They seem so seductive and so *chosen*, like a little club, a little society of the five of them.

No, not five, I think, taking in the scene with fresh eyes. *Four.*

St. Sebastian is not part of the group.

It's not only his T-shirt and jeans compared with the careless sophistication of everyone else, but it's also the way he's standing with boots planted and arms crossed, almost as if he's waiting for someone to tell him to leave. My chest pinches at that, both in sympathy and empathy.

I feel apart too. Young and poor and cheaply dressed. And indecently fascinated with the interesting people in front of me.

I turn to say something to St. Sebastian—I'm not sure what, but I don't like this weird fault line running through the hallway, this fault line I don't understand—and that's when I catch Auden looking at me and St. Sebastian.

No, not looking…*devouring.*

A high flush dusts his cheeks, and his wide, boyish mouth is set in the same hungry, tortured line it was twelve years ago, right before he pulled us into a searing wedding kiss. His hands flex at his sides, as if they're itching at the memory of pulling us close. As if they ache to make us ache.

My blood is flooded with something hot, something urgent, and I hear St. Sebastian inhale.

Auden's eyes close ever so briefly as he lets out a breath, like he's searching for control, and when he opens them again, he's back to how he was. Indifferent and the tiniest bit scornful.

You are not going to be stupid. Spoiled rich boy, remember?

No one seems to notice what's happening between the three of us. Becket, Rebecca, and Delphine are still talking over one another, and anyway, the moment is so short that I think it's only lasted a handful of breaths. Then St. Sebastian is back to scowling and Auden is back to that crooked smile, and I'm grabbing for my suitcases and making excuses about needing to change.

"Yes, yes, really," Auden says in exasperation to the others, "there's going to be plenty of time to catch up later; you're making me out to be a terrible host." He does a very good job of not looking at St. Sebastian as he takes a suitcase handle and shoulders a bag for me.

I turn again to St. Sebastian, knowing I should say goodbye…and what? That I want to see him again? That I'd like to grab coffee? As soon as I think it, I feel flushed and girlish. It would be easier if St. Sebastian weren't so himself, maybe, if he weren't exactly the kind of person I've always been attracted to. Broody and pierced and a little angry. The diametric opposite to my dreamy tweediness.

But St. Sebastian is already backing outside, one fist against the doorway as if he needed to hit something or someone, and then he's fully turned and disappearing into a fresh spate of winter drizzle.

It's the exhaustion and adrenaline of travel that makes my stomach twist so hard at him leaving without a word, I'm sure of it. He'll be around the house, and I'll find him, and we'll talk and it will be…fine. Probably.

With a smile I summon up from somewhere, I swivel away from the sight of St. Sebastian vanishing into the rain. I take my other suitcase in hand and gesture to Auden. "Ready when you are."

My room is winsomely old.

A few large rugs are scattered over wide wood planks, and there's a canopied bed piled thick with blankets and snowy pillows. A small stone fireplace has a wood-burning stove fitted in, and there's a low bench before a row of arched, mullioned windows. A small desk, large dresser, and end table complete the furnishings, along with two small tapestries covering the stone and plaster walls.

"I'm sorry it's so primitive," Auden apologizes as we wheel my things in. We're alone for the moment—the others having bustled off to get tea ready for me—and it feels quiet. Too quiet.

"I don't think I stayed here last time," I say, looking around. "I must have stayed in a different room."

"You would have stayed in the south wing, I'm sure. It's the most 'modern,' although modern is a very generous use of the word. It's what's currently being renovated and extended. But this wing will have its turn too, and in a few months, we'll all have to decamp to the new section."

"'We'll all'—so everyone is really staying here?"

"Just like old times, right?" Auden says, moving my suitcase against a wall and carefully setting my bag beside it.

"Just like old times," I echo. It's what I've wanted for so long—and thought myself ridiculous for wanting. Who wants to see the people from their childhood so badly? Like really?

"Becket doesn't live here, obviously," Auden says, wandering over to the window. "His church is in Bellever. But he comes here quite a bit since I came back."

"When was that?" I ask, curious. "When you came back, I mean?"

I wonder if he's felt the same pull to Thornchapel I have, if he even could, since I suspect part of my fascination with the place stems from its distance from my life, its inaccessibility. It would always be a mystery to me, this hovering dream just out of waking reach. But I wasn't a Guest, I wasn't tied to the place as Auden was. It wasn't mine.

"After I buried my father in the St. Brigid's graveyard," Auden says after a minute, his eyes on the rain-soaked forest outside the windows.

Well, shit. I feel idiotic for not having thought of that, especially after I'd only just talked to the cab driver about it. I make a pointless gesture with my hands—not that he can see it, since he's still looking outside. "I'm sorry about your father."

"I'm not," he bites off.

"Oh."

He scrubs his hands through his hair and blows out a breath. "I'm sorry. That was churlish of me, especially given what happened to your mother. What I should say is that we had a complicated relationship and none of that complication was resolved at the time of his death."

"But your own mother…" I say, then stop, wishing I could take it back. It's another consequence of my half-dreaming brain. Sometimes the words escape me before I can think them through.

"She drank herself to death," Auden says, finally turning to face me. "If you were wondering."

She drank herself to death. My father had told me when she'd died a few years ago, but I hadn't known…I'd only known that Auden's father had written to my father, and that when my father read the letter, he'd been angrier than I'd ever seen him. He'd burned the letter and gotten drunk and told me I was never, ever allowed to return to Thornchapel, not as an adult, not as an old woman, not ever.

"Anyway," Auden says. "My father dying only meant I was an orphan in truth rather than in spirit. A mere formality."

"Oh Auden," I say, because I can't help it, because it's what I would say to anyone. No matter how handsome and sad and angry they look framed by a medieval window.

He sighs and I see him reaching for his mask again, the one that makes it so easy for me not to fall in love with him. "At any rate, we were talking about my little house party. After *he* died, I felt like I needed to…I don't know, erase all my memories of him, I guess. I sold off the townhouse, donated all his things. I thought I'd find a way to blot out Thornchapel too because I hate this place, I hate it so much, but when I walked in the front door, I—"

Auden breaks off, as if he isn't sure what he was or what he felt. He blinks at me for a moment, as if I'll have the answer.

I don't, but strangely, I wish I did. Or maybe I just wish I knew the question better.

"Well, regardless," he says, shaking off whatever thoughts he'd been having, "I began to think maybe I couldn't sell it. Maybe I should tear it down. Burn it and salt the earth where it stood."

His voice is just a touch too wry, a bit too self-deprecating, for it to be hyperbole, which means he's telling the truth. He really did want to burn Thornchapel to the ground. It's almost like hearing blasphemy, and I'm surprised at how horrified the thought makes me.

"But then," he continues, "I just *couldn't*. I just couldn't. I don't know why. I still don't."

He gives me a helpless kind of smile, as if I'd blame him for *not* destroying his ancient family home.

"I suppose you know I just finished my master's in architecture?" he asks.

I make a vague nod, not wanting to admit exactly how Drunk Librarian I'd gone on him before I came here.

"Well, I'd just taken a job with a firm, and I had the idea—why not hire myself? Why not get my practical experience working on someplace that belongs to me? My boss agreed so long as I keep up my work on my other projects, and so now I'm here." He waves a careless hand. "Playing architect to a place I might still hate."

"Might?"

More helpless smiling. "I guess I'm hoping I'll figure it out by the end."

"And the others?" I ask.

"Will they figure it out—Oh! Why are they here, you mean. Well, Rebecca is a couple years older, I think you remember, and our resident genius. She's already got a global reputation as a landscape architect."

"You're going to redesign the gardens," I realize.

"*Rebecca* is going to redesign the gardens," Auden clarifies, "and I don't really care what she does to them. Whatever it is, it'll be good because *she's* good, and it will be different. It won't be the same as it was when, well…you know."

"As that summer?"

He nods.

I chew on my lip. The thought of the cloistered English gardens being demolished, with their tousled riots of flowers and statues of veiled women and hidden benches…the thought of the *maze* being demolished…

My head snaps back up. "You're not going to do anything with the thorn chapel, are you?"

"It's not scheduled or anything, so I *could*," Auden says, with a strange note to his voice, like he himself has just realized he's committing some kind of blasphemy. "But I don't know yet. I don't have any plans to at the moment."

Relief seeps through me. "And then Delphine? Why is she here too?"

"Well, we're engaged," he murmurs. "So it just seemed natural she'd come live with me."

The relief stops; all other feelings stop. I'm suddenly very, very still. And numb.

"Pardon?" I ask.

"We're engaged to be married," he repeats, slightly louder, as if he thinks I asked pardon because I didn't hear him. "I proposed last year."

"Oh," I say. My voice sounds dull, and I try to brighten it. "I didn't know."

"We haven't formally announced it; you know, in the papers or anything like that. My father didn't approve, and then after he died, Delphine wanted to wait until it was more…seemly, I suppose. Only her parents and our close friends know; she hasn't even posted about it online, I don't think."

I *know* she hasn't posted about it online because she'd also been a victim of my Drunk Librarian research.

"Congratulations," I say, with a fake-jolly expression that makes me wince, but Auden doesn't see because he's turned back to the trees.

"Yes," he says to the glass.

Yes.

Not *thank you*, not any expression of excitement or endearments of his future bride. It's strange, but I take less notice of it than I should because I'm still fighting against that awful numb feeling.

Auden and Delphine.

Engaged.

It makes a terrible kind of sense—of all of us, their worlds are the closest aligned, and even downstairs they looked like a matched set—her with her Peter Pan-collared blouse and skirt, him in his trousers and clinging sweater—offhandedly rich without being flashy about it.

I have to change the subject, and I cast around desperately for something, anything, that will move the conversation away from the idea of Auden and Delphine getting married.

"And St. Sebastian?" I ask quickly. "Is he staying here? I saw him working..."

"He moonlights for the local building team I hired," Auden says tightly. "He is *not* living here."

I wonder what possible reason he could have to be so hostile about St. Sebastian. "Oh."

"I think he's still living in his mother's old house in Thorncombe," Auden says after a mutual pause.

"Her old house? Did she move?"

"She died."

"Jesus."

"Yes. Seems to be a theme with us." Auden's voice is flat, and he's still looking out the window, his hands in his pockets.

I don't know what to say next; my brain is completely wrung dry from the travel and the time change and seeing everyone and I just can't think.

I need a nap, I think with the fervor of an addict. *Just a small one.*

Luckily, I'm saved from having to speak by the cheerful clicking of paws on the hallway floor outside, and then by the appearance of a very handsome dog who noses a snout into the crack of the door and then pushes his body inside.

I drop to a crouch and invite him over for pets. "Hi there, good boy," I croon as he trots toward me, tail and ears up. He plops down to sit after a cursory snuffle around my hands and feet, and when he opens his mouth to pant, his tongue falls out of the side. I'm in love immediately, and prove it by scratching behind his ears, which earns me a lick on the face.

Auden turns again, and when he does, both the angry vulnerability and the indifferent mask are gone. He gives me and the dog a real smile, with that damn crook in his upper lip, and I have to look quickly away or I know I'll blush and he'll see.

They always see when I blush.

"That's Sir James Frazer," Auden says, seeming pleased to see me and his dog getting along. "I hope you're not allergic…?"

"Not at all. My dad has three dogs at home, and I've always planned on adopting one once I got my own place."

"Then I hope you'll consider Sir James a surrogate while you're staying here," Auden says. "Not that he'll give you any peace anyway. He gets very snuggly with everyone he meets."

Sir James Frazer licks me again on the face, as if to agree.

Auden seems to come to some kind of realization and shakes his head at himself. "I'm so sorry. I've been keeping you occupied up here—I'm not sure what's gotten into me." His mouth slants ruefully. "You're very easy to talk to, you know."

It's something I've heard all my life, and I'm used to it, even if it sometimes makes me feel a little lonely. The person that everyone talks to, but who never gets that comfort in return.

Oh, stop it, Poe. I'm not melancholy by nature, and I don't intend to start, even if I'm basically on the set of the underrated 1994 adaptation of *The Secret Garden*, and even if I am sharing a room with an expert brooder.

I give Auden a smile. "I promise I'm usually a bit better at keeping up my end of a conversation, I just—" another dizzying yawn interrupts my words.

Auden holds up a hand. "Say no more. And actually, I insist you take a nap before I refresh your memory about the layout of the house.

The bathroom is just down the hall—apologies for that in advance, you'll be sharing with Rebecca when she's staying here, but she's here even less than me, so hopefully it won't be too inconvenient."

"I don't mind sharing," I say foggily, going to sit on the bed. "I just…one moment."

I have a long blink. I know these blinks. It means sleep is creeping up on me too fast for me to stop it, and my head is drooping as I fade…

My head snaps up and Auden is next to me, helping me lie down.

"Are you okay?" he asks, clearly concerned.

"Fine," I mumble. "Just need a moment."

"Take as long as you need," he says, and I feel warm, blunt fingertips brushing the hair from my forehead.

It's the last thing I remember before sleep closes over me like water, and I'm lost.

3

My father always used to joke that I dreamed on my feet, but when I was sixteen, we discovered that I was quite literally dreaming on my feet. After a series of unspeakably boring and uncomfortable studies, I was diagnosed with narcolepsy without cataplexy—which is just fancy medical talk for saying that a part of my brain eats itself, and as a consequence, I am a very, very sleepy person.

And also I dream too many dreams.

When I wake up from my nap, there's a scream balled in my throat, but I can't remember why. Just something about the thorn chapel and Auden and there was a knife maybe, and sparks spitting from a fire.

A fire burning against the night.

I press the heels of my palms against my eyes and take a deep breath. I dream like this all the time and have ever since I can remember. And sometimes I have waking dreams, as I'm falling asleep or waking up, so vivid that when I claw free from them, I burst immediately into tears.

This is nothing new, Poe.

But it was so real, so urgent, and I can almost still smell the smoke burning my nostrils and hear Auden's razored breaths as he stood at a door in the thorn chapel…

No, that can't be right. There's no door in the chapel ruins.

Just a dream thing.

Right. Just a dream thing.

I sit up and feel the relief only a narcoleptic can feel when I check my watch. I've only slept an hour or so, which sounds like a lot, but I've been known to lie down for a nap and wake up the next morning, so I'm calling it a win, even though I know I'll feel a little sheepish going downstairs. That's the thing about naps. Everyone knows what you've done, and there's something that feels lazy about it, shameful, even though I don't have a choice about my brain cannibalizing its own proteins, and really, everyone sleeps.

I decide to take some extra time, since that hot tea waiting for me is already cold and they'll need to make a fresh pot anyway…and if I have to make the nap walk of shame, I think I'll feel better doing it with clean hair and fresh clothes. I grab new clothes and underthings, and my travel-sized toiletries—I'll need to head into Thorncombe soon to stock up for real—and strike out for the bathroom I'll share with Rebecca.

The dream still clings to the corners of my mind as I find the bathroom and familiarize myself with all the light switches and shower workings. It bothers me as I scrub my skin and wash my hair. And when I finish up and stow my dirty laundry back in my room, it's still the only thing I can think of.

Just a dream thing, Poe. Just bad brain chemistry.

It better be.

In between pulling on fresh clothes, I text my ex-girlfriend that I'm here, and after a moment's hesitation, I finally text my dad.

Me: I made it here safely. Love you.

He responds right away—like he's been keeping his phone close—but the answer is short, the meaning clear.

Dad: It's not too late to come back.

I don't reply. We fought bitterly enough about me coming here when I took the job, and I don't see how either of us can have anything new to say. I close my eyes and remind myself of how pointless it would be to fight about it again.

"You can't go," he begged. "You promised you wouldn't."

"Dad, they're paying *me to go. To do a job I'd do for free if I could."*

He'd leaned over his kitchen counter then, his hands balled in fists and his posture that of a broken man. "It's too dangerous. Your mom and I—we learned the hard way how dangerous it is. She'd want me to keep you safe now."

"But the note she sent—"

"She didn't send it, Poe, she couldn't have!" he exploded. "She's dead or she's forgotten about us in some new life, and she's not sending you notes in Latin!"

His words stung. They stung enough that I had to sit down on a kitchen chair and stare at the floor for a minute.

"Poe," he said after a minute. "I'm sorry. You must know that this hurts for me too."

"You never had a service for her," I whispered. "You never tried to have her declared dead, even though you could have. Why not, if you don't still secretly hope she's alive?"

He took off his glasses then, wiping them on his shirt to avoid looking at me. "I don't know," he said finally. "I don't know why I didn't. Maybe it felt like Thornchapel would win if I did."

Thornchapel. It always came back to Thornchapel.

"What did you do that summer?" I asked, lifting my face to his. "What had you locked up in that library for weeks and weeks?"

He stared at me for a moment, his forehead wrinkling as if he were trying to find a way to convey, finally, why we'd all gone to Thornchapel in the first place. An explanation I'd only been brave enough to ask for a few times, and that he'd always refused to give. But maybe now with this mysterious note, maybe now with me on the verge of going there again—

"Just don't go," Dad said, looking away. "Please."

I let out a long, disappointed breath and stood up. "Bye, Dad," I said. "I guess I'll call when my plane lands."

I put my phone in the pocket of my skirt, determined to put my father out of my mind for the moment. We've always been close, we've never really fought, and so I promise myself he'll come around. After all, I've been a model daughter—I got my grad degree before most people even get their bachelor's, I've never been in trouble at school or with the law, and I always walked the dogs and helped with dishes.

He'll forgive this little rebellion, I'm sure, because it's my first, and really, it's all in the name of library science, and he should understand that, scholar that he is. Right?

I've never felt more like an underpaid academic librarian than I do when I walk downstairs and find the others—minus St. Sebastian of course—curled into armchairs in front of a fire and arguing about something over the din of hammers and saws. My hair is still wet, because I don't have a blow-dryer that works with English outlets—and if I'm very honest, and why not be, I never blow-dry my hair anyway. It's always seemed like a waste of time when I can be doing so many other things—reading or studying or sleeping—and so I usually just braid it into a wet rope and deal with it later. Which is what I've done now, but one glimpse of Delphine's flaxen blowout and Rebecca's artful updo make me regret it. Along with my suitcase-wrinkled blouse and skirt, both of which were bought on clearance, I'm sure I don't present a very compelling picture.

But they all pop up and exclaim over me, and I fight through my nap-shame and my irritation with my father and smile back at them.

Everything is possible.

Those were the last words my mother ever spoke to me, and I planted them in my heart like seeds and made them grow.

Everything is possible.

Even making friends with people while I'm all wet hair and sleep-flushed cheeks. While I have to constantly smooth my skirt behind me because I forgot to pack another pair of tights and my welts are one too-quick turn away from revealing themselves to the world.

"Now, *how* was your flight?" Delphine asks in this *I insist you tell me everything because we're the very best of friends* voice that nice popular girls have.

"Exhausting, obviously," Rebecca says, rolling her eyes and giving me a *what are we going to do about her* look. Becket bustles off to get the tea, and Auden gets up from his chair and gestures toward the door.

"Let's show you around a bit so you're not lost in your own home," he says, and then Rebecca and Delphine erupt in protests.

"She hasn't told us about her journey!"

"Becky *just* left for tea—"

Auden heaves a giant, exaggerated sigh. "Poe came all this way to work in the damn library, and I'm guessing she's eager to see it again, aren't you?" He says this last bit to me.

I give the others a sheepish look. "I really do want to see it."

Delphine makes a pout and then flops into her chair in a very adorable way. "It hasn't changed a bit, you know. It's still a big old room full of books."

"She hasn't seen it in twelve years," Rebecca points out, although I notice there's the hint of an involuntary smile about the corners of her mouth, as if she can't help but find Delphine the tiniest bit adorable too. "And *you* aren't going to have to spend the next year digging around in there and *she* is."

Delphine huffs.

"*Goodbye*," Auden sings at them, taking my elbow before I can get caught in any more pouts or protests and leading me out of the sitting room and into the main hall. Which, because this is the medieval part of the house, is literally a fucking hall, with a lofty ceiling and a massive fireplace and flagstone floors that must have seen hundreds and hundreds of feasts and revels.

No revels now though. Only piles of construction supplies and a random metal folding chair. Auden leads me past it all, his arm still on my elbow, and I feel like my elbow is now all of my body, it's the only part that exists. His hand is warm through my blouse and it's the style of authoritative contact that makes me melt.

He really shouldn't be holding me like this, he shouldn't be touching me at all, because aren't engaged men supposed to keep their hands to themselves?

Do not fall in love, Proserpina Markham. You are not stupid.

But I'm so susceptible to this kind of touch; I bloom like a rose when I'm handled like a weed, and I'm going to have to put a stop to this right now. His stride is eager and energetic, and so I slow down just enough that he has to pull his hand from my elbow to avoid yanking me ahead. He doesn't seem to notice.

"I promise to show you everything else soon," he's saying as we walk. "But if you're anything like me, you'll want to see the work first. And there's so much to be done, and I still can't believe that we've found *you* to do it. The odds of that are...well, they're staggering."

It *is* strange. It's been one of those things I haven't looked too closely at since Auden's lawyer called to offer me the job. To tell me that the estate wished to hire a specialist to archive their family library, and that I'd come personally recommended. That it would be at least a year of cataloging, scanning, annotating, and arranging for the repair and stabilization of any damaged or decaying volumes. It could possibly be many more years, since no formal survey had ever been undertaken of Thornchapel's library and no one could say for certain exactly how many books were in there.

And of all the lengths I've gone to in order to try to come back to

Thornchapel—even going so far as to book a plane ticket once during my sophomore year in college until I confessed to my father and he convinced me not to go—I have to say that concentrating my master's in the digital preservation of rare books was not one of them.

"I'm damned lucky Ryan Belvedere recommended you," Auden says as we walk down a narrow walkway lined with arched windows. It leads from the main hall to the Jacobean portion of the house where the library is.

Ryan who? "I don't know who that is."

Auden pauses and looks back at me. "You don't?"

I shake my head.

"How curious," he murmurs. "He came here looking for a book last month, for a someone named Merlin. We had someone else in at the time to put together a catalog for an auction house—all the old art, you know—and he mentioned the state of the library was appalling. Which it is, you'll see soon enough for yourself. And that's when Ryan said we should call you. And obviously when I realized it was *you*—well, it just had to be you."

"I'm glad it's me," I say.

"So am I," he says and then he takes my elbow again.

I let him. There's something electrifying about having him touch me like this, in this sort of peremptory, possessive way. Half like he's a gracious host and half like I'm getting hauled off to be punished. I adore being hauled off and punished, and the bruises on my thighs and ass sing to me again, ready for Auden to add to their number.

This time my blush actually burns my cheeks. I use my free hand to tug at the hem of my skirt again, keeping all those singing spots on my body hidden.

Stop. It. Poe. You. Pervert.

He has to let go and turn away as we approach the library's double doors. It's the first chance I've had to study his body without the fog of exhaustion clouding my eyes, and it's doing nothing to help my blush.

He's taller than me—well, everyone is taller than me—but he's objectively tall, at least six feet. He's that heady combination of lean but muscled, with the curves of his biceps and shoulders swelling under his sweater, and the flat of his stomach leading into narrow hips hugged by expensive trousers and an equally expensive leather belt that would hurt like hell on someone's backside. His trousers cling to firm thighs and an equally firm and tantalizingly pert ass. The kind of ass that would have dents in the sides when he stood still.

But even all of that isn't enough to explain the pull of Auden Guest—even the hazel eyes and crooked grin and sad, rich-boy disposition aren't enough.

I can't say what it *is* that makes Auden so…so Auden, and that's professionally irritating. I'm a librarian. I like to catalog things. How can I annotate his metadata on my mental card catalog if I don't know what to annotate? If I don't know how to describe him or his effect on me?

Looking like something out of a men's fashion magazine, Auden gives me a smile over his shoulder and pushes open the doors. And then all my other thoughts fade away as I take in the room I've flown across an ocean to see.

Northerly light, pale and diffuse, fills the room from the dark wooden floor to the delicately plastered ceilings above. The center of the room is open all the way to the top, a full two stories, and the sides are flanked by rows of bookshelves like marching soldiers, both on the bottom level and the top, with ladders studded at intervals to assist in getting things from the highest shelves. The top level is ringed by narrow galleries and accessed by small but elaborately carved staircases near the stretch of multi-paned windows at the end of the room.

A massive fireplace yawns against one side, disrupting the otherwise symmetrical layout of bookshelves, and several chairs and a couple sofas have been arranged cozily around it. A drinks bar and random spills of throw blanket finish off the inviting space, and I lose myself to a momentary dream of curling up and reading while the fire and the window-glass keep the winter at bay outside.

The narcoleptic in me can't help but think of all the lovely naps to be had here. The librarian in me notes the generous stone hearth and the healthy distance between it and all the books.

There are two long tables stretching down the length of the room, a massive Victorian globe, and a few glass cases with motley collections of Roman coins and artifacts of metal and bone. And other than the ornate ceiling—all white, but molded in what appear to be geometric patterns of roses and branching thorns—the only real decoration is the books themselves. Leather spines of claret, cinnabar, and citrine, clothbound tomes of sapphire and sage…and the requisite scatterings of umber and filemot and terra-cotta, which are the very picture of Serious Books with their sepia colors and peeling lettering.

It should be grim, this room, it should be forbidding. The stark white of the ceiling and the near-black of the dark, dark wood should make it somber and churchlike, the cool light pouring in from between the stark trees outside should make it lonesome and cold.

But by some kind of magic, none of that is true. Maybe it's the variegated strata of books, or maybe it's that I feel at home in rooms like this anyway. Maybe it's because it's Thornchapel and I love

Thornchapel, and when I think about it, the whole house is like this. Three stories of cold stone and glass should in no way feel as inviting and as enchanting as they do, and yet I feel utterly invited. Utterly enchanted.

I give a very long, very happy sigh.

"Do you like it?" Auden asks quietly.

I realize I've been turning in wondering circles for the last God-knows-how-many minutes, and I feel like an idiot—until I see Auden's face. He must have been watching me go all dreamy and hazy over his library, but he's not looking at me like I'm an idiot at all.

He's looking at me like I've just told him a secret.

"This is the best place in the world," I declare, and he laughs.

"We need to take you more places then," he says, but he's wrong. I wouldn't be able to burrow into other places, I wouldn't have the promise of spending days and days rifling through all this arcana, of touching each and every forgotten page. It's the best place in the world because it will belong to me—not in a legal sense, of course, but in the caretaking sense, in the spiritual sense.

"Did you remember it much?" he asks as I drift over to one of the glass cases to examine the curios. "From that summer?"

"Barely," I admit, running my fingers along the glass. It's dusty, as if the room hasn't been cleaned in a while, even though the fireplace area looks well used. I have a sudden image of Auden and the others camping in this house like children, eating out of cans and making tents out of blankets. "The adults always chased us off, remember?"

My only memory had been of a cavernous space filled with books, of temptation incarnate for a girl like me—but it was a temptation I never satisfied. My parents—and Becket's, Rebecca's and Delphine's—had all been kind and warm to us, herd of feral children that we were that summer, but Auden's father terrified me. It had only taken one barked warning from him when he caught me running down the Long Gallery to know that I never wanted to be in trouble with him ever again.

So I stayed far away from the library, even though it called to me. Even though I felt its presence in the house like a flickering lamp—beckoning me, brightening the shadows, promising secrets.

"They were so ferocious about us being in here," Auden agrees, coming over to join me at the case. "Do you...do you know what they were working on?"

He sounds so hopeful, and it's a hope I know well because it's mirrored inside me. All these years I've asked my father, straining my memory for anything I could have heard or seen, all for nothing.

"My father would never tell me. What about your parents? Did they ever say anything to you about it?"

Auden shakes his head. "And same with everyone else. Whatever they were working on, they abandoned it that summer and decided to take it to the grave. Literally, in the cases of some of them."

Disappointment makes hatch marks over my good mood like frost on a window.

"All I remember is that they needed the library," he says. "And they had books and things spread out all over the tables. And one night they went out to the maze"

"I didn't know that," I say. "When?"

"August first. Lammas. I remember because our cook made us little bread people, do you remember?"

I have a murky recollection of holding a bread person in my hands, of being sullen that Delphine's little bread girl was prettier than mine, but that's it.

"I was eating mine in my room that night when I saw them go into the maze. I stayed up for hours waiting for them to come back, and they didn't return until after dawn…"

"And you don't know what they were doing?"

"No idea. Maybe they went to the thorn chapel to get married. Like us." Another crooked smile and my heart flips over.

He shifts closer, ducking over a verdigris-covered figurine of a man with antlers. There's only a few inches between my shoulder and his arm, and this close, I can smell traces of his scent. Something with citrus and pepper and pine…and lavender? I want to press my face against his neck and suck it in. I want to smell it as he's pinning me to the floor…

Engaged, Poe. Engaged. And you're not stupid.

I'm stupider than I give myself credit for, apparently, because that pepper and lavender smell is all I can think about. "Blenheim Bouquet," I say. Randomly. Like a random asshole.

"Pardon?" Auden asks, startled.

"Blenheim Bouquet. That's what you're wearing, right?" I say, trying to fill in this awkward conversation crater I've just made. "Delphine's father wore it. I remember that day St. Sebastian found it in their room when we were looking for spare change to go to the shops, and he broke it on the floor."

"Oh God, I'd forgotten," Auden says, pressing a hand to his hair. "We tried for hours to make that room smell right again. And it didn't matter because they'd immediately known what we'd done."

"And you confessed," I add, just now remembering that part. "You confessed so St. Sebastian wouldn't get into trouble."

"Well, it's not like Delphine's father was going to yell at *me,*" Auden replies with a charming dimple.

I don't think he knows that I also remember the bruise he had on his cheek after his own father got done with him. I move away to another case, pretending to be absorbed in the shallow dishes and bone knives inside. Auden follows me.

"Proserpina," he says quietly, and the sound of my full name is so lovely in his voice, I have to look up. "Why did you come here? Why did you come to Thornchapel?"

Is he joking?

"This is every librarian's dream," I answer quickly. This is the line I've been feeding everyone—my startled roommate, my former boss at the University of Kansas, my ex-girlfriend/Domme. It's true, even if it's not the entire truth about why I agreed to take the job. "You have an untouched library, and I could be the first person to learn its secrets. It's like an untouched canvas to an artist, or a new dig for an archeologist. How could I resist?"

He studies me, hazel eyes kaleidoscopic under those long, dark lashes. "But there must be something else," he murmurs. "Something else to make you want to uproot your life and come all the way out here."

The trouble with being hopeful, with feeling like *everything is possible*, is that it can sometimes come at the cost of dignity, which is a trait I'm reluctant to sign away, even when I'm being forced to kneel with a gag in my mouth. The need for dignity is partly why I'm trying to resist the pull of Auden, not to mention the lure of the glossy group outside.

If I tell him about the *convivificat* and all my secret hopes about my mother, does that make me *less*? Will Auden think I'm foolish or deluded? Will he look at me with pity?

And does it even matter?

He might know something about my mother or the note that can help. I'm *here* for her, or at least, I'm here *about* her, and even if I'd planned on waiting until longer than my first afternoon here to ask, there's no point in being coy about it.

I relent, and surrender my dignity, as hope so often demands.

"Actually," I say, reaching into my skirt pocket. "There was one other thing."

4

Auden takes the piece of paper from me and steps a little closer to the wall of windows, which sends light glowing over his hair and face, catching on his long lashes and along the sculpted cut of his jaw.

"It...revives?" he asks, peering down at the paper. His brows pull together. "No, it wakes."

I don't bother asking how he can just whip out a random Latin translation, because everything about Auden screams *boy who learned Latin in school.* But I do register a tiny tick of disappointment at his genuine confusion; he's never seen this before, which means he doesn't have the answers I need.

"It quickens," I say, trying to sound like that's a totally normal thing to be written on a piece of paper and mailed to me. "Or that's what my friend in the Classics department told me at least."

Auden glances up at me, head tilted. "And you got this in the mail?"

"Yes. It was mailed on my birthday."

"Happy belated birthday."

"Thank you. It was mailed from here."

His brows pull together even more, making a little crease between them that I'd like to lick. And then be punished for licking. "Mailed from *Thornchapel*? You're not saying that one of us could have written this…? I mean, I suppose we could have, in a technical sense, but why?"

I'm already shaking my head. "It wasn't one of you. At least, not one of you who wrote it. That's my mother's handwriting."

Auden's lips come together and then part. "Poe."

"I know. I know."

He angles the paper in the weak sunlight, bending over it. "I can't tell how old this paper is."

"It's got a high cotton content. It wouldn't show its age for at least another few decades."

He nods to himself, eyes still scanning the paper. "Meaning it could have been written the day it was sent or twenty years before."

"Exactly."

"You can tell it was underneath another paper she'd written on—there are indentations of other letters on here. *S-e-c-r-a-t-i-o-n…?*"

I've already been down this river of thought. "Either obsecration or desecration is my best guess."

"And then here's an *L* and a *C*. Capitalized, it looks like. Underlined too."

"Short for limited liability company? Library of Congress? Lacuna Coil?"

Auden's lips twitch. "Lacuna Coil? Really?"

"My point is that those letters could be anything. An abbreviation. A call number. A test to make sure her pen works."

Auden makes an *mmm* noise.

"I have to ask, Auden. Does any of this seem familiar to you? Have you heard or seen anything about my mother recently?" I rush through it, hearing how desperate I sound. How naive.

But when Auden looks up at me, there's no pity in his eyes. If there were pity, I might have left. I might have cried.

There's only understanding. His own vulnerability shining through.

"No," he says softly. "I'm sorry."

My shoulders droop. "Maybe one of the others..." I trail off. I don't really believe that. I'm not sure what I believe, what I hope right now, but it's not that the others will know something.

Auden hands the paper back to me, his eyes searching my face.

"It's what I expected," I say hopelessly, feeling suddenly and painfully tired. I need to sleep again. "I didn't expect to find her. Or for anyone to know anything. I just thought...I don't know. I guess I thought that I'd come here and the note would suddenly make sense. Like I'd find a giant stone plinth engraved with this Latin word and she'd be buried there."

"Not knowing is the hardest," Auden says.

I remember his mother, and what she did to herself, and I think our losses are cousins to each other. Like me, he'll never know what his mother thought while she bore down into the pit of her addiction, and there won't be any answers or closure. Just a seeping wound that sometimes bleeds and sometimes doesn't.

I don't know what to say, so I only nod and tuck the note back in my dress. To change the subject, I ask, "So you really don't know how many books are in here?"

Auden cups the back of his neck with a hand, looking like he wants to say more about mothers and Latin, but he's too well-bred to push, I suppose. "Yes, that's right. There was a Victorian lady of the house, Estamond Guest, who undertook a partial survey when she married into the family, but she didn't get very far. Cremer says he heard a family legend that she found some kind of heretical tract and it shocked her pious sensibilities, but I think it's more likely that she was too busy having piles and piles of Guest babies to catalog old books."

I wander over to one of the shelves opposite the fireplace and run my fingers along the spines. "Do you still have it? Estamond's survey?"

"Oh yes, no one ever throws anything away at Thornchapel. It's actually at the top of that shelf there, the one right in front of you. Do you see?"

I look up, and just as Auden said, there are two large books on the highest shelf—propped on top of the normal row of books. A big no-no, and I let out a disappointed huff at whoever did it. I slide that bookshelf's ladder over to the middle and mount the first rung, flinching at the ominous wooden creak under my foot.

Auden, ever the gentleman, sweeps over to steady the base of the ladder as I climb—and presumably to catch my fall if the old ladder collapses. "Is it really necessary for you to get them right now?" he asks pleasantly.

"Yes." I could explain about the additional weight and potential trapped damp of keeping the ledgers like this, or I could confess that I can't even wait for the equipment to get delivered before I start assessing the library, but I've already got a hold of the ledgers and it's taking all my concentration to lever them free and tuck them to my chest. They are mercifully dry, and my worries about damp are allayed.

They're bound in a cloth that's faded to the color of dried blood, and when I crack open the top book, I see a flowery, scribbled signature.

Estamond Guest. The *m* has an extra hump in it, like Estamond had dashed it out too fast to keep the letters neat.

Feeling victorious for no real reason, I turn to smile down at the gentleman holding my ladder and find that his eyes are not on my face but on my ass, which at this angle is surely visible from under my skirt. Conflicting reactions blaze through me—embarrassment, anger, lust—and when he drags his eyes away from my bottom to meet my gaze, I realize that he has only one look on his face.

Anguish.

Utter, violent anguish.

His beautiful mouth is tight at the corners but parted ever so slightly in the middle, and he's breathing hard, hard enough that I can see the rapid rise and fall of his chest. His hands are gripping the ladder so hard that they're blanched around the knuckles, and his eyes—

I think I might be burning alive from those eyes. Burning alive like a saint tied to a stake.

For a long minute, we do nothing but stare, and my body flames with awareness of him, with the want of him, but the moment collapses faster than I want it to and he pushes himself away from the ladder with much more force than necessary.

"I trust—" he clears his throat, not looking at me. "I trust you'll be able to make it down on your own. I need to step out for a moment.

Excuse me."

And he's moving to the door before I can say anything in response. Before I can even sputter a protest.

Do I want to sputter a protest?

No, no, of course not. Of course he should leave. He's engaged and I'm not stupid, and there's no world where he should have been looking at me like that regardless of those two things.

The others push through the door just as Auden's trying to leave, and Delphine gives him a playful smack on the arm.

"The tea's been ready *forever*! What was taking you so long?"

To Auden's credit, the question doesn't fluster him. He merely drops a quick kiss on Delphine's cheek and murmurs an excuse as he slides out of sight. Becket watches him go, holding the tea tray and frowning.

"Everything all right?" Rebecca asks, looking between me on the ladder and the door.

"Totally all right," I lie. But it shouldn't be a lie. Or should it?

I want to hit myself in the face with Estamond's ledgers. This is *exactly* what I'd wanted to avoid when I came to Thornchapel. This exact situation.

Becket sets down the tea things in the middle of the room, presumably to help me, but Rebecca is already on her way over. "Do you want to hand those to me?"

"Yes, please," I say gratefully, twisting enough to pass them down, and then I hear her suck in a breath. I crane my neck to see what she's reacting to, but it's not necessary. At that same instant, I feel her finger trace a line over the marks on my thigh.

Oh, holy fuck. The marks.

Rebecca's face is thoughtful. "This looks like a cane."

I don't answer. I can't. I hadn't planned on ever revealing this part of myself here, and while I'm not ashamed, I have no rehearsed lines and clear explanations to pull out of my brain. My brain is blank.

"And a paddle too."

She pokes a bruise, and I gasp, nearly dropping the books.

"Give those to me before you fall."

Disoriented and not a little panicked, I obey immediately, and this sends a small smirk curling at her mouth. "Well, well, well," she says, taking the books. "Proserpina Markham is a little sub girl. Who would have guessed?"

"I don't—" I look over at Becket, who's turned back to the tea and is currently pouring Delphine a cup. They can't hear us. "I can't—"

"You don't have to justify anything. Not to me," she says. There's a world of understanding in her deep umber gaze.

"You too?" I whisper.

"I'm the one who gives little submissive girls what they're looking for. Stay there one moment." She sets the books carefully on the closest table, and then angles her body so I can climb down the ladder without exposing my marks any further. Which is only half a relief because she still knows they're there.

And—oh God—Auden.

Auden knows they're there. That's what he saw, that's what sent him fleeing from the room like he was being chased. And as I step off the ladder and smooth my skirt down my legs, something obvious becomes clear to me: Auden knows what these marks are.

He knows what they mean.

If he'd thought I'd fallen or that I was being abused, he would have said something, asked after my welfare. But instead he'd gone rigid and silent and then left.

Was he aroused? Disgusted? Both?

He's your employer, Poe, however much it doesn't feel that way. You need to explain.

"Have some tea!" Delphine chirps from beside the fireplace.

"I, um…yes, I'll have some tea in just a minute. Where's the nearest bathroom?"

"You'll have to go upstairs," Rebecca says, her eyes on my face. I get the feeling she knows I'm lying, but I also get the feeling she's not going to press me on it. Yet. "Up the back stairwell and take a right."

"Thank you," I say and go to find Auden.

5

I expect to have to search the house for Auden. I assume I'll have to tramp over the barely unfrozen grass across the gardens to find him.

But no. I walk down the narrow corridor connecting the east wing of the house to the main hall and there's Sir James Frazer whining at the doorway—whining at Auden actually, who's just outside the threshold talking with someone. The huge double doors are propped open by buckets of paint, and when I step all the way into the hall, I can see that he's talking with one of the workers.

St. Sebastian.

Both of them are squared off to each other, and St. Sebastian's arms are crossed while Auden's hands stay by his sides. Only the occasional flex of his fingers betrays the depth of his agitation—his voice is low and calm, although whatever he's saying has St.

Sebastian's mouth going tight, his plush lower lip flattening under his lip piercing.

This is none of your business.

It feels like it is, though. I need to talk to Auden, I already planned on finding St. Sebastian again. And I can't repress my librarian-ish need for more information, just to know *why*. Why do they dislike each other so much? What's happened in the years I've been gone to curdle their boyish affection into this hatred?

I step closer, but I don't announce myself yet, and they don't notice me, caught up as they are in their conversation.

"I never would have allowed you back into this house," Auden's saying. His hands twitch again. "You know that."

"My uncle needed the extra help today." The rain is only halfheartedly dribbling down now, barely enough to take notice of, but still enough that St. Sebastian has to keep shaking it free of his so-long-it's-unholy eyelashes. "I wasn't going to leave him hanging just because the job site belongs to an asshole."

"Is it for the money? I'll pay you whatever he's paying you for you to go away."

"It's *not about money*," St. Sebastian seethes. "I'm doing just fine, fuck you very much for asking, and I'm only here as a favor."

"It's always about the money with you," Auden replies coldly. "One way or another."

"Spoken like someone who's always had it."

"You weren't so proud when you were begging me to—"

It happens in an instant. One moment St. Sebastian is standing there glowering, and the next, he's slamming Auden to the ground.

They land—Auden first, St. Sebastian on top—with a thud and then a crunch as they start wrestling on the gravel. And for a split second—no more than that, because I'm not a *total* sex monster—I can't help but notice how beautiful they both are like this. St. Sebastian with his threadbare T-shirt hiked up around his abdomen and Auden's entire body a long, lean arch of strength as he bucks up against him.

Then I come to my senses and run toward them, shouting at them to stop. The dog has the same idea, tearing over the gravel to go bark in their faces and prance around them, as if he can't figure out if he should protect Auden or if it's a big play party and he wants in.

I reach them just as St. Sebastian's pinned Auden's hips between his thighs and fisted Auden's sweater in one hand. The pose you assume when you're about to hit somebody as hard as you can. I do the only thing I can think of—which is to throw my arms around St. Sebastian and pull him off my host.

My body is somewhere between the model-slim Rebecca's and the summer-blown curves of Delphine's, not really enough to tackle a full-grown man, but enough to knock him off balance when he's not expecting it, and together we tumble to the cold, wet ground. Before I can process my new position, however, Auden's on top of us both.

He freezes when he realizes he's on top of more than just St. Sebastian.

We're all completely still. St. Sebastian under me, Auden on top, me in the middle, and for a single moment we're breathing as one, our chests filling and emptying, our hearts pounding in time. There's a buzzing in my blood, and it's along every stretch and tuck of my skin, like I've become electrified, like I'm sharing something deeper and more elemental than breath and a wedge of cold gravel with these men.

And then Auden shoves himself up to his feet and the moment ruptures wide open, spilling its guts and dying. There's no more electricity, no more buzzing, no more of that heady awareness. We're just three cold, damp people with gravel embedded in our palms.

Auden stands over us, furious and ferocious, and St. Sebastian sits up and angles his body in front of me as I struggle to sit too, as if he's trying to protect me.

Auden scowls at this, scowls harder at where St. Sebastian's forearm brushes along my bare legs. He yanks once at his hair, then storms away without another word, Sir James Frazer trotting behind him.

St. Sebastian and I sit there and stare at the doorway for a moment, and then with a sigh, he gets to his feet and extends a hand to help me up.

"I'm sorry," he says after we're both standing, but I'm not sure what he's apologizing for. There's no doubt in my mind that Auden knew his words would hurt St. Sebastian. That he intended them to be a provocation of the highest order.

"He started it," I say.

"No, I started it," St. Sebastian answers wearily. "Years ago."

I brush the extra gravel off my shirt and dab at my rain-wet face with a rain-wet sleeve. "You didn't deserve all that though."

"Didn't I?" St. Sebastian says, and he turns before I can read his expression, before I can ask him to explain. "It was good to see you again, Poe," he adds over his shoulder. "Take care."

Wait, I want to say. *I want to see you again. Talk to you again.*

I want to look into your inky eyes again.

Feel my body on yours again.

I screw my lips shut. None of that is really appropriate in this moment, and maybe it'll never be appropriate. Maybe I'm just being a sex monster again.

So instead I say, "Good to see you too," as he climbs into a work van. With a small wave, he drives away. And with a deep breath, I steel myself to go back inside.

When I get back to the library, there's no trace of Auden, but there is a cup of tea waiting for me, and I manage to pass off the rest of the afternoon in facsimile of pleasantness, even though I'm exhausted and confused and my hand stings with the tiny bites of countless pieces of gravel.

And when it comes time for dinner, there's still no Auden. We make spaghetti in the kitchen and eat in the library, Becket genially covering over any awkward gaps when my sleepiness gets too intense for me to focus on conversation. Delphine repeatedly apologizes for Auden's absence, saying he needs to work, and Rebecca keeps shooting me glances that indicate I'm going to be pulled into a corner and questioned soon. My jet lag makes an excellent excuse to bow out early, and by nine o'clock, me and my scraped palms are in bed asleep.

Auden, Delphine, and Rebecca are not in the house when I wake up the next morning.

I'm not totally surprised, as Rebecca told me over dinner that today is their day for traveling back to London, but it's still strange to wake up and know that I'll be the only person inside the house. At least the only person who's not currently tearing it apart. Even Sir

James Frazer has gone to stay with Becket at his rectory; I'm truly alone.

I go down to the kitchen, sleepily make some toast and eat it, and then go back up to my bedroom to change—which somehow results in me curling up on top of my bed again and falling asleep for another four hours. I could claim jet lag, I guess, but that's not really the whole of it. It's the narcolepsy, and I'm flushed and shameful when I wake up in the early afternoon, having done nothing with my time except dream wild, fretful dreams. It's hard to shake off the uneasy fog that clings to me after I wake up for good, a fog that seems to be about everything and nothing all at once.

If I'm honest, a lot of my uneasiness is about Auden. I never had the chance to correct whatever assumptions he'd made after seeing my legs, and our last moment together was with me and St. Sebastian tangled on the ground, with *that* look on his face. A look of primal fury...and raw betrayal.

The whole episode is sitting heavy in my chest, but I'm not sure why. I think I might be angry or defensive, but I'm also strangely worried. I want Auden to like me.

It's a stupid thing to want, and I push it out of my head, determined to get some work done in his absence.

I know from my correspondence with Mr. Cremer that I can expect my equipment tomorrow, which means there's no time to waste today. I need to make a preliminary assessment of the collection before I start handling anything, and I need to make a plan. Thornchapel is so isolated that it would be logistically difficult to move all the books offsite—the ideal situation for cataloging and then re-shelving according to the new classifications—but also the other large rooms in the house are currently being attacked with saws and drills, so I'm limited inside the house as well. I think over all this during my shower, mentally reviewing the layout of the library shelves while I brush my teeth.

After I give myself a quick, encouraging little orgasm, I dress and fortify my brain with coffee. And then I go to the library and stand in the doorway for a long time. Just holding the coffee mug in my hands and dreaming.

Dreaming boxes of books in one corner and then in the next. Dreaming the best spot for the massive book scanner that's coming and then for the computer station that will go with it. Dreaming where I'll take humidity and temperature readings and what I'll do if they come back with dire results. Dreaming of classification systems and sympathetic but clear labeling for the shelves, and dreaming of cloud storage and external backups and servers.

When I've dreamed my dreams enough to start anchoring them to plans, I find my laptop and then settle in at one of the long tables with my coffee to work. I write down my notes and any potential supplies I'll need—archival boxes for sure, playbook binders, some document cleaning powder—and things I'll need to clear with Auden, like environmental appliances for the library and any extensive book repairs that I won't be able to do myself. And then I take my phone, open up a blank note on the screen, and start counting books, starting at the shelves by the door.

I'm lost in the numbers when a murderous barking spikes my blood with adrenaline. I spin, holding a book in front of me like maybe I can defend myself with it, but then it's just Sir James Frazer skidding into the library and cantering toward me with his tongue hanging out of his mouth. He shoves his nose in my crotch before licking my hand

and then he trots back to the door where Becket appears in his priest's collar and black slacks, out of breath.

"I'm so sorry, Poe," he gasps, holding on to the doorframe and leaning over to breathe. "He didn't scare you, did he?"

"Only a little," I say dryly and set down my book-weapon. "What are you doing here? You said you'd be back at your rectory today."

Becket catches his breath enough to transfer himself into one of the chairs at my worktable. The winter light catches in his sandy-blond hair and casts a soft shadow under his long, long legs. He makes a very romantic figure in his collar, his chiseled profile limned by the pinkening late afternoon glow. Like some kind of Scandinavian saint or northern martyr.

"I finished with my homily early, and I wanted to make sure you were settling in okay," Becket says, giving me a warm smile. He pulls out a chair and pats the seat, and when I sit, he folds his hands together on the table and tilts his head to look at me. It's very priestly, but also very Becket—even the patient expression on his face can't erase the far-seeing shimmer in his eyes, like he can see angels. Like he knows their names.

"Thanks," I say, and I mean it. Back home, my life was brimming over with drinks fun and kinky fun and everything in between. But here…

I mean, I *want* to be here. I chose to be here. But still, there's something lonely about being in a new place and knowing that your old place is so very, very far away. Even if you've chosen your new place with a whole heart. "I might be a little homesick."

"I was too at first," Becket admits with a smile. "It's different from home, you know?"

Which of course it is, every place is different from everywhere else after all—but in this moment, with just the two of us and the pacing dog, I know exactly what he means. He means that the sun sets too soon and that range cookers are completely baffling to the uninitiated and all the snacks in the pantry are strange. He means that every voice you hear is different, and that when you hear your own voice out loud, it starts to sound different too. He means that when you fall asleep at night, you're bereft of the night sounds you've clung to for years, whether they're sirens or cicadas or the television in your neighbor's apartment, and when you wake up, your body has forgotten the oceans you've crossed and the roads you've driven and it still thinks it's home.

"Are you still homesick?" I ask softly.

"Yes and no. It's been almost a year, and there are times when *this* is home, no doubt about it. But then there are times when I miss Virginia so much I could cry."

Sir James comes up and sniffs at my hand, then sits expectantly. I pet him as I ask Becket, "Why work here? Why not work in Virginia?"

A pause. Not long. Just long enough for me to know that he considered his words. "I could ask you the same," he responds in a gentle tone.

I think of the *convivificat* up in my room, tucked safely into a dresser drawer. I think of my dreams, filled with Thornchapel and all the people I knew here. I think of Auden's hazel eyes full of scorn and frolic, and of St. Sebastian's lip ring glinting against his soft mouth.

"Lots of reasons," I finally say, not sure how much I can tell Becket without sounding delusional or obsessed.

"I'll go first then," he says. "I came back for this place. For Thornchapel."

He says it without any shame or self-deprecation, like of course he's not delusional to want Thornchapel, and it makes me feel less delusional too.

"Same for me," I whisper.

"Even though I left it, it never left me. I never stopped feeling like I should be here...that for some reason, I belonged at Thornchapel and I could never really belong anywhere else. We have, well—" Now Becket does look embarrassed and he clears his throat. "We have a family friend who's a cardinal. He helped, ah, *arrange* for me to find a situation in England, close to here."

"You nepotist!" I poke him in the arm.

He gives me a look. "Well, I'm not exactly proud of it," he confesses. "I wrestled with my conscience daily before I came, wondering if I was forcing a way open when I was supposed to wait and serve some other parish first, but then I came here and it just felt right. It felt like a knot in my chest had finally been loosened. I could breathe for the first time in so long."

"I know exactly what you mean," I murmur, looking past him to the window. The trees scratch against the blue-pink sky outside. "I used to dream about it. For years I've dreamed about it."

Becket doesn't say anything, experienced confessor that he is, and so I find myself explaining about the note in my mother's handwriting, about how I want so much to know what she was doing here and why. How I still harbor a secret little hope that I'll find her one day, that she's been on some sun-drenched dig in the Levant for twelve years and simply forgot to call. I tell Becket about the dreams too, although I do leave out how thoroughly those dreams starred Auden and St. Sebastian. I leave out being a sex monster and how much it hurts to burn with desires I also haven't let myself satisfy.

"Do I sound bananas?" I ask after I'm done talking. "Do I sound obsessed?"

"No more than the rest of us are," he assures me. "When it comes to Thornchapel, none of us are immune."

"Auden might be," I muse, thinking of his words in my room yesterday.

Burn it and salt the earth where it stood.

Becket shakes his head. "No. Auden most of all."

I want to ask him more about this, but a chime comes from Becket's pocket and he pulls out his phone and taps the screen. "Ah, I've got to get back. We have a First Communion parent meeting tonight. Much more dull than spending the evening with you, but alas, duty calls."

I stand up with him. "Do you want to leave Sir James here?"

"Oh, no. The only reason those kids come to church is hoping he'll be there."

Sir James wags his tail in agreement, which continues all the way through the walk to Becket's car.

"Oh!" I say just as Becket's about to climb inside. "Do you know where I can find St. Sebastian? I thought he was working on the house, but he wasn't around today and I think…well, I think Auden drove him off."

Becket sighs. "Yeah. I suspected that might happen."

"Do they fight often?"

"No, thank God." Becket's fervent tone tells me he's actually thanking God for this. "Yesterday must have been the first time they've seen each other in years."

Years? What the hell had happened between them?

"Saint works at the public library in Thorncombe," Becket goes on. "Most weekdays."

"St. Sebastian is a *librarian*?" I ask, shocked.

Becket cracks a wide smile, looking like a charming, eligible clergyman from some *Masterpiece* show. "He looks too sexy to be a librarian, doesn't he?"

"Becket."

"Don't worry, you do too," he says, with an angel-eyed wink I wouldn't have thought him capable of giving.

"*Becket!*"

The priest just laughs, shuts his door with a wave, and then drives off, Sir James Frazer barking back at me the whole way down the drive.

6

The equipment comes the next day, and supervising the delivery and installation takes almost until dinner. By the time the too-early dusk comes, I'm almost too tired to make myself a quick sandwich, but I force myself, knowing I'll probably sleep for twelve or thirteen hours, and I hate waking up with low blood sugar. I eat, brush my teeth, and then fall into bed like I've never been there before. I do indeed sleep for twelve hours.

But the next day, I go into Thorncombe around lunchtime, after I've worked a few hours in the library getting the digitization software up and running. After a pie and a beer—and a second beer for courage—I walk down to the library, which is off the main street through the village on a small side road that has an arresting view of the St. Brigid's graveyard.

High in the far corner of the cemetery, a glossy black headstone frowns over the weathered gray teeth of the other markers, gleaming and distinct. GUEST is printed across the top in massive letters, with two sets of dates underneath, and there are no flowers decorating it, no wreaths or plants, just a rectangle of grass that looks newer than the rest.

Auden's parents.

I stop and take it in for a minute, the graveyard and the church, and after a while, my gaze drifts to the rest of the street, so pretty and so lonely all at the same time. While there are signs of modernity—a banner flapping against the fence for the church's nursery school, a pharmacy, a bank—it feels shoved to the background, as if the stones and streets of the village itself refuse to be dragged into the present day. A beautiful spot to visit, but it makes me a little wistful...and a little unsettled. It's like the village is keeping secrets, just like the estate it originally served, and there's this feeling—thin and filament-like, too fragile to really examine—that it's all connected, that Thorncombe is keeping Thornchapel's secrets or vice versa, that somehow this deep seam of river and forest in the middle of nowhere knows something I don't.

It's a feeling only strengthened by the way people look at me while I walk around. I'm from Kansas: I know small towns. And so for a while, I chalk it up to the usual *who are you* vibe people give off when they see a stranger. But I can't deny that there's something different too; it's not clannishness or suspicion—or not only those things. It's expectation. Like they're waiting for me to say something or do something, and I have no idea what it is. Apologize for being here? Explain *why* I'm here?

Not drink two beers by myself in the middle of the day?

I'm relieved when I push my way into the Thorncombe Library and find it empty. And though the building itself is all old stone and brick, the inside is fairly modern, if displaying the usual public-building shabbiness that American libraries also have in abundance. I step onto the industrial carpet and walk past a cheerful children's section and a bank of public computers—all empty—until I find the desk in the back, which judging from the scribbled notes littered around the keyboard and the carts of books lined up behind it, doubles as a reference desk and a circulation desk.

No one's there.

Life would be so much easier if he had an Instagram or a Snapchat or a Twitter account like everybody else, but no, St. Sebastian is one of *those* people, and I feel distinctly stupid as I look around the empty space.

Is this how people really used to find people before iPhones? By asking other people? Out loud? With mouth-words?

Ugh.

The longest rows of stacks continue on from the desk, and I can make out a half-empty cart at the end, so I decide to go ask whoever's shelving if they know St. Sebastian.

But when I find the row the librarian is currently shelving in, it's *not* other people, it's St. Sebastian himself. He's half-kneeling, one arm laden with books, a hand expertly wedging a title between the others on the shelf. And with the messy hair and lip ring, I expected him to be in a T-shirt and boots again, but he's in slacks and glossy shoes and a charcoal zip-up with a collared shirt underneath. Cheap business casual, but on St. Sebastian's tight body, it looks delicious.

"May I help you find something?" St. Sebastian asks without looking up.

"Yes," I say. "You."

He nearly drops the book he's trying to shelve, just barely managing to catch it between his palm and his knee with a *thwacky* sound. "Jesus Christ," he mumbles, finally looking up at me. "Proserpina?"

"Poe is easier," I suggest, shrugging off my coat and draping it over the cart. I kneel next to him and take a couple of his books. He starts to protest, but I give him a look. "I have my master's in library science. Do you really think I can't handle shelving large-print mysteries?"

His sigh is one of defeat, and I take that as permission. We start shelving side by side, finding an easy, efficient rhythm that's unbroken by words until he finally asks, "Why are you here?"

I decide to ignore his grouchy tone. "I wanted to see you."

He makes an impatient noise, shelving his last book and turning to face me. "But *why*?"

I still have books to put away, so I don't return his gaze. "Because we knew each other as kids and now I'm back. Isn't that enough?"

He steps over to me, taking a few of the books out of my arms. His warm hands brush against my arm, and I can't help but remember yesterday, what it felt like to be stretched out on top of him, what it felt like to have my legs tangled with his. His hair isn't long enough to tie back but it is more than long enough to tug on, to twine my fingers through. To feel brushing over my stomach as he kisses his way down to the wet place between my legs…

I blush and look back at the two books left in my arms, staring at the labels on the spines while I try to force my mind away from sex.

Which should be easy, because I've actually never done it. Not once, not with anyone.

When Emily was my Mistress, she would welt me and spank me and call me her slut, but there was nothing more than the punishment—no oral, no digital, no toys. It's ultimately why we broke up—and why I broke up with the boyfriend before her—because they were ready for more and I just…couldn't. Despite the raging libido and the insatiable need for kink, I've never been able to join with someone that way.

Sharing pain?

Sure.

Sharing pleasure?

Way too much.

But despite this weird hitch in my soul, I want sex constantly. Emily used to call me the Literal Madonna-Whore, since I think about sex all the time, almost all of my dreams are sex-filled, and if I don't come at least once a day, I'm miserable. And yet, I still haven't had sex.

This would be so much easier if you'd let me fuck you, she'd told me once, near the end. *Can you at least tell me why you aren't ready?*

The truth was—and is—I didn't know. My family's Catholic, but the easygoing kind, and any faint flickers of discomfort with my queerness were doused early on. I was raised to be sex-positive. I found kink online as a teen and went to my first club on my eighteenth birthday. I'm not afraid of pain and I don't have any kind of aversion to tongues, fingers, toys, or cocks.

I've felt this way with both boys and girls, I've felt this way in dark clubs with music thumping through the walls and in cozy bedrooms surrounded by pillows and posters. I've felt this way drunk and felt this way sober, with people I loved and people I merely found sexy as hell. With every person, in every place, I haven't been able to do it, and the only constant has been this feeling inside of me, this *not yet* feeling.

Like I need to wait, but I have no idea what for.

Love? I'd found it. More than once.

The perfect blend of affection and torture? Also found that.

Marriage? I didn't even know if I wanted to get married. Leaving aside the wedding I'd had as a girl to Auden and St. Sebastian, of course.

Maybe it's been too long. Maybe I've let it become this all-important gateway in my head, when it's not a gate at all, it's just another step, another footfall on a path that can lead anywhere I choose.

I look back at St. Sebastian and wonder.

Why not him? Why not now, in this new life?

Everything is possible, right?

He has no idea I'm dreaming about my weird, complicated virginity however, because he takes one of the two books I'm still holding, shelves it, and says, "Lots of people know each other as kids. I'm not sure it has to mean anything now."

I'm yanked away from my reverie by a small puncture of hurt. "What does that mean?" I ask, wounded. "You don't want to talk to me?"

"No!" he blurts out and then jams the heels of his palms into his eyes. "Maybe? Christ, I don't know, Poe, I really don't."

"I'm not asking to move in, St. Sebastian, just to hang out."

"It's just Saint these days," he says tiredly, dropping his hands. "It's easier...like how Poe is easier. Easier to say."

That's true. It suddenly strikes me that both of us have modified our names since the summer we knew each other, like if we changed our names, we could escape their meanings. We could escape the now-painful memories of the mothers who gave them to us.

"And I don't know if us hanging out is a good idea," he continues. "Auden won't like it."

"Who cares?" I say, my words bolder than my feelings.

If he sees through my lie, Saint doesn't call me on it. Instead he says, "Maybe you should care. He's paying you."

"I doubt Auden would go so far as to fire me over it. And he's gone so much anyway. Tuesday through Friday evening, I'm at the house alone."

Saint toys with his lip ring, catching it between his teeth and tugging while he thinks.

"What about just dinner tonight?" I say. "For old time's sake? Or at the very least as my prize for helping you shelve this cart?"

That makes him smile the tiniest, tiniest bit...and I know I've won.

We meet at The Thorn and Crown a few hours later. I walked from the house, even though Auden's graciously left me the use of a car. One of his few, which is a little upsetting when I consider how casually he just...has more than one car. I think it would be even more upsetting to actually drive it, so I don't—but as a consequence, I'm both fucking freezing and completely winded from the steep walk by the time I blow into the front door of the pub.

It's not full by any means, but a good handful of people turn to stare at me with that expectant Thorncombe stare, made even more awkward by the fact that they're clearly having some kind of miniature community meeting.

St. Brigid's Day Planning Committee is on a battered poster board sign leaning against a table. There's a man with a notepad, a woman with a toddler crawling around her feet, and two people with dogs. They look at me like I should know their names, but when I wave, they all turn quickly back to themselves and start talking, without waving back.

If my cheeks weren't already chapped raw by the wind, I'd have blushed.

As it is, I'm already too hot in the stuffy pub as I spot Saint hunched over a book in the corner, and I'm stripping off coats and gloves and scarves as I approach.

"Hi!" I say breathlessly.

He looks up over his book and gives me a hesitant smile. It doesn't reach his eyes, which are so dark in the dim light of the pub that they remind me of Dartmoor itself, of its nights so lightless you can't even see your hand in front of your face.

I have the same feeling looking at him as I do looking at the winter hills and leafless forests. I'm fascinated, I'm drawn, I want to touch all that loneliness with my bare fingertips and take it inside of myself.

"You're so—" he stops saying whatever it is he's about to say and shakes his head at himself.

"What?" I ask with a laugh, still trying to pile all my winter shit onto the seat next to me.

"You're so colorful," he says. Quickly. "I mean with your cheeks being so flushed and your eyes being so green right now—"

He breaks off and looks away, his expression stony. Like Auden, he has a mask he wears too, except instead of Pouty Rich Boy, it's Broody Poor Boy. I think about this while I finish wedging my coat through the back of the chair so it will stop sliding off. And when I look up again, there's a faint ruddiness under the bronze of his cheeks, like he's embarrassed.

Maybe that's what draws me to Saint—the blush under the composure, the small signs that under his bitter aloofness is a river of dammed-up emotion threatening to break free.

"So there's a meeting here tonight, huh?" I say in a small-talky kind of way while I glance at the menu.

"Yeah, the St. Brigid's Day festival."

"Sounds Irish to me."

"St. Brigid is an Anglican saint too," Saint says with the tired patience of someone who's explained this before. "The village gets very into it, since the church is—" Saint waves a hand in the direction of the church, which is also named for St. Brigid.

"Well. A festival sounds fun," I say, flipping the menu over. "I love festivals. And fairs. And carnivals. And parties."

When I look back up, Saint is staring at me like I've started speaking in tongues. "*Why*?" he asks.

"Because they are fun and I like fun things. Easy question."

He studies me, all sullen, sexy scrutiny, and I'm suddenly not sure what to do with myself, with my hands or my face or my eyes.

"I don't think any questions are easy when it comes to you," he says after a minute, and my heart climbs right out of my chest.

Everything is possible.

The moment hovers between us, him studying me and me dying to be more than studied, to be *handled*—and I know I should yank it all back down to earth, bring us back into real life.

"I heard about your mother," I say out of nowhere and then wince inwardly. If I'm trying to coax Saint into being my friend—maybe even coax him into taking an unimportant, not-a-gateway step with me—bringing up a recent tragedy is probably not the way to do it.

But weirdly, my little outburst seems to anchor him. He slips into his pain like a familiar suit. "Yes," he says. "It was last year. An infection."

"God. I'm sorry."

He lifts up a shoulder. "I'm heading up to the bar to order—do you want anything?"

"Yes, duh." My food appetite is equal to my sexual appetite, and both are currently in full swing. "The pie please. And the mushroom starters. Oh, and bread!"

I almost get a real smile for all that. "Anything to drink?"

"Um, just a beer that's not an IPA. Thanks!"

Saint goes to order for us, and I slide his book over to my side of the table. It's a popular fantasy novel, and I page through until he gets back.

"We have a copy at the library," he says, nodding to the book as he sets down our beers and sits. "You know, if you're interested. It's pretty good so far."

I push the book back to him, take a sip of beer, and then blurt out, "Were you here when she got sick? I'm sorry to ask, just with my own mom…I don't know, I'm morbidly curious, I guess."

Saint's clearly surprised that I'm taking us back to this, but it doesn't seem to upset him. When he speaks, his tone is weary but level. "I was. When I was a teenager, I did—well, something happened—and I couldn't bear to stay here any longer. So I went to live with my grandparents in Texas for the rest of school. I'd even started college there. But I think she was lonely, and she was struggling with money…"

"So you came back to her," I realize.

"Middle of my sophomore year," he says. "To help with bills. I'd been here two years by the time she got sick."

"You put your life on hold to help her. That's amazing, Saint. I think a lot of people wouldn't have done that."

"Yeah." He takes a drink. A big one.

"So why are you still here?" I ask. "Why not go back to Texas and finish college?"

This question strikes a nerve, I can tell. He takes another drink, looks down at his glass. "I don't know," he says. "When I got here, I found the job at the library, and my dad's brother is a contractor, so there was enough work to compensate for the library not paying much. And then I just kind of…fell into a life. And I guess that moving away, you know, *after*…after she's died…"

He trails off, takes another drink.

"It makes it real," I finish for him, thinking of my own mother. "If you leave, it makes it real."

"Yeah."

"Do you feel like your life is still on hold?" I ask.

Saint laughs—he actually laughs! And when he laughs, I can see that one of his front teeth is ever so slightly longer than the other. And the cleft in his chin smooths out, and his dark brown eyes sparkle. Life and spark hidden under all that winter cold.

"Fuck, you're nosy," he says, still laughing. "Christ."

I give a sheepish shrug. "I'm sorry. I like to know things. Don't answer if you don't want to."

He takes a drink, but this time it doesn't seem like he's doing it because he doesn't want to say more, but because he wants a minute to think.

"On every objective level, yes. My life is still on hold. I'm in a job that pays pennies, and without a degree, I'll never get to the next job up on the ladder. I'm taking some online classes, but at this rate, I'll be thirty before I get my B.A., and I'm not even sure what I want to major in, anyway. I took over my mom's lease because it seemed easier than trying to find a new place and figure out what to do with her stuff..." He catches his lip ring in his teeth for a moment, then continues. "But it's so strange. Every time I think of leaving, I ache with wanting to stay. I can't make myself go. It's like I've put down roots without even wanting to, and I don't mean family roots, because my aunt and uncle have always been here and I only barely remember my dad and his parents. I don't mean friend roots, because I don't really have any of those. I mean the kind of roots that happen privately between you and a certain place. Like you come to a place, and instead of planting a flag and saying *mine*, the place plants something in you. The place claims you, it knows your name and the crooked corners of your heart, and you've pledged yourself to it before you've even realized what's happening. *That's* why I've stayed, *that's* why I can't leave. Thornchapel knows my name and the crooked corners of my heart, and it wants me to make promises that I'm going to keep."

7

Hail, Holy Queen, Mother of Mercy

That night, St. Sebastian walks Poe back to Thornchapel. It's cold as fuck and windy as shit, and her teeth chatter the entire way. He wants to fold her into his arms, he wants to unzip his coat and tuck her against his chest. He may not be good for much, but he could do that.

He could warm her up.

But all told, it's a short walk, and there's no need. They get to the front door and she's fine, and it's only him who's not fine, only him who's jumbled up inside with all the things he *could* do. He could shake her hand. He could hug her. He could kiss her cheek.

He could kiss her mouth.

He could tell her that he can't stop thinking about the way her eyes look like summer. He could tell her that he wants to bite the point of her chin and the arch of her throat. That he's shaking and sick with wanting to touch her. Wanting to watch her gasp and laugh and smile. Wanting to reach that ever-unfolding bloom of her spirit and cradle it in his palms.

He could tell her that they did get married once, after all, and why not play husband and wife for a couple hours and drive back the cold and the dark? Why not pretend Auden was there too, pretend each other's hands were his hands, and each other's mouths were his mouth?

In the end, he tells her none of these things. He sees her inside and mumbles something in noncommittal agreement when she talks about calling him. He listens to his better nature; he keeps his distance. Even when she wheels abruptly around and pulls him into a hug, he manages to keep himself from pressing close, from putting his lips against the wind-tangled silk of her hair.

After all, he knows things she doesn't know.

He knows the things the village knows.

She can't be his.

When he gets home twenty minutes later, he stands in his dead mother's living room and takes in the carcass of his life. His mother's burned out saints' candles that he feels would be cowardly to throw away, even though they gouge a hole in his heart every time he looks at them. A mostly empty sketchbook. A secondhand guitar that's never been played. An old laptop he bought for writing two years ago, the case covered with a film of indifferent dust.

All the relics of a boy who wanted to create, who wanted to be different and interesting and chosen. Who wanted to be the lord of the manor like the flop-haired boy with hazel eyes and too much money.

And instead, all St. Sebastian has to show for his life is an unfinished degree, the scattered remains of abandoned hobbies, no friends, no pets, no lovers—and a lip ring.

He's alone, and he deserves it.

Becket is not a monk, but he abides by his own little monastic rules. He likes the structured focus of ordered days, the quiet asceticism of plain meals, the undeniable rewards of regular prayer. Auden teases him about his daily penances, and Becket can't find the words to explain that these practices are to *protect* him, to keep him from going too far, to make sure that he *does* eat and he *does* sleep.

Zeal, his confessor had once told him, *is a curse as much as it's a blessing. Don't let it consume you like a fire; keep the flames of it small.*

And so the zeal must be dampened. Smothered. He prays at regular intervals to keep himself from lying face down on the floor in ecstatic devotion for hours. He eats plain meals so he won't be tempted to forgo every nourishment except the Host itself. He punishes his body gently with running and exercise so that he won't be tempted to punish it with whips and hair shirts and other unsanctioned mortifications.

His zeal is a secret, almost like a sin itself, and it's only through his gritted teeth that he manages to keep it at bay.

It eases, however, around his friends. Delphine and Rebecca and Auden, Poe now too, if he can count her as a friend, and he hopes he can. It eases around St. Sebastian, whom he leaves the church unlocked for, whose lip ring glints as he bows his head and murmurs empty prayers.

Yes, around them, the zeal dims, and he feels like a different version of himself, the version he might have been if the zeal had never found him. He can be naughty and fun, smart and lively. He can feel comfortable with the desires that burden him, the desires that overwhelm him when they walk hand in hand with the fervor of his faith. With his friends, he eats and drinks and keeps late hours, with them he is only a human and not a saint.

But he's not with them tonight, and so there's only been a plain meal of unbuttered bread and broth. He's done push-ups and sit-ups until his muscles shake with exhaustion. He's prayed the Rosary, the Chaplet, his various devotions, and spent time in silent, contemplative meditation with his Lord.

At nine, he finishes his prayers, checks the side door of the church to make sure it's unlocked in case St. Sebastian wants to come in. St. Sebastian, the unbeliever, who still comes in and prays and kneels and sighs. Who sits and stares at the tabernacle as if he expects God himself to crawl out and apologize to him.

Becket the priest reads for thirty more minutes in bed, a book of Celtic mythology he ordered online last week. It's a secret fascination of his. He tells himself it's purely academic.

When he goes to sleep, the zeal comes for him in his dreams. It shows him dying kings, dying gods, rain pattering on the summer-spread leaves of Thornchapel's forest.

And Proserpina in the middle of it all, haloed and radiant. Waiting.

There's an old warehouse in Peckham, and in that warehouse is a trendy flat, and in that flat there's a woman in bed asleep. She's on her stomach, naked and without a cover, and her bottom is a thing of beauty. Bruises, red and purple like Valentine's Day flowers, have turned her backside into a postmodern canvas of torment and affection. The arnica gel on her skin shines in the glow from the window.

Rebecca watches tonight's submissive sleep for a moment, then slides out of bed to walk to the windows and stare down at the empty street below. It's wet from an earlier burst of rain. An indeterminate clump of litter has caught against the curb, and there's a fresh spray of graffiti on the building opposite that she hasn't noticed before.

It looks cold.

She loves her flat, wedged as it is between a car mechanic's and an art gallery. She loves the little neighborhood it nestles in—she loves the impossibly hip restaurants and speakeasies cropping up between the African food shops and the tattoo parlors and the upstairs churches.

The inside of her home is both a hymn to natural light and an adoration of the city at night—the walls are more glass than brick, and from almost any place in the flat, Rebecca can look up and see the sky. She can access the fresh air and the wind and the rain, something she likes to do often when she's folded into the city's fussy, concrete arms.

She accesses them now, stepping out onto the balcony Auden designed for her when he helped her renovate the flat. It was his first project out of school, and though it feels like a million years ago, it was only three.

Only three years for her to know what forever feels like.

She knows why that is, but she's not going to admit it to herself, at least not tonight. Just like she's not going to examine why she took a curvy blond sub to bed either, not when she's tried so hard to stay away from the blondes, not when she's made sure any white girl she plays with has red or brown or pink or blue hair.

She can tell herself the truth about this at least: the idea of white-gold hair brushing against her thighs is like a kick to the chest. She thinks of it and then she can't breathe.

Rebecca leans against the railing and lets the wind nip at her fingers and toes, and she tries to pretend that tomorrow she will be back in control. Tomorrow, when she goes to Thornchapel, she will know herself again, and in that knowledge there will be no room for wanting the person she also hates.

On the other side of the Thames, Delphine debates whether or not to stay with her fiancé for the night. She stays often, she adores his high-ceilinged townhouse with its combination of newly fitted skylights and original features, the place he bought after his father's death for a fresh start. She doesn't adore her own flat, a glassy, soulless cove in a City high-rise. There is a spa and a swimming pool, however, and a view that is almost worth the millions of pounds the place cost her parents.

It makes for good Instagram pictures.

Truth be told, she *wants* to stay the night with Auden, and so she agrees. She loves him, of course she does, and she reminds herself of this as she changes into a borrowed T-shirt and brushes her teeth. If she didn't love him, then why would she keep a toothbrush at his house? Why would she have consented to marry him?

He saved her life once, and how could she not love the boy who saved her life?

Auden showers while she changes, and then he climbs into bed with her still warm and damp, and clad only in boxer briefs that cling to the sinful curves of his tight ass and strong thighs. That reveal the heavy, lazily thickening shape of his cock.

He wraps her in his arms, his chest to her back and one of his legs sliding easily between hers. She knows that he does it so he can snuggle her close without also pressing his erection into her bottom. It's thoughtful, because Auden is thoughtful. It's gentle because Auden of all people in the world knows why she needs gentleness.

He kisses the back of her neck. "Good night, Delphine," he says, and nothing else. He expects nothing else, because he's good. He's just *so good.*

"Good night, Auden."

And they slowly circle the well of sleep together. There's no sex, there's no kissing. No playful fondles or cupping favorite parts of each other's bodies. There's only this chaste snuggle, the way friends might snuggle, if one ignores the massive erection that occasionally grazes her backside whenever Auden shifts.

She and Auden have been engaged for a year—dating for another year before that—and it's always been like this. They've never fucked. They've only ever kissed, and Auden's been nothing but patient. He never pushes her, never asks for more, even though she knows he wants her. When he holds her, she can feel his muscles trembling with pent-up need, she can feel his hands shaking when they slide over the dip of her waist and the generous flare of her hips. Once she caught him masturbating to a picture of her in a bikini that she'd put on her Instagram.

It was so sweet and cute that she almost wanted to have sex with him right then just as a reward for being the most adorable fiancé ever.

But she simply can't bring herself to, and she doesn't know why. She's been in therapy since…well, since *it* happened, and she carries out all her therapy assignments dutifully. She can masturbate, she can communicate. Whenever she looks at Auden, all she feels is safety and warmth. And when Auden looks at her, she knows all he feels is sweet, affectionate need.

It should be the easiest thing in the world to part her legs for him. She should have done it months ago. She wants to do it, in an abstract, intellectual kind of way. But whenever she imagines Auden tenderly making love to her, imagines his sweet kisses and gentle, careful hands, her body just refuses to respond. It stays asleep.

And she has no idea how to wake it up.

In London, the witching hour is no darker than any other time of night, something that should be comforting, and instead is disorienting. Auden rests his head against his study's window and looks out onto the quiet Knightsbridge street below. The leafy square outside is kindled with pretty lamplight, and some of the other houses around have one or two windows glowing against the shadows. The ambient light of the city turns the sky into a haze of purple-gray.

At Thornchapel, the witching hour is so dark that he can't even remember what the light looks like, what it feels like.

He's come to his study to do something shameful, which is to slacken the hot ache in his body now that Delphine is asleep, and he closes the curtain against the glass so he can be alone with his sins.

It would be so much easier if he didn't have these hungers so *often*, if they weren't so fierce, if they didn't continue tangling inside of him like ever-growing, ever-knotting thorns. He feels insatiable sometimes, he feels like he's choking on the weight and the heat of his unending needs.

He needs to fuck. And he can't.

Or rather, he won't, he won't ever do anything that could hurt Delphine.

He doesn't settle in, he doesn't need to, lots of practice has made sure of that. This is something he has to do at least two or three times a day, and he's as embarrassed by it as he is helpless to stop it. He's learned how to be fast and quiet. Ruthless with himself.

He loves Delphine, and so it's her on his mind when his hand finds his thick, rigid organ and clenches a fist around it. But as always, his thoughts slide sideways, away from the sweet, passionate lovemaking he should be thinking about and back to the urges that afflicted him as a young man, the urges that afflict him still.

He wants to fuck and fuck and fuck, he wants to paint more bruises on Proserpina's pale legs and he wants to pin St. Sebastian to the ground and screw an apology right out of him. He wants to share Delphine, he wants Delphine to share him, he wants to feel the sting of flesh against his hand when he spanks someone and he wants them to love the sting so much that they'll do anything to have it again.

He wants to hurt and be hurt in return, although he wants the hurts in different ways.

He's already hurting now.

He comes with a grunt and then an ashamed sigh. He comes feeling like he's being unstitched at the seams. And tomorrow he'll have to go to Thornchapel and see Poe and maybe see St. Sebastian again and have to pretend he's not unraveling. Pretend he isn't growing a tree of thorns inside his chest and that those thorns don't have names.

Delphine. Rebecca. Becket.

St. Sebastian.

Proserpina.

His thorns, his regrets.

His hurts.

8

The next day is Friday, and I continue my informal census of the books, counting by shelves to get a rough idea of how many books I'll be working with. They'll all need to be cataloged, but not all of them will need to be digitized if they already exist in digital form thanks to another library.

Cremer has responded to an email I sent a couple days ago, and I'm given permission to order all the boxes and storage containers I'd like, which I do. I also order a dehumidifier for the room, although I'm mostly pleased with my humidity readings, given the age of the house. I respond with a query about our budget for data storage and backups, and then by lunch, I find that I'm ready to truly begin. I'm starting at the far corner by the window and pulling down the first shelf's worth of titles when I hear Saint say my name from the doorway.

I turn, arms full of books, and smile big. He must not have to work today, because he's back in a T-shirt and jeans, and with a leather jacket and that lip ring, he looks like every bad-boy fantasy I've ever had. I want to kiss him, and I want to feel his lip ring against my clit, and I want him to be the one I break my strange little virgin curse with. This bad boy with eyes like winter trees who'd rather talk about death than friendship.

I hop down from the ladder, set the books on the table, and bounce over to him. "Hi!"

My cheerfulness cracks his guarded expression the tiniest bit; there's a small tip to his lips that wasn't there before.

"Hi," he says. Almost shyly. "I shouldn't be here, but I just—I knew Auden wasn't going to be home yet, and I thought you might be hungry." He holds up a plastic storage container of what looks like homemade soup, and then he looks incredibly pained. "This is stupid. I'm sorry, I should go."

"No, wait! Stop!" I move over to him and grab at the soup container like it's the last bottle of wine in a hotel room at a library conference. I clutch it to my chest and beam up at him.

He does stop, he stays right where I've ordered him, but he doesn't smile back down at me. Instead he stares at me like I'm a vase he broke. A pearl he chipped.

And when he stares, his eyes in the full sunlight are so rich and so dark that I can feel myself drowning in them.

"Why would you think this is stupid?" I ask softly, still cradling the soup to my chest. "It's actually very kind."

He takes a long time to answer. "It's stupid because it's a bad idea."

"Us being friends?"

"Yes." He closes his eyes for a minute, opens them. "I should stay away from you."

That's the most nonsensical thing I've ever heard. "Why?" I say, taking his hand and leading him to the kitchen so I can have my soup. "Why does it matter?"

He heaves a beleaguered sigh. "It just does."

When we get to the kitchen, I put the soup in a pan to warm it up and get him a beer from the fridge. He shucks off his jacket and leans against the counter while he drinks it, watching me bustle around the kitchen with a kind of wary fascination. I chatter at him the whole time, asking him about his library and what hours he works and what music he likes and what other fantasy novels he's read and does he want water? Tea? More beer?

He answers in a slightly bewildered way, but by the time we're sitting down with our soup, I've almost got him into something like a real conversation. As I pull words from him like teeth, I think of the boy I married in the thorn chapel, the boy who crackled with mischief and life.

How did he turn into this man of frost and doubt? And why?

I'm about to ask him this exact question—yes, I know it's blunt, but I can't help it—when there's the sound of the side door in the kitchen opening, and Becket blows in with the wind and a happy Sir James Frazer, who barks once at Saint, then decides to lick his hand instead.

"Saint," Becket says in pleased surprise. "I didn't realize you'd be here."

Saint looks a little panicked. "I should go."

"At least finish your soup," I playfully plead. I feel like a teenage girl scheming to get just five more minutes with her crush. "Don't rush off with an empty stomach."

I don't need to look at Becket to know that he's probably staring at me with piqued interest, but like any good priest, he stays silent.

Saint lets out a breath. Picks up his spoon. "Okay. I guess."

I watch him eat, my own hunger tearing at me from the inside. The careful press and touch of his lips against the spoon is killing me. I think I'm just going to have to tell him the truth. Tell him that I'm a virgin and a sex monster and I want him to fuck me. He can even fuck me vanilla if kink isn't his thing. But I want to have sex with him and I want to do it as soon as possible.

Funny how I spent years not being ready, and now within the space of a day, I'm so ready that I'm crawling out of my skin.

When I look away, Becket is studying me, and I flush, because he's studying me like he knows what I've been thinking. Like he can see me struggling not to squirm in my seat, can see me wondering how I can convince Saint that I'd be a lot of fun to sleep with, despite the whole virginity thing.

But before he can say anything about it, or I can say anything to draw attention away from how obvious it must be that I want Saint, I hear voices in the hallway outside—one voice low and polished, the other one sweetly musical. Auden and Delphine. Hours ahead of schedule.

Saint gets to his feet just as they come into the kitchen looking like a magazine ad for beautiful people in love. Delphine is all blond hair and riotous, wool-covered curves in her cigarette pants and bright red coat, and Auden's in this denim shirt and sports jacket outfit that should look like a mess, but on his perfect frame and with his hair doing its perfect hair thing, it looks amazing, of course. Their hands are linked, and Delphine is mid-laugh at something Auden has said to her, and he's looking down at her like he's never seen anything prettier or better than Delphine Dansey—because, let's face it, he probably hasn't and two million Instagram followers would agree.

Jealousy punctures me like an arrow. I hate it.

I hate feeling jealous of Delphine, who is so nice, and I hate that I can't clamp off this burgeoning attraction for Auden. I hate that just ten seconds ago I was watching Saint's mouth with a hunger that almost scared me, and now I'm doing the same with Auden's.

Do I just want to have sex with everybody? Is that it? Auden *and* Saint? Hell, maybe even Delphine and Rebecca and Becket?

After years of saying no, I want to say *yes* to five different people I barely know? What the fuck is wrong with me?

While I'm thinking all this, a small tableau of frozen shock and resentment has assembled itself before me. Auden and Delphine are stock-still in the doorway, that beatific look in Auden's eyes replaced with something close to fury.

Saint's on his feet, ready to bolt, and Becket's risen too, as if he thinks he might have to physically intervene between the two men—which, given the events earlier in the week, might be necessary. Who knows with these two?

I stand as well, touching Saint's arm to underscore what I say next. "I invited him here," I half-lie to Auden. "I know you two don't get along, but he's here for me."

Auden's eyes, which were trained on the press of my fingers against the bare skin of Saint's arm, snap up to my face at my words. "We 'don't get along' is a very mild way of putting things," Auden says.

"I should go," Saint says to me, moving away and grabbing his jacket. My fingertips tingle with the memory of his skin against them.

"I'll walk you out," Becket says quickly, shooting Auden a look that says *stay put.* "Be right back, everyone."

And they leave through the side door. Only Auden, Delphine, and I are left in the kitchen.

I should apologize, I think. Or acknowledge that there's a new net of tension over us that wasn't there before.

But as usual, it's the curiosity that wins out.

"Why do you hate him so much?" I ask Auden. I'm angry enough that I want him to know I'm angry. I'm irritated and defensive and still fucking jealous of beautiful Delphine with her beautiful fingers still laced with his.

Auden's face is unreadable, but those eyes glitter, green and brown and hard. "I could ask him the same question about me."

"That's not an answer," I say, still furious.

He's still furious too, and there's a moment when his mouth flattens, when his jaw goes tight and his pulse hammers in the column of his neck…

There's a real ripple of power from him, and it's like kicking through cold water to feel the heat of the sun. When he straightens up and looks at me like that, he looks like a king. He looks like he wants to have me chained and whipped for my insolence, he looks like he did on the day he yanked both Saint and me to his mouth for a kiss.

A bolt of real, true fear flies through me; it leaves wet need in its wake. My knees feel weak and unsteady. I want to drop to the ground and press my forehead between his expensive brown Oxfords and wait for him to dispense justice. I want to earn his approval; I want every depraved, sick, and delicious thing a submissive wants—and more.

Auden finally speaks, his voice low and tight and furious still. "I hate him because he deserves it. I hate him because once upon a time, I gave him a piece of my heart."

He closes his eyes, a muscle in his jaw jumping. "And then he fed it to the wolves."

9

I retreat to the library and work well past darkness, starting the laborious process of building a catalog from scratch, building it one shelf at a time. With each book I enter into the system, I research whether or not the book has already been digitized by another library somewhere in the world, and by the end of the first shelf, I have a good five or six books that haven't. Those are the ones I'll digitize myself—slowly, of course. This whole thing is really a job for at least three or four people, which I suppose is job security, so I can't complain.

I'm starting on the first scan when Delphine comes in.

"Auden and Rebecca are working on more house stuff, even though it's a weekend and he promised to work less." She pouts. "I'm bored."

I make what I hope is a sympathetic noise, while I put the book

I'm scanning—*An Amateur History of the Thorncombe Valley and Its Environs*—in the machine and fiddle with the width of the cradle until it's narrow enough for the little book. Then I adjust the lights in the hood above, lower a V-shaped glass plate that rests on top of the book itself to keep the pages flat, and start scanning.

"Poe," Delphine whines. It should be annoying, but she's so pretty and darling, and when I look back at her, I find she's perched herself on the table and she's kicking her powder blue ankle boots back and forth. She's kind of irresistible. My jealousy of her coils into something more protective, more vital. I think if I were Auden, I'd probably be engaged to her too.

"I'm sorry, I'm sure this is just as boring," I say. The scanner is the fastest one I've ever worked with—it only takes a few seconds for each page. There's a slow pulse of light, a quick glance over to the monitor to double-check the image, and then the hiss of the glass plate going up while I flip to the next page. Then the glass goes back down, ready for the new pages to be imaged. And repeat.

"It *is* just as boring," Delphine says sadly. "What are you even doing?"

"Ah!" I say. "I'm so glad you asked. I'm making digital surrogates for any books in here that haven't been digitized yet. I'm more or less doing it concurrently with cataloging because I don't have all the things I need to go hard with the cataloging yet, but eventually I think I'll have to pick one or the other to focus on."

Hiss goes the glass plate coming down. Pulse goes the light.

I glance back and Delphine looks sadder than ever. "Oh, Poe," she says. "I hope this doesn't hurt your feelings, but I think you should know how boring that sounds."

My feelings aren't hurt in the least. The magic of Delphine is that she can say things like this and it doesn't feel hurtful—if anything, it feels like she's trying to help you. Plus, she looks even prettier when she's sad.

Hiss. Pulse. "I completely understand why you feel that way," I tell her. "My ex had a 'no library talk' policy after dinner. She was getting her grad degree in film studies, though, so, you know."

"I don't think I do know," Delphine says politely.

I squint down at the latest page to make sure I'm not seeing a mold spot. "We fundamentally disagreed about the value of each other's mediums."

Delphine straightens a little bit; I mistakenly think this is because she might have an opinion on different mediums herself, but then she scolds, "You should have posted your girlfriend more on your Insta."

It's not mold, just some kind of ink blotch from its printing. I hit the scan button. "That wouldn't have ruined my brand?" I joke.

"Your brand is a mess," Delphine says, and I laugh, but when I look back at her, she's giving me a very solemn look.

"Well, I mean, I don't really need a brand," I say, flipping a page. "I'm not selling anything."

I hear the sound of adorable ankle boots kicking a table leg in frustration. "It's not about selling things. It's about building a presentation of yourself that you can use for anything. For potential employers or potential lovers or potential friends. It's a place where you can compile the most salient expressions of yourself—expressions that *you* choose, *you* curate—and create a living biography. A testament to your life and the space you deserve to occupy."

I stare at her, speechless.

I like Delphine and I definitely think about kissing her sometimes, but I have to admit I didn't think she was capable of whipping out a word like *salient* in everyday conversation.

"You've given this a lot of thought," I say, turning back to the scanner to hide my surprise.

I hear her boots kicking against the table, slower this time, as if she's thinking. "For a long time, I was the only fat girl in my circle," she says pensively. "Or even in the circle outside of that one. I started the Instagram account because I needed to feel like *all* the parts of myself were real, and that they were real all at the same time—that I was well-dressed *and* interesting *and* cultured *and* fat."

She takes a breath. "It sounds so shallow, like needing pictures of yourself to self-validate is weak. But the truth is that I only saw pictures of people who looked like me in the worst possible ways. Headless bodies for news stories about obesity or as the butt of a joke in a cartoon. So why should I be judged for creating something positive on social media? The one medium I can control? It seems unfair to me."

Delphine is so effortlessly beautiful, so at home with money and stylish clothes, that I've never thought of her as having anything other than total confidence about her body. Even as a girl, nothing ever seemed to discompose her princess-like bearing, not even the cruel words of the village kids. But of course she's had to grapple with this, and in a moment of shame and epiphany, I realize that if Delphine with her money and whiteness and traditionally feminine beauty has been hurt, then how many others without those things have been hurt even worse?

"I've been unfair to you too, Delphine," I admit. "I assumed there was something narcissistic about people who post themselves a lot, but I never considered…well, I guess I never thought that there could be real work to be done with it. That it was contributing something."

Delphine waves away my apology. "I'm used to people not understanding." She gives me a warm smile; a dimple appears in one perfect cheek. "It was nice of you to own up to it, though."

The scanner lights pulse again and I go back to flipping pages. "It was generous of you to explain it to me."

"*Anyway,*" Delphine says, as if I'd purposefully pulled us off topic. "You only have pictures of coffee and books on your Instagram. They're over-filtered and repetitive. You need pictures of yourself—and the people in your life."

"I'm too preoccupied *being* with the people in my life to take pictures," I say.

My "being in the moment" doesn't seem to impress her. "Be less preoccupied then."

"You're bossy."

"I know. Look, your bio is excellent: 'queer Sagittarius librarian.'" She says the last part in such a way that I know she has her phone out and she's looking at my account. "I want to get to know *her*. Not her coffee."

"Point taken." *Hiss*. Pulse.

"I know what we could do!" Delphine says after a minute, so suddenly and so loudly that I nearly tear a page clean off.

"About my Instagram?"

"What? *No.*" She sounds exasperated that I haven't followed her to her new train of thought. "We should have a party for you! Tomorrow night. We'll get some champagne, have Abby make something special."

Abby...I search my memory and come up with nothing. "Abby?"

"She does the dinners. She's marvelous, really. Like a one-woman wonder." Delphine says *marvelous* in only two syllables, but the continued swinging of her feet keeps it from sounding too much like she's fresh off the set of *The Crown*. "She had some time away, a sick sister or something, but she's back now. Making dinner tonight, actually."

"Ah." Of course this all seems perfectly natural to Delphine. Of course there's just someone to make the dinners, of course that's totally normal. I chew on the inside of my lip so that I don't blurt out anything idiotic or totally déclassé.

"Anyway, it'll be just a cozy, fun thing here at the house, and we'll get Becky in too, of course."

Becky, I'd learned earlier, is their pet name for Becket, *not* a nickname for Rebecca—who is Bex. Auden is Audey, but only from Delphine, and sometimes he's simply *Guest* to Rebecca and she is *Quartey* to him, in that collegiate way of theirs. Delphine is Delly—except sometimes she's also Delph or Dee or—inexplicably—Pickles. It seems like the one rule is that you aren't allowed to make the ridiculous nicknames for yourself; they must be awarded to you by your friends who have their own ridiculous nicknames—which explains their shock at my declaring that I wanted to go by Poe, I guess. I should have waited until they decided to call me Prosey or PoPo or Patches or whatever.

"That sounds delightful," I say. I wasn't lying to Saint—I really do love parties.

I'm toward the end of scanning the book now, and when I move to flip a page, it falls open with barely any help from me. I have only a brief second to think *spine damage?* before the cause becomes clear.

There's a picture wedged inside. Not an old one either. At least, not as old as the book would lead one to believe.

I lift the glass plate a little higher while Delphine chatters behind me about what she'll have Abby throw together and what I should wear and how much champagne she should get. I pull the picture out and study it.

The corner bears the time-stamp common to digital cameras of a certain age, and it's stamped with the date of that summer, *the* summer.

The summer we were all here.

There are nine adults in the picture. My parents, Auden's parents, Delphine's parents, Becket's parents. Rebecca's father alone because her mother had already moved back to Accra by that point. Neither of Saint's parents because they weren't part of the strange little house party; his father was already dead, and his mother lived in the village. He'd joined our troupe by sheer accident of proximity.

The adults are smiling in the picture, all of them smiling like they have a secret. And they're here in the library, standing in front of the huge windows, bathed in light and alive. My mother is near the center of the group, something narrow and circular glinting in her hand that she's trying to put around Auden's father's neck. My own father watches fondly, one hand at the small of her back, his other hand laced with Rebecca's father's. Auden's mother watches her husband and my mother with a pained smile, but the way she leans into Becket's parents suggests familiarity, just as the way they have their arms entangled with Delphine's parents' suggests possession.

It's a strangely intimate scene, and yet I can only look at my mother, laughing and alive. Keeping whatever secrets that would lead her right back to Thornchapel a couple months after this picture was taken. Secrets that would lead her to her death.

Have hope, Poe.

Everything is possible.

I stare at her, my teeth digging so hard into my lower lip that the pain there is almost a counterpoint to the sharp, lonely pain in my chest.

Almost.

Closure isn't too much to hope for, I remind myself. I might not find her, I may never see the grass growing over her grave, but I might learn *why*. I might learn *how*.

I might discover how a Latin word scrawled in her handwriting ended up in my mailbox.

"...and I'll take some pictures of you and you'll see what I mean by posting more of yourself. Poe? Are you listening?"

I extend the picture to her, and she slides off the table to investigate. She takes it and examines it, her honey-brown eyes soft when she looks up at me. "Where did you find it?"

"In this book," I say, looking back down at the *Amateur History of Thornchapel*. "Stuck in the pages."

Delphine steps closer and peers over the glass plate at the book below. "There's the thorn chapel," she says quietly. "Golly. I haven't thought of that place in so long."

She's right, the thorn chapel's right there and I missed it, absorbed as I was with the picture itself. On the pages below, there's a colorless sketch of the ruins, looking much the same as I remember it—standing stones and rubble covered in thorns and roses.

Except there are people in the sketch, several men and women with lanterns. One woman stands in the center, her robes simple and unadorned and her lantern raised higher than the rest. She's faced by another woman and a man, and behind them is the gentle grassy swell of the old altar.

Déjà vu has me sucking in a fast breath, like I've been struck.

"Many traditions survived late at Thornchapel," Delphine reads from over my shoulder, "and the rural folk even until recent memory have carried on their superstitions, celebrating feasts like St. Brigid's Day in the most rustic and profane ways. Some say these country heresies were even led by the lord of Thornchapel himself..."

She stops reading, gives a long, pouty sigh. "I wish we still got to do fun things like this."

"Like what? Cavort around in the dark with lanterns?"

"Yes! Wouldn't that make all these dreary, gray weeks seem brighter? Knowing we'd get to do something pretty and playful at the end of them?"

"It would," I murmur. My own heart beats a little faster at the idea, but not because I necessarily *want* to wander around the ruins with lanterns and robes.

But because I've dreamt it.

I've dreamt it so many times that it's begun to feel real.

Just a dream thing, Poe.

"Anyway," Delphine says, breaking the spell, "I'm simply *starving.* I'm going to go have a little pre-dinner tipple to take the edge off the hunger. You want to come with me?"

"Yes, yes, I'll join you," I say, but I'm not looking at her. I'm looking back down at the sketch, where the man in the middle is greeting the maiden by the altar. He has something slender around his neck; it looks like a torc, like something an ancient Celtic king would have worn.

In fact, it looks like the very same thing my mother is holding in the picture, the thing she's trying to put around Ralph Guest's neck.

What were you doing that summer? I ask my mother silently.

And what went so terribly wrong that you had to come back?

10

Auden's mask is back in place.

Throughout dinner and the drinks after, he's charming and interesting and such a careless, beautiful boy that I can't even remember what I'm supposed to feel. Except that I'm not supposed to fall in love with him because he's engaged, and because it would be stupid, and because he's been so awful to Saint for no reason I can discern—

And yet even his carelessness snares me, even his casual literary references and his haughty looks make me blush. I think about glimpsing his anger and his power in the kitchen. I wonder if he's ever thought about BDSM, if he's ever wanted to tie someone down just so he could stand over them, if he's ever wanted to mark someone's skin just to know if they'd let him.

I wonder if he and Delphine are kinky.

I wonder it so hard that I strain my ears that night to see if I can hear them make love.

I can't.

But I get myself off just thinking about it, and then I roll over onto my back wishing I could slap myself in the face.

I'm jealous of Delphine and yet turned on by Delphine. My skin is haunted by the ghost of Saint's lip ring...and I haven't even felt it yet. I wonder if Rebecca is willing to take me on as a sub, and I wonder if Becket ever breaks his vows. I can't stop thinking of the expression on Auden's face when he was hoisted over Saint and me on the gravel, I can't stop thinking about those hazel eyes and how they would look burning over me in the heat of power and play.

Even for a sex monster, it's just too much, but I'm helpless against the churning of desire. I can control *myself*, I can keep my actions sane and respectful, but inside—inside I am seething and roiling with a hunger so acute I think it might kill me.

And the worst thing is I don't even want to stop feeling this way. I like it too fucking much.

"Put all of that away at once," Delphine declares to me as she glides into the library the next evening. She's waving in poor Abby, who's rolling a tray laden with pies and miniature quiches, and rolls and ham, and bowls of salads and slaws that look like they took a long time to make. I suddenly feel very embarrassed at the effort that's been expended on my account, and I close down my scanner station so I can help Abby set up a buffet of sorts on one of the long tables.

Delphine helps too, to her credit, and between us, we have the work done quickly.

"I told Bex and Audey to get down here pronto," Delphine says, pulling out her phone and starting to experiment with camera angles. "They're plotting some new garden thing, I think. And Becky should be here any minute."

"I found another book about people cavorting with lanterns today," I tell her, walking over to get myself a drink.

I have Delphine's full attention now. "In the thorn chapel?"

"In the thorn chapel," I confirm, trotting back to my workstation to grab the book. "I kept it out for you."

"Kept what out?" an elegant voice says, and I turn to see Auden leaning in the doorway, hands in his pockets. His eyes glitter over me, and I have to remember how to breathe.

"It's just a book," I whisper.

"Oh, Audey, it's so much fun!" Delphine says, practically bouncing over to her fiancé. She gives him a quick kiss on his cheek, and then beams at me as he slides a hand around her back. "Poe found some old books with pictures of parties in the thorn chapel."

I hate myself for how much the sight of his hand on her back bothers me.

"Well, I don't think they were *parties* as such," I say as I approach them. I hold out the book, open to the page I'd bookmarked for Delphine. "They sounded like rituals."

Auden's eyebrow quirks the tiniest bit. "Rituals?"

I meet his gaze and try not to shiver as something vivid and uncomfortable arcs between us. I think I've dreamed this too, this moment, this part where I hold a book open for him to read, and the déjà vu is dizzying.

"Yes, rituals," I say after clearing my throat. "See?" I gesture down at the open pages, one of which is a lithograph of the chapel ruins, showing it overflowing with roses and empty of people.

Auden and Delphine bend over the book, with Delphine reading aloud from the page next to the picture. "The thorn chapel was required for the seasonal ceremonies then common to the valley," she begins. "The first was Imbolc, when the folk would bless the village's well, and afterwards, would go by torchlight to the forest sanctuary where its lord awaited them. The next ceremony was Beltane—what is called May Day in other, more civilized, parts of the world—then there was Lammas Feast, and the unholy frolic of death on All Hallows' Eve. There are unspeakable rumors of many heathen acts done at these country revels; thankfully these crude and unschooled rituals have been burned away by the light of modernity, and Thornchapel is now regarded in its valley as an upright and Godly place."

We all let out a breath as soon as Delphine finishes.

"Does it say *what* they did on Imbolc?" Auden asks.

"No," I say. "But I think the 'lord' it mentions must be the lord of Thornchapel—or at least that's what the other book implies. And torches or lanterns seem to be required. But what happens when they get to the ruins—none of these books say." Then I quickly describe the rest of what Delphine and I learned from yesterday's book.

Auden makes an unimpressed noise. I peer up at him.

"It seems a bit gossipy to me," he says. "All these books have are rumors and hearsay and the usual kind of illustration Victorians go mad for, with the gowns and flowers and things. Nothing of substance."

I think of the picture I found in the book last night, of the torc my mother had laughingly held out to Auden's father. The same torc in the first book's illustration. "So you don't recall any talk of things happening in the thorn chapel? It wasn't something your family did?"

Auden shakes the hair out of his eyes to study the lithograph more closely. "No," he replies. "I saw the ruins before I'd ever even heard about them—with you all that summer. And I assume they went out to the chapel on Lammas night, if they went through the maze, but I don't know that for sure."

"It's too bad," sighs Delphine. "I thought it would be fun for us to have our own little Imbolc."

Auden blinks at her as if she's suggested we all join a cult. "*Why*?"

She shrugs. "I don't know. It just seems like a lark, a little bit of an adventure. We used to have them in school and now we don't do any fun, uncivilized things anymore. We're such adults and it's *very boring*."

I trail a finger over one of the chapel's walls in the illustration. "There would be a certain symmetry to it," I remark.

"Would there?" Auden asks, looking at me like I'm just as delusional as Delphine.

When I close my eyes, dreams crowd against my eyelids. I see Auden and the thorn chapel, I see a door behind the altar that's not supposed to be there.

I blink the memory of my dreams away and try to sound rational. "This is your time with this house, isn't it? You are the lord of Thornchapel now. Why not bring back an old tradition, just the once? Why not do something your father never did, claim a part of Thornchapel's history for yourself?"

Auden's mouth pulls over to one side as he stares down at the image of the chapel. "It is a thought," he says softly.

Our moment is cut short by Rebecca, who comes in wearing a sapphire-blue jumpsuit hugging her narrow body like a dream. She has her braids down and hanging almost to her waist, and there's a long gold pendant dangling between her breasts. She looks every inch a glamorous architect from London, even down to the *we have a problem, let's find a solution* expression on her face.

"I know that look, Quartey," Auden says. "Everything okay?"

"Everything is *fine*," Rebecca emphasizes. "Becket is coming in now, and he brought someone with him, and everything is *fine*."

Auden frowns. "He's bringing someone with him? But who—"

His question is answered before he can even finish asking it, as Becket appears in the doorway of the library...trailed by an uncertain Saint.

Silence fills the room; the fire pops once, loudly.

"Um. Hi," Saint says. Everyone stares.

I'm the first to break the scene, and I stride over and give him a big, old American hug. "I'm glad you're here," I say as I pull back, and Saint looks a little grateful. Becket smiles at me, also looking grateful.

"I was driving past Saint's house on the way here," Becket explains as he walks over to the drinks bar, "and it just seemed like such a waste not to have us all back together again."

I don't need to remind him that the last time Saint was here—yesterday—it ended with Saint fleeing out the side door like a fugitive. Becket clearly remembers this, and it's in the look he gives Auden before he starts pouring a glass of wine. A calm, blue-eyed gaze that says *behave*.

I still have an arm around Saint's waist, and Auden's eyes light on it as he says, "I think I'll have a drink too." And he abruptly turns and walks away to the drinks bar.

"That went better than I thought," Saint mutters to me, and I laugh. He looks surprised, as if he weren't trying to be funny, but my laugh seems to make him happier. He studies my face for a minute; his own mouth eases around the edges a little.

I want to run the tip of my tongue over his lip ring so badly that I'm worried I might do it, everything else be damned. Just once, just to feel if it's cool, if it's warm, if his lip gives under the pressure of my kiss.

"Why did you come here if you thought it would go badly?" I say, trying to tear my eyes away from his mouth.

"I wanted to see you," he says. "I shouldn't, because—well, I just shouldn't."

He said something like this the other night, like he thinks Auden will fire me if I'm too friendly with him. Which is unfair to Auden, because he may be a spoiled princeling, but I don't think he's vindictive. Or at least if he is, he saves all his vindictiveness for Saint.

I'm about to say just that when Saint reaches up and brushes the hair away from my face, his fingertips ghosting warmth across my skin. His dark eyes follow his own movements, the path of his fingers along my temple, the places where the silk of my hair sifts through his fingers. A slow-rolling shiver moves down my spine, settles low in my belly.

"When Becket gave me the choice to either see you or not see you, I realized it wasn't a choice at all," he says, his eyes still on his fingers in my hair. He meets my gaze. "I had to see you again," he finishes simply. "I had to."

"And Auden?" I ask, and when I ask it, I mean *what about Auden*, I mean *is it okay that you have to see him in order to see me?*

But that's not what Saint hears, I think, because he closes his eyes for the briefest of seconds, and when he opens them again, they're full of deep, frozen pain. "I lost the right to have any choices about Auden a very long time ago," he says.

My lips are parted. I have a thousand things I want to say, a thousand questions I want to ask, but nothing will come, nothing makes it out.

Saint misinterprets my silence for something judgmental. "Don't worry," he says, dropping his hand away from my face and looking across the room at the fireplace, where the lord of Thornchapel himself leans against the mantel and scowls into the fire. "Auden's been punishing me for it ever since."

Dinner is predictably awkward, but the more we eat, the more we drink, and the more we drink, the looser the noose around the room becomes. The conversation slides from the usual dinner chatter to something freer and more intense. Becket and Rebecca begin debating the purpose of labyrinths and mazes and whether they have any secular use, and Delphine waves us around the room like we're mannequins so she can take pictures of us or the food or the fire or whatever strikes her fancy.

Before Abby leaves for the evening she brings in a tray of delicious little tarts and hot coffee and tea, and clears away the old food. The fire continues to burn, and outside the massive library windows, the wind whips through trees and a cold rain begins spattering at the glass.

I go over to one of the long tables to refill my drink, but I'm arrested by the sight, by the black trees and the black rain. By the contrast of the winter night with our fire and food and loud debates about architecture.

"You need something stronger than coffee now," Rebecca says from behind me, and when I turn, she hands me a glass of something amber-colored. I take a deep gulp and then sputter helplessly.

"A nice Speyside," she says as I cough. "It'll warm you up faster than anything else."

I take a second, more cautious sip. "Thanks."

Both of us angle toward the rest of the room, watching Saint and Auden doing their very best not to watch each other. Watching Delphine animatedly tell a story while an amused Becket teases her.

"I don't know what Becket was thinking," Rebecca says, quietly so that only I can hear. "Bringing that boy here. He hurt Auden so badly, so fucking badly, and I was the one who found him. I was the one who had to—"

She breaks off, clearing her throat. "Well, I haven't forgotten what happened, even if I did promise Auden I wouldn't do anything about it."

I glance over at her, her profile lovely against the rainy glass behind her, her high cheekbones and delicate jawline burnished with the fire's light. She looks every inch the Domme right now as she gazes over at the others. Serene and perceptive.

If anyone would tell me the story, it would be her.

"What happened between them?" I ask.

She turns that Domme's gaze on me, and like any good submissive, I instinctively lower my eyes, then raise them back up when I catch myself. That earns a small laugh out of her at least.

"You need to find someone kinky here, and fast," she says. "I think you're hard up for it."

She has no idea.

"I'm in agony to be in agony," I admit. And then I narrow my eyes. "You didn't answer my question."

She twists her mouth. "It's not my story to tell."

I think about this a moment. "Does it make a difference that I really, really want to know?"

"It could, if it were up to me. Which it's not."

For a minute, there's only the rising wind and the rain hurling itself against the house.

"Are you going to fuck Saint?" Rebecca finally asks, still quietly enough so that only I can hear, but frankly enough that I let out a surprised laugh. "Because you look like you want to fuck him."

"I like you," I tell her, grinning into my drink. "And I appreciate your candor."

"I'm allergic to bullshit," she says. "Now confess."

"I *want* to fuck him," I say, risking a more direct glance over at him. He must have worked today—either that or he felt the need to dress up for dinner. He's in a mostly unwrinkled button-down and slacks, department store shoes on his feet, and it looks like he's tried to smooth back his longish hair, but it keeps falling into his face anyway. He's leaning forward and looking down into his whisky, and there's a restlessness moving through him that reminds me of the winter storm outside.

"He might not be kinky," Rebecca cautions.

"I'm not planning a wedding or anything. Just sex."

"Can you even come from vanilla sex?"

Question of the century. "Well, I, um. I don't know what makes me come during sex."

Rebecca turns to me, head first, then the rest of her body. "You don't know," she repeats slowly. "What makes you come during sex."

I scrunch up my face in embarrassment. "I've never done it."

"Is this some heteronormative 'never specifically had a penis specifically in your vagina' thing? Or are you saying you really, truly haven't had sex?"

"No sex," I respond. My cheeks are on fire. "Nothing."

"So the person who gave you those welts…?"

"Just gave me the welts," I confirm. "No orgasms involved. I mean, I got myself off later, alone, but not with her around."

Rebecca looks stunned. "And how long have you been doing kink?"

"Formally since I was eighteen."

"And you're how old now?"

"Twenty-two. Look, I know what you're thinking, and it's not anything like that—I'm not scared, it's not a religion thing, I've been in love before. It just hasn't felt right, that's all."

Rebecca thinks about this a moment. "Interesting," she muses. "And now it does?"

I'm dying for whatever Domme insight she has. "Now it does. Does that make me strange?"

She looks back at Saint rolling his glass between his fingertips as the others laugh and talk around him.

"No," she says heavily. "It may make you foolish. But it doesn't make you strange."

Which is when Delphine pops over, her cheeks rosy with booze and fire. "You two are being so secretive over here," she scolds. "Come back to the fire, I have a game for us to play."

Rebecca sighs a certain sigh I've come to identify as her Delphine Sigh. "I don't want to play a game."

Delphine gives Rebecca a pout, and I do believe if she were any younger she would be sticking her tongue out at Rebecca. As it is, she just grabs my hand and yanks me back toward the group, and Rebecca follows with another Sigh.

11

"Let's play Spin the Bottle!" Delphine declares once we're back in the glow of the fire. Her voice has the fearless optimism that only comes from a lifetime of cosseted extroversion and a bottle of champagne mixed together.

"Are you *insane*?" Rebecca demands from behind us. "We aren't children!"

"Of course we aren't," Delphine says in a voice that says *well, obviously*. "That's the whole point."

When I glance over at Auden, he's looking at me, but he looks away as soon as he sees me looking at him.

Saint is still staring at his whisky glass like he's wondering if he can drown in it.

"Delphine, be reasonable," I say, although I've had just enough Scotch that kissing beautiful people by a fire sounds like heaven. "You and Auden will have to recuse yourselves and so will Becket. And without the engaged people or the priest, there are only three of us left, and that's hardly enough for a game."

Delphine turns to us, bottle in hand and eyes narrowed. "Who said anything about recusing?"

"Of course we can't play, Delly," Auden says. "Becket can't either."

She sets the bottle down on the low table between all the sofas and chairs, and then puts her hands on her hips. "And why, exactly, is that?"

Auden looks surprised, then swiftly protective. "I won't kiss anyone but you. And our priest has his vows."

The priest in question polishes off his flute of champagne. "Actually," he says, "I don't see the harm in it."

Now we're all surprised, staring at him with open mouths and slack expressions. He regards us with amusement. "Well, it is just kissing, after all; I don't plan on breaking any vows for real. I haven't had *that* much champagne."

"Isn't kissing against the spirit of the vow though?" Saint asks quietly. It's the first he's spoken in at least an hour, if not more.

"Jesus kissed his friends," Becket replies, his words untroubled, but I didn't miss the barely there flinch he gave at Saint's question. It makes me wonder exactly how Becket feels about his vows—and kissing—and his friends.

"It doesn't matter because we are not playing," Rebecca announces. "We are too old—"

"That's exactly it!" Delphine interrupts, glowering at Rebecca. "We are too young to be so old! I'm so tired of not doing anything fun ever."

"You are such a child," Rebecca accuses, crossing her arms and glaring at Delphine. "The minute people aren't falling all over themselves to entertain you—"

"Erroneous! I've been entertaining myself just *fine* while you and Auden spend hours and hours talking about the house stuff. I *do* have a job too, you know, and—"

When Rebecca cuts in to disagree, Becket stands up. "We all know you two can go like this for hours," he says kindly. "But we also all know the secret, and the secret is that you don't actually hate each other."

The glares Delphine and Rebecca trade between them would suggest otherwise, but Becket keeps going. "*I* think it does sound fun. And I'm not ashamed to admit I miss the feeling of being kissed, even if it's by a friend."

I try to sound very Sober and Adult when I chime in, "I also think kissing sounds fun!"

"Of course you do," Delphine replies. She walks over to Auden and stands between his knees, taking his hand in hers.

"I know you love me," she says, and she sounds less tipsy now, and more wise. "I know how faithful you've been to me and at what cost. Just like we all know that Becket loves God and has been faithful to him. Kissing someone in a game doesn't change any of that."

"What if it does?" Auden whispers up to her. His hand is tight in hers and his eyes are more brown than green in the glow of the fire.

And then they slide to me.

And then to Saint.

He looks back up at Delphine. "Sometimes a kiss is more than a kiss," he says, and there's a faint edge of hoarseness to his voice. Saint's fingers whiten around his glass, and I wonder if he's thinking of that summer, of that wedding kiss the three of us shared.

Of a kiss that was so much more than just a kiss.

It was an omen.

An anointing.

Delphine squeezes his hand. Her engagement ring sparkles. "I won't think less of you for kissing someone, and I know you're too generous to think less of me."

Auden doesn't answer, but he does pull Delphine's hand close to his mouth and he brushes his lips over the back of it.

"Is that an 'okay'?" she asks.

For a minute, the wind picks up and rattles the glass with fierce, noisy gusts; the rain hammering the window sounds like it's turned to sleet. Almost as if the forest itself wants to answer for Auden.

Finally he says, "Okay."

Delphine turns to the rest of us. "And it's okay with the rest of you?"

I look to Rebecca, who throws up her hands. "*Fine*," she says. "But if I kiss someone, I'll kiss them my way. Is that understood?"

We all nod.

"Poe?" Delphine asks.

"Yes, please!" I say eagerly, like the horny librarian I am. Then I clear my throat and try to sound normal and not perverted. "I mean, as long as everyone else is okay with it."

And then we look to Saint. He drains the last of his whisky and puts the glass on the table. "Yes," he says. "I'll play. If you are willing to have me."

There's no doubt that by *you*, he means Auden, and the faintest frown pulls at Auden's mouth at his words. But he gives a short nod.

"Excellent!" Delphine exclaims, clapping her hands together. "Let me just clear off the table here and get our bottle ready."

I decide to refill my glass—as do Rebecca and Saint—and by the time we're back, the table in the middle is clear, save for an empty bottle on its side, and the drumming, manicured fingers of an eager Delphine Dansey.

"This is perfect, you know," she says, as we get settled around the table. I choose to sit on the floor next to Saint, and Rebecca perches on the arm of the sofa. "We never got to have this kind of fun as a group when we were in school. Now we can make up for lost time."

I have to admit that if life had been different, if for some reason all six of us had been able to keep seeing each other, I'm sure we would have done lots and lots of wild things, and I'm sure at least some of them would have involved kissing. Maybe Delphine is right, and we're reclaiming something that ought to have been ours to begin with.

"I think Becket should go first," Delphine says. "Since he was the first to agree to my game. And also he's the oldest."

Becket smiles and leans his long frame forward to reach the bottle. The firelight gilds every exposed inch of his pale skin, his blond hair and eyelashes, and when he spins the bottle, the light glints and fades in a slow strobe on the glass.

The strobing light abates, the bottle slows. The bottle points at St. Sebastian.

"Well, Saint?" the priest says softly. "Are you ready?"

Saint takes a long drink, but it doesn't seem like it's for courage. More like for a moment to compose himself, so that when he answers, his voice is perfectly even. "I'm ready, Father Becket."

"This would be hotter if Becky had his collar on," Delphine whispers. Rebecca shushes her.

Becket goes to Saint and squats down, so that he's eye to eye with the man he's about to kiss. Even without his collar, there's still something priestly about him. Maybe it's the dark pants clinging to his long thighs, or the black shoes that give off a dull gleam from the fire. Maybe it's in the way he presses his long fingers under Saint's chin and lifts his face to his own. Or maybe it's his expression, intense and holy, as he lowers his mouth and kisses St. Sebastian Martinez on the lips.

None of us speak a word—in fact, I don't think any of us even breathe—as the game becomes real, as we watch Saint's lips part under the pressure of Becket's firm, surprisingly practiced mouth. His fingers are assured and insistent on Saint's chin, and I can tell the moment his tongue strokes against Saint's, because Saint gives a shudder that I can practically feel myself, feel all the way down into my toes.

I'm hypnotized, and everyone else is too. All the doubts, all the reservations and reluctance, are melting away in the heat of their kiss, and when I hear the sound of someone trying to control their ragged breath, I know without looking that it's Auden. I know that no matter his earlier doubts, he's caught up in it now, he's as ensnared as the rest of us at the sight of our priest gently making love to St. Sebastian's mouth.

When Becket pulls away, Saint looks dazed. "Thank you," he says, rather distantly.

"Thank *you*," the priest says graciously.

Although as he takes his chair once again, there's something pained in Becket's expression that doesn't look gracious at all. It looks like he wants to do so, so much more than kiss now, and who can blame him? I'm burning alive and I only *watched*.

Delphine's spin lands on her own fiancé, and she giggles as she goes over to kiss him. "This is exactly what you would have wanted," she says, leaning down and clearly planning on giving him a quick kiss on the cheek.

He catches her arms instead and pulls her to his mouth, nothing long or involved, just a real kiss, and when Delphine pulls away, her smile is pleased and affectionate and even happy—but it's not the smile of someone who's aroused. It's like she just finished kissing a cousin or a fellow actor…or someone she had to kiss for a party game. There's warmth, but no heat.

"Your turn," Delphine tells her betrothed. "Don't land on me, we don't want to be boring."

"I wouldn't dream of it," Auden says, a bit dryly, and leans forward to spin the bottle. He gives it a quick, indifferent spin, as if already trying to absolve himself from the consequences of where it lands.

It should land on Delphine. That would be the safest alternative, the alternative that would keep our dinners friendly and our evenings free of awkwardness. But I'm just drunk enough that I don't want it to land on Delphine.

I want it to land on me.

I want to be stupid. I want to admit to myself that I like Auden, that I ache for his touch, his crooked smile, and all this after only a week here.

Stupid, stupid, stupid.

And spin, spin, spin goes the bottle.

It swings past me once, quickly, then twice, going slower now, and then a third time. I breathe out a long, silent breath of either disappointment or relief—I'm not sure which—and then the bottle keeps going. Slower and slower, but it keeps moving, gradually, gradually, appearing to stop in front of Saint.

The air itself seems to crystallize; next to me, Saint's entire body trembles. But then the bottle nudges just the tiniest bit left so that it's pointing at the spot between Saint and myself.

I swallow.

"I think it's Poe," Delphine says, having apparently nominated herself the moderator of our game. True to her earlier confidence, she doesn't sound jealous or bothered in the least as she coordinates her fiancé kissing another person.

I look up and meet eyes with Auden. He stares back at me, shocked.

"Go on," Delphine urges. "I won't be upset." Indeed, she even seems excited, and I try to use this to mentally clean away my own worry and guilt.

It's just a game, Proserpina. Just a kiss.

But there's nothing *just* about the twisting thrill in my stomach as I get to my feet. Auden stands too, and we meet in the middle, neither of us seeming to know where to look or where to put our hands. For a minute, I feel like we really are teenagers, not adults at all, with nothing between us but nervousness and hormones.

"Hi," Auden says as we finally meet.

"Hi," I say back.

"I suppose we've already done this once before," he says. "Nothing new."

"Right," I say back. There's something violent threatening to shiver through me, and if I let it, it will shiver my body right apart. I'm so aware of Saint behind me watching us, of him seeing my reaction to Auden, and I hate it, I hate that I'm so stupid, I hate that I want two people at the same time—hell, *five* people, if I'm being honest—although it's only Saint and Auden that make me feel like my very life depends on touching them. I hate that they can see me wanting them; I hate that all the wild desires curling through me like vines have become so tangled and thick.

I hate that at Thornchapel, I'm both not myself and more myself than I've ever been.

"It's just a game," Auden whispers to me, his hand sliding around to cup the back of my neck. "Just a kiss."

Please, God, let this kiss be just a kiss.

My hands come up against his chest, almost of their own accord, spreading against the soft cashmere of his sweater and the warm, firm lines of his chest underneath. His hand at my neck slides up through my loose hair to cradle the back of my head, and it feels so good I want to purr. Maybe I even do purr a little, because the hesitation that had been written all over his face disappears in an instant. And in its wake is the same hungry ownership I saw in his face when we were children.

I want to tell him to tighten his fingers in my hair, I want him to wrap his other hand around my throat so I can feel the pressure of his touch against my pulse. I want another wedding, another crown of flowers, I want to be his in all the bruising, sighing, sparking ways I can.

He dips his face low and pauses for the barest second. In that pause, I see his eyes are the perfect fusion of my vivid green and Saint's deep brown. A starburst of emerald around the black pools of his irises, ringed with a dark coffee that reaches inward in ever-lightening shades to mix with the green. His eyes are hypnotic, his eyes are everything.

His eyes are like windows to summer and winter all at the same time.

The pause ends in the space of a single breath, and then he lowers his head all the way down and we kiss.

12

The touch of his lips on mine is the most powerful thing I've ever felt.

More powerful than caning, than flogging. More powerful than suspension or bondage, more powerful than having all of my senses denied me or being so overwhelmed with sound and noise and touch that I want to cry.

Auden's kiss is all of it. Every single bit of it.

Like being hurt and loved all at the same time.

His lips are firm, but they're not sure. They're not certain. There's hesitation in each brush of his mouth over mine, his hand in my hair is shaking, and I can feel every rigid muscle in his chest quivering under my palms. Like he's as terrified as I am.

Like he knows this kiss is not just a kiss.

His lips part ever so slightly, and mine follow suit, and then there's the flicker-fast silk of his tongue against the top of my lower lip. I don't know what he tastes there—Scotch, most likely—but whatever it is has him giving a soft, tattered sigh against my mouth. His fingers in my hair tighten to the point of pain, his other hand finds my upper arm and grips me tight, tight like the way I want, tight like the way I crave, and I'm yanked in even closer. Suddenly, he's in all of my senses, his body pressed so completely against mine that I can feel his erection against my belly and the fast heave of his chest against my own. I can smell that pine and pepper and lavender smell of him, a smell that should be feminine, but it's not, it's so very masculine, and on him it seems like what Thornchapel itself could smell like. Forests and flowers and danger.

Then there are those noises that seem torn from the very heart of him—quiet and urgent and meant only for me.

Then there's the taste—scotch like myself, and underneath it, mint.

And then there's the sight, because when I dare to peek through my lashes at his face, I see him already watching me with winter-summer eyes.

And it's as our eyes meet that he truly invades my mouth. His tongue flutters past my own in a touch so erotic that I whimper into him. He angles my head farther back, tilting my mouth to where he wants it, and then for a heady instant, I forget everything, everything. There's only this, only this intimate touch, only this kiss like he wants to kiss my very dreams out of me. There's only him, and only me, and only Thornchapel around us—

A shattering crash breaks us apart, our kiss ending abruptly as everyone jumps to their feet. Only Auden's hand still on my arm is a testament to what we were just doing, to how lost I was only a second ago. That and my lips, which buzz and tingle from the memory of his.

Well, okay, those two things *and* the heat gathering wet and low in my cunt, because he kissed me the way someone kisses the person they're about to fuck. And my body is screaming at its abandonment, protesting its loss.

I press my thighs together under my skirt to try to soothe away the ache.

"It sounded like glass," Becket says, surveying the tables and our drinks.

"It *was* glass," Rebecca says. "I'm sure of it."

Saint has already gone to the library doors to look over the windowed corridor connecting the library to the hall. He disappears, and then there's the sound of tinkling glass and something clunky dragging across the flagstones. He trots back in, sleet caught in his black hair and across his wide shoulders.

"A pane shattered in one of the windows," he confirms, ruffling his hair to knock out the ice. "I found a big square of chipboard to lean against it, that should keep the worst of the sleet out for now. I'll tell my uncle, and he can take care of it when they come back Monday—but in the meantime, everyone should be careful walking through there."

Auden's hand on my arm doesn't move, but his entire focus is on Saint. "Thank you," he says politely. Maybe even a little gratefully, as if he hadn't thought Saint capable of enough courtesy to put a board over a broken window.

Saint just nods.

"Well, I don't think anyone is going to beat the glass-shattering kiss, *but* there are still more turns to go," Delphine the Kissing Czar declares. "It's Rebecca's turn now."

Auden squeezes my arm and lets go.

"That was nice," I say, trying to keep a grip on all the feelings threatening to quaver through my voice. "Thank you."

Auden doesn't answer verbally, but he gives me a pained smile. No dimples, only the asymmetrical tilt to his upper lip. His eyes are no longer windows, but doors and mysteries and gates that I'll never unlock.

That privilege belongs to someone else.

I get settled right as Rebecca spins the bottle. Saint's sat on the floor too, and I can see the leftover sleet still in his hair, sparkling in the light like a strange frozen crown. I'm so intrigued by it that I don't notice when the bottle lands on me. Again.

The room breaks into laughter.

"This is Poe's lucky night!" Delphine chirps, and strangely, she almost sounds like she's forcing her cheer this time. More so than when her fiancé's erection was pressing against my stomach and he was sighing into my mouth.

Rebecca stands and walks over to me, extending a hand, which I take. When I'm on my feet, she leans in and whispers, "Are you up for a little kink?"

Oh God, yes, yes, that sounds like the absolute best idea after that wrenching, confusing kiss. I'm wet and flushed and horny, and I've drunk enough to be brave, and I'm sober enough to consent.

"Yes," I say. "I'm yours."

Hot approval flashes through her dark eyes. "That's what I like to hear," she replies in a voice a little huskier than normal. And to everyone else she says, "I told you I was going to play my way. I'm going to make Poe earn her kiss."

I can tell by the way Delphine tilts her head that she has no idea what Rebecca means, but a new interest thrums through the others, a new kind of silence. This was already a dangerous game, but Rebecca's just raised the stakes.

Rebecca quickly appraises the scene and what she has to work with—honestly, not much, unless she wants to whale on my ass with a book, which I'd only object to for the sake of the books. Their fragile leather bindings wouldn't do well with the repeated blows, I think.

Rebecca seems to make up her mind about something. "Okay, your safeword is Thornchapel. I want you to lay over Auden's lap—"

"What?" I blurt out at the same time Auden goes, "*Rebecca*—"

Rebecca points a finger at all of us. "I didn't finish. Poe, I want you to lay over Auden's lap so that he can hold down your legs—and press down on your upper back to keep you from squirming, if need be."

It's easy to see why she chose Auden—he's the only one situated in the middle of a sofa. Delphine is sitting on the arm of the same sofa, Becket's in a chair, Saint's on the floor. It's not like there's a handy coil of rope on the floor for restraints. Auden and I look at each other, and I think we feel the same mutual panic—like we both realize what we shared during our kiss is best left alone, best kept in a box somewhere without air or light. Something best starved and not fed.

And I fail to see how me wriggling in his lap as Rebecca dominates me is not going to feed it.

But the Kissing Czar is suddenly delighted by this turn of events. Maybe it's the novelty? Maybe she has a secret fetish for seeing Auden with other people, like a compersion thing? Who knows, but she's up and tugging me over to the sofa before I have time to figure it out.

"Auden, move back a little so she has plenty of room," Delphine chides, and then moves some throw pillows out of my way so I can lie down. I look at Auden one last time, and he's searching my face.

"Is this okay with you?" he asks.

"Is it okay with you?"

He closes his eyes once, briefly and with torment.

"Yes," he admits.

And I think I might die at that one word.

"Then yes, it's okay with me," I say. "I'm not safe-ing out." That last part is meant for Rebecca.

She nods with that preternaturally knowledgeable look most Dominants have. "I know. Now get up there."

I've draped myself over Auden's lap in so many waking and sleeping dreams that it almost feels familiar, like I'm remembering it instead of doing it, but I know that's not right. I know this is the first time because every detail is so painfully crisp, like this moment is reaching into my mind and etching itself there. There's the heat of the fire tickling my shoeless feet, the cooler air of the cavernous library against my face. There's the sound of sleet on the glass, of someone else in the room shifting to get comfortable, the almost-silent exhales from Auden as he tries to control his breathing.

I adjust myself so that my upper body is supported by my elbows, with my head hanging down, and so that my pelvis is squarely over Auden's lap.

There's an unmistakable length of male arousal under my hip.

I try to move, because it must be uncomfortable for him to have my weight pinning it like this, but once I start squirming, he seizes my thigh and spreads a hand at the small of my back.

"Be still," he begs quietly. "For the love of God, be still."

I go still.

I'm not sure if anyone else heard that little exchange, but Rebecca's voice is careful when she says, "Is everyone ready? Auden, you can hold her steady?"

"Yes," he and I answer at the same time.

"Excellent. Poe, I'm going to spank you and that's how you'll earn your kiss from me. Do you want my hand over the skirt or under?"

Auden shudders underneath me, and I feel his cock swell even bigger.

I know how he feels. My cunt is swollen too, and wet, needing to come. I try not to grind the front of my pussy against his thigh, and mostly succeed.

"Under my skirt," I say.

"Bare-arsed?"

"If everyone is okay with it," I whisper. "I like the sting."

"Of course you do," Rebecca says soothingly. And then to the rest of the room, "Is everyone okay with this? You can safe out too, if you'd like."

There's no answer from the others—no verbal answer, at least. I can't see anyone's face except Saint's, and even then, I'd have to turn my head to look at him, which I'm too cowardly to do now. Not because I'm embarrassed that I'm about to be spanked in front of a little crowd of onlookers—that's essentially just another Saturday night for me. But I'm embarrassed that he must have seen how much I liked kissing Auden; I'm embarrassed that he might be able to guess how much I like being over Auden's lap just now.

I wish I could tell him that this doesn't change anything about *us*, that I haven't picked Auden's side over his, that I still want to be friends. That if he's suspected that I like him, that I want him, he's not wrong.

I wish I could tell him I'm just as confused. Just as lost.

But I'm a coward, so I don't look and I don't tell him. And then the moment is gone anyway, because Rebecca flips up the skirt of my dress and pulls down the thick tights I'm wearing to my upper thighs. She does the same with my panties, and I have a moment of panic when I realize that if someone looked at just the right angle, they'd undoubtedly be able to see my pussy. They'd be able to see how wet and swollen I am, how much I want to be touched.

I shiver as her fingers leave my skin after they finish baring my flesh. There's nothing between me and the others now, except maybe the lace of my panties and the tights where they stretch along the crease between my thighs and my cheeks. Though I haven't known Rebecca long as an adult, she strikes me as the kind of person who would take care to make sure I wasn't unduly exposed beyond what we agreed. On the other hand, she also strikes me as the kind of person to leave me in torment about whether she was unduly exposing me or not.

I can't tell.

And I can't tell who can see what, but I do know that it's a forcefully erotic idea. That if they wanted, my friends could see my cunt. Maybe they could pet it, maybe they could lean down and kiss it to make it feel better.

I could almost cry with how much I want that.

The size of the room and the broken window in the hallway make drafts unavoidable, and so there's a tantalizing play of cool and warm air over my skin. There's no forgetting that my bottom is shamefully bare while the rest of me is not.

A hand touches me, giving one of my cheeks a fond squeeze. "How many spanks do you think? To earn my kiss?"

This is a trick question, I know it is. Too low a number, and I'll be given more spanks for my impudence, too high and she'll say, "Ahhh, a pain-slut then? How about we double that amount so you'll enjoy it more?" Or something to that effect.

Of course, the problem is that if a Dominant has decided there's no right answer, then there's really no right answer. It's just easier to pick a number and get on with the consequences of being wrong. And consequences are half the fun anyway.

"Fifteen," I say, feeling like it's a nice middle amount, not too low and not too high.

"Fif*teen*," Rebecca repeats. "As in five plus ten?"

Oh boy. "Yes?"

"Even Delphine could do fifteen," Rebecca says, and it's a testament to the spell she's slowly casting around the room that Delphine doesn't erupt in protest. "And I'd like to think my kisses are a little more valuable than that. We'll do thirty…plus five more for your cheek in suggesting fifteen."

Thirty-five will probably hurt her hand as much as it hurts my ass, but I'm not foolish enough to say anything about it. Thirty-five spankings for a single kiss is bad enough—I'd hate to see what she'd cook up if I actually mouthed off.

The first one comes with no warning, crackling across my skin like a firework, pleasant and pretty.

"One," I say.

The second comes a bit harder, right on the same spot. The crackling comes again, the firework-bite of it sparking a little deeper this time.

"Two," I say, turning my head a little so I can see the sapphire-blue of Rebecca's jumpsuit. She's standing with her legs just on the outside of Auden's, leaning over me the slightest bit, and I'm suddenly very grateful as strikes three and four come that she doesn't have anything more rigid than her hand, and that we're in such an improvised position. If I were bent over one of those tables, and she could really put her shoulder and back into each swat, I have no doubt that I'd already be whimpering.

As it is, I keep my cool until number ten. And when number ten lands right on the tender strip of flesh between my ass and upper thighs, I finally let out a muffled noise.

"What was that, Poe?" Rebecca asks pleasantly.

"Nothing!"

"Hmm."

I'm punished for that particular lie with several fast swats to the same place, so fast I can barely keep up with counting and breathing at the same time. When she's done, we're at seventeen, and my ass is rocking in the air, that senseless rock of trying to move away from the sting. I'm mostly only sensible of the burning along my ass, but I can feel Auden grow more and more restless underneath me, his cock like an iron bar against my hip and his thighs locked rigid and tight under my own. It seems like he's lost control of his hands, however, because the one on my thigh has started kneading the flesh there ever so slightly, and the hand that was spread at the small of my back has now moved up to my nape and is playing with my hair.

"You can push her down if you like," Rebecca says to Auden. "I bet she'll even like it."

Ohhhh, I do, I do like it. Auden's hand is warm and rough, and more certain than I've felt it yet tonight, as if he's discovering a natural aptitude for pinning librarians down by their necks.

And the sound he makes when the change in position forces my ass higher arrows right through me. It's a low, satisfied groan, it's the groan of someone who can't help himself. I squeeze my eyes closed, as if that will stop up my ears, as if that will save me from the intoxicating presence that is Auden Guest.

Rebecca goes again, and I count through the thudding breathlessness she's created, I count even as I try to wriggle away and Auden has to hold me even tighter. Until she gets to number twenty-five and lays one so hard on my sit-spot that I give a little scream and try to arch away. Auden's holding me too well, and so all I accomplish is rucking down my tights and revealing my cunt for real.

There's an audible reaction the moment it happens, a caress of cool air on my wet folds, and I realize that all the wiggling around has finally accomplished what I fantasized about earlier. I try to squirm back down, but I can't seem to find a modest angle, and I'm stopped anyway—by another five, vicious spanks from Rebecca.

"Thirty," I manage, my eyes wet. My throat and chest are all knotted up with the pain, and I'm hovering in that space where I can't take another spank and also I could take thirty more. Nothing matters and everything matters. Everything hurts, and everything is just starting to feel good.

I feel as much as hear when Auden drops his head back against the couch, as if hearing my shaken voice as well as seeing my naked ass at the same time is too much to handle, and that's when Rebecca says, in a voice so intentionally denuded of emotion that I wonder if this was her goal all along, "My hand hurts, Auden. Maybe you could do the last five?"

Auden's hand on my thigh tightens, then relaxes, then tightens again. "Pardon," he says. His voice is calm, but I can tell the lie—under me, his cock is rock-hard and throbbing, and his chest is heaving like he's just run a race. "But you'd like me to what?"

"It's only five," Rebecca explains. "And there's not much you need to know. Just stay away from her kidneys and her spine and you'll be fine."

I hear Delphine shift on the arm of the sofa. "Auden, I don't mind if you do," she says, and there's an odd mix of relief and fascination in her tone. "I really don't, darling."

Even with Delphine's sanction, I still expect Auden to protest more—but he doesn't. "Very well," he says, sounding resigned. "Ready to count, Poe?"

I almost want to shake my head. My ass is screaming, and I'm very, very aware that Auden has a much better angle for spanking than Rebecca did. And a fresh hand. And no idea what the hell he's doing.

On the other hand, do I want Auden to spank me? Do I want to be exactly here, thrown over his lap with my skirt flipped up and my backside ready for his punishments? Yes, yes, of fucking course I want this; I've only been fantasizing about exactly this moment since I arrived at Thornchapel a week ago.

And anyway, it's only five. I can do five of anything, right?

So I nod.

Without another word of warning, he connects the flat of his palm against my rump, and somehow he makes one swat feel like ten, like twenty. I cry out from the impact, the air gone from my lungs, and before I can even finish whispering *thirty-one*, he's at the other side, right on the abused skin of my upper thighs. I cry out again, a couple tears dropping out of my eyes and clinging to my eyelashes. Through the tears, I can see that Saint has moved closer. He looks entranced by the scene, his gaze caroming up to Auden, then down to where his hand cracks across my ass again, and then to my face. And I wish I could speak, I wish I had the air in my lungs to say that for me this moment is as beautiful as it is sordid, that the tears beading on my eyelashes feel good, that the breathless knot in my chest is actually loosening far more painful knots in my mind.

I wish I could tell him about the endorphins, which even now are coaxing heady, dizzy bliss to the surface. I wish I could tell him how the red heat on my ass has sunk into every secret place in my body, kindling warmth at the tips of my breasts and at the juncture of my thighs. I wish I could tell him that he's beautiful. As beautiful as this spanking feels, which is the kind of beauty that comes with bitter pain and is all the better for it.

Auden's about to do number thirty-four now, and I'm unable to stay completely still. I'm squirming in his lap, and each squirm adds a delicious grind of friction from my clit against his thigh, and also sends me grinding against his cock too.

This time, Auden doesn't ask me to stop.

A massive *thwack* makes the whole room suck in its breath, even Auden—who is undoubtedly feeling the sting in his hand right now. I manage to moan out *thirty-four*, almost beyond all thought, beyond anything but the heat on my bottom and the yanking, angry orgasm building behind my clit. For the first time in my life, I'm about to come with someone else. With *several* someone elses.

And also for the first time in my life, there's no feeling of *wait*, there's no sense that somehow this isn't right. It all feels right, nothing feels wrong, and maybe it will happen, if I could have just another moment of grinding against Auden's muscular thigh…

Spank number thirty-five makes me scream. It sears through me, it sets every nerve ending jangling with a surfeit of pain, and I'm rolling my face against the couch cushions, the cushions that are wet with my own tears. My orgasm is hovering, hot, ready to tear me apart if only I could just—

Two things happen at once.

Firstly, Rebecca kneels beside the sofa and gently turns my head toward hers. Her lips brush against my tear-wet mouth, and then she gives me a deep and appreciative kiss. I moan into her mouth, into the softness of it, the satin touch of her tongue and the warmth of her lips. I moan again when she pulls away and the kiss is over.

And secondly, I notice that Auden is completely frozen underneath me, not moving at all—except for the hand that's come to rest on my bottom, that seems to be reflexively soothing the place he just hurt. I also notice a hot, wet feeling against my hip.

Auden came.

He came from *spanking me.*

I brace up on my elbows and look at him over my shoulder. He looks stunned, lost, no longer the spoiled boy-king, but the wandering knight who's just seen the Grail...only to have it disappear before he could close his fingers around it.

Those long, long eyelashes flutter as he closes his eyes and drops his head back against the sofa, and the silence around the room breaks when Becket says quietly, "Saint's gone."

13

Somehow, Auden and I manage to extricate ourselves with minimal embarrassment. The dim room hides the evidence of the pleasure he took in my spanking, and when I stand and Rebecca helps me pull up my tights—checking my ass first to make sure I don't need any other care—the expressions on Becket and Delphine's faces are not condemning or concerned. Both of them look near drunk—pale skin flushed with hungry, glassy eyes—the expression of voyeurs with whetted appetites.

But I can't sate those appetites right now. The only thing I want to do is find St. Sebastian and…well, I don't know yet.

Just find him, I guess, and hope that I haven't irreparably broken something.

The minute my skirt is back down, I'm padding quickly across the floor and out into the corridor, shivering against the cold air seeping in from the broken window. I wrap my arms around my chest as I go into the main hall and see that Saint has opened one of the big front doors and is about to leave.

"Wait!" I call out, rushing forward. "Don't go!"

Saint stops, but he doesn't turn and neither does he close the door, which sends the icy wind whipping through the high hall, and sleet bouncing against his feet.

So I shut the door for him, firmly, standing between him and it until he looks at me.

"What is it?" he asks tiredly.

"That's my question to ask," I say. "You should be riding with Becket if you want to leave. Not planning to slog home in the ice and wind in order to prove a point."

He lets out a joyless bark of laughter at that. "To prove a *point*? Is that what you think I'm doing?"

"Well, isn't it? You don't have to pretend with me, St. Sebastian, I'm not afraid of your honesty. And I'm not new to people having ideas about the things people like Rebecca and I enjoy—"

Saint braces a hand against the door next to my head and stares at me with those dark eyes. He's nibbling thoughtfully at his lip piercing, as if choosing exactly what he wants to say next.

"I've never done what you did in there," he finally says. "Or what Rebecca did. I've never hurt someone, and I've never been hurt—for fun, I mean. For—" there's the faintest flush under his cheeks now, "—for *pleasure*. But that doesn't mean that I haven't wanted it, you know. That doesn't mean I haven't been craving it for years, that I don't fantasize about it—"

He catches his breath; there's shame everywhere through him, and it's so delicious that I just want to lick it right off his body and make it my own. "Look at me, Poe," he pleads, and when I search his face, he shakes his head and dips his chin. "I mean, *look*."

I look down, and there's the firm, heavy proof of his response.

Fuck. Me. I slump against the door, lust coiled so tightly in my belly that it almost hurts.

"Oh, Saint," I murmur. "Was that because you wanted to be me? Or Rebecca?"

"I don't know," he says helplessly. "I always thought I wanted to be both, but then when I saw Auden's face—"

And here he cuts himself off for good, refusing to say more.

"Saint…" I try to nudge, but he seals his lips closed, looking like he wants to punch himself for even uttering Auden's name aloud. The little metal ball underneath his lip is pulled tight enough that it dents the soft skin there, and I can't stop staring at it. I can't stop thinking about what it would feel like to take that little ball between my teeth and tug.

In an ideal world, I'd be spanked again for taking such a liberty, but alas…

"I want to kiss you," I blurt out and his eyes widen, then darken even more as his eyes dip to my mouth. "I'm sorry and I know that's a strange thing to say, but I just had to tell you—"

His lips are hard against mine before I can even speak another word.

The kiss is desperate, grasping, gasping, with tongues and teeth, and everywhere touching, everywhere my fingers digging into Saint's arms while his hands clutch and fist at my skirt. I can smell him, and he smells like Thornchapel too, except smoky and crisp somehow, the way a fire smells burning against a cold night.

The kiss is like fire too, consuming, roaring, volcanic. I feel wild, unstable—and Saint is even wilder than I feel, cupping my ass and shoving me up against the door, pinning me there as he plunders my mouth with vicious, fitful frenzy. His lip piercing digs insistently into my lip, and I want to die it feels so good, I want to worship it and write poems to it, and every time he moves his mouth, I feel its delicious little path over my lips; I chase after it with my tongue.

I circle my legs around his waist and my arms around his neck, and the pain of my sore bottom against his palms is like heaven as we kiss and arch together, his erection finding *just* the spot to grind against, his chest pressing hard against my swollen breasts. I can't breathe, I don't want to breathe, and with my hurting ass and the rough, cold door behind me, I have such a perfect balance of pleasure and pain that I know I could come from this. My thwarted orgasm from earlier is tightening and tightening, it's beckoning me, it's begging me, and I'm ready to follow, I'm so very ready—

Saint breaks our kiss, our faces still so close that our noses nearly touch, and he blinks a few times, as if he's not sure where he is or what he's doing. I try to pull him back, I want more, more, more, but he sets me down and takes a big step back, his hands balled into fists and his expression anguished. When he meets my confused stare, he looks at me like I've accused him of something.

But I haven't, I'm not, I don't understand—

"This can't—" his voice breaks and he looks away, swallowing. "This can't happen. We can't happen. Do you understand?"

"No, I don't fucking understand," I say, my not understanding slowly giving way to hurt, humiliated anger. "I don't know what to think at all right now."

He sucks his lower lip into his mouth, toying with the barbell. He looks miserable.

It would be so easy right now to whip him with my words and scourge him with all the bitter rejection I feel. And I want to, *really* want to, even though I've never been a whipper—never before St. Sebastian at least. I also want to plead, to coax, to chase him away from *we can't happen.*

I want him to be mine. Or I want to deny him the right to ever call me his.

I want to heal him and I want to hurt him.

All because of one broken kiss.

I take a deep breath, I remember who I want to be. That I want to believe the best of people, that I want to be honest and resilient—not someone who doesn't listen, not some discourteous, feral sub girl who lashes out with hurt pride.

And if that's who I want to be, then I owe Saint what he's asked for. My understanding.

"I like you," I say finally. "I like you a lot. Not just because we were kids once, but because I'm intrigued by the man you are now. I'm…I don't even know how to describe it without sounding trite, but I'm drawn to you, St. Sebastian. I'm coded to you somehow, like every part of me just *responds* to every part of you. But it's okay if it's not reciprocated, if you don't feel the same way, because sometimes that's just what happens, and I promise to honor that."

Saint looks angry and pained at turns—he pivots to face the far end of the hall, like he needs to see something other than me while he thinks, and then he pivots back. "It's reciprocated, Proserpina," he says in a low, tight voice. "It's very, very reciprocated. But there are other things to consider. Auden—"

"—is not going to fire me," I interrupt, completely and utterly done with this excuse. "I know you've had your differences, but that's not something he'd do."

Saint's voice is still tight when he says, "There's more to Auden than you think. He can be incredibly cruel when he likes."

"Is that truly it? You're worried I'll be fired if we fuck?"

Saint winces at that word. "Poe."

I study his face, and suddenly I get the creeping feeling that there's more, that there's something else. "What aren't you telling me?" I ask. "What aren't you saying?"

Saint takes so long to answer that it's almost its own answer. I rest my head back against the cold door with a sudden wave of exhaustion.

The sleet that had blown in earlier is now melting around my tights-covered feet into a frigid pool of wet.

"It's complicated," he tells me. "And I am reasonably certain you wouldn't believe me even if I did tell you, because I don't even believe it myself. Not really."

"What the fuck is that supposed to mean?" I ask.

He pushes his palms into his eyes. "Nothing," he mumbles through his hands. "It doesn't mean anything."

"This is bullshit," I say, any nice and *understanding* words turning sour in my mouth. "You won't kiss me because of a reason you won't tell me and that you don't even believe yourself? You know, all you had to say was 'Poe, I don't want to kiss you.' You don't have to make fools out of us both to make sure we don't do it again."

His hands drop away from his face, his eyes blazing with an inky heat. "Jesus *fucking* Christ, Poe! What about that kiss would make you think I wouldn't want to do it again?"

"I don't know!" I shout back, fully aware that I've abandoned all my good intentions not to be the feral sub girl, but I can't help it. *None of this makes sense*, none of it, and I may not deserve much, but I at least deserve the truth. Or even a better fucking lie. "I don't know what to think at all!"

His lips press together in a bloodless, angry line, and he slams his hand against the door by my head. Just like he did earlier when we were kissing, except this time when he ducks his head low, it's not to touch mouths but to utter low, acid words.

"You want to know so fucking badly? *Fine.* The entire village of Thorncombe thinks that you should marry Auden. Auden's father wanted you to marry Auden. Everybody in this goddamn place thinks you should marry Auden, except Delphine."

And Auden himself.

I try to speak the words out loud, but I can't, I'm too stunned, my mind still tripping over this weird and untrustworthy little speech of his. "The village doesn't know me," is all I can manage, all I can produce as a somewhat logical response.

"Don't they?" Saint asks bitterly. "You haven't noticed any stares as you've walked around? Any people watching you?"

I open my mouth to protest.

But I can't.

Saint goes on, nodding at my aborted response. "They've known about you since you were a child, or at least they've known about Ralph Guest's plans to marry you to his son once you two were old enough."

"That's—" I shake my head, still not making sense of anything Saint is saying. "Why would it matter what Ralph wanted? Why would it matter to the people in the village?"

"Of course it matters what the Guests want. You don't pick up on the vibe here? Like this whole place is cloistered in a strange, timeless little bubble? Like a Sarah Waters novel but with pizza delivery?"

He's right, but he goes on before I can agree with him.

"I don't know why or how, but somehow they learned Ralph thought you were destined to marry his son, and that was that."

"But that's stupid," I protest. "He's engaged. Surely they know that from Abby working here."

Saint's hand falls from the door and he sighs. "They know. And they still think you're some kind of chosen bride for the lord of the manor."

"It's...it's just something for people to gossip about, that's all." But even as I say it, I remember Auden's words in my room on my first day here, I remember him saying his father didn't approve of his engagement to Delphine. Could that have possibly had anything to do with *me*?

No. No, that's ridiculous. Bananas. Saint's got the story mixed up somehow, or maybe the villagers do, but there's no way any of this can be true. "I'm not a chosen bride," I say firmly. "For anyone. I don't belong to Auden just because his father willed it so, and I'm certainly not going to worry about what the people of Thorncombe think."

Saint almost speaks then. He lifts a hand and parts his lips, and whatever it is that he's about to say has him even more bitter than before.

But he doesn't say it. Instead, he closes his mouth and then regards me with half-lidded eyes, more of that watchful hunger he seems to have around me so often.

After a long moment like this, he finally speaks, and when he does, he speaks softly. "I have to care what they think, Poe. I don't have friends here and I barely have family. I don't have a real home, I don't have anything I can call mine. All I have is this small, scratched-out life, and if I want to keep scratching it out, I can't be any more of a pariah than I already am. I want you more than words can say, but I also want to survive here when you're gone, and for that to happen, the most we can be is friends."

The words drop through the air like swords. Terrible and final.

He leans his forehead against mine, his eyes closing. "Can you understand now?"

Defeated, I nod.

What is my lust compared with his future? What are kisses when he needs neighbors?

"Yes, Saint," I whisper as he lifts his head away from mine. "I see now."

He stares down at me, and for a moment, I imagine I see something else in his face—guilt, maybe? A certain evasiveness?—but then it's gone, and he leans in to give me a cautious, chaste kiss on the cheek.

"I hope we can be friends," he says in a quiet voice. "I hope there's at least that."

I don't like the way the words feel leaving my lips, but I say them anyway. "We'll be friends, Saint, and that will be enough."

He lets out a breath, as if he doesn't like hearing the words any more than I like saying them, but before either of us can say anything else to disrupt our new balance, Becket comes into the room with Saint's coat in his arms.

"I think the party's over," Becket says, walking toward us and extending the coat, which Saint takes with a nod. "Auden spent about ten minutes glaring at the fire and then stalked upstairs, and then

Rebecca decided she'd had enough too. It's just Delphine in there now."

"I'll go help her clean up," I say. "Goodbye, Saint. Becket."

Saint doesn't look at me as he reaches for the door. "Good night, Proserpina."

Becket gives me an apologetic sort of kiss on the cheek, as if wanting to make up for Saint's curtness, and then he follows Saint into the cold, leaving me alone in the hall.

When I get back to the library, Delphine has almost everything picked up, and we work together in companionable silence until the room is back to rights. Together we cover up the remaining logs in the fireplace and turn out the lights.

My mind is on Saint the entire time. I don't cry, I don't breathe a word of anything to Delphine, but I feel it huge and hulking inside my chest, like some awful tree with burrowing roots and crowding, scratching branches.

It scratches rejection and disappointment everywhere inside me.

I try to ignore it.

After we're done and we're walking up the stairs, Delphine says, completely out of nowhere, "Did you like it when Rebecca spanked you?"

Surprised—and a little grateful to have something to think about that's not Saint—I shoot a glance over at her. "Didn't it look like I was enjoying it?"

"Well," she says, a little self-consciously, "I could see your…you *know*. And it was wet."

I nudge her shoulder with my own. "Are you embarrassed to say the word pussy?"

"No!" she protests. But then she glances over at me and amends, "Maybe a little."

"Yes, Delphine, my pussy was wet. Yes, I enjoyed the spanking very much."

She thinks about this. "But you also cried. And screamed."

We are to my bedroom door now, and I stop and look at her for real. She doesn't look as puzzled as she sounds—she looks thoughtful.

And she looks very, very interested in my reply.

"There are as many different reasons to enjoy kink as there are people who enjoy it," I say. "But for me there's something fundamentally beautiful about pain and pleasure mixing together, because that's real life, right? Being alive means the harsh is mixed in with the good, and every time I get to choose the harsh for myself, it loses its sting. Every time I taste the bitter and survive, I'm all the stronger to enjoy the sweet."

"What about the parts that aren't about the pain? The parts that are about—" and I can't tell in the dark hallway, but I think she blushes "—about doing what someone says?"

Mmm. Those are my favorite parts. "It's like being loved," I say. "Like loving."

"But Rebecca doesn't love you," Delphine says sharply. "She hardly knows you."

"I didn't say she loved me. I said it's *like* being loved, it's like—"

I break off, not wanting her to misunderstand. After four years of BDSM, you'd think I'd be better at explaining why I do it in the first place.

I start again. "Maybe it is love in a way. You don't have to know a person's favorite movie to show them that they're human and beautiful and sacred. You don't have to know their middle name to prove to them that they're worth cherishing and spoiling, even if it's only for an hour. Or for thirty-five swats and a kiss. And taking the time to prove to someone that they're worthwhile and enough…isn't that love? Isn't that what love is for?"

I say this, and I try not to think about what it means that Auden and I shared the bitter and the sweet together. I try not to think about the kiss I'll never get to repeat with Saint, because showing him love right now means not *making* love.

Delphine tilts her head, her mouth pulled to the side. "You make getting spanked sound like going to church."

"It is when I do it," I say.

She looks down the hallway, I assume at the door she shares with Auden, and when she turns back to me, all her curiosity is gone, replaced by something tired and sad.

"Thank you for explaining it to me," she says. "Good night."

"Good night, Delphine."

It doesn't take me long to get ready for bed, and it's not nearly long enough for my mind to settle around everything that happened tonight. The spanking and the kisses—Auden's and Rebecca's and St. Sebastian's—and the reason why the people in Thorncombe look at me like they've been waiting for me to get here.

Some kind of chosen bride for the lord of the manor…

Lord of the manor… "the lord of Thornchapel," as those old books so grandiosely put it. I think of the illustration in the book with the women and the lanterns, and the man at the altar with the torc around his neck. I think about my mother holding the same torc, trying to give it to Ralph Guest.

It stirs, was what that strange note said. *It quickens.*

Or as Auden translated it—*it revives. It reawakens.* As if from sleep, as if from death. I fall asleep thinking of that one word.

Convivificat.

14

The nights go like this: I fall asleep in a fit of keening loneliness and tumble straight into the same vivid, grasping dreams of the thorn chapel. I wake up, ready to scream or ready to come or both, never able to remember much about why the dream made me that way. Only that there were thorns and hands on my body and Auden silhouetted in shadow in front of a door I've only ever seen in my mind.

The days go like this: I catalog, I scan, I scan some more, and then I find Saint or Becket to help me pass the time. When they're in from London, Auden and Rebecca are busy with the ongoing construction and destruction of the house and grounds, and I use my lunch hour to take restless, dream-filled naps in my room, so aside from the occasional glimpse of Auden's shoulders bent over his office desk when I walk past, we don't see each other until the evening hours.

On Sunday mornings, we go to Mass at Becket's church—all of us except for Rebecca, who stays at the house and works instead. Once, we saw St. Sebastian scowling and pouting in the very back pew, but only once. Becket tells me Saint usually only comes to the church at night, alone, to continue his ongoing argument with God, and hardly ever comes to Mass. I save a spot next to me in our pew anyway.

Just in case.

While I catalog, Delphine wanders into the library at intervals to chatter or just to sit on one of the tables while she works on her phone, and gradually I begin to see the amount of time it takes for her to keep up her job as an influencer. There's not only her content to produce and plan out, but emails and phone calls and an unceasing rain of comments and DMs that she answers to boost engagement.

When we do talk, it's usually more questions about kink or speculating about Thornchapel's old rituals.

Becket joins us often. Saint stays away when the others are in.

None of us talk about the kissing, there's no more *chosen bride* talk from St. Sebastian, and if Auden and I have trouble making eye contact or being alone together in the same room, no one seems to notice, which is for the best. No more kisses for me, unless they come from Rebecca, but she seems preoccupied after the game, working at every spare moment, even when we're all curled up with drinks by the fire, so I don't ask her for a repeat session.

"Auden's asked her to build a new maze," Becket explains to me one day after they've gone back to London. "And I think it's not coming easily."

"I wish they'd leave it alone," I sigh, looking out the large windows at the south end of the hall. I can only just make out the leading edge of the maze before it recedes into the mist.

Becket makes a noise of agreement. "Me too."

But we both know that Auden's drive to reshape Thornchapel is driven by forces deeper than our shared nostalgia, and he's determined beyond measure to carve it up beyond recognition, as if by carving it up, he can excise his childhood from the landscape. The very fact that we all have memories of the maze would be more proof to him that it needs to be peeled off the face of the earth.

"I don't know what it would take to convince him to keep it," I say. "You'd think he'd direct more of this animosity toward the house itself, because surely that's where he remembers his father the most?"

Becket follows my stare to the mist-veiled maze, and we just stare at it for a few minutes. "He just has to see how it matters," Becket says finally. "He has to understand it. Thornchapel, I mean."

I look at Becket now, questioning. "You think he doesn't understand his own house?"

"No," the priest says, returning my look with a sad smile. "I don't think he does."

"You have to stop doing that," I scold St. Sebastian as he sets another armload of books down on the long table. "You need to *relax*."

Saint gives me a very small, very reluctant tip of his lips—which I've learned is the closest thing to a real smile I can coax out of him. "I actually like doing this," he says, sitting down and opening up the first book. With a piece of paper and a pencil, he starts scratching down some of the easy-to-find information I'll need to build the title's metadata entry. "There's something satisfying about it. Also it feels weird to sit here and watch you work."

"Sorry," I say, my attention back on the computer I use as a cataloging workstation. "I'm trying to do at least a shelf a day. There are *so many books*."

The sheer number never ceases to astound me—in fact, I think I'm even more in awe than when I first arrived, because now I fully appreciate just how many there are and how long it will take to put this place in order. No wonder poor Estamond Guest gave up on her ledgers.

Saint makes a soft noise that could almost be a laugh, and I jerk my head up, hoping to catch a smile. No such luck, but I am treated to the vague tilt of amusement to his eyes as his long fingers flip through the pages of the book he's making notes on. It's a younger book—at least, compared with most of the books in here—with a tattered paper jacket showing a clumsy illustration of a clapper bridge and a river.

"What's so funny?" I can't help but ask. I want to know everything he's thinking all the time; it's like some weird supply-and-demand thing where he keeps himself locked so tight that *anything* from him feels like a gift of gold. And even though these last two weeks between us have been strained and chaste, we can't seem to stop seeking each other out. I can't seem to stop wanting to kiss him. Or right now, wanting to straddle him and lick his neck.

"Our friend Estamond," Saint says, his eyes sparkling as he pushes the book toward me. "She was quite the scandal back in the day."

I reach for the book and tug it toward me. It's a motorist's guide to Dartmoor, published sometime in the fifties, and there's an entire chapter about Thornchapel, which back then was open to visitors one day a week. I start reading at the top of the page.

Visitors will find the grounds enchanting, especially the maze to the south of the house. Originally constructed in Tudor times, it's said that it was built atop the ruins of a medieval labyrinth, but this seems mostly to be local legend, as the housekeeper said there's no family record of that being true. In any case, the maze was given new life under the dashing and vivacious Estamond Guest. Born Estamond Kernstow to an ancient and worthy family here in the moors, she was only nineteen when she caught the eye of the much older Randolph Guest. By all accounts, however, it was a happy marriage, and Randolph indulged his young wife by letting her host extravagant house parties with some of the best and brightest of the day. Poets, painters, thinkers, and novelists all came to spend quiet days and cheerful nights on Thornchapel's inspiring grounds.

Estamond's bohemian taste in company, however, led to unpleasant rumors about her character. These rumors only grew after she commissioned a full repair of the overgrown Tudor maze—and commissioned new statuary for the middle. The centerpiece in question was a depiction of Adonis and Aphrodite in an unmistakably amorous embrace, leading to speculation about Estamond's personal morals.

Despite the gossip, however, Estamond carried on with her parties and changes to the house, and over the course of their short but happy marriage, she bore Randolph four children. She died after delivering their fifth. Visitors today can not only see her legacy in the maze and the walled garden to the southeast, but in her great personal collection of paintings still on display inside the house.

I look at Saint. "Quite the scandal," I repeat faintly.

"Is something wrong?" he asks, looking closely at me. Very closely. "You seem…upset."

"I'm not upset," I say quickly. "I'm intrigued, actually, because if

Estamond commissioned that statue, then surely she's the one who built the tunnel we found as children, right? A hidden way out to the thorn chapel—it seems like exactly the kind of thing she'd like."

Saint keeps examining me. "Okay."

I shut the book and slide it back to him, and then I turn back to my monitor and the entry I was working on before he interrupted. There's no point in telling him what really unsettled me, what was like seeing a ghost curl up from the page. There's no need, because it's simply a coincidence, and he would agree with me that it's just a coincidence, and then it would have been a waste of breath for both of us.

It doesn't matter that Kernstow was my mother's maiden name. It doesn't matter that I've never come across it anywhere else, ever in my entire life. It doesn't mean anything.

Unless it meant something to her. Unless she has a connection to Thornchapel I never knew about, not by interest or archaeology or friendship, but by blood.

Unless coming to Thornchapel for my mother was coming home.

Over the next few days, a warm wind buffets in from somewhere, the sun burns off the mist, and I can pretend I remember what spring feels like. I wake up one day feeling less sleepy than normal, less haunted by dreams, and I decide to take a short walk before I go to the library to work. It's been the first day really nice enough to do so, and I want to see the maze and Estamond's walled garden. If I'm honest, I'd really like to visit the chapel ruins too, but there's not enough time between work and the early sunsets here.

This weekend, I promise myself. I've been here almost three weeks, and I still haven't gone to see it. And I'm not entirely sure why—it's certainly been prohibitively cold and nasty, but I've spent twelve years dreaming about the place, surely I'm not deterred by some rain?

Mind made up that I'll go on Saturday, I get dressed for my walk. I check my phone after pulling on a jacket and my bright blue rain boots, but my dad still hasn't responded to a text I sent him asking about the name Kernstow and if my mother had any family here.

I sent the text two days ago.

Frustrated, I go into the south wing—already grating with the noise of construction at this early hour, and then find the door that leads to a large paved terrace looking out over the grounds. The trees and hills thwart the earliest light here, so there's a kind of sleepy murk clinging to the estate still. It's as romantic as it is disquieting, as if Thornchapel is reluctant to give up the night and its secrets.

To my left is the herb garden, nestled fairly close to the kitchen, and Estamond's walled garden, which, as I recall, is home to some more eye-raising statuary—a boozy Dionysus, for one, and Leda with a swan nuzzling her breasts—their naughtiness snuck between the usual veiled women and small fountains. All of the statues are surrounded by crowds of lavender, lamb's ear, and lady's mantle, and hollyhocks of crimson, pink, and cream. And all of that is surrounded by high stone walls, interrupted only by a single wooden door.

In front of me are shallow stone steps leading down to a long, green lawn. The grass stretches down to a valley cradling the narrow River Thorne, and then it stretches back up again to an arresting sweep of hills. Elsewhere, the trees press in close to the house, as if wanting to protect it and keep it safe, but here, right here, I can glimpse heather and granite crags and the frowning bleakness that crouches in wait outside of the lush Thorne valley.

Again, I feel that curl of fascination, that hunger to gobble up all the desolation around me and pronounce it delicious. To tramp through wet grass and squint into the wind and feel so very, very alive in all the slumbering wastes around me. To find the tiny flecks of life in the midst of all the winter—tiny snowdrops and buttery celandine and sprays of blackthorn blossoms, new and fragile against the chilly air.

I've always been a summer girl. The girl who spends hours and hours at the pool, the girl who loves heat and thunderstorms and gardens, and trees so heavy with leaves that they whisper in even the barest breath of wind. But here…here I think I could be a winter girl too, I think I could learn to love the cold and the wet and the quiet.

I think of Saint's winter eyes and sigh.

Though it's warm enough that my sweater and jacket suffice, the air smells cold, and I remember Becket saying last night that we'd have snow this weekend. Determined to get my vitamin D while I can, I stride across the terrace and down the stairs to the crushed gravel path that leads to the maze.

I'm not alone when I get there.

I find Rebecca in a white trench and designer rain boots—as stylish as they are functional—with her iPad dangling from gloved fingertips. She's staring at the maze like it owes her money.

"Good morning," I say, tromping over. "Isn't it…a little early to be working?"

"I needed to see it in the dark," Rebecca says, not even bothering to look over at me. She's still glaring at the maze. "And in the first light."

"Oh," I say, glancing over at her and then trying to see the maze as she's seeing it—as a problem to be solved. But I can't. It just looks mysterious and inviting and perfect to me. "Has it helped? To see it in the dark and in the sunrise?"

"No," Rebecca says flatly. "Nothing's helped."

I sneak a look back over at her, wondering what I can do. Normally, Rebecca is all cool equanimity and analytical composure, and she takes everything in stride—with the possible exception of Delphine. Nothing ever seems to disrupt her confidence…apart from this snarl of hedge and gravel.

"I was going to walk through it," I say. "Do you want to walk with me? And even if it doesn't help, you'll have at least spent some time with your best friend Poe."

She sighs—but it's not a Delphine Sigh, it's a smiling sigh, which I think means I've won.

"Okay, Markham," she says, waving me forward. "You're right. Let's go for a walk."

The maze is still shrouded with gloom and shadows when we walk through the entrance. A marble Demeter and Persephone flank the entry arch cut into the hedge, their outstretched hands reaching for one another, their expressions joyful and their bodies frozen in the act of flying into a desperate, happy embrace.

"Estamond really liked her mythology," I say as we start walking.

"I know," Rebecca says. "And she certainly didn't mind the raunchier myths either. For a Victorian."

We turn our first corner, immediately turn again. It's dark enough in here that I'm almost tempted to use the flashlight on my phone.

"Saint and I read that she was very improper, what with her sexy statues and inviting poets to come get drunk at her house and all."

Rebecca laughs a little. "She sounds like someone we would like."

"She does." I stop at a junction and try to orient myself, but it's hopeless. There are too many little dead ends and spurs, too many turns to keep track of our direction. Rebecca picks a path for us and we keep going. Neither of us knows the way, but with each corner, Rebecca seems to ease more and more, as if the very challenge of the maze is relaxing, as if the difficulty of it reassures her somehow. She leads us closer and closer to the center, choosing paths with startling ease.

I remember Auden telling me that Rebecca is a genius.

"I also read that this is very, very old," I say, after several long minutes of us crunching over the crushed gravel. "Estamond renovated the maze and put in the statue at the center, but there was a Tudor maze here first. And before that, maybe a labyrinth."

Rebecca is walking slightly ahead of me now, peeking around a corner and then doubling back to take the last turn we saw. "Labyrinths are not the same as mazes," she says as we walk along her new route.

"I know!" I say, wounded that she would think I didn't know that. "It was interesting is all. The possibility that there's been something in this spot for over a thousand years, maybe even with the center in the same place—"

Rebecca stops right in the middle of the path and I almost run into the back of her.

"With the center in the same place," she echoes, staring straight ahead, as if she's seeing something I can't. "Ah. Of course. A *labyrinth*. Like a turf maze, maybe, or paved."

"Well, the book didn't say *what* the labyrinth looked like, just that there was one—oh." Rebecca's pulled her iPad out and she's started making notes for herself. "Has that helped? Did I help?"

She looks up at me with one eyebrow arched high. "Given that I still have the entirety of the design and planning to do, and given that I'm still the one who had the idea to begin with, I'd say the help was limited."

"*Pleeease*?" I wheedle.

She sighs at me bouncing on the balls of my feet, but there's a distinct smile pulling at the edges of her mouth. "Okay, fine. You helped."

I beam and she rolls her eyes and mutters something like *subbie*, although I can't hear for sure. But I don't mind, either being a sub or purring under her praise. Who doesn't like praise? Surely even Dominants do. And she's smiling anyway.

She and I decide to make it to the center before we head back, and when we step into the silent, hedge-lined enclosure, I feel the same dazzling air of mystery I did as a child. There's something about the statue, Adonis and Aphrodite, this mortal man clutching his goddess, something tragic, erotic, timeless.

Something hiding even deeper secrets underneath.

"I want to go there again," I say, kneeling near the fountain to see—ah, yes, it's still there, still like I remember. A narrow notch only two feet wide between the fountain's base and the statue's plinth, disguised from almost every angle by the crescent shape of the fountain's basin, which nearly wraps completely around the plinth itself. In the slow-brightening light, I can barely make out the steep steps that lead downward.

"I've been once since we were kids," Rebecca says, joining me by the fountain. "Five years ago. I was staying the weekend with Auden, and we went out there together. Just to see it."

"And?" I ask, facing her. I want her to tell me that it was magical, alive, filled with fairies, and maybe there was a conveniently dropped letter from my mother explaining why she left her child and her husband and if she'd ever come back.

"It was lovely," Rebecca says, "but it was wild too. The grass was so tall you could barely see where you stepped, and it was so still that the air itself felt thick. Like you could suspend things in it, like you could grab hold of it."

And then Rebecca—confident, left-brained Rebecca—shivers, the few braids she's left out of her low bun dropping in front her face as she does.

"It felt like it wanted something," she says quietly, tucking the braids back. "Like it was waiting."

"Waiting?"

She gives a quick nod, looking away, but her expression as she looks away isn't one of sheepish admission. It's determined. Watchful.

"It was waiting for me to do something. I didn't know what—I still don't know what. But I feel like I'm about to find out."

15

The others leave for London, they come back. I play in the library the whole time, happy and sleepy and sadly still horny—but the last can't be helped, so I take the edge off when I can, and try not to think too much about Auden and Saint when I do.

I mostly fail.

At night I dream more dreams of fire and pain and sex.

I dream about a door that doesn't exist.

On a Friday afternoon, just after Auden and Delphine and Rebecca arrive in their usual formation of good looks and Keats references, and just before the clouds begin emptying their bellies of snow, Saint touches my arm in the library.

I nearly jolt out of my chair.

"Jesus *Christ*," I say, my hand to my heart and trying to remember how to breathe again. And then I glare up at him. "What the hell?"

Saint's lips tip at the corners. "I thought surely you'd hear me come in. You must have been completely absorbed." He nods toward the book I was reading.

I have a moment—a Rip Van Winkle moment I'm very familiar with as a narcoleptic and also as an avid reader—when I realize a *lot* of time has passed. I'd carried this book over to an armchair and started skimming so I could give the highlights to Delphine, because I knew she'd be interested, and somehow that skimming turned into two or three obsessive hours. It's dark now, the only light coming from the single lamp I'd turned on before I sat down, and snow has started dancing down outside.

"It's, um, a book about Imbolc." And then I add, because I am aware that not everyone has fallen down the Thornchapel rabbit holes I have, "it's an old seasonal holiday, on the same day as—"

"—St. Brigid's Day, yeah," Saint says. "She was a goddess before the Church turned her into a saint, you know. So Imbolc and St. Brigid's Day are basically two sides of the same coin. Pagan and Catholic, old and new."

"*New*?" I ask, dipping my eyes to the dusty book in my hands.

"Fine. 'Less old.' There's really a whole book about this?"

"Even better," I reply, holding it up with my finger still on the page I was reading. "It's about Imbolc in Thorncombe specifically. Imbolc and the other seasonal festivals; the residents here had their own particular ways of celebrating them, I guess."

"It's not very long," Saint observes, and he's right, it's actually a very slender volume, compiled by a local clergyman from a nearby parish with admirable directness and efficiency.

"Yes, but get this—he wrote this in the 1860s. After a certain someone gave him use of her library…"

Saint raises his eyebrows. "Estamond?"

"Yes!" I say, getting excited all over again. "Apparently he'd petitioned Randolph Guest before, but Randolph couldn't ever be bothered to answer his letters. But after Estamond became lady of the house, she allowed him use of the library and grounds to put together his history. Which is interesting, because it's a bit scathing for all that. I get the sense that he probably would have disapproved of Estamond's behavior, given how much he fusses about the 'heathen practices' and 'licentious, immoral antics' in Thorncombe."

Saint extends a hand, and I reluctantly pass him the book, after noting my page number, of course. He flips through it, casually at first, but with more and more interest as he goes on.

"You'll notice," I say, getting to my knees on the seat of the chair so I can lean over the book too, "that for someone who's very insistent that all of this is evil and pagan, the clergyman sure does spend a lot of time detailing and describing said pagan acts."

"He was probably fascinated despite himself," Saint says as he turns a page and reads some more. "And then that fascination made him ashamed. People like that aren't motivated out of holiness, but guilt."

"You think our clergyman felt guilty?"

Saint checks the cover of the book before going back to the page he was reading. "Old Paris Dartham of Blackhope Parish? Oh yes. He wouldn't rail so much about it and then spend paragraphs imagining every single detail."

Saint's handing the book back to me when I hear footsteps and look up in time to see Auden stopping in the doorway of the library. He's staring at Saint. And me.

And I realize how intimate the scene looks: me up on my knees like an eager schoolgirl, my head bent close to Saint's as we murmur back and forth.

"St. Sebastian," Auden says.

That's all he says. That seems like all he can say, judging from the shock on his face.

A muscle jumps in Saint's jaw as he straightens up. "Auden."

"I'd ask what you're doing here, but I see you're visiting Poe," Auden finally manages. "And I'm clearly interrupting. Forgive me, I'll come back later." He moves to leave and I scramble out of the chair to stop him.

"Auden, wait."

He stops, shifts ever so slightly. He won't look at us, and I'm suddenly unsure which one of us it is he can't stand to see. I recall the torment in his face when he looked down at us pinned to the ground underneath him that first day, and I almost want to see it again. Convince myself that it was real, that I didn't conjure it up in some dark, airless dream.

"What did you want?" I ask softly. "When you came in here?"

"I wanted to—" he breaks off and runs his fingers through his hair in that way he does when he's upset. "It wasn't important."

I don't know what to say to that, or if I should say anything at all, or if I *can* say anything, because my heart has started beating very, very fast. God, I hope Saint can't tell. This is awful, being strung between the two of them like this, and it's even worse because one man is in love with someone else and the other man won't have me.

I'd be better off longing for the priest.

Saint scuffs a foot against the floor. I know he's about to go, I know he's about to dodge away, and I hate it, I hate that we can't be like we were as children—together. Despite our fights and scrapes and petty competitions, *together* was the default, it was the understood mechanism of how we were. We could fight and complain all we wanted, but at the beginning of each new day, we came together once again.

There are lots of good reasons why adults don't do that. Pain and boundaries and new lives, but God—just for us, just for this thorny little family of ours, I wish we could be more like the children we were.

"Auden, Abby says dinner will be ready in half an hour, and Becket's just called, he's almost here and he says the roads are bad already so he might have to stay the night..." Rebecca comes around the corner and stops at our silent tableau. She assesses Auden, and then assesses Saint and me. "So Saint's joining us for dinner then?"

"No!" Saint and Auden blurt at the same time—and then glower at each other for having the audacity to say the same word aloud.

Rebecca gives them both an impatient look. "He's here. Dinner is soon. Roads are bad." She relays all this like she's writing an algebra formula on a board, the solution going unspoken because it's just so obvious. "I'll tell Abby that we'll have another at the table, excuse me." And she goes back out.

And so it's decided. Saint's staying for dinner.

There's a bunch of London talk during the meal—Auden is working on a large project that involves renovating a school and its attached church, and Rebecca and Becket have lots of opinions. Delphine is mostly on her phone, and Saint is his usual wordless-around-Auden presence, although I notice he has more than his customary single drink with dinner, as if he's not unaffected by what happened between all of us in the library earlier. I treat myself to an extra drink too, as a reward for surviving the barbed coil of tension circling the room.

It's a relief to move on to drinks in the library, and when we get there, I finally spill the good news to Delphine while the others continue talking architecture and Sir James Frazer gnaws loudly on a rubber toy near the fire.

"I think I found an Imbolc ceremony for us to do," I tell her.

"Oh my *God*," she says. "Really? *Really* really?"

"Really really."

"Oh God, tell me everything. Like everything right now."

I trot over to find the clergyman's book, and we sit together on the sofa, the one facing the big windows so we can see the snow swirling and whirling against the glass. We hold the book between us, and Saint kneels behind the sofa with his arms crossed along the back so he can join in. His extra drink seems to have relaxed him somewhat, because he's almost smiling when he joins us, and when his hand brushes my shoulder accidentally, he doesn't jerk it back like he normally does. In fact, he leaves it there, warm and insistent, and I have to force myself to breathe normally, to think about ancient pagan ceremonies and not St. Sebastian's hand.

"So a Victorian clergyman came into the Thornchapel library," I start, "and apparently found some old pamphlets, books, and journals that mention the different ceremonies they used to hold at the chapel.

And while he rants about the 'unfaithful flock' occasionally, he does give a *lot* of the details he uncovered..."

Delphine takes the book from me, her eyes bright and her lush mouth open like it gets when she's excited. She's got these slightly-too-big front teeth and an upper lip that naturally curves up in a plump arch, meaning its only when she's thinking about it that she can keep her mouth closed, and times like now, when she's utterly wrapped up in something else, her lips are enticingly parted.

It's the kind of mouth that teenage boys and horny librarians dream about, and between that and Saint's hand still casually against my shoulder, I think I might go up in flames.

I turn the pages for her until we get to the section on Imbolc, trying to focus. "Here he says that after the villagers blessed the well of St. Brigid, they went by lanterns and torches to the chapel ruins. That's where the lord and lady of Thornchapel waited—or sometimes just the lord? Sometimes Dartham says 'lords' or 'ladies' plural, so I don't know. It sounds like the main thing was that there was some kind of representation from the manor, whether it was more than one person or not."

Delphine nibbles on her lip as she traces her fingers along the page, reading as I talk. "This sounds familiar from the other books. What happened next?"

I tuck my legs underneath me as I keep going, and the movement means St. Sebastian has to drop his hand—until I get settled again and he puts it back.

On purpose.

I'm trying to be annoyed, I really am, because he's the one who won't have me, who won't kiss me again, and yet it's impossible to be annoyed with him touching me like this. Maybe it's supposed to be friendly, brotherly even, to cup my shoulder as he bends his head close to mine and reads, but it doesn't feel brotherly in the least. It feels probing, possessive, like he can't stop himself from doing it—and oh, that shouldn't be so sexy, but it is. Like I'm watching his good intentions crumble to dust and they're crumbling because of me.

"The villagers picked a maiden every year to be St. Brigid," I manage to say over the bratty, needy pulse deep in my clit. "She was the one who actually blessed the well, and she was the one who led the procession to the ruins. When she got there, she would promise to keep the fires burning and the waters clean. She would bring the lambs and the new shoots out of the earth. She would—" I find the passage again so I don't misquote it "—'bless the village and be its blessing in turn. And then the maiden would light the fire, and there at the altar be made a bride by thorns.'"

"How romantic," Delphine sighs happily.

"How cold," Saint says pragmatically. His thumb makes the slightest brush against my shoulder, a tiny arcing rub that sparks across my skin, even through my thick sweater. "February? At night? Outdoors?"

Delphine scowls at him. "That's *what the fire is for*. You don't have any imagination, do you?"

"I think I have too much," he mutters, and she waves him away, bored with his practicality. I'm not bored with anything because the only thing that matters is Saint's thumb doing the thing again, which it does. One slow arc, as if daring me to stop him.

"Is there anything else?" she asks.

Fuck, I don't know, I want to say. *Can't you see this fucking thumb doing a fucking thing on my shoulder?!*

Oh my God, I have to get it together. I've been clamped and flogged in front of hordes of people and I'm losing it over a goddamn thumb? From a boy who's made it clear we can't be anything together?

I try to ignore his touch, don't succeed, and then force myself to answer anyway. I scan the page really fast to make sure I've covered everything. "Just that after she's 'made a bride by thorns,' whatever that means, she's given cakes and wine, and then the entire village can share them. Oh, and the same maiden is also the May Queen on May Day."

Delphine claps her hands together. "Oh! We should do a May Day party too!"

Her enthusiasm has caught the attention of the rest of the room, and as always, my gaze goes first to Auden, who's staring at Saint's thumb on my shoulder like he wants to bite it off.

"What should we do on May Day?" Becket asks, curious and seemingly oblivious to the drama playing out on my shoulder. The drama between Saint's mixed signals and my growing need to pounce on him and kiss the sullen brood right off his mouth.

The drama Auden seems very, very aware of.

It's Delphine who answers. "Never mind that right now, because first, we are going to do something next weekend and it's going to be *such* a delight." She launches into a fairly accurate recounting of what we know about the ritual, and then immediately starts talking about how we'd recreate it. "I mean, torches are a bit *primitive*, but wouldn't lanterns be pretty? And Auden can be the lord of the manor, and I can be the bride, and we'll have Abby make the cakes—"

"There's nothing that says the bride and the lord have to be a woman and a man," Becket points out.

"I think etymology says," Rebecca remarks dryly.

"Okay, okay, but I mean for *us*. Because it would be ours, right, our own thing? Our own ritual, our own celebration? There's no reason we can't reclaim it and make things less…" Becket temples his fingers and stares at us gravely, as if he's at his pulpit giving a homily "…gender essentialist."

"My good priest, you aren't actually considering this madness, are you?" Auden says, finally breaking his gaze away from my shoulder to stare at Becket with pained incredulity.

"Why not?" I ask, a little indignant on Becket's behalf, at the same time Becket himself replies, "Well, why not?"

Auden sits up, setting his whisky on the table with a glassy *plink*. "Firstly, it can't be very Catholic to trounce around in the dark with lanterns while a young maiden promises to keep the livestock safe and then eats a cake."

"St. Brigid *is* a Catholic saint," Becket interjects, but Auden keeps going.

"Secondly, the practicalities are almost insurmountable. Who would play which role and would someone feel left out if they're just some sort of lantern-holding extra? How are we going to explain whatever the fuck these cakes are to Abby? How are we going to get out to the chapel without anyone breaking an ankle and then stay warm enough to light a fire, have some odd little marriage rite—and we have no idea what this rite consists of, by the way, except that it involves thorns—eat some cakes and then walk back uninjured and not hypothermic?"

"Oh, don't be such a *bore*," Delphine groans. "If they did it back in the—" she waves a hand at the book "—in the whatever times, then we can do it now! We have *coats*, Auden," she adds, as if this is a closing argument.

Auden ignores her. "Thirdly, why? Why the fuck would we waste a night in the cold making idiots of ourselves? We don't believe that wells or livestock or fires need to be blessed anymore, so what's the point in pretending that we do?"

"What's the point of any ritual, then?" Becket points out. "Rituals aren't for wells and livestock, Auden. They're for the people performing them."

"Well, then? What do those people get out of it? Because they're not getting magical protection, and they're not getting the attention of gods who don't exist. And I'll make this question more than academic—I'll make it individual to the six of us."

Behind me, I hear St. Sebastian catch his breath.

Auden said *six of us*. Not five.

Auden continues, "What do *we* specifically get out of tramping through the frozen grass to light a fire and eat cake? We're doing that tonight and all we had to do was walk to my fucking library."

Becket temples his fingers again, staring serenely at his friend. "I think you're answering your own question. We would tramp through the cold grass precisely *because* it's not normal, because it's not what we do in our daily lives. That's how we demarcate the sacred from the profane—it's how we communicate to ourselves that this day or thing is special, that it matters."

Auden gets to his feet in agitation, giving all of us an imploring, frustrated look. "But why does it have to matter? What is this day to us that we need to make it special?"

"It could be Thornchapel coming back to life," Rebecca says. We all look over to where she's standing by the fireplace, her gaze turned toward the snow and one foot idly rubbing at Sir James Frazer's fur. She looks back to us. "Right? Isn't that what this festival is about?

Marking the coming end of winter? Celebrating the earth reawakening?"

The word *reawakening* cuts through my thoughts like a knife.

Convivificat.

Oh God. I drop my eyes back to the book, not seeing the words, not even really looking at them. I'm seeing instead my mother's sharp, aggressive handwriting.

It quickens.

There's no way my mother could have meant this, there's no way she could have meant this particular date, this particular festival—there's no way that note can mean anything at all close to what I'm thinking.

But I also know it doesn't matter, because I still have to do this, I still have to…try? To hope? Hope that there might be meaning here, something more than coincidence, and that it will bring me closer to learning why she left?

Everything is possible. Maybe even this. And initially I'd wanted to do this because it sounded romantic and mysterious and it was hard not to get swept up in Delphine's enthusiasm, but now—

I think of the torc my mother held in that picture. The same torc from the drawing.

It quickens.

Auden is looking a little betrayed by Rebecca's words; clearly, he considered her an ally in fighting off our enthusiasm. "Quartey, you can't believe in this blessing nonsense like the others."

She fixes him with a steady look. "I believe in the grounds. The earth and the trees and the water—that's my job, to believe in them, to make them into shapes that inspire people, to mold their potential into something memorable and powerful. Something like this acknowledges the work we're doing. It would be a way for us to signify that we are bringing Thornchapel back to life. A new version of itself that we all shaped together by choice." She pauses before she adds for emphasis, "That *we* shaped and not Ralph."

Auden's mouth tightens at the mention of his father.

"Is it so odd to want to mark all that?" she asks. "It's not even my home or my family's legacy, and I still want to mark it because it's my work. And because I care about this place, even if you don't."

Auden ducks his head, mouth still grimly set, and then he looks up at me. "You seem enamored with this idea," he says, and it's not unkind the way he says it, but more like my being enamored is bothering him. Like it's a weakness for him. "Why, Proserpina? Because you like old things? Mysterious things, like the books in this library?"

I don't want to share my thoughts about my mother's note and what it might mean about this ritual, but I don't want to lie either. Auden deserves honesty, I think, and so I find another truth to tell, even if that other truth is equally incredulous. But what about any of this doesn't beggar belief? It's all incredulous, and there's no point in pretending otherwise.

"I've dreamed about it," I say. "About us in the chapel together. There were thorns and there was touching and fire, and there was a door behind the altar that doesn't exist. And it's not just one dream one time—I feel like I can't *stop* dreaming about it, like it's waiting for me every time I fall asleep, and it's always with me. Like a memory, except it's never actually happened."

"So you want to make it a memory?" Auden asks, searching my face. "You want to make this dream real?"

St. Sebastian's thumb—which I'd forgotten almost all about, what with the *convivificat* and Auden's protests—tightens against my shoulder. I wish I knew why, but then again, I wish I knew why he was touching me in the first place.

"Yes," I say. "Rebecca cares about the land and Becket cares about the ritual. Delphine cares about *us* and wants to give us something special to brighten up the last days of winter." I don't mention St. Sebastian because I don't know that he cares at all about recreating an Imbolc ritual from an old book. But I feel his touch loosen ever so slightly as I speak, as if he's noticed my omission and is stung by it.

I go on making my point. "We all have reasons to want this, but I think you have the biggest reason of us all, and that's why you're fighting this so hard right now."

A dimple dots the smooth line of his cheek as he gives me a rueful smile. "Oh really?"

I refuse to be deterred by how cute he is. "You keep denying your place here," I tell him bluntly. "*This* is your home, *this* is your place in the world, and instead of giving it the best of yourself, instead of looking after it, you're doing everything you can to pretend you don't care. You refuse to let it have you, and that refusal is robbing you of something. I don't know what exactly it's robbing you *of*, but I do know that you're only ever going to be a shadow of who you could be if you keep refusing to face what you've inherited."

The dimple disappears. "What I've inherited," he echoes flatly.

"Yes," I say. "It's cowardly."

If he weren't already on his feet, he would have shot up in protest. "Cowardly?" he exclaims. "Cowardly? I'm here, am I not? I'm not abandoning this heap of stones, I'm not tearing it to the ground, and I'm not even selling it off! I'm putting in bigger showers and bi-fold doors, I hardly think that's some kind of abject dereliction of duty—"

"You're upset right now because you know I'm right!" I'm also on my feet, my shoulder feeling uncomfortably cool after losing the warmth of St. Sebastian's hand. "It's not about the actual work you're doing to the house—it's *why* you're doing the work. You're tearing the house apart out of disgust and bitterness and because you're holding Thornchapel responsible for the people who lived in its walls, and you know that's not fair! You know you owe this place a chance! You owe it the best parts of you, even if it's only for one night."

When I stop, the room is quiet. Auden is turned half away from us, facing the books, the hollows of his cheeks and throat pooled in shadow. Everyone else is staring at me, as if they still can't believe I called Auden cowardly.

"This place, it infects people," he says into the darkness. "I can feel it infecting me. And if I let it—"

He breaks off, but I think I know what he was going to say.

If I let it, I will become my father.

The silence pervades the room, and I know I should say something kind, something conciliatory, especially after calling him a coward in front of everyone else, but I *can't*. I'm too choked off with my own anger. Here he is, the pretty lordling of a pretty castle, with all his family and history spread out around him, and he can't be bothered to take any part in it, can't be bothered to step up. While I'm here chasing ghosts and maybes for even the tiniest whisper of my own legacy.

Doesn't he know how lucky he is? To call such a place a home?

To know the grass that grows over his parents' graves?

Auden takes a single heave of a breath and then turns to us, shoving a hand through his hair. "Fine," he says. "Fine. You all win."

Delphine squeals and pops off the sofa to kiss him on the cheek.

"How wonderful, darling!" she says. "I mean, I would have done it without you anyway, but this will be much more fun. You'll see!"

He endures the kiss gracefully, but his eyes are glittering and dangerous as Delphine bounces back to the sofa and starts making plans for us. And rather than join the chatter about weather reports and whether or not we should wear robes or something more practical, he wanders over to the window to watch the snow.

"Do you think the people from Thorncombe still go up to the chapel after they're done with the well?" Rebecca asks, and I hear Saint answer as he gets up from where he's kneeling behind the sofa and comes to sit on the arm.

"They don't. I've done the festival a few times with my mom, and it begins at the well and then ends at The Thorn and Crown with beer." There's a shy quality to Saint's words, as if he's nervous and happy and uncertain about being included in all this. It pulls at me, both with sadness and with pleasure, because I'm happy he's a part of this, but I'm also pained that it was ever a question to begin with.

"It looks like the clergyman mentions a single title repeatedly," Saint says, reaching for the book as I take a drink in hand and stare at Auden's back across the library. "*The Consecration of the May Queen.* It was old even in Reverend Dartham's time. Maybe if we can find it, we can figure out a little more about the ritual in the chapel itself?"

"And the book is here?" Becket asks.

"Presumably, unless it's been removed," Saint says. "Poe, do you know where it might be?"

I'm chewing my lip, watching Auden while dreams and memories of dreams threaten to push through into real life. "No," I murmur distractedly. "Maybe Estamond's ledgers? She has shelf numbers marked on there, so if she'd cataloged the book, we might be able to find it."

There's a general flapping of excitement about this, and within a few minutes, Rebecca and Becket are poring over one ledger while Delphine and Saint take the other. And while they're searching for the paper needle in a paper haystack, I make a choice.

I steel myself with a long swallow of scotch, and then walk across the library to go apologize to Auden.

16

He's facing the snow when I get to the window, the fingers of one hand splayed against the glass while his other hand fists and unfists in slow, methodical pulses. This deep into the night-gloom of the library, he's only the barest highlights of himself—eyelashes caught with shadows like drops of water, the wide mouth, the patrician nose and elegant tumbles of light brown hair. He'd dressed simply today—or as simply as he ever does—in dark red trousers and a white button-down, and the collar of his shirt is open enough for me to trace the strong lines of his throat and the mesmerizing crescent of his collarbone. I still feel that primal urge to go to my knees and beg him to pull my hair, but I ignore it. I refuse to kneel to a coward.

I may apologize, but I won't kneel.

"You were right," he says without looking at me, before I can even speak. "You were right about what you said."

I think about this a moment. "I came to say I'm sorry, and I think I still should. I shouldn't have said those things in front of everyone else. I know what happened between you and your father was painful."

His eyes are still on the snow. "Painful," he says. "Yes."

"And I shouldn't have shamed you for how you're handling his death." Guilt tightens my throat as I realize that I did fuck up pretty badly back there. "You're grieving and you are grieving a man who was cruel to you, and I…I should have known better."

"Yes," Auden says, finally turning to face me. "You should have." He sighs and scrubs at his hair. "But you also weren't wrong. It's easier to draw up wiring schedules and review wood samples than it is to think of Thornchapel as my own."

He looks at me for a moment, then extends a hand. It's cool from the glass, and I feel that coolness everywhere as I give him my hand in return.

"I want to show you something," he says, pulling me away from the window. "In the south tower."

I follow him, but I do tug my hand free, feeling strange about holding hands with him and not wanting Delphine to get the wrong idea as we go past the group by the fire. I needn't have worried though; they're so absorbed with the ledgers that they don't notice us leaving the library at all.

Snow buffets the windows of the corridor leading back to the hall, gusting against the newly repaired windowpane and piling atop the sills. We take another corridor to the south wing, passing more windows looking onto a paved courtyard with a single bench and empty fountain, and then into the locus of the renovation mayhem, stepping over wood planks and spools of wire and random piles of tarp and scrap. We go up the stairs to the first floor, where the renovated bedrooms are mostly finished and awaiting final coats of paint, and then up another floor to the former servants' quarters, where Auden's studio will be.

And then the last flight takes us up into the tower, which is a squarish facsimile of a medieval tower, but with the telltale faux-Gothic trappings of an enthusiastic Victorian builder. There are windows overlooking every direction—the forest to the north, east, and west, the majestic stretch of lawn and river valley to the south, the snow-hummocked maze and walled garden to the southwest and southeast respectively. The middles of the windows are inset with stained-glass roses and thorns twining in curlicues from windowpane to windowpane, and the tops of the windows are capped with stone quatrefoils.

"It's very fanciful," I say politely.

Auden laughs a little. "It is. The view is amazing, but I don't think anyone could ever accuse my Victorian ancestors of restraint."

I step over to the north-facing windows, peering out against the snow. The lights on the front of the house illuminate the flakes from underneath, showing exactly how thick and fast they're falling. I can't even make out the orange glow of Thorncombe less than a mile off.

"Anyway, I didn't bring you up here to make you look at the Gothic architecture," Auden says. "I wanted to show you this."

When I turn back, he's kneeling in front of a trunk that's been shoved against the wall—in fact, there's rather a lot of stuff that's been shoved against the wall here, like this tower room has been more like an attic than an observatory. There's more than the one trunk, and a few battered cardboard boxes, and even a tricycle for a very small child. A small child in the 1950s, one would guess, given the amount of dust clinging to it.

Auden stands up, holding a framed painting in one hand while he turns on his phone flashlight with the other. The painting is only a foot square—nothing like the massive ones still hanging in the Long Gallery—and the frame is almost simple, just some polished, beveled wood. Nothing ornately gilt or carved. But what's most remarkable about the painting is the image itself, of the young woman it depicts.

She stands alone in the middle of the chapel ruins, holding a lantern aloft while a white gown billows around her bare feet. Her long, dark hair is unbound and tangling over itself in the wind as she looks back over her shoulder to the painter. She's nearly as pale as her gown, her cheekbones high and wide, her full mouth parted ever so slightly, as if she's startled. Her eyes have been painted so green that they nearly glow from the canvas, like a cat's.

The distinctive arc of the golden torc dangles from the hand not holding the lantern.

I should be focused on that, I should be consumed with that little detail because that torc seems to be everywhere—but I'm not, I'm back to staring at her face, struggling to believe what I'm seeing.

"Uncanny, isn't it?" Auden asks softly, and I don't have to look to know he's gazing intently at my face, at the face that so closely resembles the painted one in his hands. "You could be sisters. Mother and daughter."

"Who is she?" I whisper, only barely stopping myself from touching the canvas.

"This is Estamond, your Victorian party girl and amateur librarian. Her husband Randolph seems to have had a particular fondness for this painting—after her death, he kept it in the master bedroom. I heard my grandfather say once that Randolph even traveled with it, although that might just be family gossip."

I can't stop staring at her, this Victorian doppelgänger of mine, Estamond Kernstow Guest.

Kernstow, I remember. *Your mother was a Kernstow.*

Can it be a coincidence? Can it really? How many things are going to happen around my mother and Thornchapel before I stop dismissing them as mere accidents of fate?

I wish my father would text me back about my mother's family. My grandparents died long before I knew them, and unlike many other librarians, I never entered the cult of genealogy research. Partly because it held no charm for me, and partly because I couldn't bear to fill out any family tree knowing that I'd have to put a question mark as my mother's year of death.

I finally look at Auden. He's staring back at me with a thoughtful but heated expression. His eyes dip to my mouth once, just briefly, just long enough that I know he's thinking about our kiss. That he might even be thinking about spanking my bare ass while I writhe and cry in his lap.

"I noticed the resemblance right away," he says with a small smile that doesn't cool the heat in his eyes. "I used to come here often as a kid. My father hated it up here, and so it was my safe room of sorts. I used to pretend I was a prince with a wicked king for a father, and that when he died, I was going to be a merciful, strong ruler in his place. And Estamond would be my queen." He rumples his hair in embarrassment. "A stupid, childish game."

"It wasn't stupid," I say quietly.

"It was." He's bitter again. Bitter with himself, and with this tower and everything surrounding it. I can tell.

"Maybe it was a little childish fantasizing about your ancestor," I say to try to tease away some of the bitterness, and he looks up at me with surprise.

"Oh, Estamond isn't my ancestor," he says. "All of her children and her grandchildren were dead by the time of the War. It was Randolph's nephew—his brother's son—who inherited Thornchapel. My great-great-grandfather."

I think of the entry Saint and I found, about her happy but too-short life. "That's so sad. All of her children and grandchildren?"

Auden nods. "Randolph let the place fall into ruin after her death. He would occasionally visit his children in London, but gradually, he fired most of the staff and became a recluse. He watched his own line die out."

I feel a pang for the old Randolph, alone in this empty manor with only his painting of Estamond for company. And a pang for Auden, the equally lonely boy, hiding up here from his father with his imaginary kingdom and an old tricycle.

"I'm sorry again," I say, squeezing his hand and thinking of that little boy. The tower is freezing, and so now both our hands are cold when we touch. "I shouldn't have said—"

"Maybe not to someone else, but I'm glad you said it to me," he says, catching my gaze with his. His eyes are serious. "I have been blaming the house for him. And I'm letting him take up all this space in my thoughts like he's still alive, like he can still hurt me, because if I stop letting him into my thoughts...If he's really dead—then maybe it means I'm someone different now. Part of me must have died with him and I'm not sure what's left. What can grow into the vacant places."

"They'll be good things," I tell him confidently. "Strong things. That's what Imbolc is for, you know—new beginnings."

"At least according to the Reverend Paris Dartham," Auden sighs. Then he gives me a real smile—half hopeful, half mischievous. "Are you really sure you want to act out a scenario laid down by an obsessive clergyman?"

I'm still squeezing his hand, I realize, as I look down at the woman in the painting. "It looks more like we're following Estamond than him."

"You're right," he says. "Well, that's a comfort. I much prefer Estamond to old Dartham."

I let go of his hand and point at Estamond with her torc and her vivid eyes.

"You'll finally get to be with your queen," I say, thinking of his boyhood games, but Auden gives me an odd look, as if unsettled by what I just said.

"My queen," he answers slowly. "Yes, I suppose I will."

We end up bringing the painting down to show the others, who are predictably excited and fascinated with it, and we all have another round of drinks while Delphine makes me pose like Estamond in the picture to gauge the resemblance for herself.

It's decided—by Delphine and Rebecca, in a rare show of solidarity—that Becket and Saint should spend the night in the old wing's remaining spare room, and that the planning for Imbolc would resume tomorrow. Saint makes a faint noise of protest at this, but there's no arguing the blizzard outside, no denying the snow falling so thick and fast that even the forest can't be seen from the windows.

So after dousing the fire, we stumble in a boozy haze up to our rooms, and after a general hubbub of brushing teeth and hunting for extra blankets and making sure Becket and Saint found everything they needed and also would both fit on the spare room's bed, we close our doors and prepare to sleep while winter screams outside.

It takes me almost no time at all to fall into the dreams.

And when I do, there are thorns biting into my wrist and there's a fire hot on my back and when I look down, I'm clasping St. Sebastian's hand. Auden's hand covers both of ours, and all of it is wrapped in thorny vines, stiff enough to make a cage, but tight enough to make all three of us bleed. We're handfasted.

"A bride by thorns," dream-Auden says.

Except then it's not him, it's Delphine and me, bound together with blood and thorns and she's shivering against the pain, but with delight—and then it's all of us standing in a circle, thorns between our palms and clasping hands tight so that we'll each be pricked.

"Are you ready to lie down, Proserpina?" dream-Auden asks gently, and I am, I am finally ready to lie down.

There's a door behind the altar.

I stare at it as I slowly spread my legs and am made a bride.

17

Our Life, Our Sweetness, and Our Hope

The bed is almost too small for Becket and Saint together, but the priest is conscientious and Saint is exhausted. He came to Thornchapel to drop off a public library book for Proserpina, a fantasy title he knew she wanted to read and that he'd checked out under his account so she could take her time with it without worrying about late fees…but even at the time he knew it was a pretense. She hadn't asked for the book and he hadn't offered it—there was no reason for him to come to Thornchapel other than that he was crawling out of his skin from not having seen her that day. And if there was the danger that Auden would be there, the danger that he might see the same look of mingled hunger and anguish on Auden's handsome face as Saint saw that night when he hurt Proserpina's bare bottom for everyone to see…

It had been a danger that didn't feel like a danger at all.

And then when Auden said *six of us*. Not five. Not them minus Saint, but them *plus* Saint...

He didn't even know what he felt then, except that it was almost like panic but sweeter. Honeyed like bourbon and the lies he tells himself at night with his hand on his cock and his mind full of Auden.

Saint rolls onto his side and stares at the window, even though there's nothing to see but snow and darkness. He doesn't need to see to know the window looks out over the south gardens, over the maze. He knows exactly which stand of trees conceals the tunnel exit from the maze's center, and which almost indiscernible path leads to the chapel ruins.

He knows because he goes there often. Like a poacher in the woods, treading soundlessly through the back paths and hidden inlets onto the Thornchapel grounds, he's learned to come and go without being seen. Unlike a poacher, he's not hunting, he's not looking to take anything that isn't his—all he does is search out the ruins and sit, as if the wildflowers and dead stones have answers for him.

His mother's family was a family of devout Catholics, and his mother had grown up with faith as inescapable and natural as breathing. She lit her saint's candles, she prayed her devotions, and she went to Mass faithfully, every week. At his birth, she named her only child after the patron saint of saintly deaths.

And for all that—for his mother's fierce faith and his own name—Saint had never found any faith of his own. It all felt hollow, and after watching his mother die, it now feels worse than hollow—it feels pointless.

Except there are these times...these strange, ephemeral times when he almost feels...*something*. He doesn't know what to call it, how to think of it, and he doesn't even know if he likes it, because whenever that something brushes up against his mind, it's so dizzying and potent that he feels like he could lose himself in it without a second thought. And for a man who's clawed for every scrap of identity he has, the thought of losing anything is terrifying.

What he does know is this: any time he's ever felt whatever it is, magic or God or the collective energy of the universe, it's been in the thorn chapel.

It should feel ridiculous, what he's agreed to do with the others. In fact, he half expects they'll all wake up and remember their drunken declarations with shame, and the idea will be quietly and gratefully forgotten.

But for St. Sebastian, nothing could be further from ridiculous. Nothing could feel more necessary right now. He may not believe in anything, but if he *could*, it would be there in that place and it would be with them, and it seems right somehow to try. Like doing anything else might actually tear him apart.

Father Becket is at peace until he dreams. And then the zeal opens its pitiless mouth and chews him with eager, champing teeth.

He's told himself precious few lies over the course of his life; he prizes honesty as the king of virtues. And while he learned compassionate silence with others so that he could comfort them without prevarication, he forbade himself the same comfort. He would always tell himself the truth—the zeal demanded it—and so any lies he told himself were lies he sincerely believed. A lie, for instance, that his interest in Celtic mythology was merely an academic response to his surroundings.

Of course, he'd reasoned to himself, he'd be fascinated here, in this lonely corner of the country still studded with fragments of Brythonic place names and scattered with dolmens and menhirs older than the Celts themselves. It was intellectual curiosity that sent him searching for books and rambling over the moors to see each and every standing stone or ruined church or hill fort for himself. That was all. Nothing more.

The lie had dissolved tonight. He could no longer pretend to himself that his fascination was intellectual. It was personal, deeply personal, rooted to his very soul somehow. And despite the dispassionate and worldly air he'd put on downstairs, he's troubled by it. He's troubled by the pull he feels toward this place. He's troubled by the feeling that it needs him.

It's not the unorthodoxy that troubles him, at least he doesn't think so. He's an unorthodox priest anyway, being openly bisexual—if celibate—and encouraging his parishioners to think critically and constructively about their faith. He is fond of other religions and their rituals, he enjoys learning about them, and he sees this Imbolc as more of a cultural exercise anyway.

Or at least he should.

Instead, he's terrified that the zeal waits for him in the chapel ruins. And when he dreams—dreaming of the summer he came here in college, alone and with the zeal blazing so hot inside him that he couldn't even think—he dreams of being in the thorn chapel. He dreams of standing in front of the altar and feeling like a pillar of fire because he was so consumed with a desire to know his god.

And when he wakes up, he wakes up with his skin burning against the air, like he's aflame with righteous hunger once again.

The storm howls on through the morning, and Rebecca wakes at her usual early hour to find that it feels like day hasn't broken at all. There's a vague sort of brightening in the white maelstrom outside, like somewhere high above the world the sun does, in fact, still exist, but it's dim enough that Rebecca has to turn on the light in the kitchen to make her tea while she hunts down an apple for breakfast. She decides to work in her favorite spot, which is a corner of the old hall, on a window bench overlooking the terrace and south gardens. Of course today she won't be able to see much outside, but she'll be cozy with her pile of blankets and the space heater she keeps over there.

Strictly speaking, she shouldn't be working. It's Saturday, and Rebecca has been trying to work less, to keep normal hours, to be the kind of woman who has enough free time to take up a hobby besides flogging strangers for fun. But she also can't seem to rid herself of this suspicion that free time is wasted time, that she's cheating herself out of her own future if she doesn't pour everything she has into the present. A belief no doubt planted in her childhood, when those early tests revealed exactly how gifted she was, and a belief watered daily by her boss—who is also her father.

She supposes in an ideal world, there'd be something easier about working for one's father, relaxed expectations maybe, or just a surfeit of understanding and compassion. But the truth is that her father is all the harder on her for their connection, demanding more of her than he does of any of his other architects. She knows he loves her…she knows that in a way, expecting so much from her is his way of showing his love. He wants her to succeed the same way he succeeded—against the odds and tirelessly.

And she understands, she *knows*, she'd felt her neck burn and her shoulders creep forward those days in sixth form when she'd walk in and realize she was the only black girl in the class. She'd felt helplessness and frustration dig inside her chest when she'd had to work doubly hard as the white men in her master's classes just to have her projects graded the same. She knows tirelessness, she knows when the world wants her to bite down her words and her feelings, she knows that she's not ever, ever allowed a moment's rest, a moment's weakness, a moment when she's not the best and the most graceful and the most patient.

She just thinks it would be nice if her father didn't demand all the same things too. If he could give her the space to breathe she doesn't have anywhere else.

In any case, Rebecca has never been the type to linger over wishes and unmet hopes. Truth be told, it's too late for her to be anything but a workaholic, and she's found places where she doesn't have to swallow her bitten-down words like she does in her father's office—places where *she* can do the biting, the speaking, the winning. It's the one thing she has that's hers and only hers, and it's the one thing that keeps her job and her father's all-consuming expectations of her from swallowing her whole.

Rebecca thinks with some wistfulness about how it will be another few days until she's in London again, until she can find someone to play with and until she can shuck off the exhaustion that comes from being entirely perfect all the fucking time.

And that's a few days *if* the storm lets up…

Christ.

She's just getting settled in her corner and pulling out her laptop when Delphine drifts down the stairs, looking unfairly cute and sexy with her hair piled on top of her head and wearing one of Auden's old Cambridge sweatshirts. Her curves strain at the material, they strain her unicorn-patterned sleep shorts even more, and her soft flesh makes a distinctive and inviting *v* between her legs. Rebecca looks away quickly, her heart beating faster.

"You're up early," Delphine yawns, trundling forward in Auden's slippers, which are too big for her and so she has to shuffle to keep them on.

"I'm always up early," Rebecca points out. "You can't have failed to notice this about me over the last two months we've been living in the same house."

Delphine just tilts her head, blinking sleepily at Rebecca. She's shivering too, her legs covered in goosebumps, which for some reason irritates Rebecca rather a lot.

"Get under here," Rebecca says, a bit gruffly, holding up the big, fuzzy blanket that's currently over her lap. Apparently too sleepy to remember to argue, Delphine obeys; she crawls onto the window seat next to Rebecca, tangles their legs together, then drops her head onto Rebecca's shoulder like it's the most natural thing in the world.

"Are you going to help me plan the Imbolc thing today?" Delphine asks on another yawn.

Rebecca had nearly forgotten about all that, too wrapped up in her usual morning routine of tea and work. "I really should complete this proposal," she says.

"And then you'll help me," Delphine decides, as if it's that easy, as if all Delphine has to do is wish it and it's so, like a storybook princess.

And the strangest thing is that Rebecca almost feels like indulging her. Right now with her pressed warm and lush against her side, with that mass of golden hair brushing against her cheek with faint whisper-scents of something expensive and floral, she wants to pet her and spoil her.

"Why aren't you still in bed, Delphine?" she asks, trying to sound normal, trying to sound like she's not committing the smell of her hair to memory.

"Sir James Frazer," Delphine answers dozily. "He wants to be in the bed with Auden when it's cold, and there's just not enough room..."

"So you came down here, where there's no bed at all?"

"Thought I'd—" a yawn "—come get—" another yawn "—some tea..."

With a sigh—she chooses not to examine how almost-content her own sigh is—Rebecca opens up her laptop and begins working, Delphine's head on her shoulder the entire time. And within moments, Delphine is fast asleep.

When Delphine wakes up for the second time that day, she's alone in the hall. Someone has tucked the big blanket around her and given her a pillow, and she notices that whoever did it also angled the space heater toward her and made sure to wedge a couple cushions between her and the glass, to keep the window from leeching away her hard-won warmth.

It must have been Rebecca. For some reason, that makes Delphine smile, thinking of Rebecca pausing budget calculations or parsing environmental impact studies so that she could tuck Delphine in. And then she thinks of Rebecca spanking Poe, of the slaps and cracks that echoed through the room, and her smile slowly fades. She digs her teeth into her lip, spreads her legs ever so slightly under the blanket. Just enough that she can feel the empty air against her swelling clit.

All this time when she couldn't wake her body up enough to want sex, was it because she was wanting the wrong kind of sex? She'd been imagining something gentle and patient and sweet with Auden, and every time she imagined it, it felt like the imagining was more than enough, like she'd choke on it.

But she didn't choke on anything when she watched Rebecca and Auden spank Poe, she didn't choke on anything at all except how much she wanted to be Poe just then. How much she wanted just to cry and feel things and then have someone kiss her and tell her what a good girl she was.

She should ask Auden to spank her. That's what she should do. That would be the sensible thing, and she knows he wouldn't judge her for asking. In fact, after watching him spank Poe, she has to wonder if he *wants* her to ask, because the way he looked when he was spanking their friend was the way a sinner looks at the cross. Like salvation was just within reach.

But Delphine doesn't go ask him, even though she knows he's probably awake by now. Instead she takes a final peek around the hall to confirm that she's alone, and then she moves her hands deeper under the covers and begins to rub herself.

When she closes her eyes, it's not her fiancé's voice she imagines, but a woman's, and it's not his hand cracking pain along her backside, but Rebecca's. And when she's finished, she's limp and warm and full of questions she's not sure she's ready to ask herself.

She holds up her hand and stares at her engagement ring as it glitters in the faint, gray light.

She stares at it for a very, very long time.

It's unthinkable that Abby should try to come in with all this weather, so the impromptu Imbolc planning committee fends for itself with cheese toasties and leftover soup. Auden brings the food into the library where everyone is clustered over the old ledgers and around fresh notebooks, and he has a moment looking at them when he feels something so powerfully *right* that his heart flips over inside his chest.

Maybe it's the nostalgia of having everyone in one place again, or maybe the excitement of the ritual is starting to seep into his blood too, but whatever it is, he has the sudden and fierce urge to give them something, anything and everything, just to keep them all here like this, under his roof and nestled close. Even St. Sebastian.

Even St. Sebastian.

He thinks of Poe, of how her firm, plump bottom felt against his hand, and then he wonders what it would be like to do the same to St. Sebastian. To have the only person who ever hurt him worse than his father draped over his lap and trembling. Would he be hard?

Would *Auden* be hard?

Yes, yes of course he fucking would be, because everything he's kept locked up inside of him is just spilling out now, tearing free of him, and it won't be long before his tattered hungers make themselves known…

No. God, no, what is happening to him? Of course he won't do that, he's stronger than that. He has to be.

He finishes delivering the food to the gratitude and cheers of all, and then he murmurs something about finding his own laptop before he strides out of the room to collect himself.

To the tower he goes, his frozen aerie, and he sits on a trunk and shoves his face in his hands, his sides heaving. He can't stop this ache, this need, for two people who are not the one person he is supposed to ache for, and it's killing him. He has to burn it out of himself somehow, *dig* it out if it won't be burned, and soon. He refuses to hurt Delphine, he absolutely won't do it; she's the last person in the world who deserves that after all she's been through.

And yet…and yet when he thinks of Poe's soft mouth yielding under his, of feeling her squirm in his lap with her mewling little cries while her cunt grew wetter and wetter…

With a groan, Auden gives up. He slides the clasp free of his trousers, zips them down, and hooks a thumb in the waistband of his boxer briefs to allow his cock to push free. He doesn't play games with himself—he never does—but he imagines making Poe play games with him. Imagines spanking her until she's wet and crying, and then pushing her off his lap so he can pin her to the floor and push his cock into her pussy. He imagines St. Sebastian there too, imagines Saint's soft lips around his dick, the metal ball on his lower lip stroking against his shaft while Poe watches…

He's about to erupt…he can feel that point of no return just within reach—

There's a creak on the stairs; a man's hand appears on the railing and then a head full of ink-dark hair—

It's too late. Auden's erection gives a thick, swelling throb just as St. Sebastian fully emerges into the tower, and cum pumps in hot, fast spurts all over his fist. Pulse after pulse of it, dripping from the plump tip and then to his fingers, and while he comes, he can't help stroking himself a little bit more, can't help the quiet grunts that tear out of his throat from the sheer fucking relief of it all.

St. Sebastian looks like a man who's just fallen into a trap, like any movement could mean some bitter and untimely end, and Auden can't help but savor it a little as he rides out the last few squeezes. He wants to see St. Sebastian at the edge, at the limits of his endurance, and then he wants to see St. Sebastian ragged and thrashing with the need to come. He wants to be the one to ease that need, but he also doesn't know what that means because he hates St. Sebastian, he's hated him for years—

Holy fuck.

St. Sebastian no longer looks like he's trapped, or if he does, he looks like he's decided that this trap is the only place he wants to be for the rest of his life. He's stepping forward now, one heavy, booted foot after the other, his lip ring tucked between his teeth and his eyes tormented in the snowy twilight of the room.

And then he kneels in front in Auden, his knees between Auden's light brown brogues and his hands sliding up the insides of Auden's thighs.

Holy fuck holy fuck holy fuck.

St. Sebastian gives Auden one last look—a look Auden can't even begin to interpret, a look he's not even sure if he *wants* to interpret—

and then lowers his warm mouth to Auden's still-thick shaft and gives it one long, lingering pass with his tongue.

Auden hisses, all control gone, all reason gone, nothing left but thorns. "*Yes.* Do it. Fucking do it."

Saint's tongue moves again, warm and wet, lapping up everything Auden had spilled, as if it's too precious to waste, too treasured to let drip onto a dirty floor. His lips are somehow firm and soft all at the same time—plush and silky and yet still a man's lips, still a man's mouth—and that lip ring, it's everything, it's fucking everything, Auden can feel it along his shaft and against the creases of his fingers when Saint kisses his hand clean, he can feel it along the creases and tucks of his testicles when Saint kisses those clean too. He threads his clean hand into Saint's hair and shoves Saint's mouth even harder against him; he lets out a feral groan when Saint sucks his too-sensitive cock into his mouth. He feels himself swelling hard again—he could keep Saint here just like this, he could fuck Saint's pretty mouth and then he could reward him with callous pets and pleasures until Saint came too, and it would be revenge and lust all tied together—

No.

Oh God, oh no. No, no, no.

"Saint," Auden says hoarsely, pushing him away, "stop, *fuck*. Stop."

Saint looks up at Auden from his lap, his lips swollen and his eyes darker than anything Auden's ever seen, and Christ, he's so handsome and so pretty and it's not fair, it's never been fair that St. Sebastian Martinez could be his undoing when St. Sebastian also could hurt him so much, so fucking much.

"I can't do this," Auden manages. And he's about to say, *I can't hurt Delphine*, when St. Sebastian gives a jerky nod and gets to his feet in an equally jerky movement.

"I know," St. Sebastian says. He sounds hurt, and not in the way Auden's fantasized about hurting him. He sounds hurt in a way that makes Auden hurt too somehow, and then he's gone before Auden can say anything to fix it.

He's gone, and Auden is alone in the tower with nothing but thorns in his chest and the memory of Saint's lip ring on his skin.

18

Six Days Later

"*Gotcha.*"

There's plenty of light here on the second story of shelves, and so when I finally find what I'm looking for, I don't bother to climb down to one of the tables with their lamps to look at it, I stay up here on the balcony.

The book is mid-eighteenth century, quite small, but the printing is clear and straight, and the handsome leather bindings show expertise and care. There's only one word tooled onto the spine, *Thornechapel,* but the title page reveals that it is indeed the book we've been looking for: *A Record of Thornechapel Customs, including the Consecration of the May Queen, Stories taken from Ancient Sources and Explicated Herein.*

Dartham's chief source.

Delphine and the others did their best scanning through

Estamond's ledgers this last weekend, but reading old, faded Copperplate is tricky work unless you've had practice, and it finally fell to me to finish combing through the entries. It took me almost a week to find the entry itself, and after figuring out Estamond's shelving system—a system that could kindly be called eccentric—it only took a half hour of hunting to find it hidden in the upper stories, wedged between guides to monastic gardens.

I prop my shoulder against the side of the shelf while I carefully page through the book. It only takes two pages to find mention of Imbolc and the other feasts Dartham complained about, and it looks like there's a fair amount of detail for me to sift through. Deciding that I should go down to the table after all, I'm about to close the book, and that's when I see the handwriting.

On a page depicting the now-familiar scene of a woman standing in the chapel ruins with a lantern, there's a caption that says, "The consecration of the May Queen on Beltane night."

And someone has crossed out *Beltane* in one decisive stroke, and written *Imbolc* instead. The *m* has an extra hump in it, as if whoever wrote it was in a hurry. I think of Estamond's signature in her ledger and smile. It had to have been her.

But interestingly, the word *Imbolc* is underlined with a different pen—a blue ballpoint pen. A modern pen. There's also an exclamation point after, pressed into the paper in the same blue ink, slanted and emphatic.

Stop seeing your mother's ghost everywhere, I chide myself. *This can't be her handwriting; there's simply no way for you to tell.*

But I can tell for certain that I'm not the first person since Dartham to find this book, and I still can't help the weird spike of intuition that the last person to find it was my mother.

As if enervated after the storm, winter has retreated into the shadows of trees and the cover of night. The days have grown milder as the week goes on, and eventually the swells and drifts of snow are melted into a cold, gloppy mud.

I'm slogging through it now in my blue rubber boots, the *Consecration* book tucked securely in my coat pocket and my thoughts racing. Racing through the much more explicit description of what kind of wedding rite the lord of the manor and the bride are supposed to perform.

Not just the promise, but the consummation—not just words, but flesh.

The bride and the lord are supposed to fuck. *During* the ceremony.

There at the altar be made a bride by thorns was what Dartham had said. And there's a hot, tight feeling between my legs as I recall reading what the *Consecration* author had described, and God, if it were up to me, if it was to be me holding the lantern and walking toward Auden…

But it's not going to be you, I remind myself. I'm a pervy little sex monster, and the ritual described in this old book is exactly the type of thing I'm hardwired to find delicious. Being bathed and groomed and robed, married to a tall stranger by firelight and then claimed in front of everyone—

It's not going to be you.

It's supposed to be Delphine. Delphine being claimed by firelight, by the man she's going to marry anyway. I try to ignore the lance of pain that goes through me as I imagine watching the two of them together, fucking and rutting by the altar. It's paired with an equally potent lance of arousal, and I want to shake myself.

Why am I so messy? So eager? I feel like an overgrown garden, lush and crowded, rioted and jumbled, except instead of leaves and roots and petals, I'm jealousy and hunger and pain and thrill.

All the bitter and all the sweet, all mixed together.

I keep walking and I force my mind back into reality. Or whatever counts as reality here at Thornchapel, where six educated adults have decided to act out an ancient winter ritual for six entirely different reasons. And the reality is that the bride is going to be Delphine.

Even so, everyone will need to consent to taking part, even as a witness. If it was necessary for us all to consent to being present for a short spanking, then it would definitely be necessary for a ritualistic deflowering, and *oh my God*, never mind about reality, this can't be reality, why am I even thinking through this?

For a moment, I almost consider not telling the others. I could pretend I never found the book, and we could move forward with the ceremony as we'd planned. Just some lanterns and some cakes, with a few stilted phrases read aloud in between.

Just the game we thought it was going to be.

But the librarian in me feels firmly that they deserve to know. Information is information, after all, and we can decide as a group whether we want to do anything with that information or not. Probably not, considering exactly how lurid and impossible that information is, but still. I won't make that choice for anyone else. I can't.

Anyway, I'm already halfway to the chapel ruins, and I don't want to have taken this long, muddy walk for nothing.

When I get to the clearing, the others are there, standing next to the stone row that leads to the chapel and arguing about something. Sir James Frazer is circling around the clearing, shoving his nose into every clump of grass he can find.

"…just because it's there doesn't mean we have to use it," Auden is saying.

"It's there to be used," Rebecca argues. "It's been there to be used for close to four thousand years."

"And why wouldn't we use it?" Delphine demands. "What a silly thing to say, Auden, really."

Auden looks up at the sky for patience. "I'm the one being silly?" he mutters to himself. The others ignore him.

They'd all come up from London first thing this morning, and so they've already changed into their "let's go hunting with the dogs" clothes—even Becket. Saint's the only exception, in his usual boots and jeans. He stands apart from the group, not wearing a coat, and scowling. Even Sir James Frazer gives him a wide berth.

"Ah, Poe," Becket says as I approach. "Did you have a nice walk up here?"

"I had a *muddy* walk," I grouse. "My boots are about five pounds heavier than when I started. Saint, aren't you cold?"

"No," is the short reply.

"It's supposed to rain tomorrow night," Rebecca says to me, "so I think the mud is here to stay."

"We should add umbrellas to the list," Delphine says.

Auden makes an apologetic face. "Delph, it's going to be hard enough walking with lanterns and our supplies, we can't add umbrellas too."

"Rain ponchos then," she counters.

"God help us all when you start planning the wedding," Saint remarks, and it's an innocent enough—if sarcastic—joke, but Delphine stiffens at it, her full lips pursing together in a frown.

"They haven't even set a date yet, so there's nothing to plan," Rebecca cuts in, and it's hard to tell from her tone of voice whether she's defending Delphine, accusing Delphine, or just annoyed we've gotten off topic.

Delphine frowns even more.

Auden is frowning too, not at Saint or Rebecca, but at his fiancée and her troubled expression.

I decide to change the subject. "Did you guys figure it all out?" I say, gesturing to the stone row and the church. They came out here about an hour ago to assess the ruins and plan out the physical part of the ceremony, and it looks like they've also carried in a few bundles of firewood and a tarp.

I assess it all myself, taking in the wet, bare trees and trodden, brownish grass. Mist sparkles in between the branches and in a faint haze around the chapel walls, and the air seems curiously muffled. No wind, no woodland noises. Even our own voices seem to come from a great distance.

Everything is wet and cold and quiet.

It's so far away from the Thornchapel of my dreams, from my memories of a vivid, whispering place, that disappointment tugs hard in my chest. A little embarrassment too, because I've been so excited for our Imbolc ceremony, and I'd been picturing something magical and evocative, like in the painting of Estamond. But right now it just looks like a place. Lovely with its mist and its quiet, but still just a place, still just an ordinary clearing with an equally ordinary historical site.

Not the kind of place a smart girl should have spent twelve years dreaming about and making the locus of her every fantasy and desire.

I suddenly feel very stupid and obvious.

The others, however, don't pick up on my mood, except maybe Saint, who's watching me more closely than I would like. I flush and look away while Delphine chatters out an explanation of how it will all work tomorrow.

"Rebecca says she's getting the thorns for us, and Auden found some lanterns out in the shed. They look like they're made for parties more than anything, so they may be fragile, but they'll work. Oh! And we'll have all the cakes and ale out by the altar, all ready to go after the bride says her whole bit about cows and wells and stuff, and then we move on to eating."

The bride. Ah.

I clear my throat. "Actually, that's what I came out here to talk to you all about." I extract the book from my pocket.

"It looks like there's more to being the bride than we initially thought."

"Of course, it should be out of the question," I say.

It's nearly an hour later, and we're all around the kitchen table now, stripped of damp clothes and cupping mugs of tea between our chilled fingers. Sir James Frazer is dozing on a large cushion by the range, and the book in question is in the middle of the table. Becket and Rebecca look thoughtful, Delphine looks positively aglow with excitement, and Auden and Saint wear matching scowls.

Everything about them should be a contrast—light brown hair to dark, hazel eyes to near black, tailored wool to mud-streaked denim—but when they both frown, they almost look like brothers. It's those proud cheekbones and carved jaws, I decide, and maybe also the long eyelashes and too-pretty mouths. A mixture of young male power and vulnerable beauty.

I go on with my half-explanation, half-apology. "It's obviously a very, very old rite, and my guess is that it predates Christianity by a big measure of time. And if we had trouble reconciling ourselves with the Victorian version of our ceremony, then I imagine we'll struggle even more with this. But as Becket said, this is *our* Imbolc and we get to shape it however we wish, so we don't have to do anything with this book. We can put it back on the shelf and forget about it."

Auden pushes back from the table and stands up, going over to a large window that looks out onto the driveway. "But that's not what you want to do, is it?" he asks.

I swallow down the denial wanting to worm free from my lips. I refuse to be ashamed of the things I like. For the most part. Unless the shame is part of the fun.

"What I want is immaterial," I say diplomatically. "It's up to Delphine. And of course, she won't—"

"I think we should do it!" Delphine says. Every face in the room except Sir James Frazer's turns toward her in shock.

"What?" she asks, surprised by *our* surprise. "Why not? What's so different about it than playing Spin the Bottle?"

"A *lot*," many voices answer at once.

She waves a hand. "We're not all such prudes as all that, are we? It's just sex."

"Kinky, ritualistic, muddy sex," Saint observes. The light catches on his lip ring as he leans back in his chair and crosses his arms, his eyebrow raised as he looks at us. "If we couldn't handle a kissing game, how are we going to handle watching two of us fuck?"

"Well, it'll be Delphine and Auden," I say in a placatory voice. "So it's not such a radical—"

I don't break off because Saint scowls again, but because Delphine corrects me.

"It won't be me."

I turn to face her. I've been framing this entire discussion around the fact that if we *did* do this bananaballs thing, it would be the two of us who were already paired off, the two who were already having sex. And I've been doing a very good job of pretending it didn't bother me too. "Delphine, you wanted to be the bride in the beginning, remember? It was one of the first things you wanted from this, and if this makes you feel like you can't be the bride, then we're not doing it. End of story."

"No, not *end of story*," Delphine argues back. "I wouldn't have known that I wanted this until you told us about it, but don't you think—" her voice drops and pink rises to her cheeks "—don't you think it sounds like fun?"

Well, I can't lie about that.

"But it can't be me," she says. "This book says she's supposed to be a virgin, and I'm not."

Becket, Rebecca, and Auden clearly know something Saint and I don't, because there's an explosion of angry protests at this, protests so heated and fast that I can't make out what any individual person is saying before she flaps her hands at them to get them to shut up.

"I know, I *know*. But there's more to it than that. Honestly, I'm not sure how I feel about the whole 'bride' thing anyway."

She says this last part lightly, but after she finishes speaking, her eyes drop briefly to her engagement ring. I can't help but glance over to Auden, who's also looking at Delphine's hand, and there's so much grief in his face that I hate myself for every moment I ever wished the two of them apart.

He loves her. Whatever else is true about Auden, he loves Delphine Dansey.

My sadness at that comes with a wave of exhaustion so severe that I make myself stand up and pace so I won't fall asleep at the table.

"So," I say, swallowing down the knot in my throat—a knot for Auden and Delphine—and for me too. "You're saying we should do this, but you don't want to be the bride."

"Exactly," Delphine says, all beams and bounces once again. "Now, who in here hasn't had sex?"

Rebecca makes an impatient noise. "Virginity is a construct. A meaningless, destructive construct that I think we can all agree to ignore in this conversation."

I think about all the years I've waited, of my conclusion earlier this month that sex was merely a step and not a gateway. I think of how I feel with every person here in this room, how I feel more hunger and more rightness with any one of them than with anyone else I've ever been with—as if it was always meant to be here, always meant to be them.

Can something be meaningless and meaningful at the same time?

"I agree that it's a construct, but—" I stop my pacing to face everyone. I start over. "We're right to say that a first time doesn't have to mean everything, and it doesn't even have to mean *anything*. But it can mean *some*thing if we want it to."

"Spoken like a virgin," she replies, but her eyes are friendly.

"So Poe's a candidate," Delphine wraps up for us, taking a drink and looking over her mug at us like we're giving her gossip. "And…Becket?"

Becket blushes. Actually blushes, looking down at the fingers laced in his lap. "Ah…no. I'm not a candidate."

"*Becket,*" Delphine gasps.

"I didn't always know I was going to a priest," Becket mutters.

"I'm not a virgin either," Rebecca says. "*Not* that it matters."

We all look at Saint.

He crosses his arms even more tightly across his chest and looks at us all defiantly. "Define *virgin,*" he drawls.

"Oh, for fuck's sake," Delphine says. "Have you had prolonged contact with someone's cock, cunt, or arse?"

That wipes the sullenness right off his face. He looks speechless at Delphine's crass language, and I know how he feels, given that she could barely say *pussy* to me the other night.

"What?" she says, noticing all of our expressions. "If we're going to do this, we need to get over being embarrassed about these things."

Maybe so, but it seems to me like Delphine's changed more in the last week than I would have thought possible.

"Fine," Saint bites off. "I haven't had *prolonged* contact with anyone's genitals, and they haven't had contact with mine."

"Did any of the *brief* contact result in someone having an orgasm?"

Is it me, or do Saint's eyes flicker in Auden's direction?

"No," Saint says. "No orgasms were the result."

"This is ridiculous," Rebecca cuts in. "Orgasms can't be the metric—"

"Orgasms *or* contact," Delphine clarifies defensively.

"I think," Becket says, "this just proves how flawed the notion of virginity is to begin with."

"*That* is what I've been trying to say this whole time," grumbles Rebecca.

"But," Becket says, shooting a look over at his friend, "that doesn't mean we can't break it down and re-appropriate the parts we find appealing or useful. If we choose the elements we like, with open eyes, with intention, I see no problem with it."

Silence lays heavy in the room, Becket's assured, priestly voice ringing through our thoughts as we think this through, each of us shifting a little as the silence stretches on.

Eventually Rebecca realizes we've all started staring at her for her answer, and she heaves a giant sigh. A Delphine Sigh. "Ugh," she says. "Fine."

"So that settles it," Delphine declares. "Poe and Saint are our virgins—"

"I'm a virgin too," Auden says quietly.

The room goes still.

"What?" Delphine exclaims, her expression one of horror.

She can't be any more stunned than I am, because she and Auden are *engaged*, and if he's a virgin, then that means they've never...

God.

They've never had sex.

"There wasn't anyone else before you," Auden says, leaning back against the counter, his eyes on Delphine. "And I meant every promise I made to you about..."

He presses his mouth closed, as if deciding that's too private for the rest of us to hear, and changes course. "So by everyone else's definitions, I'm a virgin too."

"Oh Auden," says Delphine, a sad note in her voice. "I never realized…I just assumed that there must have been someone you wanted before we started dating."

"There was," Auden says tiredly. "But he didn't want me back."

Saint next to me goes very, very still. So still I think I can hear his heart beating like it's outside of his body.

"I think we should do this," Becket says abruptly, before Auden can say anything else.

"Why?" Auden asks. "And please try not to forget that you are a Catholic priest when you answer this time."

"It's my opinion *as a Catholic priest* that we're talking about this in the wrong fashion," Becket says. "These kinds of things aren't meant to be dissected in the bright light of day. Rituals are supposed to be acted out and performed. And the explanation for why they're done is always going to feel flimsy when it's held up without context and without the actions that imbue them with meaning. The doing of them *is* the explanation, it is the understanding. They are built to reach inside us and expose the things that words can't excavate, the longings and the joys that reason and logic can't puzzle out.

"If we want to consider doing this with any degree of fairness, then we'll have to set aside logic for the present moment. We'll have to listen to the parts of ourselves we're not used to listening to. The little slivers in our hearts that we've trained ourselves to ignore—those tender soul-splinters that ache when we hear the wind sighing a certain way or when we see the stars glitter over the sea. Those slivers haven't forgotten how to hope that there's something more to this world than we can see or touch.

"We can sit around this table all night and find a thousand reasons why it would be silly or prohibitively difficult to perform a ceremony we have no personal connection to. Or we can decide that we're willing to approach it the way it's meant to be approached—not cynically, not ironically, but with fascination and respect. It's the same I would ask of any non-Catholic coming to Mass."

"This is different than Mass," St. Sebastian says.

"Why?" Becket asks.

Saint swivels his head to look at Becket. "You mean aside from the ritualized sex?"

"Well, Mass has ritualized cannibalism, so I'm not sure which is more civilized in your view," says the priest in a mild tone.

"The cannibalism is *symbolic*," Saint argues. "We're talking about actual, *non*-symbolic sex."

"Just because it's real doesn't mean it's not symbolic," I interject.

"You know what I meant," Saint replies with a touch of exasperation. "And I want to do the Imbolc ceremony—I do—it's just that this part is...I mean, how? How will we look at each other afterward?"

"I managed to look everyone in the eye after being spanked, didn't I? You can still look at Becket even though he had his tongue in your mouth."

Saint's cheeks darken the slightest bit and he swallows. "That's different."

"But why does it have to be?" I ask. "Think about it—if we had a wild night, say, with lots to drink and maybe more kissing, and two of us ended up fooling around in the shadows of the library—why would that be acceptable and normal, but choosing to have sex in advance isn't?"

"Because it's *not* normal," he says. "No one else is doing this, Poe; there's not a greeting card you give to the person you're going to fuck in the mud, there's not an Imbolc Day sale on Prosecco and chocolate, teenagers aren't sneaking off to have 'Celtic goddess role-play' sex."

"I believe it's called aspecting," Becket observes.

"My point is," Saint says, talking over the priest, "we don't have any reference for this—the uniquely Thornchapel way of celebrating Imbolc. We don't have a script for what comes after. There's nothing and no one we can look at who've done exactly what we're going to do."

Unless our parents did it before us...

"I didn't realize you were such a traditionalist," Becket says.

"I'm not! I'm fucking not at all, but you all don't get it, you don't understand. You don't know what it's like to see someone you care about, someone you'd tear out a lung just to talk to, and you can't. You can't talk to them because what you've done to each other in the past is an iron door without a lock between you."

Auden doesn't speak, but he doesn't have to. He closes his eyes and tugs at his hair as he turns back to the window.

If Saint notices, he doesn't show it. He finishes, "And I don't think I can bear it if that happens with us. I'm sorry if that's too honest, if I sound too desperate, but I don't want to lose you, I don't want to lose this." He looks at all of us, Auden too, even though Auden can't see him looking. "I just got it back. I don't want to risk it. I can't."

I take a seat again, so I can put my hand over Saint's on the table. "Maybe there's another option other than it tearing us apart?"

He sighs. "What would that be?"

"It brings us closer together."

A slow ripple moves through the room as everyone processes this.

"Maybe," I continue, "maybe we do this and we're better for it. It won't be a door, but a link. A bond. A knot tying us together."

"I vote yes," says Rebecca suddenly, surprising us all. And then she makes a face at our surprise. "Well, Poe had a point about the spanking, actually. It reminds me of kink, of some of the more ritualized kink scenes I've done. And thinking of it like that…it makes a certain kind of sense to me. Not logical sense, like Becket was saying. Like an intuitive sense, I suppose. A mythological sense."

"I say yes, obviously," Delphine votes.

"Me too," agrees Becket.

"And me," I say. I look over at Auden, who's still facing the window, and then over to Saint, who's chewing on his lip ring. "But it has to be all of us. We all have to agree."

Saint shifts, scowls a little around where he's pulled his lip piercing into his mouth. "I guess," he mumbles.

"That's not exactly a ringing endorsement," I say.

"Yes," he says, louder this time. "I'm saying yes. But I'm also saying—*asking*—for this not to hurt us. I don't want to not belong again."

And then his cheeks flush very dark indeed, and he scowls even deeper, as if it cost him everything to be so honest with us. I reach down and squeeze his leg in encouragement, and to my surprise, he traps my hand there and laces his fingers through my own. The firm heat of his thigh through his jeans sends warmth everywhere through me, up to my cheeks and down to my cunt. It feels so private, so intimate, to have my hand against his leg, to be touching him under the table, and I flush as deeply as Saint does as I try to keep my mind on our conversation and not just the supple stretch of male thigh pressed against my palm.

It's just Auden left now, and I feel certain he's going to say no. He's going to say no because this is madness, or because it's not emotionally safe for any of us, or because Saint said yes. He's going to say no because he can't stop fighting Thornchapel, he can't bear for it to have any more influence over him than it already does.

He's going to say no because his imaginary kingdom never included muddy, holy, fire-lit sex in the woods.

He finally turns to face us. His hands are at his sides, and his eyes are downcast, their dark lashes revealing only a small, hooded glimpse of tormented hazel.

But it's not the posture of someone defeated or reluctant; it's more like the stillness of a prince waiting for the touch of his father's crown on his head. It's the restraint of youthful power and deep anguish—a deceptive calm held only through his strength of will while he decides what he'll do. And we're all in captivity to it, all of us enthralled and possessed as a muscle ticks in his cheek and his lips press together in finality.

I squirm in my seat at the same moment Saint pushes my palm harder against his inner thigh—like we're both undone by Auden when he's like this, like we're both ready to crawl for him, to offer ourselves to him.

We're *the imaginary kingdom,* I think dizzily. *It's us. And he's the king.*

Auden looks up, meets every single one of our gazes, holding mine and Saint's the longest.

"Yes," he says simply. Finally. "Yes."

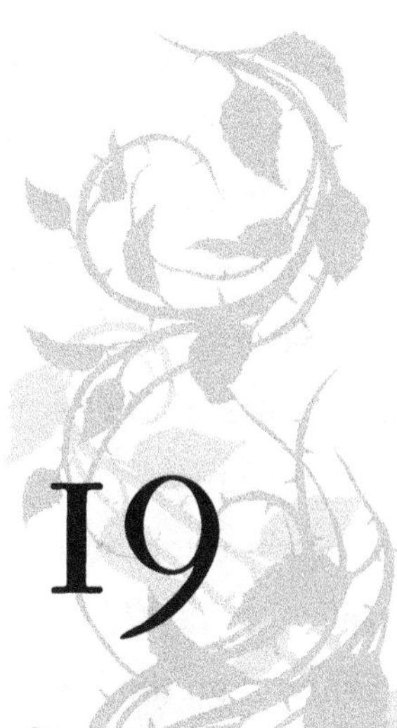

19

We still haven't decided who will be the bride or the lord, and when Rebecca suggests we wait until the morning to pick, I think we're all slightly relieved. It was hard enough to choose to do this in the first place—so having to wade through all the snarls of emotion and desire strung between us feels nigh on impossible right now.

Abby comes in from the village and makes us a dinner of roast chicken and potatoes—both sprinkled with some mysterious, addictive combination of herbs and salt. It's delicious; delicious enough that the relative silence around the dinner table feels natural and not awkward. But after the excuse of food is over and it would normally be time to go to the library and drink, it becomes apparent that we aren't sure what to say to each other, what to talk about. Tomorrow, we'll experience something that none of us have ever experienced before, and there's both tremulous excitement and shaky nervousness running through us all.

Becket is the first to leave the table—he has to have everything ready for his weekend Masses, and he'll join us in the early evening, after the Saturday service. Rebecca mutters something about getting ahead on work, and closets herself in her room with her laptop and her drawing tablet.

Auden mutters much the same, and is gone only seconds after Rebecca.

"I should go too," Saint says. "I promised Uncle Augie I'd polish up a written bid for him by tomorrow."

"Okay," I say, wanting to protest but not knowing how. He should go, he should help his uncle, and yet I want him to stay. I want to touch his thigh again. I want his thumb on my shoulder making those slow, distracting arcs.

He stands—Delphine glances up from her phone only long enough to mumble a goodbye—and then I stand too, and offer to walk him out.

"Do you like working for your uncle?" I ask as we go. I notice we're both walking slowly, as if we don't want to part, but neither of us knows how to say he should stay. Because saying it would bring all those little touches to life, it would give them meaning, it would mean risking his refusal of me again.

"I do," Saint says, and he sounds like he means it. "Augie was too busy to be a real surrogate after Dad died, but he did his best, and even though Mom and Dad never married, Augie still helped out Mom whenever he could. When I came back from Texas this last time, I was finally able to help him in return."

Seeing my questioning look, he says, "My mother's father owns a construction company in Dallas, and they do lots of big builds, like hotels and office buildings, things like that. I spent my weekends and summers helping out with the administrative stuff, learning the ropes. So when I came back and saw what a mess Uncle Augie's books were, I offered to clean them up. Sometimes I'll help on-site if they're short, but mostly I'm the money guy. The paper guy."

I bump his shoulder. "You're the money guy in a family business. And yet you still feel like you don't belong here in Thorncombe? Not even with your dad's family?"

He shrugs, like he's feeling indifferent about it, but there's something defensive in the roll of his shoulders. "My mother was Mexican and Texan and Catholic. I spent years back in America, away from my dad's family. I don't look like them, I don't sound like them." Another brittle shrug. "At best, they see me as exotic. Most of the time, I feel more like an interloper. A cuckoo dropped into their nest."

Something in my chest twists, a sharp, wringing ache. I stop walking and throw my arms around him, burying my face in his chest, and startled, he catches me up, steadying me and cradling my head against him with a large, warm hand.

"You'll always belong with me, and everyone else can fuck off if they feel differently."

"It's just life, Poe. It's just how it is."

"Fuck life," I mumble into his T-shirt. It's an old shirt, so worn through that the cotton is impossibly soft, and he smells like a bonfire in the woods, smoky and clean. I nuzzle against his chest again, relishing the feel of his firm chest all warm and strong under the fabric.

"Poe…" he says softly.

I angle my head so I can look up at him. He's staring down at me with that wary fascination again, a small frown paired with a notch between his brows. I slide a hand up the tight lines of his stomach and chest, and then trace that frown with the tip of my finger.

His hand tightens in my hair. "Fuck," he mutters. "I can't—we can't—Poe—"

I answer him by gently pushing my fingertip into his mouth, past the plushness of his lower lip. He catches it in his teeth, flicks at the pad of my finger with his tongue. I let out a helpless noise, and he shudders.

"You belong to him," he whispers, although it sounds more like he's trying to remind himself. "You belong to him and I've already taken so much from him..."

"I'm not his," I whisper back, fiercely.

And with a low, helpless groan, his mouth crashes into mine.

The piercing digs insistently into my lip, and I lick at it like I've been wanting to, I suck at the soft skin around it until Saint is growling against my mouth and yanking me close. A thick erection intrudes against my belly, and some deep-seated, unlearned instinct makes me press harder against it, sends my hand sliding between our stomachs so I can shape my palm to it.

"Fuck," he mumbles as I grip him through his jeans. His forehead drops down to roll against mine in slow, agonized movements. "Fuck."

I've never touched someone like this before, never held the weight and heat of someone's pleasure in my hand, never felt someone shivering violently against me because of something I was doing to them.

With the possible exception of Auden. Who came just from spanking me.

I'm not his.

Saint's breath ruffles the hair near my ear and warms my neck, and he moves his lips over my temple, then over my face in helpless, searching kisses, like the answers he's looking for are in the curve of my jaw and the blush warming my cheeks, like he can find the meaning of life with his lips alone.

I trace the hardness of him, I let my fingers wander up to the tip—swollen and distinct even through the denim—and then down to the base and back up again.

"Sometimes I wish you were engaged to him like Ralph wanted," Saint confesses in a hoarse whisper. "And that he was here right now. Seeing us like this."

"He'd punish us both," I say, and it comes out like I'm fantasizing because I *am* fantasizing; I am imagining being thrown over his lap again, being scolded, being fucked into dreamy submission by Auden Guest for the crime of kissing his enemy.

God. I have to stop.

"I'm not his," I repeat again.

Saint pulls back enough that I can see his blown pupils and his parted mouth, which is wet from kissing me. He cups one of my breasts in his large hand, plumping and massaging it until it's so heavy and aching that I could cry, until my nipple pulls into a tight bead against his palm. Then he gives it a vicious, unexpected twist, and I whimper in pure, clean pain.

I want to worship him for it.

Here's the thing about me:

Most people are programmed to move away from hurt, but I'm not. And it's not for any bathetic, mother-abandonment issues either—I've just always been a girl who likes it to ache. As a child, I would bite my own forearm to see the marks it would leave, I would wrap a length of scratchy rope around my wrist and tug on it for hours to feel the chafing, pretending every kind of child's game imaginable around it. I was a captive, a pirate held by an enemy crew, a princess kidnapped by an evil wizard. The pain made the games real…or maybe the games gave me an excuse for the pain. Either way, the bruises and marks and chafes gave me power somehow, some kind of strength, like they sharpened the rest of the world into a thing of fearful, breath-taking beauty, a beauty that could only be perceived through the power of hurting.

So when Saint hurts me, I don't slap his hand away, I don't leap back. Sizzle-fast agony burns through my nervous system and then vanishes in a flash; by the time I cry out and buckle against him, the pain is gone and there's only breathless, endorphin-fed eagerness in its place.

St. Sebastian winds his fingers through my hair and pulls my head back, just enough so he can search my face with dark, troubled eyes.

"Maybe you're not his," he says finally. "But you want to be."

I don't know what to say to that. Because it's true.

It's also true that I want to be Saint's.

With a sigh, he slides his hand free from my hair and takes a step back, the cool air of the hall rushing in to fill the space between us. My hand tingles with the remembered feel of his erection stiff and thick against it, my nipple aches for more cruelty, and I think I could sing hymns to the memory of his lip piercing as he browsed over my face with needy, greedy kisses.

"What's going on between us?" I ask, all of me keening for his touch again. "The other night with your hand on my shoulder, and now this…?"

He scrubs his hands over his face. "I don't know," he admits, looking miserable. "I don't know. I just—I feel like I keep telling myself what I *should* do and then it doesn't matter. There's only what I want."

"What do you want?" I ask.

Me? Auden?

Both?

But he doesn't answer. Those dark eyes grow cold, that perfect mouth pulls into a pretty sulk.

"Saint," I say, reaching for his hand. He lets me take it, but he's completely still and unresponsive when I do. "I'm waiting for you. I'm waiting for you to say *screw Thorncombe* and choose me instead."

"Don't you get it?" he asks. "I *am* choosing you. And you don't even know it."

"That doesn't make any sense—"

He gives a short, bitten-off noise of fury, and I take a step back.

"I can't be what you need!" he says. "I can't be *anything* you need. I'm choosing you by choosing to see the fucking truth."

"I don't believe that," I say. Grouchily.

"Well, I do. You know when I told you that I didn't believe all the shit the village does? I *lied*." He starts walking backward to the front door, lacing his hands behind his neck before stooping to grab the coat he'd thrown over the metal folding chair earlier. "I lied, Poe. I do believe it. I don't want to, I don't like it—it fucking kills me that you're so obviously meant for someone else. It kills me that you're this beautiful dream and I'm a nightmare to anyone who tries to love me."

"Stop it."

"I'm poison to certain people, Poe. Auden learned that the hard way. I'm not going to do the same to you."

And in the bare second it takes me to fumble for a response, he's yanked open the door and stormed out into the wet night.

I wander up to my room, stunned. There's no erasing all the mixed signals Saint's been giving; I don't feel like I've imagined something that's not there. No, it's more like I haven't been seeing something that I should have seen before. Something about the way St. Sebastian and Auden are around each other; something about how their history has scarred the both of them.

I'm poison.

Auden learned that the hard way.

It's uncomfortably like what my father said about learning how dangerous Thornchapel was with my mother, and I have a real moment where my angry, hurt feelings about Saint slide into all the angry and hurt feelings I still have about Mom. Poison and danger, daughter and mother. Alive and dead.

There's a knock at the door, and given that I've only just entered, I'm close enough to pop open the knob without taking another step.

Delphine stands there in pajamas, two colorful packets in her hand. "I want to do face masks," she declares, and then without waiting for me to answer, she comes inside my room and deposits herself on my bed.

"Um," I say.

She's already opening the first packet. "Don't you want to have clear, dewy skin for the ritual tomorrow?"

"It hadn't occurred to me," I answer honestly.

She tugs the slimy mask free and unfolds it into its horrific fake-face shape. "Here. You need it." She narrows her eyes at me as I approach and take it from her. "Have you been crying?"

"*No,*" I say.

"So you're about to cry, then."

"I'm not," I protest through gritted teeth.

"Your eyes are glassy and your chin is doing the thing. Come *onnnn*, put the face mask on, I promise you'll feel better."

With a sigh, I obey. When Delphine wants something, she is a force of nature, and I'm too tired to fight nature right now. I lie down on the bed, adjust the cold, glutinous mask over my face, and then close my eyes to wait.

"So what happened between you and Saint?" Delphine asks, settling in next to me. Even through her pajamas and my sweater, her shoulder is warm and soft, and she strokes an idle foot along my shin in a casually sexy way that raises goosebumps along my flesh.

How has Auden not fucked her yet?

Since I don't feel particularly invested in protecting Saint's pride at the moment, I answer, "Well, we kissed and then he told me he was poison and stormed out."

"Oh my *God*, really?" Delphine says.

"Yes, really. And it's not the first time it's happened. I should have seen it coming."

"You mean he's kissed you and told you he was poison before?"

"The night we played Spin the Bottle, I chased him out and we...you know. Had a moment. Then he said we couldn't be together." I feel even stupider now that I'm saying all of this out loud. When did I become a *Russian Doll* girl? Except instead of dying over and over again, I'm just doomed to repeat the same kiss and the same fight with St. Sebastian Martinez.

"Why can't you be together?" Delphine asks, puzzled.

I open my mouth and then close it again, having to readjust the mask as I think. I can't tell her about the village and what it thinks about me marrying Auden; it's too ridiculous and it could be hurtful and I'm not going to burden Delphine with it—

"Is this about Ralph wanting you to marry Auden?" Delphine says, and I freeze.

"You know about that?" I ask, shocked.

I feel her hand wave my question away. "Oh, everyone knows about that. He even told me before he died. 'If you marry my boy and keep him from Proserpina Markham, you'll be damning him to hell' or something like that. I mostly ignored him."

"Jesus fucking Christ. Delphine, please know that I don't have any intention of—"

She reaches over and squeezes my hand. "Stop. Ralph was beastly, and nobody would ever blame you for the things he said. I told him to fuck right off." She laughs. "Golly, that made him furious."

"Why was he so obsessed with this idea? Me marrying Auden? It's just so *random*."

"Well, I used to think him quite mad…but then I saw how Auden looked at you when he was spanking you, and I have to say, it didn't seem quite so delusional then."

Her voice is so mild, so unaccusing, and meanwhile my face is flaming so hot under the mask that I think it might catch on fire despite the antioxidant-laden slime. "Delphine…"

"Did I ever tell you how Auden and I started dating?" she asks softly, before I can say anything else. Before I can apologize for making her fiancé come from spanking my bare ass. Or apologize for wanting her fiancé so badly that it haunts every dream I have.

"No."

"I was raped when I was at Cambridge," she says matter-of-factly. "My second year."

"Oh my God. Delphine. God, I'm so fucking sorry."

She squeezes my hand again, not in reassurance or acceptance, but like she just wants to feel close, like she wants to hold on to someone while she talks. "They'd dragged me out of Audra Bishop's summer party, and only one of them managed to—managed to do it before they got caught—but they kept hitting me to stop me from screaming, and I—"

She breaks off and takes a breath. I tighten my fingers through hers, and she tucks our clasped hands to her belly. "Auden was at the party, and he noticed I was missing. He came out and found them in the garden, and he yanked them off me. He fought them all, you know, so viciously. Beat two or three of them to fuck and back, and then sent the rest running."

"Jesus."

"He saved my life." She sighs. "Of all the things I don't know sometimes, I do know that."

"He saved your life," I repeat, feeling the weight of that. The undeniable fate of it. How could there be anything but a happy ending for them when that was their beginning? "So then you two started dating?"

I can feel her shake her head next to me. "It took a while. I couldn't do anything at first. Most of the boys from that night were arrested—and they'd all been sent down of course, all except one who the police couldn't prove was there. Just this one boy, and we didn't even go to the same college, but the idea that I *might* run into him, that I *might* see him—it was paralyzing. I couldn't even walk to class alone. I couldn't study in the library by myself. I ordered food in so I wouldn't have to leave my room after nighttime fell. And then the trial began and it was so fucking terrible…"

Another breath.

"Auden gave me anything I needed, then, you know? He walked me to class, he studied with me. He went to all the legal bits he could. He'd sleep on the floor of my room when I was terrified someone might break in, and he drove me home whenever I needed to just be *away*. I wouldn't have finished if it weren't for him. Well, and Rebecca, but that's a different story. Anyway, when we graduated, it felt natural that we should keep it up. And then when he proposed a year later, that felt natural too."

"Of course it did," I say. "Oh Delphine. I can't even imagine. I'm so fucking sorry."

"I'm sorry too," she says quietly. "Sometimes I forget, you know? Sometimes I'm still just Delphine Dansey, and I'm the same girl who likes silly television and lipstick and lots of champagne. And then other times, it feels like it's touched everything in my life. Left smudges everywhere. Smudges and dirt."

"Both can be true."

"That's what my therapist says too," Delphine responds. "She likes the word *seasons* a lot. You know, 'there's a season for this, there's a season for that,' that kind of thing. A season for smudges and a season for normal. A season for same and a season for different. And I wonder…"

"Wonder what?"

The mask peels off my face and I open my eyes to see Delphine propped on an elbow, looking down at me. "I think I'm about to start a different season now," she says. And then she drops a light kiss onto my lips. Nothing lingering, nothing deep.

Just a soft, face-masky brush of her mouth over mine.

“I think you’re about to start a new season too, Proserpina Markham.”

“I’m not starting anything—”

She puts a finger over my lips, and then smiles. “Tomorrow night. You’ll see.”

I blink up at her. “I still think you should be the bride,” I say against her fingertip.

Her smile grows sad. “I don’t think I’m ready yet.”

“We are still talking about the ceremony, right? Not real life?”

She lifts her finger and slides off my bed. “Haven’t you figured it out yet? It’s all real life.”

And then she tosses our face masks into the trash, and leaves.

20

I'm as sleepless tonight as I am normally sleepy, which is how I end up climbing the steps to the south tower with a blanket wrapped around my shoulders and my phone flashlight lighting the way.

The darkness outside feels like a living thing, seeping inside the windows and settling in the tucks and corners of the house. It's awake, aware—but it's not sinister, and there's nothing baleful in its observant gloom as I push through it to get to the tower. It's more like the night has decided to keep watch with me, as if it wants to wrap itself around my shoulders like my blanket and follow me around. Except when I finally emerge into the tower, I see that the Thornchapel night is already keeping watch with someone else.

There's a man standing at one of the windows. A tall man, with shoulders so wide they stretch across the gothic window casings and blot out the moon-glow view outside. I don't need to see the tumbles of hair or the long-fingered architect's hands to know who it is.

I don't need to hear his low, rich voice to know it's Auden.

He speaks anyway, reaching for his glass of whisky as he does. "I keep meaning to have lights wired up here. The flashlights lose their charm after a while."

I turn off my charmless flashlight and come up next to him. He wordlessly hands me his glass. He has something closed tight in the fist of his other hand.

"I couldn't sleep," I say, after taking a drink.

"Nervous about tomorrow night?"

I take another sip and then hand the glass back. Our fingers touch briefly as he takes it from me, and I fight off the automatic shiver that comes with his touch. "I don't know."

He seems amused by this. "You don't know?"

"Well, *nervous* implies an element of fear, right? And I'm not afraid."

He glances over at me. The darkness makes it near impossible to read his expression. "No, you wouldn't be, would you? You're not afraid of anything."

"Categorically untrue."

"Okay then, Proserpina Markham. What are you afraid of?"

I cross my arms and brace my elbows on the windowsill, looking out on the gray-green paleness of the lawn, the distant reaches of the moors beyond the ribbon-thin glint of river. "I'm afraid of never finding out what happened to my mother," I say after a minute. "I'm afraid that one day I'll do what she did, and abandon someone who doesn't deserve it."

He doesn't try to talk me out of my fears, he doesn't try to reassure me. Instead he slides the glass on the sill so that it's next to my elbow, and then I gratefully take another drink.

"What else are you afraid of?" he asks, leaning down, mimicking my posture, and catching my gaze. Even in the dark, his stare is direct—convincing and commanding all at once.

I couldn't lie to him right now even if I wanted to.

"I'm afraid of you," I whisper. "I'm afraid of how I feel."

He takes in a sharp breath, but his eyes don't leave my face. They search and search and search, as if he can see right through me, right to the heart of me. Still one hand is closed tight, not a fist, but close, like someone who's caught a small insect and is keeping it trapped.

"Are you truly afraid of me?" he asks after a minute, straightening up to his full height.

I have to straighten up myself and tilt my head back to meet his stare. "Yes."

He takes a step forward, his slippered feet nudging against my own slippers, his legs pushing against the blanket. "Afraid that I'm going to hurt you?"

I nod.

Another step closer, and now his legs are flush with mine, his body warm and hard against me. He trails his open hand down the dark sweep of my hair, and then slowly wraps the length of it around his fist. I whimper at the discomfort in my scalp, at the pulse of heat between my legs.

"What else?" he murmurs.

"I'm afraid I'll like it."

The admission only hangs in the air for a second before I'm being pulled down, inexorably down, until I'm kneeling in a pool of soft blanket. He's still holding me by the hair.

I shouldn't let him do this, I shouldn't be at his feet and damp between the legs when I can still recall the tickling brush of Delphine's mouth over my own.

He's not yours.

"I'll confess something, since you confessed to me," Auden says.

"Yes?"

"I'm afraid of the same things you are, Proserpina."

My lips part, but no words come out. I don't know what to say, or if I even know what to hope about what he means by that.

His voice is gentle as he murmurs, "I want to hurt you so much that I dream about it sometimes."

I breathe in a shaky breath, meeting his powerful stare in the dark.

"I've wanted to hurt you since we were ten years old," he adds. "Sometimes *I* hurt with wanting to hurt you."

"What else are you afraid of?" I ask, echoing his earlier question. He gives me a fond smile, a sweet, crooked-lipped smile. Like he's indulging me by letting me ask such a thing, and we both know it, and suddenly I want to cry at how good that feels. To be indulged at the same time my hair is wrapped in his fist.

"I'm afraid of you letting me hurt you," says Auden.

"Why?"

"Because then I'll want to do it for the rest of my life."

We stare at each other for a long time, my hair pulled taut in his fist and his eyes glittering at me, and nothing can matter right now except us, nothing has ever mattered except us, and my hair in his fist and his body towering over mine. And if he wanted to pin me to the ground and shove his fingers into my mouth, I'd let him. I'd let him do anything.

I'd let him love me.

I'd let him make me fall in love with him right back.

I'd admit that I'm already in love with him.

He doesn't pin me though, he doesn't stick his fingers in my mouth or yank me close to his visible erection. He carefully, deliberately squats down so that we're at eye level, and then he uses his other hand to cup my jaw.

Something hard and metallic pushes against my skin.

"You deserve better than me," Auden says. We're now so close that even in the darkness I can see his eyes are rimmed with red. I can see a faint line in his cheek I've never seen before—a tiny scar that only reveals itself when the shadows are swirling just right. "You deserve someone who already knows who they are."

"I know who you are, Auden Guest," I tell him softly. "I can know for the both of us."

I reach up and tuck my fingers under his palm to peel it away, making sure not to drop whatever he was holding against my skin. I pull his hand down and look at what's cradled there. In the moonlight, a delicate ring glints with diamonds and antique filigree. An engagement ring.

The same ring that was on Delphine's finger earlier tonight.

"What happened?" I whisper, looking up from his palm to his face.

I don't think I've ever seen him look so sad. Or so beautiful.

He loosens my hair with a sigh, stands, and helps me to stand as well, taking care to arrange the blanket back around my shoulders so I won't be cold.

"I think it's fairly obvious what happened," he says, some of that bitter, rich-boy drawl creeping back into his voice. "Delphine's decided to call off the engagement. Probably the sensible thing to do, given all that I've told you tonight."

"Oh Auden," I say. His hands are still fussing with the blanket, and I see the effort it takes for him to let go of me. Like if he lets go of me, he'll sink right through the floor and into hell.

"Are you okay?" I whisper.

"No," he says. "I'm not."

"Do you—do you need anything?"

His jaw works to the side a little, but when he answers, his voice is more rich boy than ever. "I think you just gave it to me."

A horrible, awful feeling sneaks up through my heels, it crawls up my stomach and chest and balls up in my throat. The kneeling and the hair pulling and the secrets…

I whisper, "Tell me you didn't talk about hurting me because you wanted to prove something to yourself. Or to Delphine."

"What does it matter?" he asks. "It doesn't make any difference either way."

There's so much ugly embarrassment inside me that I think I might split open with it, like a dress with a cheap zipper. "It always makes a difference," I say quietly. My chin is starting to tremble now. *It's doing the thing*, as Delphine would say. "It makes the difference between us sharing and you using. I thought we shared. But instead—"

"But instead I used you," Auden interrupts. "Yes, yes, I get it. Well, I did tell you that you deserved better, didn't I?"

I grip the blanket harder around myself, staring at him like I'm seeing him for the first time. "Everything I said and did, I did it out of complete honesty."

"Oh, is that right," he says scornfully.

"Except one thing," I continue, so furious and itchy with

humiliation that I can't even look at him. "I said I knew who you were. And now I realize that I have no fucking idea."

That seems to break something in him.

"I was telling the truth too, Proserpina," he says. "Yes, maybe I'm gutted. Maybe I'm raw and angry and sad as fuck. That doesn't mean I lied."

"It means," I say, going to the stairs, "that everything we did tonight was about you and about how you feel. I don't kneel for selfish men, Auden."

"But you'll kneel for an engaged one?"

"Fuck you," I spit.

"Maybe tomorrow," he says coolly.

Oh my God. I narrow my eyes. "You're a bastard."

He stares at me a moment, mouth tight, his tall, powerful body strained with rage and pain. "If only that were true," he says finally, turning away from me.

"If only that were fucking true."

21

"Dad?"

I wince at the sunlight as I sit up in bed with my phone pressed to my ear. Pale and wintery as the day is, I'm still exhausted and bleary from fractured sleep and too many dreams. And from too many waking moments when I re-lived what happened between Auden and me and then had to scream into the pillow.

"Poe," my dad says, the *p* sound a little clumsy, the *oe* sound a little choked off.

I pull my phone away from my ear and squint at the time. It's late morning here, which means it's *late* back home. Or very fucking early, depending on your perspective.

"Dad, are you drunk?"

I hear the sound of my father getting out of his favorite leather chair—a combination of human grunts and leather squeaks. "Just had a little," he says. Slurs, more like. "Just enough to get to sleep."

"It's got to be like four a.m. there," I say. "You should already be asleep."

"Wanted to call," he mumbles. "Wanted to tell you."

Which is when the last of the sleep-fog burns off and I remember the text I'd sent last week.

"Is it about Mom's family?" I ask eagerly. "The Kernstows?"

"Should've known you'd find out," he tells me. "Such a smart girl. She was always so proud of you, you know. She'd hang up your report cards in her office at the university. Bragged about you skipping grades to anyone who would listen."

This is the most he's talked about my mother since she left, and I don't want him ever to stop, but I'm also dying to know about my ancestors. "Dad. Mom's family. I asked you about them, remember?"

"I remember," he says tiredly. "I just didn't want to tell you."

"Don't I have a right to know?"

"Don't I have a right to keep you safe?"

I kick off my blankets and stand up, grumpy. "*Dad.*"

Somewhere on the other end, there's the sound of a bottle clinking into a glass. "I know, I know. But talking about your mom's family meant talking about your mom—"

He breaks off, and my heart twists. I can't forget that he's been hurt too, that his life ended the same day mine did.

He takes an audible drink, and I pace up and down the length of my bed twice. Then he says, "You're right. Your mother was a Kernstow."

"From here?"

"From the far side of the Thorne Valley. North of Thorncombe." When he speaks again, his voice is less wobbly, more certain, as if relaying the bare facts makes speaking easier. "Can you guess which Kernstow alienated her family and beloved twin brother in the 1860s by marrying the wrong man?"

I have a guess. "Estamond?"

"Estamond." A hiccup. "She married a Guest."

I stop pacing, thinking about Estamond and her happy, fruitful marriage. About Ralph Guest and how much he wanted me to marry Auden. Kernstows and Guests, now and then.

"Was that a problem?"

"The Kernstows were forbidden to marry the Guests from time out of mind," Dad says. "That was the story your mother found. So when Estamond married into the Guest family, it caused a major rift, and led to her twin brother selling the Kernstow farmstead and moving to America with his son after their parents died. He never saw his sister again, or so the legend goes."

"I see," I say, going over to the window again. The sky has grayed over, silvering the air with rain.

"It should be a boring story," he says. There's a tired sort of irritation to his voice now. "There should be nothing to it. My ancestors left Yorkshire in 1901 and came to America, and there's no mythos around it. It shouldn't have mattered that your mother's family came from near Thornchapel, it shouldn't have made a difference to anyone or anything."

"But it did?" I ask breathlessly, sensing I'm finally about to learn *something* about my mother, anything; even the tiniest ancestral morsel that might help me understand why she came here. Why she came back.

"It made a difference to Ralph," Dad says. "He would have married her if she would have consented. Well, and if I would have given her up, which never would have happened."

"I don't understand," I say slowly, trying to fit the pieces together. "He was in love with her? Did she love him back?"

Dad exhales. "I keep forgetting that there's so much you don't know."

But that's your fault! I want to say, but I hold my tongue. I want answers more than I want to punish my father for not giving them to me sooner.

"I think Ralph did love her," Dad says after a minute. "Or at least he thought he did. He was certainly obsessed with her, and obsession can often feel like love, especially when pain is involved. Or power."

"Are you saying they had an affair?" I ask, knowing it's a tactless question, but barely caring. If she and Ralph were having an affair, then the explanation for why she went back is obvious, and I can begin to let go of her disappearance. I can stop attributing to Thornchapel all the sinister and beautiful qualities that I'd attribute to a temple or a god-garden or a cemetery. I can stop believing it's suffused with high, holy magic, and I can stop imagining that the high, holy magic chooses people for itself and pulls them inexorably back into its rustling, sun-dappled heart.

"They didn't have an affair in the sense that you're thinking of it," Dad answers vaguely.

"Then they did have an affair in some other sense?"

"I can't talk about this with you."

I make a frustrated noise. "Why not? She's gone, Ralph's dead, what difference does it make now?"

"Exactly. And what difference *can* it make now?"

"It makes a difference to me," I tell him. "I want to know why she came back here. And I deserve to know. And I deserve any pieces of her that are left, because she took herself away from me, because she left me nothing but doubt, and I'm scared of living with that doubt inside me for the rest of my life. I'm scared it will spread to everything, that it will cover over my heart like mold, and then that mold will spread and spread and spread, and everything that's fresh and bloody and alive in me will wither and decay until there's nothing left. No pieces of her or me. Nothing."

Outside, the rain picks up in earnest, coming down with soothing, steady force.

"Poe, I just need you to know that your mother loved you very much. More than anything. More than the world."

"Then why did she leave?"

This time his silence is almost comforting, and I know if I were there and we were talking face to face, he'd be pulling me into his arms. "I don't know, sweetheart. I really don't."

"Is that the truth?"

An exhale. "Yes."

"But you do know about her and Ralph," I push. "You do know if that *might* have been the reason she came here."

"I do. And it might have."

"Were they fucking?"

"*Proserpina!*" my dad says, shocked.

"I'm twenty-two, I know what fucking is," I say irritably. "I know you and Mom did it, I know you probably did with other people before you met her, I know she probably did too. I just want to know what happened, and I guess it's shitty of me to ask you about Mom being unfaithful, but it's been *twelve years* and—"

"She wasn't unfaithful," Dad cuts in. "It wasn't…*that*. Wasn't like that."

"Then what was it like?"

"It was like this: we loved each other. Sometimes we also loved other people. We never lied to each other about it, and we never chose a new lover over what we had together. That's what marriage meant to us, and that's why your mother wasn't unfaithful, not in the truest sense of the word. She didn't betray my trust, and she didn't sneak around. I knew about Ralph because I was there. I knew about Ralph because I loved Ralph too."

I drop down onto the bed, stunned. "You were in love with *Ralph Guest*?"

"Was. Past tense. I stopped even before your mom disappeared, because he was greedy. Not even with money, but greedy with people. Greedy with time and sex and feelings. He was jealous and possessive, convinced that your mother belonged to him by some ancient familial right, and it eventually tore us apart, all of us. We were too tangled by then for it to do anything else."

"You were all together? All the parents?"

"Parents are people too," Dad says in his professor voice, as if pointing out a remedial fact I should have learned long before I ever set foot in his classroom. "We fall in love just like everyone else. Although I wouldn't say we all were in love with each other, only that some of us were in love with some others. But we all shared time and affection."

I'm a very sex-positive girl, but the moment I realize *time and affection* is a euphemism for all of our parents having sex, I make a face, which thankfully he can't see.

"But it all went sour," he goes on. "Ralph had this idea that your mom being a Kernstow meant something, that your mom was another

Estamond come back to life or some fucking nonsense. He wanted her to be his, which was patently ridiculous."

"Right, because she was married to you and he was married to Auden's mother."

"It was ridiculous because she would never belong to anyone, not even me. We belonged to her, that was how it worked. That was how it always worked."

I think of his words earlier, about obsession. About how he used the words *pain* and *power*, words that can mean nothing to some people and everything to me.

"Dad, were you and Mom *kinky*?"

"I can't talk about this with you," he chides.

I want to tell him that I'm kinky too, that I understand, that he won't have to explain roles and terms to me because I already know them all, but I don't. I don't tell him. There are limits to what a daughter wants her father to know about her, after all.

"I'm taking that as a yes," I say. "You were kinky and she was your Domme."

"I'm not going to answer your questions about this."

But I'm fitting together parts of the puzzle now, reaching for the picture I keep on my nightstand and looking at it. Looking at my mother trying to put the torc on Ralph's neck. Like a collar.

"She was Ralph's Domme then too. Which means Ralph was submissive…but how could he have been?" I wonder aloud. "He was so awful to everyone around him. He hit Auden sometimes, I think, and I know he yelled at him so much, he was always angry."

"Abuse has nothing to do with kink," Dad says sharply. He sounds very sober right now. "And it especially has nothing to do with what kind of power dynamic gets you off. I've known Dominants gentler than Mother Teresa, and submissives more vicious and ambitious than you could ever imagine. Ralph was a tainted man who just happened to get off on pain. It didn't stop him from trying to control everyone and everything around him. It didn't save him from himself."

I think about this a moment. "Did Mom ever want to marry him? Like before she knew how awful he was?"

"Of course not." My father's voice is still sharp. "I told you that we loved each other deeply—we still *chose* each other, we still chose our commitment to each other and to you, and she didn't entertain his ideas for a single second. It infuriated him. Enraged him beyond all measure, but the angrier he got, the more she'd punish him, and the more she punished him, the more he wanted to marry her. It was a vicious loop, and it finally twisted hard enough that I thought it would strangle us all. Everyone had to leave before our work was finished, and it was the end of whatever we had. I haven't spoken to any of the others since."

I try to remember the day we left, if the adults had seemed angry or strained or sad. But I can't picture any of their faces, hear any of their words. I'd been too busy saying goodbye to the other children, memorizing the color of Auden's eyes and the shape of St. Sebastian's hands, and there'd been no room for me to notice how the adults felt when I felt so cheated and wronged to be taken away from my friends and the magic house of Thornchapel.

"Why did we come to Thornchapel at all?" I finally ask. "How did you meet everyone? What were you working on?"

He answers after a long pause. "It's a conversation we should have in person. It's a very long, very weird story."

"Weirder than telling me that you and Mom slept with other

people, and oh, sometimes she beat them too?"

He lets out a tired laugh. "If you can believe it, yes. It's even weirder than that."

"I'm holding you to your word," I say. "I need to know."

"You could come home now and I could tell it to you?" he offers hopefully.

"Dad."

"Just promise me you won't go out to the chapel ruins," he says. "Don't go into the woods. Especially not today. Please."

What can I say to him?

Sorry, Dad, I can't promise that because a bunch of us are going out to the ruins to have a sex party in the dark?

"Okay, Dad," I lie. "I won't go out there tonight."

"Good."

The rain's swallowed the house now, we're in a world of rain, and the narcolepsy creeps back for me, clutching at me with fingers made of yawns and nods. I manage to say goodbye to my father—after getting his repeated assurance that he will finally tell me the story of the adults that summer—and then I lie back down and disappear into dreams of mud and sex.

Dreams of tonight.

22

To Thee Do We Cry, Poor Banished Children of Eve

The sawn boards give off a pleasant fresh-wood smell as St. Sebastian carries them into the clearing. He skipped the maze and went to the ruins using one of his poacher's paths through the trees, wood lengths balanced easily on one broad shoulder. It takes four trips to get all the wood into the clearing, a final trip to bring out the tools he borrowed from Augie, and then he gets to work assembling the low platform in front of the altar.

He loses himself in the tactile, methodical comfort of building, in the music of the drill and the clink of screws in his palm. The world outside the clearing slinks away from here, and by the time St. Sebastian finishes, there's mud on his knees and his hands, and one thick daub across his cheek, as if he's been marked with the only world that matters. The only earth, which is the earth of Thornchapel.

His mind is clean and clear. He likes this work. He likes this place.

He stretches his back and examines the fruits of his labor.

The platform is much smaller than a stage, but it's big enough that six adults could lie comfortably on it. There's enough room between it and the altar that all six of them could easily congregate in front of the grassy mound, and there's enough room between the platform and the front of the chapel that they can still safely build a fire inside.

It will be warmer than laying in the mud.

It occurs to him, as he walks around the platform examining it for flaws, that this is the first project he's ever finished. The first idea sparked in his mind that he didn't eventually snuff out with his inevitable indifference or doubt. He had the idea for the platform last night as he lay awake in bed, thinking of Proserpina's kiss, of her hand on his erection, of the curve of her breast in his hand before he ruined everything. He wanted to say sorry and he wanted to atone and he also wanted to grab her by the shoulders and shake her until she admitted that he was right and she was better off without him.

He wanted to explain somehow that his entire life was defined by one moment, by one cowardly moment, and he'd never forgive himself for it and no one else should either. He wanted to explain that he'd once done the worst thing one person can do to another, and in the process, had scorched the inside of his soul beyond all redemption.

He wanted to explain to Proserpina that she scorched him all over again, but in the best way. In a way that made him feel like he wasn't such a fuck-up, that he could be good, that maybe being scorched clean actually meant that everything unnecessary had been burned away to make room for something better.

Maybe he'd been purified.

So he got up at dawn and went to Augie's workshop and started working on the platform. Not because it was a substitute for explanation—as much as he wanted to, St. Sebastian couldn't delude himself into that—but because he wanted the night to be the kind of night that lent itself to explanations. He wanted the night to be perfect, perfect for Proserpina in particular even if she wasn't chosen as the bride, and then after the perfection, he'd offer her all his imperfections.

He's done pushing her away. He's done fighting himself. She might belong with Auden in the eyes of the village—hell, even in his own eyes sometimes—but he doesn't care anymore. Auden is engaged, after all, about to marry Delphine, and so it seems the village is going to be out of luck regardless of what St. Sebastian does.

And St. Sebastian is going to tell Proserpina that he's falling in love with her and he's terrified. He's going to ask her to forgive him and then he's going to offer her his scorched heart and then he's going to pray, even though he doesn't believe in prayer.

He's going to pray that she takes it.

He's going to pray that she offers her heart back to him in return.

Becket hangs up his vestments in the sacristy, and then finishes closing up the church for the night. There's no need to leave the side door unlocked since he'll be with St. Sebastian tonight in the thorn chapel, as they watch the fire burn against the sky and two of his friends consecrate themselves with thorns and sex.

Or it could be you that's consecrated, a voice whispers in his mind.

He thinks about this as he gathers his things in the rectory and then gets in the car to drive to Thornchapel. If by some random chance the others think he should be one of the people up at the altar, should he say no? Can a Catholic priest still claim anthropological distance when he's fucking someone in the mud?

No. No, he doesn't think so.

If he does this thing, he can't pretend to himself that he's doing it as a priest, or at least as a *Catholic* priest, since in a way, they'll all be priests tonight. Priests for each other, priests for themselves. Priests for Thornchapel.

By the vows he's taken, by every creed and doctrine of the church he's sworn his life to, tonight is wrong. Immoral and unfaithful to a jealous God. That can't be denied. But the zeal can't be denied either, and the zeal is demanding mud under his fingernails and the heat of a fire against his face. The zeal is demanding thorns and blood and worship.

Primal, ancient worship.

Isn't all worship primal? Isn't all worship ancient?

Why should the zeal see a difference between muddy earth and cold stone floors? Between a bonfire and tall white candles? Between ale and wine?

Between consummation and communion?

He knows tonight can't be undone. Whatever happens tonight will stay with him for the rest of his life. It will mark him, and whether that mark will bar him from heaven, he doesn't know, but he also doesn't know if he can afford to care what the rules are anymore.

What are rules when God Himself has filled him with holy fire?

Because the other thing he knows is that tonight *is* holy. And he is a holy man.

With a short prayer and a long exhale, Becket puts the car into drive and starts down the road for Thornchapel.

It's almost dark when Rebecca gets to the center of the maze, but it's not late, it's not time for them to gather together and go to the ruins yet. Which is why Rebecca had the time to follow Delphine when she saw her going into the maze.

She didn't want Delphine to get lost and delay their ceremony. That's why she followed her, and definitely not for any other reason.

Certainly not because Rebecca could see from her window seat that Delphine had been wiping her face as she'd been walking toward the maze. That her shoulders were hunched as if she were crying. Certainly not because the idea of Delphine crying irritated Rebecca so much that she literally could not sit still while she thought about it.

So Rebecca went into the maze, deciding she'd take the route to the center first, and then if she didn't find Delphine along the way, she'd check the little dead-end paths and silent niches where the hedge was carved out to accommodate a bench or two. Fortunately, none of that was necessary, because here's Delphine, precisely where she should be. In the center of the maze that Rebecca is planning to rip down.

Delphine sits on the ledge of the empty fountain, her feet where the water will be once the weather warms enough and her coat wrapped tightly around her. She's staring at the statue of Adonis and Aphrodite while tears run in slow, effortless tracks down her face.

She doesn't wipe them away.

Neither does Rebecca, even though she is close enough to after she sits down on the ledge next to Delphine. Rebecca could so easily steal a tear off Delphine's cheek and lick it off her finger to taste the salt.

She takes a deep breath and looks away so she won't be tempted to. So she can stop seeing how beautiful Delphine is when she cries.

Instead she asks, "Is everything okay?"

"I broke up with Auden," Delphine says with a tiny hiccup as she pushes down a sob. "Last night. I guess it's just catching up with me today."

Rebecca feels like the world has suddenly rolled over on its side. "You what?" she whispers, completely shocked. "You *what*?"

Delphine just shrugs unhappily. "I couldn't do it, Rebecca. I was marrying him for all the wrong reasons. Because he's a good man and one of my best friends and I love him in the way that I've always loved him. Because it felt like the thing I *should* do, even if it wasn't what I really *wanted* to do."

Rebecca can't stop her thoughts from circling, racing each other faster and faster. Delphine and Auden were supposed to be a constant, a known variable. A stable, unchanging factor in their lives.

"What changed?" Rebecca asks. "What made you realize all this?"

Even in the dusky light, Delphine's blush is apparent. "Well, if you must know, it was watching you spank Proserpina."

The place between Rebecca's legs gives a single, tight throb, and she forces herself to ignore it. "Oh?"

"Yes," Delphine admits, her face still bright red. "I watched it and felt like—oh, I don't know how to say it. Like I was waking up. Or like something in maths finally made sense or like I'd finally figured out how to ride a bike. It was something that had always been there, been true, and I just hadn't put it together yet. I hadn't seen it."

"And what hadn't you seen before that night?" Rebecca asks in a low voice, almost not sure if she wants to know the answer. Not sure if the answer will change something that's best left unchanged.

"I saw Poe and I realized I wanted to be her," Delphine says simply.

Rebecca realizes she already knows this.

She's known this for three years.

But she doesn't let herself think about that week three years ago right now. She doesn't ever let herself think about it.

Delphine goes on. "I wanted to have that same expression on my face—the ecstasy, but also the pain and the trust. Ever since it happened everyone has been so good to me, so kind, and sometimes I feel smothered by it. But at the same time, if I'm brave, if I try to be strong, then I still want people to be kind and good to me after. I want to be rewarded and petted, and what I saw that night with Poe was that I can have both. I can be tested, I can be brave, and then afterwards, I'll still get to be coddled. It seems like the best of both worlds."

"People shouldn't want to be consensually hurt so they can feel brave," Rebecca says.

"Well, Poe told me that there's as many reasons for doing kinky things as there are people who do them, so there." Delphine sticks a tongue out at her, and it's so ridiculous, so adorable, so sweet with her face still stained and shiny with tears and her nose red from the cold, that Rebecca laughs.

She laughs so she doesn't kiss her.

Then Delphine's face changes, and she looks down at her hands in her lap. Rebecca has a sudden foreboding that Delphine's about to ask the obvious question.

Will you hurt me like you did Proserpina? she'll ask, and what could Rebecca possibly say but yes? For the sake of kink, of course, not because she likes Delphine, not because the idea of Delphine cuffed to her bed makes her want to growl with hunger.

But that's not what Delphine asks this time. Instead, she asks, "Rebecca, why have we never gotten along?" And then she turns those big, honey-brown eyes up to Rebecca, and Rebecca suddenly thanks Jesus in heaven that Delphine is not actually her sub, because Rebecca would be in so much trouble. That fuck-me mouth, those huge, liquid eyes.

They wouldn't leave Rebecca's bed for days.

"I think we're just incompatible," Rebecca says. It's another constant of theirs, another known variable, and so she's never given it a lot of thought. They simply don't get along and they never have, and that's that. It doesn't bear further examination.

"Incompatible because you're a genius and I'm just a blond on Instagram?" Delphine doesn't sound accusatory or defensive, only curious, and something about that makes Rebecca's chest ache. Like Delphine is so used to being told she's silly or pointless that she's accepted it herself.

"You're not just a blond on Instagram," Rebecca says. "And my IQ is only part of me, not all of me. No, I only meant that you're bossy and I'm bossy, and we both like having our own way too much."

"You could spank it out of me," Delphine offers with a laugh, standing up.

"Maybe I will," Rebecca says, and Delphine laughs again, but Rebecca doesn't. She means it.

She wants it.

But she still doesn't like Delphine, she's certain of that—or mostly certain, at least. This incessant craving for her is just an itch, that's all.

Just one of those itches that you have for three years, and which burrows its way into every thought, feeling, and hunger you have.

Rebecca guides Delphine out of the maze, and Delphine is grateful, because she thinks she only found the center on her own through sheer luck and she probably wouldn't have found her way back out again. She's only been through the maze a few times in her life, and only ever with someone else who knew where they were going, so it's nice to have Rebecca leading the way.

No, it's better than nice. It's *good.* Fun. Rebecca sometimes puts a hand on Delphine's back to guide her past corners where the hedge has gone a little scraggly, or sometimes she'll just tug impatiently on Delphine's coat when she thinks Delphine isn't walking fast enough, and now that Delphine knows Rebecca likes to spank people, she sees it everywhere in Rebecca's behavior. She's been doing a lot of research since her talk with Poe, watching a lot of porn and reading lots of books and forums and internet posts, and so she wonders about all the things Rebecca must do for fun. If she does more than spank people, if she flogs them and paddles them and ties them up and drips hot wax on their skin.

She wonders if Rebecca fucks them after. If Rebecca's ever wanted a sub of her own.

Not just a friend to spank for the night, but someone who would crawl for her all the time, who'd be available for her use always and in all ways.

It could be her. It could be Delphine.

Delphine could be available for her use always and in all ways.

As soon as she thinks it, she flushes again, but thankfully, Rebecca doesn't seem to notice, and when they get to the house, Rebecca darts away faster than Delphine can say anything else, although she's not sure what she would say. *Hey, I know you hate me, but please spank me and whatever else comes to mind?*

Hey, I think I may have ended my engagement because I can't stop thinking about you hurting me for fun?

No, she couldn't say that. Not that it matters, since Rebecca vanishes.

But Delphine feels better for having talked with Rebecca; she feels stronger, happier for having her coat tugged and her skin saved from the hedges by Rebecca's careful guidance. It was as if Rebecca was thinking, *if you get hurt, it'll be by my hand and nothing else.*

Rebecca probably wasn't really thinking that. But Delphine thinks she would like it if she had been.

So, with her better and stronger self, and her nose still red from the chill and her eyes still swollen from crying, Delphine goes to find her ex-fiancé in the one place he likes best to hide.

Auden's in his tower, head bowed, hands braced on a windowsill as if he can't hold himself upright without support, and Sir James Frazer is a sprawl of fur and dream-twitching paws on the floor. There's a laptop and a couple sketchbooks on a trunk, as if he'd tried to work earlier, but he's still in the same wrinkled clothes he was wearing last night and his hair is tousled in uneven tumbles, which doesn't seem like a good sign.

Delphine's throat tightens. She hates that she's done this to him, she hates that she's made someone she cares about so sad, and yet—can't he see this is for the best? Not just for her, but for him too? She saw him when he was spanking Poe, she knows that there's something inside him aching for their friend—not to mention the fact that he's obviously still in love with St. Sebastian, despite what St. Sebastian did to him. He wants two other people as much as or more than he wants her, and everyone knows it.

So surely he feels freed? At least a little?

"You were very kind last night," Delphine says to his back.

He doesn't turn to face her. "Why wouldn't I be kind, Delphine?" he asks. "I love you. Of course I'd be kind."

"I hate doing this to you," she says. "You're just so good."

At that, he finally turns. Anger and hurt are everywhere all over him, in the knots of his tensed, furious muscles and the tremble of his hands by his sides and the fast blink of his long eyelashes. "I am *not* good," he says in a low, shaking voice. "I am not good and I am not kind. Please don't say that about me."

"You are good," she counters. "A good man wouldn't have agreed to wait to have sex with his fiancée, and you did, you did agree. And it's been two years and I still wasn't ready, and you've never pushed me once. You've been so patient."

He shakes his head, a hand coming up to pinch the bridge of his nose. "I haven't been patient, Delphine, not in my thoughts. I promised you I would wait for you, and I might have kept that promise in the most objective sense, but God, if you knew how unhappy I was sometimes, the things I thought about, the things I wanted—"

"Then see? This is all for the best."

He closes his eyes. "There's more to love than sex."

"For some people, I think? Because some people only need a little or they don't need it at all, but lots of people need a mix of the two. And then there are others who need it more than the rest, and I think that's you, Auden. I think you're starved for it."

He opens his eyes and looks at her. "I'd starve for you."

"Because you'd starve for any one of us—even St. Sebastian. Because that's the kind of person you are!"

He drops his hand, then turns both toward her in a gesture of pleading, of offering. "Tell me what I can do to change your mind, Delphine. Tell me who you want me to be, what you want me to be, and I'll be it. And I'll wait forever if you aren't ready—"

"I think I'm ready now," she blurts out. "Just—just not like how it would be with you."

His hands slowly sink back down. "What does that mean?"

Delphine flushes hard for the third time that day. "I think I'm cut out for something…different. Like what Rebecca did with Proserpina."

"Kink?" he asks.

"You know what she does?"

"I was there for the spanking, too, Delphine, given that it happened on my lap. Yes, I know what she does. I've known it since I designed her loft with hooks in the ceiling and racks for flogging."

Delphine's been to the loft once, but she doesn't remember any rings or racks. She's disappointed in herself for not noticing.

"I can be kinky," Auden says. "I *want* to be, but I didn't want to frighten you."

Delphine weighs this, just like she weighed it last night when she argued with herself about whether or not to break things off. She could ask Auden to be kinky with her, she really could, but…

"No," she says. "I want to *be* someone else and that can only happen *with* someone else. I was with you because I was grateful for all you've done, but I can't do it anymore. I just can't."

Auden flinches.

"If we decide it's me tonight, I'm going to do it," Delphine says. "And if we decide it's you, you should do it too. And maybe it will be a nice way for us to say goodbye to each other?"

"You're saying," Auden says slowly, "that you don't want to marry me, but you'd be happy fucking me in a ritual? After you've broken up with me?"

"Yes. I'm changing, you know," she explains, after seeing his incredulous reaction to her answer. "I'm waking up. Except I wasn't asleep."

"What are you waking up to, then?"

She shrugs. "What I really want. Pleasure. Pain. Magic in my life."

"We all want those things," Auden says. "I want those things. Why can't we want them together?"

He looks so sad just then, so tired and alone silhouetted with the expanse of Thornchapel behind him, that Delphine goes up and hugs him. She hugs him like she used to hug him when they were children, when they were both adolescents in the same stuffy and luxurious world. She hugs him like someone hugs their best friend.

He takes in a deep breath, his muscles tight under her arms, but after a long moment, he carefully hugs her in return.

"I'll always love you," she whispers. "Always."

"I know," he sighs, and she can hear the rumble of his voice with her face against his chest. She can feel the breath entering and leaving his body.

"And if it's us tonight, I want you to know that I'll be glad, because even if I can't marry you, I still trust you with my body. I still love you."

He holds her tighter but doesn't say anything.

"And if it's you and someone else, then I'll be excited for you." He doesn't respond to that either, and eventually the hug ends.

He breaks the awkward silence as they step apart. "I hope you stay here at the house," he says gruffly. "We'll get you your own room and everything. But I like having all of us together too much to see you go. Even if it's hard."

"I think I'd like that," Delphine says, feeling lighter. She'd been worried about that, anxious that Auden would excommunicate her from the group for the crime of not marrying him, but she should have known better. Whatever he likes to say, he *is* good, and she'll be allowed to stay. They'll be all together, and that's what matters.

It's fully dark now, and Becket should be arriving any minute, but Auden decides to go out to the chapel one last time before they go there as a group. He uses the excuse of bringing some blankets out to use later, but really he just wants to see it by himself, see it in the cold beam of his flashlight before it's lit in the glow of lanterns and fires. He wants to lay down his feelings about Delphine and everything else before he picks up a lantern and pretends to care about this ceremony.

He skips the maze and hops easily onto the path as it emerges from the maze's tunnel and meanders into the trees. The clever topography of the grounds means the route can't be seen from the house or from the lawn, and only someone who knows Thornchapel's every last secret knows about the deep-sliced trail at the border of the woods. Being its lord, he knows every last secret—or at least he's pretty sure he does.

He eats up the walk with long, impatient strides, very aware that the others will soon be waiting on him, waiting for a ritual that might rip apart the perfect little world they've built. The tiny, perfect kingdom of his favorite people—well, his favorite people and St. Sebastian—nestled in the heart of Thornchapel, protected and happy and his.

And maybe they're about to throw that all away.

Christ.

His chest hurts with Delphine's decision, but it hurts even more knowing that he's not as crushed as he should be. He aches with his own selfishness, the selfishness that tells him he can finally stop hating himself for wanting Proserpina, the gross relief that he can finally release all the perverse needs inside him.

How fucking miserly is he? How callow? That he feels owed somehow for all the years he's held back?

That he wants to make up for lost time and he already knows with whom he wants to do it?

He's not good, that's for certain. And if he ever had doubts about that before, he knows it now, when he should be bent over with heartbreak, and instead his body is already yearning for someone else.

God, what if it's him and Proserpina chosen tonight? What if he gets to have that petite body under his, her wrists bloody with thorns and her neck arched with pleasure-pain as he fucks into her sweet cunt? What if he gets to tell her something like what Delphine told him tonight?

I think I need more of what Rebecca showed us, I think I might be like her.

I think I need to spank you and then fuck you and then spank you again.

Even just thinking about it has him so hard that he feels like a walking obscenity crime. It's a good thing he's alone and it's dark, because there'd be no mistaking the swollen length pushing against his zipper.

Except then a figure resolves itself out of the darkness, coming toward him with a fluid and wary grace. Auden's flashlight catches the glinting metal of a lip ring, and then Auden lowers it, so it won't blind St. Sebastian.

"I was just about to head back to the house," St. Sebastian says, "but I wanted a few more minutes here alone. You know?"

Auden can't stop watching Saint's mouth in the indirect glow of the flashlight. It's all shadows and metal, and his cock wants it, his cock wants back inside that shadow mouth, and his hands want Saint's hair to twist and yank, and his own lips buzz with the need to kiss and suck the strong, supple curve of Saint's throat.

Fuck.

He hates Saint. He can't ever forget that. He can't ever forget what it felt like to have his cheek taped back together and his broken arm set. He can't forget what he felt like to breathe with a cracked rib for weeks and weeks.

He can't, he can't, he can't.

"You don't know," St. Sebastian says, surprised, and Auden realizes he's been staring at Saint's exposed throat for so long that he thinks Auden isn't going to answer. "I thought you might understand how this place feels sometimes. Like when you're alone here, you're alone with God."

"You don't believe in God," Auden finally manages to say, over the roar of his lust and angry memories.

"No," St. Sebastian agrees thoughtfully, "no, I guess I don't."

Auden wants to grab him and shove him to the ground, drive

Saint to his knees and make him swallow his aching length. He wants to feel that piercing against his shaft, and see Saint's long, dark eyelashes fluttering up at him, wet with breathless, cocksucking tears. It's all Auden wants right now, it's consuming every thought, every sense of self-preservation he has.

"Well, I guess we should head back," Saint says, oblivious to Auden's struggle. "The others are probably waiting."

Saint starts to walk past Auden, and Auden grabs his arm.

Saint stops immediately.

Not because Auden forced him, not because Auden wrestled him to a stop, but because Saint felt Auden's hand on his arm and stopped on his own. He stopped like he was being obedient. And then when he looks over at Auden, when his so-dark-in-the-darkness eyes dip down to where Auden's hand circles his bicep, he bites his lower lip and says, "Yes, Auden?" in the way that someone might say, *ask me anything and I'll say yes.*

Blood pools even more in Auden's groin; he could come just standing there and listening to Saint talk to him in that voice. So he doesn't speak at first, he only squeezes ever so slightly, testing the hard curve of St. Sebastian's upper arm. The muscle is so firm that Auden has to squeeze hard to feel the flesh denting under his fingertips.

Saint goes completely, utterly still.

"You're not wearing a coat," Auden says after a long minute.

"I'm not cold."

And indeed, even though he's in only a T-shirt and jeans, both smeared and flecked with dried mud, Saint's not shivering and there are no goosebumps under Auden's fingers. Saint's skin is almost hot to the touch, so hot Auden almost wants to slide his other hand up Saint's shirt to warm it up.

He doesn't though. He says the thing he stopped Saint to say. "What if everyone else picks us, St. Sebastian? You and I?"

"Us for the ritual?" St. Sebastian asks. "Like one of us is the bride?"

He laughs, as if Auden made a joke, but Auden doesn't laugh back.

Saint sobers.

"I'm okay with that," he says, his words quick but quiet too. "Are you okay with that?"

"You really think it would be a good idea for us to fuck?" Auden asks. "Really?"

Saint shivers again, like Auden's chill is finally succeeding where the damp, Dartmoor night couldn't. "It doesn't mean anything," Saint whispers. "Tonight is just a game."

"People keep saying that, but it doesn't make it true. And you better believe that if I fuck you, it's going to mean something."

"Like what? Revenge? Possession? Finishing what you started eight years ago?"

A low noise rumbles in Auden's throat—a rough, animal noise. "*All of it.*"

Saint bites his lip again, and now Auden can't help it, he just can't, no matter how much he should hate the boy who hurt him all those years ago, no matter how much he should be mourning Delphine. He twists his other hand in Saint's shirt and wrenches his pierced Judas up to his mouth.

The kiss is a crash and their lips meet in a collision of flesh and teeth and metal. There's breath and taste and ferocious, feral energy, as if they're trying to fight each other, trying to eat each other, and they only have this moment to do it in. And then Auden yanks Saint even closer, one hand moving to thread through Saint's dark, silky hair and the other hand dropping to the unbelievably tight curve of Saint's arse, kneading the flesh there as if it already belongs to him. Auden's just that little bit taller, just enough that Saint's swelling organ has nowhere to go but against the base of Auden's own erection, and he wants to stay like this forever, devouring St. Sebastian's mouth and rubbing his cock against St. Sebastian's cock and listening to every helpless noise Saint makes as he does.

He wants to.

He also wants Proserpina.

He wants both of them so much he thinks he might be entirely made up of want, he thinks all his thorns are finally puncturing through his skin and out into the real world and everyone will see and they'll know. His darkness and his light and all the twines and ravels of his depraved, thorny heart.

He breaks off abruptly, terrified of that, terrified of himself. Terrified of how St. Sebastian makes him feel.

He releases his old enemy and Saint staggers back, wiping his mouth and looking stunned.

"What…what was that for?" Saint asks in a whisper.

Auden doesn't have an answer.

"It could be us," Saint says. "If it's us, we could be okay. We could be…you know. Good. It could be good."

Fuck, fuck it could be. Auden can picture it, can see Saint's bared skin, a darker gold than normal in the glow of the fire; he can see the curve of Saint's backside and the velvet throb of his erection as it beads helplessly with pre-cum at the head. He could pin Saint down and slick up his arse while the others watched, he could push into him with his forearm on the back of Saint's neck and the fire warm on their skin.

He could wrap the thorns around his and Saint's hands until their story was written in blood from both of them, not just Auden's blood alone. He could make Saint feel once, *just fucking once*, how much it hurts to want him.

It hurts so much.

It hurts more than stitches, than bleeding. It hurts more than breaking.

If Auden hurts any more with it, he'll die.

"It can't be us," he manages to say. "It *can't*."

And before he can see how much his words hurt Saint, he turns away and starts back for the house.

23

No one looks at the bowl on the table.

"I think it's the best way," Becket says finally. "I've thought about the consequences of us picking ourselves, and I think this might give us more freedom. To feel like the choice was taken away. And I think it will also free us from arguing about virginity as an abstract patriarchal concept for another hour, because this way the bride can be anyone. So can the lord. And we've all said we're clean, so there aren't any health worries to affect our choice either."

We're in the library right now, all fresh and showered, because the *Consecration* called for a ritual cleansing beforehand, and no one had been ready to suggest we actually bathe each other, which somehow feels like an even more intimate act than sex. So separate showers it was, and now we're in warm clothes with our lanterns on the table and raincoats draped across chairs. Half-Christian as the ceremony is, our supplies aren't what I would have expected from the handful of times I've been in the new age shop in Lawrence, Kansas. There are no ceremonial knives or wands, no ornate chalices or bowls of salt.

And we couldn't find robes, which is just as well, because even though the rain has stopped, there's no doubt that it's going to start up again.

Becket has helpfully printed up a paper script of the ceremony for each of us, cribbed from the *Consecration* and Dartham's book, and those rest in a neat stack next to long, whippy cuts of roses wrapped in tissue paper. Our thorns.

The cakes and ale ended up being small shortbread cookies Abby made for us and a bottle of Prosecco from Delphine's never-ending supply. Abby made the cookies stamped with a St. Brigid's cross on top because we told her we were having a St. Brigid's Day party, and they're nestled artfully in a picnic basket along with the wine and some slender glass flutes.

That's Thornchapel for you. Even when you're on your way to the muddy, magic sex rite, all the little details must be handled with class. No Tupperware and plastic cups shoved into backpacks at Thornchapel.

"What happened to choosing with intention?" Saint asks. "I seem to remember you giving a little speech about that."

Becket's about to answer, but I cut in. "I think this is the best way too. If someone gets chosen and they just can't do it, then we'll choose someone else, no big deal."

Saint darts a fast look over at Auden, who's currently squatting down to pet Sir James Frazer. "I guess," Saint says slowly.

I'm still not over what happened between us last night, so my voice is sharp when I say, "Look, no one wants to nominate themselves—that would feel weird and greedy—but it's impossible to nominate someone else for something like this. The only choice is no choice."

"Maybe fate will decide," Delphine says wistfully.

"Fate is a lie," comes Rebecca's predictable answer.

Becket rocks up on his heels, like he's getting ready to launch into a sermon about cynicism, and Saint looks like he's about to argue some more, and Auden just keeps petting the dog, like our squabbling is some kind of relaxing background noise that he doesn't need to pay attention to. Except then his green-brown eyes flick up to mine with a perceptive heat that makes me shiver, and I recognize that he's been paying attention all along.

"Draw, Proserpina," he tells me. "You go first."

It's not an exhortation but a command, and I'm obeying before I even understand why I'm obeying.

Not that I need long to understand why I'm doing it.

It's Auden. It's because it's Auden, and I'm still angry over what happened in the tower, I'm still angry about what I confessed and am embarrassed that he only pushed me into confessing because he was heartbroken over Delphine—but my anger and embarrassment still isn't enough to stop the curl of pleasure I get when he nods in approval at my obedience.

God, this would all just be so much easier if Saint and Auden weren't here.

But then if they weren't here, would I still be trembling with hungry, horny eagerness as I stick my hand into the bowl of paper and pick?

Becket made the slips, and he kept them simple—a black circle for the bride, a black X for the person who will play the lord. So there's no mistaking what I'll be doing when I unfold the paper and see the crooked *O* scrawled in hasty marker.

My blood is running so hot and fast that I think I might be catching fire. Tonight is the night I finally take my not-a-gateway step, tonight is the night when I'll lose my construct-or-not virginity.

I want this.

I want this.

And I don't even care who the lord is. I glance around at all my friends, all their eyes trained on me, and I know I'd be safe and happy with any one of them. If it's Becket, then I know he'll be thoughtful, and if it's Delphine, then I know it will be sweet. If it's Rebecca, and I hope it is, she'll know exactly what a sub girl needs for her first time.

If it's Saint or it's Auden—well, then I don't know anything except what it's been like in my dreams, and in my dreams, it's always been a gorgeous, filthy fuck that leaves me gasping and begging for more, more, more. Even if I hate them both a little bit right now, that hate is only a thorn on the stem of something much bigger and much older.

"I'm St. Brigid. The bride," I tell them, my mouth dry with excitement and maybe a little bit of fear, but the fun kind. "I'm going to keep it. I mean, I want to do it. I want to be her."

"Okay then," Becket says. Behind me, I hear Auden stand up, but I don't dare look at him right now, or Saint. I don't think I can bear it if they see all the things I feel made obvious in my red-stained cheeks.

There's a pause when no one really knows who should go next, and then Saint just mutters, "Fuck it," and grabs the bowl off the table, holding it out for everyone. And all at once, the five others reach in, fingers and palms moving past each other in a jostling foreplay of what's about to come, and everyone seems to realize it all at the same time, that soon it will be just more than hands and wrists touching. There's a slightly awkward moment when everyone pulls back at the same time, looking down at their papers to avoid looking at anyone else.

"It's not me," Becket says, and when I look over at him, his face is inscrutable. I can't tell if he's disappointed or relieved.

And I don't know if I'm disappointed or relieved when Saint says, "Me neither."

"It's not me," Rebecca adds, showing us the blank paper.

Auden runs a hand through his hair and then drops it to his side. I try not to remember the memory of that hand wrapped in my own hair as it pulled me down to my knees. "It's not me."

Delphine gives a shy little beam and then shows us the *X*. "Looks like I'm the lord of Thornchapel tonight."

If it bothers Auden that Delphine is representing his home for our ritual when she could have had that role in real life if she'd married him, he doesn't show it. Instead he nods, a little furrow pulling between his brows as he mentally assesses our supplies and then checks his watch.

"It's nearly nine now," he says. "I think if we have everything we need, we should head out there while the rain is holding off."

We all start getting our things, and I walk over to Delphine and squeeze her hand.

"I don't know what to say to someone I'm about to have sex with," I whisper, and her giggle fills the room.

"Me neither," she says back, a little gleefully.

"Is this the fun adventure you wanted?"

She dimples at me. "It is." And then she squeezes my hand back.

"I've been thinking, you know, about what everyone said yesterday about virginity and first times and what they mean. And I think if we get to pick, then I'm going to pick this as my first time. I'm going to lose my virginity with you, Poe Markham, and I couldn't be happier."

We were too shy for the ritual bathing, but otherwise we're trying to follow the *Consecration*'s rubric for the ceremony as closely as we can. So Delphine ventures down to the thorn chapel first—after both Rebecca and Auden make sure her phone is with her and charged and also that she has a small flashlight in case the whole lantern thing doesn't work out—and then we follow about fifteen minutes later.

At first, I feel very silly as we grab our things, light our lanterns, and make for the south wing. Even after we come out onto the terrace, Becket closing the door behind us and giving the whining Sir James Frazer one last affectionate scratch before locking him in the house, I still feel like we're about to play a very awkward party game. Like we're going to get there and no one is going to be feeling it and it's going to feel so forced and embarrassing and we'll realize we're not children anymore and the time for games and play is over. And then we'll trudge back home, moody and chilled, in a humiliated silence that will stretch beyond tonight and into tomorrow, into the next week and the week after that, until it becomes obvious to all of us that we can't be friends any longer.

And then I'll have nothing.

Not better knowledge of myself, not better knowledge of my mother, not even a fun memory to mark the time I spent here. Nothing.

But that's not what happens.

The farther and farther we get from the house, the more real everything starts to become. The homey light from the windows spills only halfway down the terrace steps, and then, more suddenly than you'd expect, we're in darkness as we walk across the lawn.

The low rain clouds above push the dark down onto us; the trees on either side press it in. The dark rolls down the moors like fog, settling more deeply in the low places and thickening the air until every breath is a lungful of wet, Dartmoor night. Only our lanterns beat it back, but even then it's only barely, and every step we take down to the concealed path coming out of the maze is a step away from comfort and the known. A step away from reason and modernity and all the things I hadn't realized I depended on so much until suddenly I'm in the cold, damp night with only a lantern to light my way.

No music, no podcasts, no blue-glow screen to connect me to anything other than this moment right here. This single line of us moving wordlessly toward the woods and stepping between the trees, this darkness and these dancing flames trapped behind glass as our lanterns sway. The crunch of the occasional leaf or stick as we step, the puffs of exertion as we walk, the rustle of hidden animals under the cover of night as they go about their animal business.

"Can you feel it?" someone whispers, and I realize it's Becket. He sounds rapturous. "Can you feel it?"

For a moment, I don't think I can, I think I'm only feeling the usual fascination I have toward the winter landscape, but after a minute or two, I start to sense it. A prickle at the back of my neck. A strange hum in my chest.

Heat at the back of my eyelids, like I'm about to cry, except I'm not sure if they're happy tears or sad tears or both. It's more like I'm remembering something I've forgotten, and I've forgotten so long ago that the remembering of it feels like discovery.

It's like the memory of my mother calling my name or the feeling of my first library card, plastic and colorful in my hand. It's like kissing Saint or kneeling before Auden. It's like having someone trace pain up and down my body until the world makes sense again. It's like the smell of old books and the sound of thick-leaved trees in a summer storm and the chatter of a clear river over bright stones.

It's home and it's not. It's old and it's young, and it's far and it's near, and it's in my body and also dancing along my skin, dancing away too fast for me to grab at it.

It's loving and it's stern.

It's generous and it's cruel.

It's every feeling I ever associated with God, but instead of a church of stone and glass, it's here in the woods, suffusing every particle of air and darkness and damp with burning, bright life.

"I feel it," I murmur, and at the same time I hear Saint say, "Yes, I feel it too."

Rebecca doesn't answer, but Auden does pause for a moment. He's behind me, at the very back of our line, and when I turn to see why he's stopped, he's standing there with the lantern by his side and his head bowed, as if he's praying. But when I lift my own lantern to see his face, I see more than awe and humility there, I see something else. Something wild and new and feral.

Something awake.

My mother's word comes back to me then.

Convivificat.

Something inside Auden is stirring, and as soon as I think it, I perceive that maybe the same is happening for me, that each breath I breathe of this God-filled winter air is a breath that's changing me. Like the magic of Thornchapel is coming into my lungs and from my lungs to my blood and from my blood to every beating, living part of my body, until my heart and my mind and every curve, corner and plane of my skin is tingling with it.

Our eyes meet through the bright haze of the lantern light and I think I see him swallow.

"Let's go to the thorn chapel, Proserpina," he says. "Let's finish this."

And he's not asking, he's not suggesting. He's telling, and so I turn and together we walk into the heart of the magic and into the living air of the thorn chapel.

24

Delphine is waiting for us by the altar, all faint flickering light and glimpses of long gold hair. And there is something very lordly about her as we approach the two menhirs that guard the entrance to the stone row. Even in her red wool coat and rain boots, she looks regal, and even though she's been alone in this buzzing, magic night for at least fifteen minutes, she seems nothing short of confident and brave.

Sweet, bubbly Delphine is the lord of the manor for real right now, and somehow that makes perfect sense. Somehow it feels like it couldn't have happened any other way.

One by one, we enter the stone row, Rebecca first, then Becket, then Saint. I follow them, dreaming on my feet, my skin and lips and breasts tingling with whatever is in the air tonight, nature or God or many gods or even just the manifested energy of enormous, thrilling potential.

And because I'm dreaming, I'm not ready for what I feel as I pass through the guard stones and begin my walk to the altar.

I feel drunk, even though I haven't had anything to drink, and I'm sure I must be asleep, even though I'm more awake than I've ever been. I can sense the weight of this stone-lined path, the sheer gravity of it, as if it gathers everything to itself so that it can run like a river down to the altar at the end. With each step closer I get to the end, I hear impossible things. Music, voices, drums. Sounds from nowhere, sounds from another time.

And then I'm within the ruins of the chapel, and the drums recede ever so slightly, although they don't entirely go away. They stay just within hearing, just within awareness. They match the pound and pulse of my heart; they match the fall of my feet on sacred ground.

I tell myself I'm dreaming.

I tell myself it can't be what I think. I'm too fanciful, too ready to believe, too eager.

But even Rebecca—the least eager of us to believe—looks troubled as we meet Delphine at the altar. She keeps glancing around the ruins and into the trees, as if she's trying to locate the source of a sound, and I notice Saint is too.

Auden has eyes only for the altar. Or rather, a point just beyond it, a point where a door could be if a door existed, which it doesn't.

But before I can ask him what he sees, Becket starts the ceremony, having memorized the script as if it were one of his normal priestly duties. As if it being about St. Brigid just makes it another arcane Catholic rite, and nothing more.

"Lord, we bring you your bride, St. Brigid," he says. "What will you have us do?"

I expected this to be awkward too, like when students are forced to read a play aloud in class, but maybe the long walk in the dark woods has pressed all the awkwardness right out of us or maybe those otherworldly drums are encouraging us or maybe it's that Becket says his part so surely and so seriously it feels impossible not to be sure and serious along with him.

Or maybe it's because this is all a dream, and in a dream, you can do anything you want without shame.

Delphine already has her paper in her hand and glances down at it once before answering. "Make a circle of light around us and then bring her to me."

Rustling over the wet grass, we walk a circle around Delphine and set the items we brought down at the altar as we finish. Then we each find a place to set our lantern down, until they're in a circle around the altar and us and a low wooden platform that must have been built this morning. I wonder who built it until I see Saint watching me examine it. I give him a tentative smile, still upset about what's between us, but thanking him for his thoughtfulness. Tonight when I share my body with someone else for the very first time, I won't have to do it in the cold mud and that's because of him.

My smile seems to surprise a vulnerable near-smile of his own right out of him, but he clamps down on it quickly, returning to his usual closed-off expression.

Becket told us earlier that the circle is one of the most important parts of the ceremony, that it represents protection and the sacred, that it marks the space we'll move in as holy. And so accordingly, four of us have arranged our lanterns to line up with the four cardinal directions, and as we all set them down, we each said a prayer to St. Brigid, asking her to protect us and protect our circle as we celebrate her feast.

And then we turn back to Delphine, all of us in a circle of faint light. The darkness pools in the corners of the chapel and in the center of our circle, but it's not ominous, it's not frightening. It feels like a shadowed library or a dark beach. Awake and inviting. Quiet, except for the low pulse of drums that can't be seen and the snatches of whispers coming from the woods.

Rebecca keeps glaring around her with narrowed eyes, as if she expects to catch the source of the noise and scold it for not falling in order with the known universe.

I withdraw a long, white taper from my coat pocket and walk to the south lantern. I remember this part without looking at my paper, and I murmur, "St. Brigid, patron saint of cattle and newborn babes, wardeness of fire and sweet water, we light this flame thinking of you."

I kneel and open the little glass door of the lantern, touching my taper to the big, sturdy candle inside. The flame hisses and jumps to life, and I close the lantern and stand, hardly able to see over the dancing brightness of the flame.

"Bring my bride to me," Delphine says once my candle is lit, and it's so unlike her, so unlike her usual girlish self. It's commanding and almost arrogant and deeply, deeply sexy. My pulse starts thudding deep in my cunt when Becket takes my hand and leads me to her, my lord for the night.

And so I'm brought before the altar.

There're so many differences from the times I've dreamed this. The rustle of my coat, the sound of sodden grass under my boots. The huff of my breath in the air and the twist in my stomach and the burn of the others watching my back as I walk. I'm not bearing a torc like in the pictures, and I'm not in a robe, but it doesn't take away from how inevitable it feels to slowly make my way to the lord who will extract promises from me. How heady and how divine and how *right*. Like this one moment, this one night, is what I've been seeking my entire life without knowing it. Like every answer to every question about myself and my mother and her past and this house and the boys I hate myself for loving is waiting just beyond a veil I can't see, and if I can reach through it, if I can part it with reverent fingertips and step in...

Reach for what and step where, I'm not sure. But I am sure that I can't stop myself from trying. I am sure touching that veil might be the most important thing that's ever happened to me. It's the closest to God I've ever felt, and I don't know if that's okay to feel, if that's allowed, to have Catholic feelings inside an arguably pagan space, but I do. I do, and they're all jumbled up together so thickly I almost can't remember what they felt like separately, and then when I stop in front of Delphine and she cups her hands around my face, I think this must be what Becket feels every time he performs the Liturgy of the Eucharist and fuses the holy into the profane. Except right now, *we* are the wafers being transfigured, all six of us; we are being made into something other and better and sanctified as we stand in a circle and act out the ancient human ache for renewal and spring.

Becket, who turned out to be something of an expert in Celtic paganism, explained to us that there's a difference between evoking someone like St. Brigid and *invoking* St. Brigid—meaning that we invited our saint to our ceremony, meaning that we asked her to protect us, but we didn't ask to *be* her. So in theory, I'm only playing a role, I'm only echoing the words she would say if she were here.

But I feel a kick of dizziness when Delphine asks, "St. Brigid, we beg your blessing on us," and I say, "You have it."

Wax drops from my taper onto my hand, hot and clinging, and the pain takes the dizziness and marries it to a breathless sort of hyperreality, grounding me to this moment even though I'm dreaming it too.

Delphine replies, "Then bestow your blessing upon all who ask."

Another kick of dizziness when Becket presses three candles into the soft grass covering the altar and I lean down to light them with my own candle.

"I promise to keep the fires burning," I say as I light the first one, feeling like I'm floating outside of myself…or maybe I'm deeper inside myself than I've ever been and that's why I'm so dizzy, that's why I feel like something shimmering and hot is pulling my chest tight with love and fear.

"I promise to keep the waters clean," I say, lighting the second one. A tear spills free and slides down my cheek and I barely feel it, all I can feel is what God and St. Brigid and priests must feel when they cup blessings in their hands like water.

"I promise to bring the lambs through birth safely and to bring the new shoots from the earth," I finish, lighting the third candle. I straighten up and turn to the others. More hot wax runs down my fingers and wrist, sending echoes of its heat to my breasts and belly.

"I promise to bless all of you and be your blessing in turn."

"Then light the fire," Delphine says softly. "So that we may feel your blessing warm us all."

I cross the circle to the cone of wood and kindling that's been covered with a tarp, and Saint is there, pulling it away and readying it all for me, and then I kneel down and touch my taper to the crumpled newspaper underneath the wood.

There's a hush all through us and through the trees themselves as the paper catches, as the small sticks above those catch, and as finally, finally, the big split logs catch too. It reminds me of the Catholic tradition of Candlemas, of bringing in your candles for the year to be blessed, and the idea of keeping the same sacred flame burning all year long.

One flame to another flame to another and another and so on, until everything is connected, everything is hallowed by memory and hope.

When I walk back to Delphine, I set my taper in the grass of the altar too, right in the middle of the three candles I lit earlier. It's so soft and muddy that the candle goes easily in, and then I take a deep breath and turn to my lord.

"Undress, Proserpina," Delphine says as she takes several steps back to give me space, and it's not part of the ritual really, she's just giving me my cue. But either way, the words send a reverent shiver through me. I'm about to undress as I'm playing a goddess-turned-saint and then I'm going to bind myself to the lord of the manor with thorns and then I'm going to lay down between the fire and the altar and spread my legs for her.

I'm shivering hard enough that I'm fumbling with the zipper of my coat, and after a long minute, I feel someone come up behind me and reach around my waist. I look down to see Auden's long fingers easily finding the tab of my zipper and tugging it down, and then his hands are peeling the coat from me, laying it in a neat fold on the ground.

He helps me with my sweater next, his cool fingers brushing

against my bare stomach as he pulls up the hem, and then his hands carefully smoothing out my hair after I'm free of the soft wool. And then he does something even more unexpected as I shiver there in my bra, and he gets to his knees in front of me.

"Auden," I whisper.

In the orange-red light of the fire, it's impossible to tell if his eyes are more green than brown when he looks up at me. "Let me," he says. "Let me do this."

I can't speak. All I can do is nod.

I don't know if he's atoning for what happened last night or if he merely wants to help the girl who's about to bare so much in front of so many, but either way, there's something powerful in the way he reaches for my boots and slowly works them free of my feet. Something that's not submissive at all, even while he's doing an act I've always associated with submission. I try to imagine Emily or any of the other Dominants at my old club doing this, willingly kneeling in the cold mud to pull off someone else's muddy boots and I just can't. Many of the Dominants I know don't even like it when their submissive walks ahead of them down a hallway.

But that's not Auden. His shoulders are still wide and strong as he works the second boot off, his power and restraint evident in every careful tug and pull. He still looks like a prince, still moves like a prince, and when he glances up at me to check on me, there's nothing but command in his gaze.

It's like all the bitterness, all the entitlement, everything that came with being the heir to so much money and the recipient of so little love, is burning away here by the Imbolc fire. Inside our circle, by the altar, surrounded by friends and enemies and priests, he's being purified. He's returning somehow to the boy who stood at this altar twelve years ago and yanked both me and Saint into a wrenching, unforgettable kiss.

And so when he finishes with my socks and stands to unbutton my pants, I have the only reaction I can to the force of his presence, and I bow my head. Like I'm before a throne.

Auden's fingers are deft with the button and zipper of my jeans, and then he ducks his head to mine so he can whisper low in my ear, "How can I serve this goddess right now?"

My breath is stuck somewhere in my chest and I can't get it out. "I think you mean 'saint'," I finally whisper.

"I don't serve saints. And anyway, you're a goddess."

"So? You're the real lord of Thornchapel."

"Not tonight," he says.

God, the things I want with him. The things I've wanted for years and years. The dreams I've had...

I turn my face just enough that it brushes against his—my smooth cheek against his hot, stubbled one. I hear his breath catch, feel his fingers curl around my waistband as if to steady himself.

I look past him to see the others, all of them talking in a low group on the other side of the circle and giving Auden and me privacy while I undress, and I feel a curl of bravery. "I want to know what you want," I tell him.

My bravery is rewarded.

Auden's breath is warm on my ear and on the corner of my jaw as he speaks. "Here's what I want, Bride of Thornchapel. I want to touch your cunt. I want to slide my hand down your panties and then push my fingers into you. I want to see if you're wet. I want to know if you get wetter when I'm inside you."

I try to breathe, I really try, but his words heat my blood so much that everything seems impossible. "Oh?" I manage.

"Yes, *oh.*" He pushes his face farther in, burying his nose in my neck. "I want to touch you as if you were mine."

My heart tumbles around all over my chest; if I thought I was breathless before, it's nothing compared to now. The word *mine* out of those charming, crooked lips, the word *mine* murmured against my skin…

"As if you were the lord tonight and I was your bride, or as if I was yours outside of here too? Because you must know by now what it takes for me to belong to someone. For me to be theirs."

"One must earn you," he says softly.

"Yes. Someone would earn me by seeing to my needs, indulging me, pushing me to be smarter and kinder and braver. They earn me by hurting me when I ask for it and taking care of me after, they earn me with tenderness and pain and love and depravity. I'm not saying I can't do anything else—" I think of Saint as I say this "—but if someone wanted to catch me and keep me for good, that's how they'd do it."

"Proserpina, if you knew how much I wanted that, you'd run straight out of here."

My heart pulls up into my throat at the same time my eyelids burn with tears. God, I want him. Want his pain and his care and his affection—

A thought intrudes, sharp and digging and unwelcome.

Remember last night? He doesn't know what he wants.

"That's the breakup talking," I say, speaking the words aloud as soon as realization blooms in my mind. "This is your breakup talking right now—"

He silences me with one hand over my mouth and the other hand down my panties, and within an instant, he's got two blunt fingertips teasing at my clit. Pleasure sears up every pathway, burning away every thought and every word I meant to say.

Fuck, that feels good. I can't remember what I was accusing him of or why, because all I can think of is how good it feels to have him tickling over my secret curls and exploring all the places I fold or swell or both. No one has ever touched my pussy like this, no one but me, and I never knew how different it could feel with another person, how electric, how dirty and how good. I don't even care that he's confusing the hell out of me with all his post-breakup feelings, I don't even care that he doesn't know what he wants, I only care that he keeps doing *this* and making me feel *that*.

I buck my hips against him and whimper against his palm.

"Bite my hand if you want me to stop," he says quietly, and I roll my lips inward so there's no chance of me doing it accidentally.

He gives a dark chuckle at that.

I look again at our friends, who can't hear us, but who can definitely see Auden's hand over my mouth and his fingers in my panties, and they've stopped their conversation now. They're watching us. My cheeks flush with shame, but it's the kind of shame I like, the kind of shame that gets me wet and squirmy, and Auden notices.

"Ah, fuck, Poe," he mutters, his clever fingers sliding even lower and discovering for himself how much I like the shame. "You like them watching? You like them seeing how much you need your cunt played with?"

I nod against his hand and he gives me that lopsided boy-king grin, the one I can't resist, and then I nod even harder.

Oh God. I'm so fucked. All he's ever going to have to do is smile at me and I'll be his, no matter what.

"I'm going to finger you now," he says. "Just a little. Just enough to make sure you're ready for your groom tonight. Bite me if you want me to stop."

No. No, I never want him to stop. I want him inside me, rubbing me, getting his fingers dirty with me. I want to be his, even though tonight I'm already promised to someone else. And so since I don't bite his palm, he begins. With enough tenderness to be sweet and enough prerogative to be interesting, he pushes the tips of his fingers inside of me, widening me. Spreading me.

"You're so wet," he whispers. "So fucking wet."

He carefully pushes in and out, testing where I'm tight, pressing against something inside me that makes me moan in pain and then moan again as the pain dulls into pleasure.

I'm quivering so much now, making more noises against his hand, because I want him deeper, want him wider. I want his mouth on me, I want his cock wedging me open. I want it all, I've been waiting for too damn long, and I want it right now—

"God, I could play with you all night." And with a regretful sigh—the kind of sigh one might make at leaving a good drink unfinished at night's end—Auden slides his hand free of my pants and drops his other hand from my mouth. "Open," he orders, and with an instinct I've never had a chance to use before, I part my lips.

He pushes his fingers inside my mouth—the two that were just inside me—and virgin though I am, I've watched enough scenes to know what he wants. I suck them clean.

Once I'm done, he continues undressing me with the patient efficiency he used before, like he didn't just finger me…but also like he could finger me again if he decided he wanted to. The effect is that I'm trembling and confused and horny by the time he's done, and I can't tell whether I want to prostrate myself before him or maybe slap that dimple off his cheek.

Either way, I'm now naked and barefoot, and Auden brushes his hand against my hand as he steps away. An almost shy touch considering what he did not moments before, as if he wanted one last moment of connection with me before he surrendered me to someone else.

My other hand goes to the place where he touched, like I'm trying to push his touch deeper into my skin. My cunt still pulses wetly at the memory of his fingers.

Delphine quickly undresses too, and I think she's uncomfortable walking up to me naked. She has her hair covering her breasts, her arms wrapped around her stomach, and she takes small, light steps, like she's aware of how her naked body moves when she moves.

If only she could see herself like I see her right now, with her rosy nipples peeking through the sliding silk of her hair and her hips flaring into irresistibly grabbable curves. Her thighs are soft, enticing, and even when she walks, her legs and her gold-covered cunt make a plump *V* that my hand aches to cup and press.

When she's in front of me, I pull her hands away from her belly and take them in my own. "You're gorgeous," I tell her. "I can't wait to fuck you."

Her chin is doing the thing, but she manages a smile at me. "I didn't realize how hard it was going to be to be naked," she says quietly. "I've never been naked with someone else. Not even when—"

She breaks off, and I lean in and kiss her.

I mean to kiss her out of reassurance, out of comfort, but the moment my lips touch hers, I want more, I want the kind of kiss a bride deserves. I dance my tongue against the seam of her lips, and when she finally parts them to let me inside, I find her tongue and show her all the things I want to try with other parts of her body. Things I've never done before with anyone, but that I will do tonight as her bride. And she responds in kind, in hunger, wrapping her arms around me and pulling me closer and closer until our bare feet are tangled in the same cold grass and our breasts are mashed together so tight you couldn't get anything between them if you tried.

When we finally break apart, gasping, I manage to ask the one thing I should have thought of earlier. "Is this going to be okay? With…everything…?"

She beams at me. We're both shorter than everyone else, but share the same height, which means I can see right into her dark honey eyes when she says, "Yes. I'm going to be okay."

"If you need to stop…"

"Then I'll stop. But I want this, and I think—" she looks around at the fire and the altar and the lanterns and her best friends in the world "—I think this might be the safest and best way."

"Is there anything I shouldn't do? Or should do?"

"You're perfect," Delphine says. "You're perfect and tonight is not a night of smudges. I'm not saying there won't be nights that are, but right now I'm ready and I want this."

"Okay," I say, giving her a quick kiss on the cheek. "Then let's get fake married at the altar. I should probably stop after this one though, so I don't make it a habit."

That makes her laugh. "Come along, bride," she says, pulling me to the altar. "Our thorns await."

25

"By your own vows and your own blessing, you the bride and you the lord of Thornchapel are bound together. For the good of all assembled here, for the good of the earth on which we stand, it's now time for you to join together and seal your union with promises exceeding words."

I can barely hear Becket over the sight of my wrist wrapped in thorns.

Rebecca did well finding these—they're green and bendy enough to loop around our wrists and then cinch tight, but firm enough that the thorns dig unrelentingly into our skin. I feel like my entire heartbeat is in my left hand; I think I can feel Delphine's heartbeat in hers. Tiny drops of blood weep from pricks and scratches and cuts, and when I meet Delphine's eyes, her lips are parted and her eyes are glassy and I see the flushed, rapid-breathed expression of a masochist experiencing safe pain for the first time. Pain without fear—or maybe pain with only the good kind of fear, the fear that comes from roller coasters and scary movies and walks through the woods on Imbolc night. Pain with trust and warmth.

I give her a dizzy, giddy smile, thinking about how much I love her, how much I love everyone else here. How alive I feel, how satisfying it is to watch our mingled blood drop in small tears onto the ground, as if we're feeding the earth together.

Handfasting over, Becket cuts us free of the thorns, and for a minute, Delphine and I don't let go. We keep our hands clasped, slick with little rivers of blood, cold and hot all at once, aching with pain but also aching with something else, something sweeter.

For a moment, I forget I'm not really a bride, not really St. Brigid, and I forget Delphine isn't my lord. I forget all the way over to the platform, where the others wait, all while Delphine coaxes me down onto the piles of blankets someone brought in earlier. I forget the cold, forget the mud, because it's warm here by the bonfire and my hand is hot with pain, and when Delphine kneels in front of me with her erect, pink nipples poking through her hair and her soft pussy glinting gold whenever the fire jumps just right, I'm hot everywhere. My cunt alone feels hot enough to smelt copper, but I'm certain that sparks are going to fly up off my skin when she runs a slow finger up my calf.

"Please," I say, not really sure what I'm asking for in a specific sense, but knowing I'm ready for it, I'm ready for anything.

"Please, what?" she teases, but she bites her lip right after and she's nervous, I see it now. And of course she is—it's her first time having sex *and* she has an audience *and* she's the one expected to take the active role. The masculine role in the ceremony, I would have said until earlier today, when Becket chided me for it.

God isn't male or female, God is God. So let's be careful how we bring gender into ritual space, mm?

So says the man who prays to the Father, Son, and Holy Spirit.

Becket had smiled then. *The official stance of the Church is that all gendered language is allegorical.*

I'd groaned then. *Fine. But I think it's sexy, the whole bride and lord thing. Can't I have it both ways?*

You can have it any way you like, as long as you think about it first and it hurts no one else.

There's no doubt that I like it this way, plush and curvy Delphine raking her eyes over me like I'm a spill of glittering treasure laid in offering at her feet. There's no doubt that I like the idea of her being the lord, the man, while I'm the incarnated saint she'll fuck as both duty and ecstasy. All the things that are good about this ceremony gleaned away from the bad, from the binary, as Becket would say. Any of us can be anything. All of us can be all things.

What's the point of searching for the divine if that's not true once you find it?

There is one extra complication, however, beyond blowing up essentialism and binaries, and that's the very nature of Delphine herself, her burgeoning identity as a sexual and kinky person. She's a submissive and she's supposed to take charge right now, and I can tell she's worried. I can tell she's not sure where to begin.

I rise up to my elbows to help, suddenly very aware of everyone around us. Auden's on my left, reclining on an elbow like a Roman emperor watching a bacchanal, his eyes raking over my naked body and Delphine's naked body, one hand flexing and relaxing as if itching to touch us. His other hand is predictably in his thick, beautiful hair, twisting it in a slow anguish. He's wearing one of his *Brideshead*

Revisited outfits, wool trousers and a tweed jacket layered over a sweater and button-down, and there's no mistaking the big erection pushing against his pants. I wonder if he's ever seen Delphine naked; I wonder if he still wants to have sex with her; I wonder if I should be jealous.

I wonder if it's strange that jealousy is such a fucking turn-on.

Saint's on the other side of me, kneeling like he's at Mass, his glittering eyes and glinting lip ring flashing with light from the fire, and he has his eyes on me, only on me, while Becket sits at my feet, his eyes on everyone, eyes so blue that even the flames can't change their color.

And Rebecca is settling next to Delphine. She's graceful and assured as she uncuffs and rolls up the sleeves of her nearly sheer white silk blouse. She discarded her coat a few moments earlier, and her boots, but there's still something so effortlessly dominant about her, even in bare feet and riding pants and an untucked blouse. The fire gilds her cheekbones and the sharp point of her chin, and that same burnish highlights the delicately fluted line of her collarbone.

"I have this, Proserpina," she says, noticing me sitting up to help Delphine.

She tosses her braids over her silk-clad shoulder in an audible waterfall, and she puts the back of one slender hand on Delphine's cheek. "The *Consecration* is quiet about what happens here, and so I think given the circumstances, we can be inventive. I'm going to guide you." She turns her hand to cup the side of Delphine's heart-shaped face. "Tell me if you don't want that."

Delphine nods, her full mouth parted. "I want it."

"Good girl," Rebecca says quietly, and the change in Delphine is immediate, a glowing happiness suffusing her entire body. Rebecca smiles at that, but her smile looks troubled, the smile of someone who's just now realizing they might be in danger and they're not sure how to escape. But it's gone before I can analyze it any further, and Rebecca is all calm, teacherly Domme again.

She uses her hand to slide the thick hair off the back of Delphine's neck, and then Rebecca begins running a slow, soothing hand from the nape of Delphine's neck down to the small of her back, whispered touches of reassurance all along the valley of Delphine's spine.

"Proserpina is already having fun," Rebecca says to Delphine, and then she asks me, "Aren't you, Proserpina?"

"Yes," I whisper.

"Show us," Rebecca commands, and next to me, Auden makes a noise at how quickly I obey. At *how* I obey, which is by letting my knees fall open to expose my wet, swollen cunt.

"Fuck," Saint says on a guttural moan from the other side of me.

"See?" Rebecca tells Delphine. "See how wet she is already? Can you see how red and flushed her cunt is? That means it wants you. It wants you to kiss and rub it. And do you see this?"

She takes Delphine's hand and guides it right to the plump berry of my erect clit, strumming their fingers across it, and sweet, needy pleasure sings up my body.

"Oh God," I pant, trying to squirm back toward their touch for more.

Rebecca laughs a little. "I think Proserpina might be a little slut, Delphine. Which means she's our little slut tonight. Our little virgin saint-slut. Doesn't that sound fun?"

Next to me, Auden drops his head back in unadulterated agony. I manage to look away from the tormentors between my legs to see the strong column of his throat working in long, tortured swallows.

"It does sound fun," Delphine says, sounding braver and happier again.

"You know what little sluts love best? Other than being fucked, of course?"

Delphine shakes her head.

"They love hearing all the ways you're going to fuck them. Put your hands on her thighs and push them farther apart; there you go, sweetheart, that's lovely, just lovely." Rebecca puts her hand on the back of Delphine's neck, not gripping hard, but holding her with just enough pressure that Delphine will still feel kept and guided as we move forward.

I'm spread even farther now, the chilly breeze fighting with warm drafts from the fire and sending hot and cold air dancing over the slick split of my pussy and over the stiffened tips of my breasts. Delphine's hands are warm on my thighs, if tentative, and I watch as Rebecca instructs her to examine my pussy as if deciding whether or not to use it.

"See how silky those curls are?" Rebecca asks. "See how those little petals in the middle are unfurled?"

"Yes," Delphine whispers. "Yes."

"Your mouth is going to be there, right?"

"Yes."

"Run your hands to where her legs meet her body, that crease right there, yes—now use your thumbs to part her cunt even more. She's not allowed to have any secrets from us, none at all, because we're going to fuck every secret place of hers, aren't we?"

"*Yes*," Delphine answers, trembling.

And then I'm opened up to her eyes. To everyone's eyes, really, because even Auden and Saint shift to look at my virgin goddess cunt.

I have to resist the urge to whimper, and they haven't even touched me for real yet.

"See this tight, wet hole?" Rebecca asks. "What are we going to do with it?"

"Fuck it," Delphine murmurs, her gaze going hungry on my body.

"That's right. We're going to fuck this tight little pussy until it comes. And what about this?"

She moves one of Delphine's hands lower down, and then I feel a fingertip graze lightly over the hot button of my asshole. A place even I've never played with.

Something like fear and hunger—but filthier than both—shivers through me as they touch.

"Could we fuck this?" Rebecca asks her protégé.

I lose the war against my self-control and moan as Delphine continues stroking me, wonder in her expression as she watches me squirm with shame and dirty pleasure as she does.

"Yes," Delphine replies, her lush lips parting in that way they do when she gets caught up in something. "We could fuck it."

"And what about that pretty mouth of hers?" Rebecca asks, directing Delphine to look at my face. "Those plump, rosy lips she has, like she's always wearing lipstick. Wouldn't it feel good to fuck that mouth? Make her suck on all our secret places too?"

Delphine's eyes hood. "*Yes.*"

"Then I think that's where we should start. You are the lord, after all, you have certain rights, do you not?"

Delphine nods, mouth parted all the way now. "I am. I do."

"Good. Lay back. Perhaps Becket wouldn't mind lending his lap for his lord to recline on?"

"I wouldn't mind," Becket says huskily, and arranges himself so that Delphine can pillow herself on his thigh. I think I can see his erection even through the gleaming curtain of her hair across his lap, but I don't have much time to look, because then Rebecca snaps her fingers—a sound I'm very attuned to. I'm up on my knees in an instant.

"Do good little sluts eat their lord's pussy when asked?" Rebecca asks me, arms crossed over her chest and one eyebrow up in a perfect, demanding arch.

"Yes, Rebecca," I murmur, keeping my eyes cast down.

"And are you a good little slut?"

I shiver. "Yes," I reply obediently.

"Then it's time for your lord to use your mouth."

Without waiting for further instructions, I lower myself to a crawling position and move between Delphine's open legs, risking Rebecca's censure for dallying when I give myself a few stolen seconds of caressing Delphine's soft thighs. They're so warm, so giving, dimpled in kissable dimples that I could spend a lifetime learning the constellations of.

And then I remember Auden will never have a chance to.

Does he feel strange watching me stroke her legs like this? Watching me swirl a finger through her gold curls and part her folds so I can taste her?

Is he jealous? Sad?

Horny?

All of those things?

There's a short, sharp flick on my ass that I know without looking came from Rebecca. "Focus," she orders, and I try to forget Auden and get down to the business at hand instead.

I've never done this before, obviously, but my motto for everything from college to drinking is that you can't go wrong with enthusiasm, so I simply dip my mouth to her and begin.

My lips brush across her curls—they're soft and fine, damp and clinging to her flesh—and I kiss my way through them, feeling her quiver as I do. There's a scent to them, disturbed by my wandering mouth the same way petals release their scent when you rub them, but it's not floral. It's sweet and a little earthy and unlike anything I've ever smelled. I run the tip of my nose along the top curve of her, breathing her in.

It's an aphrodisiac, because as soon as I do, as soon as my lungs are full of Delphine, my body pulses with heat, responding in kind by slicking my pussy even more, and my mouth waters, it actually waters for the taste of her. I part my lips and let my open mouth slide down, my tongue dipping over her clit and down to her waiting hole.

Delphine cries out—a good cry, I think—given the approving noise Rebecca makes and the rewarding swat I get on my ass for it.

So I follow her cries, I follow the curl of her toes on my back and the quavering of her belly, and the eventual desperate tugs of her fingers in my hair. I trace my tongue along the inner folds and the rim of her vagina, and lap up the tart-sweet taste of her body, and then I move up and suckle her clit until she thrashes in Becket's lap. I learn what makes her moan and what makes her sigh, and when to do what to create the perfect balance of tension and languor. I alternate between balancing on my elbows so that I can stroke the sensitive skin of her inner thighs and sliding my hands underneath her so I can cup and fondle the generous curves of her ass and angle her pussy up to my mouth.

Both drive her wild, make her writhe and make her skin glisten with the fine, misty sweat of good sex, and then Rebecca leans down and brushes her hair from her damp forehead.

"Do you want Poe's fingers?" she asks softly. "They might make you come, if she puts them inside you."

For the first time since I crawled between her legs, I feel the wrong kind of tension steal over Delphine. Her thighs stop quivering and go stiff; her belly freezes along with her breath. All from the idea of my fingers inside her.

"I—I don't—" her voice is panicked, distant-sounding, as if she's getting smaller and smaller inside of herself. "I don't think I can—"

"Shhh," Rebecca soothes, moving closer and dropping kisses on Delphine's forehead. "Shhh now. This is for you, this little slut is all yours to use however you like. You don't have to have anything you don't want, ever, ever. Not while I'm here, not ever again."

I look up just in time to see the look Delphine gives Rebecca and the look Rebecca gives her right back. A look full of fierce determination and utter trust, made hot and sparkling by the light of the fire.

How can these be the same two women who fight literally all the fucking time?

That's the power of kink, I guess, or maybe even ritual space. The outside world and the past don't have to exist here: there's no logic but the here-logic, the now-logic, and nothing else matters.

Rebecca keeps her eyes on Delphine as she reaches over and flicks my arm. The message is so clear she doesn't even need to speak it aloud. Back to work, little slut.

I return my hands to Delphine's thighs so I can gentle her and soothe her as I lick and suck. So that she can feel cherished and treasured as my tongue and lips—and yes, even the careful tugs and scrapes of my teeth—coax her tighter and tighter and higher and higher.

She comes with a long, low moan that pulls deep strings in my belly, her thighs closing around my ears and her hands shoving into my hair and holding me fast to her, as if I would move away when she's contracting so sexily against my mouth, when she's giving me more and more of the tart-sweet taste of her.

After Delphine gradually comes down, her body relaxing into a stretch of satisfaction, Rebecca urges me back to where I was. I nestle between Auden and Saint, who are near-identical pillars of male torment right now, hard and flushed-faced.

"Do *you* want fingers?" Rebecca asks, leaning down so that only I can hear the question.

"Yes," I whisper eagerly.

"Do you know if you still have a hymen?" she asks, still very quietly. "Her fingers may hurt, if you do. There might be blood."

I can actually feel my eyes light up as she says this, and then she rolls her eyes.

"I forgot who I was talking to," she mutters to herself. "Fingers and hurt it is."

I lay my head back onto the blankets, closing my eyes and taking a few deep breaths. I don't know what to expect or how to feel, but I do know the way I felt with Auden's hand in my panties was enough to push me to the brink. I'm not even sure how I'll handle anything more.

Warm fingertips brush hair away from my forehead, and I open my eyes to see that Saint has moved to his side next to me, leaning on one elbow and searching my face while he carefully caresses any tickling hairs away from my skin.

"Are you ready?" he asks. "Are you okay?"

"I am," I say. "Are you?"

He takes a moment to answer, and in that moment, the fire jumps, and I see his coffee-hued eyes steeped with shameful lust. "I am. I'm more than okay."

Delphine has moved between my legs now and I hear Rebecca murmuring to her—encouragement or instructions, I'm not sure—and that's when Auden gently turns my face away from Saint's to his.

"Your mouth is still wet from her," Auden tells me.

"Yes," I say.

He doesn't answer in words. He presses his mouth to mine, and dances his tongue over my lips until he's licked off every bit of the woman he never had a chance to taste for himself. And then he parts my mouth with an insistent kiss and kisses every trace of Delphine Dansey right out of me.

I'm breathless when he finishes, breathless from the kiss itself and the jealousy behind it, from his ragged need and the expression of pained gratitude he gives me when he's finished.

"Thank you," he says quietly. "I needed that."

My heart twists—for him or for me, I'm not sure which—and I'm relieved to see that Delphine and Rebecca were so wrapped up in their soft conversation that they didn't notice anything unusual between Auden and me, they didn't notice how he kissed me as the farewell he'd never get to give Delphine herself.

Saint notices though. "What's going on?" he asks Auden and me. "Between you two?"

Now's not really the time to tell him that Delphine dumped Auden, so I only answer the question he asked. "Nothing's going on," I say, and I mostly mean it.

"Nothing *yet*," Auden murmurs in my ear and I snap my gaze over to his. His eyes burn with meaning.

"Shut the fuck up, all of you," Rebecca interrupts in a pleasant voice, finally done instructing Delphine. "Poe, spread your legs."

I do, and Delphine smiles at me. A slightly mischievous smile, as if her own orgasm has emboldened her, or maybe it's Rebecca at her side, coaching her and telling her what to do. How to lean forward and cup my pussy so hard that my back arches off the blankets. How to take my tight nipples between her teeth and tug just enough to make me cry out, suck just sweetly enough to make me melt back down into the blankets.

She does all these things and more, she daisy-chains gentle bites down my stomach and my thighs, she grinds the heel of her palm against my clit until I've completely slicked the palm of her hand. She inches back and dips her head down and seals her lips over my bud. She sucks and licks, and it's like nothing I've ever felt, it's both more delicate and also filthier than I ever could have imagined, having someone eat you there. Having their tongue flutter all silky and naughty and curious in your private places.

Within moments, I'm there, I'm about to come—so of course that's when Rebecca tells Delphine to pull back.

I whimper in disappointment, and I think maybe Saint does too. His legs and feet keep moving restlessly against the blankets, and I wonder how badly he needs to touch himself right now, I wonder if that's allowed. The realization that everyone right now is probably throbbing with the need to come shivers over me, and I have a brief fantasy of all of them—every last one of them—using my body to sate themselves. My mouth and my tight cunt and everything, until every last person is spent and loose.

I can't stop shivering now that I've thought of it. I want it, I want to be used, and I want it with a ferocity I wouldn't have thought possible before this moment. I want it like I want my thorn-bitten hand to keep hurting. I want it like I want Delphine to tongue-fuck me again.

My lord crawls over me with her hair tickling my skin and a hungry look on her face, and then she's on me, she's kissing me, she's kissing me like she owns me. Kissing me like I'm her bride, her living saint, and she's going to worship me by consuming me. Her fingers move back down, circling my clit until I'm too distracted to kiss her back properly, and then Rebecca says to Delphine, "Start with one."

Delphine starts with one.

One slender finger tracing my inner petals until she finds the place where my body opens, stroking all around until my hips are arching to her, and then with another deep kiss, she pushes her finger inside.

It doesn't go all the way in, she's stopped at the second knuckle, but the slide of it is so good, so good and I already want more.

I buck shamelessly for it, trying to chase her touch, lure her into slipping another finger in, and Rebecca just shakes her head at me, like she's witnessing something tragic.

"Our poor little slut," she says to Delphine. "I think she can't help herself. I think you better give her more."

Delphine gives me another finger, sliding the first one out and then pushing back in with two. I make a happy noise, my toes curling as she turns her hand so that her fingers drag against something swollen and sensitive inside me on her way out. Her fingers aren't as big as Auden's, so I'm not stretched too wide—at least not until she adds a third finger, and the stretch of *that* makes me thrash and twist.

"Should we have the boys hold her still, you think?" Rebecca asks Delphine.

Delphine's eyes glint down at me as she says with a wicked grin, "Yes, I think we should."

Saint and Auden need no further prodding; Saint moves so that my head is pillowed on his arm and his body is pressed to the side of mine, and Auden moves closer too, taking my bloody, aching hand in his. Both men hook strong legs around my thighs, trapping me open, keeping me spread like a pinned butterfly on a board.

And something changes then. I'm not sure exactly what, only that it does. Only that we go from two submissive virgins exploring sex with the help of a Domme back to lord and bride so fast that I can't believe we ever slipped out of the roles at all. Delphine is braced over me, fire painting every gold part of her scarlet and shadows dancing over her face as she begins fucking me in earnest, and the trees are all around us and so are the crumbled walls and the altar and the thorns hidden in the dark.

I have that feeling again, like I'm surrounded by fluttering veils, like God and magic and history are seeping out from underneath those veils and seeping into me, and just by being here, I'm being made holy and anointed. I remember the feeling of cupping a blessing in my palm, but now it's as if I'm cupping a blessing inside my entire body, and it's time for me to spill it out, and if I don't spill it out, I'll burst with it, I'll simply burst.

Rebecca doesn't need to tell Delphine to push harder, Delphine's as caught up in the moment as I am, as much the lord as I am the saint, and so she drives her fingers inexorably in, in, in, wedging me and spreading me and doing something that hurts so much that I start crying.

Delphine pauses but I shake my head at her. "Keep going," I breathe. "I like to cry."

I really do.

The pain is like stabbing or biting or—fuck, *tearing*—that's what it is, I'm being torn open, and I know the moment it happens, because I arch my neck and let out a low scream, and the minute I do, my clit swells up and my orgasm swells up right along with it, ready to pop like a balloon. Delphine fucks me with slow, wide movements, her thumb finding my clit to rub it in time with the thrusts of her hand, and the pain has spun itself into gold now, into pure, glimmering gold. It feels so good to be fucked, so good like I never want it to stop; I want to be fucked forever, I want fucking to be my new job. I could stay poised in this moment for the rest of my life, with the fire jumping and the distant beat of drums thudding through my blood, and the memory of pain feeding the greedy pleasure building in my womb.

Everything is so tight, so urgent, and my lord braced over me and fucking me is suddenly the most necessary and natural thing in the world, and I'm so frenzied and delirious with the need to come that I almost feel like I'm floating, like I'm holding every orgasm that ever was and ever will be inside my body, and that when I come, I'll flood the entire fucking world with relief and rapture and joy. The rain starts up again at that very moment, as if ready to flood the world with me, raining softly, softly, but with a proud, tossing wind that whips at the fire and creaks through the trees.

This is what I was missing, I think, feeling the blood and the pain and the weight of my temporary sainthood in my belly. *This was the gateway all along.*

This was worth waiting for.

A few things happen then, to make me flood the world, to make me uncup my saint's blessing and spill it out.

The first is that Delphine, after a long, hungry look at where her hand fucks me, moves herself between Saint's leg and my own so that she can push the wet and needy part of herself against my thigh. She rocks and grinds as her hand does the same, and when I catch Rebecca looking at her, I see a woman only the barest sliver of self-control away from taking what she wants. Like she wants to tackle Delphine and then devour her from top to bottom, which only makes me want to be devoured by both of them in turn.

The second thing is that Auden sits up, and he moves down so that he can watch everything Delphine does to me. His eyes trace hungry lines up and down my body, they blaze every trail that I know he wants to make with his own fingers, his own mouth, and then without warning, without preamble—*he does.* He does track his fingers up my leg, he does bend down so that he can kiss my thigh. And then he kisses Delphine's wrist, the base of her thumb, kisses the flexing knuckles where her fingers meet her hand, he kisses higher up still. Until I feel the painted lines of his kisses all over my cunt, against the tight, wet places where Delphine's fingers stretch me open. And he licks, nuzzles, bites, and samples me to distraction, winding me up and up and up, until he sits up again, his mouth swollen from kissing and stained red with virgin blood like a storybook vampire's.

And the third thing to happen is that Auden Guest moves back against me and crushes my mouth in a kiss like no other kiss I've ever had, no other kiss I've ever dreamed of, because it's ferocious and cruel and full of promises, and yes—it's tinged with the metallic salt of my most intimate blood. Saint utters a low curse from next to me, something fast and reckless and vicious, and then joins him in our branding, carnal kiss, seeking out my taste from Auden's lips as well as my own. Both men bend over me, their mouths fighting for mine, and maybe fighting for each other's too, and it's wet and open and raw and angry and claiming.

It's our wedding kiss all over again.

Auden squeezes my thorn-throbbing hand, and it's like someone pushing a detonator button. The pain runs through me like power through a line, sizzling right down to my cunt, and *boom*.

I blow.

I flood, I pour out, I bless. My body arches and contracts around Delphine's hand, unearthly sounds are torn from my throat and I sob and thrash and moan as Saint and Auden kiss the sobs and moans right off my lips and then kiss them right off each other's. At that moment, there's no question that I'm a saint, that I'm a goddess, that something in me has awakened, and the rain answers my divinity in kind, abruptly roaring into a windy, fierce downpour as I scream my pleasure up into the night.

And right as the hardest, tightest, best orgasm of my life peaks, lightning splits the sky open and strikes a massive tree, sending it crashing down into the chapel and onto the altar itself.

26

The tree is a problem for tomorrow, there's no question about that. Our eyes are too seared from the flash to see properly, our ears are still ringing with the earth-shaking clap of the lightning hitting earth, and anyway, the trunk is still nipping with flames, although the rain is doing its best to put a stop to that.

It's clear we need to get back to the house, but Becket insists we each have a nibble of cookie and a drink straight from the Prosecco bottle to finish the ritual. Rebecca makes sure Delphine and I only have the tiniest sips possible, but she makes us eat a whole cookie each and then shoves a bottle of water at us, like any good Domme monitoring for sub-drop would. And so, huddled under the noisy, flapping tarp, we still share our version of cakes and ale, watching the fire die and the wind yank angrily at the branches of the tree now half-laying across the altar. The blown-in rain sluices the blood off my left hand, and when I look over at Delphine, I can see by the guttering light of the fire that she has blood running from both her hands. Not much, but it's definitely there, definitely visible even with all the sparks and floaters from the lightning strike chasing across my field of view.

It takes me a minute to understand why she has blood on her right hand too, but once I do, I blush.

Becket says we have to close out the circle, and so Auden throws a coat over me while Rebecca and Becket do the same for Delphine, and wearing nothing but my coat and my rain boots, I walk through the slicing rain with my friends. We douse the flames of each lantern if they're still burning, and we thank St. Brigid.

We stop at the altar, but there's no time to figure out where the other lantern went, if it's crushed under the tree or what, because it's now so cold, so windy, that it's absolutely necessary for us to get back to the warm indoors. Auden and Becket make sure the big fire is completely dead, and then they make noises about coming back for everything in the morning, but I don't pay much attention to anything they're saying, because everything feels so blissful and unreal and marvelous.

I'm smiling when Auden takes my hand to lead me out of the ruins. The ground is now so wet that my rain boots come free with a sucking noise every time I lift my foot and they splash every time I set it down. *Suck-SPLASH. Suck-SPLASH.* It makes me feel like a little girl again, playing alone in my backyard while the rain dropped down and my mother graded coursework by the kitchen window. The memory makes me smile even bigger.

"What are you smiling about?" Auden asks, puzzled.

"Subspace," Rebecca answers for me over the rain. "Walk with her back to the house so she doesn't float off to the moon." And then she takes Delphine's arm and tugs her down the stone row, Delphine chattering happily all the while in a giddy, punch-drunk voice. Becket follows and steadies Delphine every now and again when she sways.

"Right," Auden says with a sigh. "Come on, Proserpina."

"Okay," I say dreamily.

Saint appears like a ghost next to me, mud-soaked and watchful, as we leave the clearing and enter the woods. "Do you hurt?" he asks me in a worried voice. "You're staggering a little."

"I only hurt in the best way," I smile, but even with all the endorphins and sex-chemicals crashing through my brain, I can still sense that I'll be sore as hell tomorrow.

Saint gets out his flashlight, and it's a good one, a strong one, the kind that a man who works with his hands owns, and it cuts a sharp cone of light over the path. Rain glitters in its beam, streaking in mesmerizing silver streaks, and I stumble when I try to reach out and catch one.

Auden catches me before I hit the ground.

"It's like she's drunk," he mutters to Saint, but he doesn't sound annoyed. He sounds charmed. He sweeps me up into his arms and cradles me against his chest. "This is what you're like after you have sex?" he asks me.

"Don't know," I mumble, sleepiness creeping up now that I'm pressed against such a strong, nice-smelling chest. His sweater smells like him—citrus, flowers, wood. Thornchapel. "Never had sex before."

"Is this what you're like after a scene then?"

"Mmm," I agree. "Yes."

"What would happen next?" Auden asks. He's carrying me so easily, so warmly, that I think I could fall asleep in his arms. "If this were a normal scene."

"I don't know," I whine. "It's too hard to think about right now."

"Well, you're going to," Auden says severely. "Tell me."

"Wow," says Saint sarcastically. "Are you the real deal now, Guest?"

"You can fuck right off," Auden says, and clearly whatever happened between them as they shared my mouth has been smothered along with our bonfire. Crushed, like our altar under a fallen tree. "We both know how much you can be trusted with someone else's pain."

Whatever this means, it silences Saint. The light around us grows a bit fainter, as if he's fallen back a couple of steps out of anger or hurt.

I should say something, I think. But the fog of subspace is too thick, too good, and too dizzying. I don't even perceive that I'm shivering like crazy until Auden pulls me even tighter to his chest to keep me warm. I nuzzle against him in response, and that stirs a noise out of him that seems to surprise us both. A growl of approval.

He likes holding me as much as I like being held by him.

"You'd make a good lord," I murmur as I lace my arms around his neck. I bury my face in the Thornchapel-scented curve of his neck and shoulder. "You'd make a good lord to me."

"Enough to earn you?" he asks seriously.

"Mmm. Mmhmm."

His voice is hoarse when he speaks again. "Poe, how do I take care of you when we get back to the house?"

I wasn't lying earlier, it really is too hard to think. I'm so buzzy and floaty and good right now.

The hoarseness fades, replaced by something stern. "Answer me."

That voice, like a rich boy all grown up into a rich king, cuts through the haze a little. "My pussy hurts," I say dreamily. "You could take care of that."

"I could. And your hand?"

"And my hand."

"What else?"

"Mmm, I should probably have more water and—" I yawn "—a shower. And I like to be snuggled."

There's something tender to his words. "You like to be snuggled after?"

"And held and petted and nice things said to me."

God, he smells so good. And his neck is so warm. And his arms are so strong and his steps are so sure and he holds me so firmly and so well that he even makes the rain warm and the wind weak. He even makes the darkness feel homey and inviting, he makes me feel like I'm already safe and cozy inside the house, and he even makes the creaking trees sound like the click of a happy dog's paws on the floor—

My eyes flutter open as he sets me gently on my bed and starts unzipping my coat. Saint is tugging off my boots, and within a few seconds, I'm completely naked again, and so fucking groggy I can barely hold my eyes open.

My head falls against Auden's sweet-smelling chest. "Want to sleep," I fuss against him.

I can hear the smile in his voice. "Shower first. Then we'll take care of your hand and then you can sleep."

"She can't go into the shower like this," Saint points out. "She'll fall and crack her head open."

"I'm going in with her," Auden says.

"Like hell you are."

Auden's arms tighten around me. "You have no idea what she needs right now," he says coldly. "I do."

"You can pretend with her, but you can't pretend with me. You have no idea what the fuck you're doing."

Auden's about to shoot back when I say—my voice muffled by Auden's chest—"Why don't you both come in with me?"

It makes total sense to my dreamy, subspace brain, but the answering silence is tumescent with horror. I force my eyes open and see Saint kneeling on the floor next to me, looking like I asked him to cut off a limb and toss it into the sea.

"Or not," I suggest on a yawn, closing my eyes again. "I can just shower tomorrow…"

"No, you can't," they both say at the same time.

"You have mud in your hair," Saint says.

"And you have blood on your thighs," Auden says, his voice going hoarse again.

"You can't sleep like this," Saint adds.

I pout against Auden's chest. "Fine. But no more fighting. Too tired."

The plaintive note in my voice does the trick, and there are reluctant noises of assent from both men. Auden gently presses me back into his arms, and Saint trails us as we go into the bathroom. Auden sets me down on the edge of the tub, and I blink and yawn like a sleepy kitten while he and Saint start undressing. And then there's a long blink, one of the long narcolepsy blinks I know so well, and I open my eyes to see both of them staring down at me wearing nothing but tight, dark boxer briefs.

It's the most I've seen of either of their bodies, it's the first I've seen of their strong, muscled legs and wide, naked chests and lines of hair disappearing into the waistbands of their underwear. The first

I've seen of their warm skin, their flat nipples, their lean stomachs lightly corrugated with tight bands of muscle.

Fuck, they're sexy. I want to have sex with them. Both of them, right now. I don't care about being sore or sleepy or still floating in subspace—I want to fuck until I can't move my body anymore.

But when I lift my head to tell them this, I have another long, narcolepsy blink and nearly fall off the tub. It's Saint who catches me this time, scooping me up and then walking me over to the ugly brass-trimmed shower stall in the corner.

"You have a nice body," I mumble to him as he sets me down and turns on the water. "I like it."

"I'm glad you like it," he says dryly. "Although this isn't exactly how I planned on showing it to you."

Auden steps into the shower too, just as the water starts spurting out of the showerhead. It's freezing and we all shriek and jump back—or at least try to jump back, since the stall was only made for one person, and now there's three people inside, and two of those people are big boys with long, muscled bodies. Their shoulders are so wide I feel like I'm in a second stall made of men instead of glass.

The water runs warm finally, and I relax, swaying back into a solid, unmoving chest. Saint. Two big hands go to my hips to steady me, and I sigh with contentment and lean farther back, until my head is tucked under his chin. I look up at Auden. "You're getting your boxers wet," I tell him. "You two should be naked like me."

"That's not a good idea," he responds at the same time Saint issues a flat, "No."

"Fine," I sigh, stretching my arms up behind me to lace around Saint's neck. I can arch my back like this and feel the water running hot over my stomach and over my no-longer-virgin pussy. It feels good, but the effect it has on Auden and Saint is even better. Saint freezes into a tower of granite behind me, and Auden's hands brace on either side of the shower stall, as if to keep from grabbing me.

Within seconds, the plump head of Auden's erection is stretching the waistband of his boxers, sticking out of the top like the world's most delicious forbidden fruit.

"I could suck on it," I tell him, my voice drowsy and husky all at once. "I could suck on it until you come."

With his arms outstretched like this, I can see the struggle of his restraint quivering through every part of him—his arms and his chest and even his belly. His cock is bigger, duskier now, begging to be seen too.

But when he finally answers me, his voice is controlled. "Not tonight," he says. "Not like this."

"Why not?" I complain.

"Just not like this," he repeats, in a tone that brooks no argument, and then he looks at Saint. "We should wash her."

It's ironic that just a few hours ago, the idea of bathing together seemed far too intimate to even consider—a little taboo even—and now I'm lazing against Saint as he and Auden pass things around and apply creamy body wash to loofahs and shampoo to the other's waiting palm. Saint holds me while Auden carefully and thoroughly washes every fold and tuck of my body. He scrubs the mud from between my toes, cleans away all the streaks and spatters of it everywhere else, and he gently sponges the blood from my wrist and hand. Saint holds up my leg so Auden can kneel down and wash my inner thighs, and for a moment, I think he might lean forward and kiss my pussy because he can't keep himself from looking at it. He licks his lips and I nearly die with wanting him to press that crooked-grin mouth against my cunt.

But he doesn't, and by the time Saint starts on my hair, my lazing has become something more restless. Needy. Life is still hazy and delicious, but all this touching, this slippery stroking and cleaning, has rekindled the heat in my belly.

My hands roam behind me to find the thick rod of St. Sebastian's erection through his wet boxers and play with it, and he lets me, washing my hair with admirable focus as I squeeze and stroke him as much as I can with my hands behind my back.

Auden watches it with something like agony, and he shudders when I cradle Saint's balls and Saint lets out a ragged, helpless moan.

"You're being very bad," Auden says, wrestling for his control. He reaches forward and pulls my hands away from Saint so Saint can focus and finish rinsing me off. "And we're not doing this in here."

"Then we're going to do it somewhere?" I ask hopefully.

"You're in an altered state of mind, Poe. The answer is no."

"Then what if we did this instead?" I ask, sliding my hand free from his and then guiding his hand to me. I mold it against my pussy, loving how firm and certain his hand feels against my slippery flesh. "It'll only take a minute, please, Auden, I want it so bad."

"If you don't do it, I will," Saint tells him.

Auden makes an exasperated sound, but he doesn't pull his hand away. "You heard Rebecca. We need to take care of her right now."

"Seems to me like 'taking care of her' can include lots of things. I mean, just *look*, Auden. She's not going to be able to get any rest like this."

Auden turns his gaze back to me, back down to where I'm actively arching and pushing against his touch. Even in the hot water, my nipples are still erect and tight, and I don't have to look at myself to know that I'm pouty and flushed like the little slut Rebecca accused me of being.

Almost as if it's against his own will, his fingers stroke along my seam, pushing ever so slightly into the place where I open. I lean back against Saint to give him better access, whispering *please please please* all the while.

"Okay," Auden says. "But this is only to put you to bed. Got it?"

"Got it," I purr.

"I'm new to this too, you know," he says, a bit shyly. "So tell me if I do anything wrong."

And then he starts rubbing me for real, giving me easy circles and slow, curling caresses lower down. I let out a short, needy pant and slump back, and Saint moves us so that he's leaning against the wall and I'm leaning against him. And then Auden braces one hand by Saint's shoulder, leaning in as he increases the pressure on my clit, one strong shoulder dipping down as he finally penetrates me with his fingers. He's gradual with it, nearly leisurely—but it's not tentative or hesitant how he works my cunt. There's a few times I feel him search for parts of me, see him studying my body to make sure he's doing the right thing—but he assumes the role of orgasm-giver with complete seriousness and grace. He locks my eyes with his own, and I'm burned alive with all the hazel hunger and possession I see there, I'm consumed with it, and there's no question what he's thinking as he slowly and deliberately fucks my cunt with his hand—

Mine.

He wants me to be his, he wants to earn me. He wants to know how to take care of me after a scene so that *he* can do the scenes, and the thought of that on top of everything else pushes me to the edge.

Knowing he might spank me or hurt me or even fuck me…and feeling the tense stretch of aroused, trembling St. Sebastian behind me…along with the perfect bite of pain from my sore pussy as Auden fingers me—

I come so abruptly it takes me by surprise, my knees giving out and Saint having to wrap his arms around my waist to keep me from collapsing on the floor in a climaxing heap.

"Fuck," Auden swears, because the only other thing keeping me from falling are his fingers in my cunt, and I end up impaling myself even deeper and harder—and therefore redoubling my orgasm into a yelling, crying, writhing thing. And he can feel every shivering contraction, every wet, clenching squeeze, everything and all of it around his fingers, and when our eyes meet, I know he's thinking about how it would feel around his cock.

I moan. He swears again.

He lets me use his fingers and Saint holds me up by the waist until I'm completely finished, my body wrung out and sensitive and soft, and then Auden slides his hand free. He licks his fingers without thinking twice, giving me a long, searing inspection as he does.

Then he looks past me to his enemy. "You need to come," he says.

I look back in time to see Saint shake his head in lust-glazed confusion. "I don't—I don't think so—"

"That wasn't a question," Auden says impatiently. "You need to come. I can tell."

Weak knees and orgasm-daze and all, I manage to turn to face him. The water has turned his hair oil-black and pieces of it are stuck to his cheeks and jaw, like dark slashes of ink. His eyelashes too are wet and black and spiky, blinking fast over gorgeously glassy eyes, and his jaw is clenched so hard that a muscle jumps in his cheek.

He looks vulnerable and edgy and in pain. He looks angry and sad.

Trapped, even, like a wolf with its paw caught, ready to snarl and bite at anyone who dares to help.

"Let me," I whisper to my wolf, hooking my fingers in his wet waistband and dragging the fabric down. His cock springs free, and I can't resist, I look down and murmur my appreciation, because it's perfect. So big and beautiful and thick with its one vein along the top and its flared crown all dusky and swollen.

Saint lets his head drop back against the wall, his throat a divine arch of bronze skin. The knot of his Adam's apple bobs as he swallows and swallows and swallows.

"Let me," I whisper again, and I finally get a short, agitated nod.

For the first time in my life, I wrap my hand around a bare cock, and marvel at the heat of it. At the velvet of his skin, so soft and yet stretched so thin over the hardness underneath. And when I fist my hand around him, I can feel how the skin moves over that hardness, how he swells and thickens when my fingers massage certain parts of him. I can feel the slick glaze of pre-cum covering his tip.

But for all my fondling and exploration, St. Sebastian isn't any closer to the edge than he was a few minutes ago. I could blame it on clumsiness or inexperience, but then Saint's eyes flutter open, and he says, "Please *please*," like I should know what he's asking for, and that's when I realize I'm missing something, I'm not giving him what he needs.

"Oh, for fuck's sake," Auden says and pushes my hand off Saint's cock. He replaces it with his own at the same moment he steps forward and collars Saint's throat with his other hand.

The change in Saint is immediate. Staggering. His lips part and his piercing flashes and his belly tightens as Auden jerks him off hard and rough. Wordless cries escape his throat in short, helpless pants, and his fingers scrabble helplessly at the tile behind him, like he can't even handle the feeling of being in his own body right now, but in the best possible way.

Hurt and maybe even a little indignation roll through me, because I always figured no matter how clumsy I was around a penis, it ultimately wouldn't matter, since penises usually seem very easy to please. But by the time my mouth pulls into a pout—a real one this time—I understand what's going on. It has nothing to do with how skilled I am or even how sexy I am, and everything to do with how gently I held him. How softly I touched him. I was giving him a vanilla hand job, and St. Sebastian, my pierced and sullen library boy, needs something else.

I've never hurt someone, and I've never been hurt. But that doesn't mean that I haven't wanted it, you know.

I'd asked him who he'd wanted to be, me or Auden, and he'd said he'd always thought both until he'd seen Auden's face as Auden spanked me. And then he'd trailed off, refused to answer—but I know the answer now, I see it right in front of me.

All it took was Auden's hand on his throat, and Saint was transformed. All it took was a cruel touch instead of a kind one.

Saint is as submissive as I am.

But as hypnotic as his face is right now—all open and wondering and vulnerable as Auden strokes him vicious and quick—it's Auden that I suddenly can't look away from, Auden with every single emotion moving over his face in waves. One stroke and he looks furious, another stroke and he looks anguished—and then another and he simply looks like he wants to fuck St. Sebastian right through the wall and out the other side. And his breathing is just as ragged and quick as Saint's, his sides are heaving like he's running a race, his stomach jerking with each tight, hungry breath. And I can still see the huge head of his cock above his waistband, bigger and fatter than ever. I can see it jumping in time with his pulse, with the rough movements of his hand on Saint, and then when Saint lets out a broken moan and says *Auden, you're making me come*, I see when Auden comes too.

Without being touched, without anything but the friction of his waistband and Saint's milky surrender coating his fist, Auden's cock pulses in response, white ropes jolting up against his belly and surging over his boxers. Like when he spanked me, he's getting off on the pure, uncut high of dominating someone, the giddy rush of power that comes from bringing someone pleasure or pain or both, and from the involuntary grunt he gives and the heavy rushes of semen, I don't have to guess to know that he's getting off *hard*.

The muscles in his legs and abs clench and pump as he ejaculates, but he doesn't stop jerking off Saint, he doesn't let go of Saint's throat until Saint is slumped back against the wall, and even then he puts a steadying hand on Saint's shoulder until he's certain that Saint can stand under his own steam. He looks him over the same way any good Dominant would, and I don't think it's because he knows he should, I think it's instinct, a natural impulse of his, and it makes my belly flip just watching.

I remember my observation from earlier tonight as I watched him walk toward the ruins.

He's waking up. He's becoming himself.

God help me when he's fully awake. I'll have no defenses against him.

I won't want any.

Satisfied that Saint is the good kind of dazed, Auden finally glances down at the mess he made of himself. With an inscrutable sigh, he uses his thumb to pull down his boxers and then he steps into the spray, rinsing off his cock with the detachment of a doctor rinsing off a surgical tool.

Once he's clean, he glances up at me. "You're all cleaned off?" he asks, like our orgasmic interlude was an unwelcome intrusion into our real business of washing.

"Yes," I say.

"Good."

Auden shuts off the water, helps me onto the bath mat, and then I'm wrapped in a giant towel and folded back up into his arms. I could walk right now, I really could, but I don't make a peep to that effect. I simply rest my head against his shoulder and enjoy the feeling of being carried by the boy I married when I was ten.

27

To Thee Do We Send Up Our Sighs

St. Sebastian doesn't know what to do with his hands or his face or his rapid, giddy heart.

He sits on the bed next to Poe while Auden tends to her hand. He disinfects and then bandages each tiny cut, scratch, or puncture made by the thorns, and with each one, after he cleans it but before he covers it with a plaster, he bends down and gives it a soft, reverent kiss. As if the little cuts are precious to him, as if Poe is precious to him.

Auden is unbearably handsome like this, kneeling in front of Poe with his brows drawn together in concentration and his mouth soft with tender focus. And even more unbearable is the memory of Auden's eyes when Auden held his throat and made him come.

Fuck, *those eyes*. Gorgeous and selfish and sexual and only for Saint in that moment.

Only for him.

Except they were for Poe too in a way, and the memory of her small hands exploring him makes him hot all over again. He would have come with her too, if he'd had enough time, he would have wrapped his hand around her own and shown her how to be rough with him, how to toss him off quick and mean like he does to himself when he needs to come.

She's as unbearably beautiful as Auden is handsome right now, naked and petite and curvy, her damp hair tumbling down to her waist in dark waves and her plump mouth parted as she watches Auden kiss and fuss over her cuts. Saint wants to try again—or maybe not so much *try* again as do it all over so he could watch her this time, watch her face as Auden pinned him to the wall by his throat and masturbated him. To tell her that he wants her like he wants Auden, that he wants them both, that he wants everything but he doesn't know how to hold all this wanting inside of himself without breaking.

It feels like he's been pried open, like the air is blowing across his pulpy, beating heart, and like the slightest touch on that exposed organ will kill him.

So he doesn't know what to do with himself as Auden tends to Poe and then finally finishes his work, standing up and stretching his back with a low, male groan. Poe, clean and kissed and sleepy again, lays her head on Saint's shoulder and promptly starts snoring tiny, quiet snores.

"I need to go back out to the ruins," Auden tells Saint. "We got out of there so fast, and I can't stop worrying about something still being on fire."

Saint glances pointedly at the windows, which are striped with thick rivulets of rain. "Nothing's still burning in that." It costs him something more dear than he'd like to admit when he adds, "Stay. Stay here with us."

For a minute, Auden looks like he wants nothing more in the world than to peel off his wet boxers and crawl into bed with Poe and Saint and sleep off their strange night in a warm, tangled cuddle.

But then he sighs, and with the sigh comes a look of resignation that Saint knows from long experience can't be fought.

"I won't be able to sleep until I check. But you should stay," he says. "She needs to be snuggled."

"You don't want to be the one to do that?" Saint asks, incredulous. "You'd let me?"

"I'm delegating," Auden says with a raised eyebrow. "But I'll be back, and then I'll be seeing to her snuggling myself."

He says it so soberly, so seriously, that Saint can't help but laugh a little. "You can relax, General Guest. I'll keep the snuggling beachhead safe and surrender it immediately upon your return."

Auden's dimple dents in, as if he's fighting a smile, and then it disappears again. "Keep her warm," he orders, as if Saint is his to order, and then he leaves.

I'm not his to order, Saint reminds himself as he carefully settles Poe under the covers. One soul-quaking hand job didn't erase the years of pain and guilt and anger between them. One perfect moment with Auden cracking open his every fantasy and bringing them to life didn't change the ugly, spotted truth.

They could never be anything more than enemies. Anything closer than two men who want the same woman.

He turns off the light, strips off his boxers, and climbs into the bed, pulling Poe close against him. She's dozy and limp and warm, and burrows trustingly into his chest in a way that makes him strangely and fiercely protective. Tomorrow, he tells himself, tomorrow he's going to sort this all out with her. He's going to apologize for all his indecision and all the times he pushed her away, and then he's going to choose her over everything else. Everything.

It feels like he's just had this thought, just made this promise to himself, when he opens his eyes and realizes the rain has stopped and Poe is awake.

"What time is it?" he asks, his voice husky from the sleep he hadn't realized he was having.

"Close to three," she says.

He's probably only been asleep for an hour or so, then. He blinks at the dark windows, knowing Auden is still probably out in the ruins, checking for fires and gathering their things. He feels a stab of guilt for not helping, and tells himself he'll help tomorrow. He'll take care of the fallen tree and anything else that still needs doing.

Poe's up on one elbow staring down at him, her delicate, ethereal face in an expression of troubled unhappiness.

Alarmed, St. Sebastian sits up. "Are you okay? Are you hurting? Do you need me to get anything?"

Slowly, Poe shakes her head. "No, I—God, it's the strangest thing."

Fuck. "Tell me what it is and I'll fix it."

She takes his hand under the blanket and presses it hard against her cunt. It's as hot and wet and swollen as it ever was, as if she hasn't already been satisfied twice tonight.

"Can you fix this?" she whispers. "Because it aches, Saint."

He can't help it, he explores her with his fingers, the first touch of her sweetness that he's had. She's soft there, so fucking soft, and wet in a way that makes his entire body shudder just to touch. He wants her, he wants her like this, exactly like this, and it's not that he thinks he's incapable of vanilla sex, it's just that the idea of her *needing* him to help, of him having no choice but to offer his body—

It makes it all the more rousing in a way he can't quantify. Like the difference between wine and whisky, or rain and thunder. One is good, but the other is a treat.

One is a comfort and the other is a thrill.

"You want my hands or my mouth?" he asks her. He wants to give her both, he wants to give her so much pleasure that when she thinks of tonight, she'll think of him alongside Auden and Delphine. He wants to take care of her, make her happy, because Proserpina's happiness is like a sunshine that feeds everything; it's like water trickling through him, sweet and life-giving.

He'll do anything to make her happy.

"What if," she murmurs, "you give me something else?"

It takes him a moment to understand.

"Proserpina..."

"I've been sure for weeks now," she tells him. "Since the day I found you in the Thorncombe Library. I knew I wanted to do this with you."

He runs a hand over his face, hardly daring to dream this is real. "You might still be sore, though. I don't want this to hurt."

She gives him a wicked smile. "I like things that hurt."

"Fuck, Poe. You're killing me."

She laughs, but then the smile fades a little. "Do you want to? I mean, will it be okay for you since we're both—well, I'm not—" She pauses. "In the shower, I noticed you needed—"

Saint presses a finger to her lips and she stops talking. "Yes, I want to. Yes, I'll be okay. If I need something more during, then we'll figure it out, right? There's nothing that two people who like each other can't figure out if they're willing to try."

And he means it. But really, this is enough—her needing him and his body. The illusion of having no choice but to serve her with pleasure…

Her smile comes back. "Okay."

And that's how St. Sebastian ends up rolling on a condom that Poe pulls out of her nightstand from a box she's been keeping "just in case" she managed to seduce him. The fact that she even thought she'd have to try to seduce him at all when he'd spend the rest of his life in bed with her if he could is laughable, but also brutally touching.

He's wanted. He's desired. He's so wanted and desired that the sexiest, smartest woman he's ever met has been hoping and wishing to fuck him. It makes him feel powerful and strong, and when he parts her legs with an impatient thigh and wedges the head of his erection against her cunt, he feels even more powerful still. He slides into her with one unrepentant thrust and covers her body with his own.

She comes almost immediately. He's never done this, never had any kind of sex until this very night, but some instinct makes him reach between them and fondle her clit while he strokes into her. It's hard—hard to concentrate when his thick organ is squeezed into the tightest, wettest, hottest thing he's ever known, when his climax is practically shredding the inside of his belly, when even in the darkness, he can make out the quiver of Poe's tits and the open, breathless part of her sweet mouth—but he does it. He manages to rub her clit just right, and then she's trembling and shaking and finally fluttering around him with delicate contractions that rip away the last of his control. He takes her hand and pushes it into his hair.

"Pull," he gasps out. "Pull hard."

She pulls.

Giving in to the primal, mindless urge to mate, he pumps his hips hard and deep, thrusting forcefully enough to make her cry out and bang the headboard against the wall, feeling the sweet, controlling anchor of her hand in his hair all the while. It's enough, it's more than enough, and with a low grunt, he fills a condom for the very first time in his life. Pulse after wet, hot pulse, he stays buried in her until he's drained the last of himself, until her thighs loosen from around his hips.

And before he pulls out, he kisses her mouth and whispers, "You have me, Proserpina."

And she says back, simply but happily, "I have you."

Becket is nearly violent with frustration when he gets to the south door and realizes he's not alone, but years of fighting back the blistering zeal means he's able to pretend his way to a smile and a "Fancy seeing you here," and he fakes it well enough that Auden smiles back.

"Proserpina is resting with Saint," he says. "And I thought I'd go check the ruins one last time and maybe bring some of the things back. How's Delphine?"

"Chipper. Wide awake and talking a mile a minute. So I also thought I'd check on the ruins."

Auden laughs a little and bends to pull on his rain boots, and Becket does the same. Sir James Frazer, who can hear boots being put on from two villages away, bounds into the makeshift boot room and wags his tail at Auden.

Auden's mouth slants in what seems to be a regretful contemplation of how much mud Sir James Frazer will bring back in with him, but he ends up opening the door with a sigh. "Oh, all right," he tells the dog, who gives his master a happy look and then trots out into the rainy night.

Both men pull on coats, and Auden flips open the top of a bench to extract umbrellas and an old flashlight. He hands it to Becket along with an umbrella, and then wordlessly they follow the dog outside.

It must be near two in the morning, and the darkness, if anything, is even thicker than before. The old flashlight's beam, while a pleasantly nostalgic yellow, is not much stronger than Becket's lantern from earlier, and by now, the rain has so slicked the world over with mud that the path is downright treacherous. Not that any of that slows down Sir James, who tears off into the woods at random intervals and then tears back, reappearing with even muddier paws and a few extra wet leaves clinging to his fur.

Still though, despite the unwelcome addition of another person, Becket's frustration eases. Auden is quiet as they walk, as if caught up in his own thoughts, and Sir James is always good company, and anyway, Becket is doing what he needs to do, what the zeal demands of him. He's going back to the chapel.

If there had been any earlier doubt that he'd remain unmoved during the ceremony, if there had been lingering mental distance between him and these old rituals—well, it's all obliterated now. He feels different, unwoven or unmade, like God has unknotted the bindings of his soul and let it sprawl everywhere like a mess of roots and branches and vines. He's felt this loose and grasping before, but never this much, never this wildly, and the zeal has never consumed him this deeply for so many hours at a time.

All he wants is to kneel in front of the chapel's altar and cry. With gratitude and wonder and sheer awe at the hand of God in his life—a hand that can reach him even through fire and sex and cakes and ale.

But when they get to the thorn chapel and Auden begins hunting down their things by the light of his phone, Becket doesn't go in front of the altar. Instead he walks behind it to examine the tree.

It has fallen some ways—the stump was a good ten feet outside the chapel wall, and is now a broken, splintered mess from where the trunk has cracked away and fallen—and the force of the fall was enough to drive it deep into the grass hump that served as their altar.

He tells his parishioners not to assign meaning to events like this, not to confuse coincidences with omens, but he can't take his own advice. This feels like an omen to him.

He's just not sure if it's good or bad.

I know what you did.

Troubling memories stir to the surface of his mind, and Becket takes a step away from the altar and the tree. He looks away, he tries to think of earlier tonight, of Delphine and Poe gilded into holy figures by the light of the fire, he tries to think of St. Brigid and candles and cookies and the dog and Auden moving through the ruins like a methodical ghost doomed to pick up wet blankets—he tries, he tries, he tries.

I know what you did.

It was his own voice that had said that. Not now, but six years ago. Here in this very place.

I know what you did.

He closes his eyes, but it only brings the memory closer to the fore, only shows him the ruins as they were that summer—lush and green and rippling with magic. He'd come to them on his own, rented a car and driven away from his grandmother's house in Cornwall, where he'd been staying for the summer.

He'd parked in the village and picked his way over the public footpaths ringing the valley until he'd managed to sight the house, and using the house and the river as reference points, had tramped his way through the wilderness to the thorn chapel.

For a long few hours, he'd been alone with God, his thoughts and feelings bent wholly on the contemplation of the divine and what it wanted from him.

And then he was no longer alone. He'd known it from the prickle along the backs of his arms and his neck, he'd known it from the way the breeze changed, as if it was trying to tell Becket the truth about the intruder.

Bad.

Wrong.

The intruder had been none other than Ralph Guest, Auden's father. He'd stridden into the clearing with his head down and expensive flowers clutched in his fist, and so he hadn't seen Becket until they were inside the walls together.

"You're not allowed here," Ralph said once he noticed Becket, glaring at him with that haughty, dangerous cool that only a Guest could muster.

"You don't recognize me?" Becket asked. It had been six years, after all, since he'd been here last, so he shouldn't have been surprised, but it did confuse him a little. How could he not be indelibly burned into the memories of everyone here when they were all burned into his?

Ralph's mouth had screwed up into an angry, little sneer. "Of course I recognize you."

Bad, the thorn chapel seemed to whisper around Becket. *Wrong.*

"Why do you have flowers?" Becket asked him then, but he already knew why.

He already knew where Ralph would lay them down too.

Ralph's eyes had narrowed then. "*Don't. Test. Me*," he'd hissed. "I could still call the police. It's only for the sake of your father that I won't."

The hand clutching the flowers had been shaking though.

Ralph Guest was afraid. And Becket knew why.

"I know what you did," he told the older man. "I know what you did here."

"You don't know anything," Ralph said uncertainly. Fearfully.

"*I know what you did.*"

Ralph's fear crystalized into anger, and he'd taken one threatening step toward Becket, which was all it took to send Becket running, scrambling up steep hills through the woods until he emerged onto a footpath, back sweaty and palms covered in mud from how often he'd fallen.

He'd been too frightened to return for years, too frightened even to think of it; only taking the collar had given him enough sense of safety to return. And by then, Ralph was too sick to terrorize anyone any longer, even people trespassing into the chapel ruins.

In the here and now, Becket walks back to the altar and the tree. It's too dark and wet to see much, even with the flashlight, but he knows the exact spot he's looking for.

The spot where Ralph Guest would have laid down his flowers.

In the dark and the cold, still smelling like smoke and mud and spilled Prosecco, Father Becket Hess gets to his knees.

And he prays.

Rebecca decides to admit it to herself.

She liked tonight.

She liked it more than she had any right to and far more than she thought she would. She liked the sex, of course, even if she wasn't the one having it, and she liked the cool, wet night all around her, the trees and the grass and the thorns and the rain. She even liked the ritual, though she doesn't know if she'd ever admit that to anyone else, and anyway, she was just responding to the orderliness of it, the feeling of being with her friends and marking out a fresh start.

Who wouldn't respond to that?

Unfortunately, and most troublesomely for her, the part she liked best about tonight is currently naked and wrapped in her blanket, with clean blond hair spilling every which way across her pillow.

She can still hear the sweetest word in the world coming from Delphine's lips. *Yes.*

Yes.

She relished every second of helping Delphine clean up, of bandaging her hand, of cuddling her to sleep, like she was playing house, but instead of *house*, the game was kink, the game was *Your Very Own Submissive to Keep.* The game was pretending this was their real life, where Rebecca could spend the evening whispering commands into Delphine's ear, and then spend hours afterwards petting her and coddling her.

Rebecca stands up and walks to her window, unable to see much past the rain but not caring. She doesn't feel ready to stop playing the game. In fact, her body is burning with unmet need, and while any good Domme has her share of scenes where she doesn't come, Rebecca actually feels like the hunger has gotten worse since the night's gone on. Like the ritual cracked her open, and now she's going to be a wet, horny mess until forever from now.

She risks a glance back at Delphine, at the exposed shoulder and the high curve of a breast.

God, she wants to fuck. She wants to fuck so badly she's shaking with it.

But she won't wake Delphine up; she can't. That would be beyond thoughtless, and strange anyway, given that whatever truce they've struck around the ritual is bound to be dissolved by morning. It's safer to stay away, safer not to crawl over Delphine and pin her wrists to the bed and bite her neck until Delphine is begging to eat her mistress's pussy…

Rebecca shudders, leans her forehead against the cool glass of the window.

Stop playing this game, she berates herself. It doesn't matter that the very thought of Delphine's soft, giving body makes her wet; it doesn't matter that somehow with Delphine Rebecca forgets that she has to be perfect, that she has to work harder than everyone else, that she has to earn everything she wants two or three times over.

It doesn't matter because it wouldn't make sense, this game, and Rebecca doesn't have time for things that don't make sense.

No time at all.

Delphine wakes up with a stretch about twenty minutes later, one of those long stretches that one could do forever, and then she yawns and rolls onto her side. Last night she slept in the guest bed, and now she's in a bed that smells like something clean and mossy and floral. A garden of a bed.

Rebecca's bed.

Delphine looks across the room to see Rebecca standing by the window in a nightgown, all dainty spaghetti straps and thin red silk, with her arms crossed over her chest and her head bowed. Her hair is bound up in a satin scarf, exposing the slender swan curve of her neck and the exquisite wings of her shoulder blades, and she's so pretty it hurts to look at her.

But Delphine keeps looking. She's learning she likes it when it hurts.

"Come to bed," she says. She doesn't even know why she says it, except it's the only thing she wants right now. She doesn't want Rebecca far away, she wants Rebecca close. She doesn't want Rebecca holding herself, she wants Rebecca holding *her*.

She's too tired and too wrung raw by the ritual to pretend anything else.

Rebecca finally turns to her, and Delphine doesn't need more light to know that her eyebrow is raised. "I give the orders in this room," Rebecca says, but she sounds more amused than annoyed.

"Come to bed...please?" Delphine tries again.

Rebecca studies her for a long minute. And then with a sigh so big it moves her shoulders up and down, she drops her arms and comes to the edge of the bed. But she doesn't climb in, she just sits next to Delphine and stares down at her.

"What's wrong?" Delphine whispers. "Why won't you get in bed?"

"Because," Rebecca says mildly, "if I get into this bed with you, then I'm going to fuck you."

Delphine's mouth falls open as Rebecca adds, "And if I fuck you, then I'm probably going to want to do it again, and maybe a third time, and I think you need your sleep."

Delphine shakes her head so fast she can hear her hair sliding over Rebecca's satin pillowcases. "I'm not tired. I promise. I don't need sleep."

A small and tender smile pulls at the creased fullness of Rebecca's mouth. "You do," she says, but she can't seem to stop herself from reaching down and tracing the place where the blanket covers Delphine's breasts. And then she drags the blanket down, slowly, so slowly that Delphine has no choice but to feel every fiber dragging over her sensitive nipples.

Rebecca lets out a surprised exhale once Delphine's breasts are exposed, as if she's forgotten what they look like. As if she underestimated what seeing them would do to her. "Just for a minute," Rebecca whispers, as if to herself, and then she's straddling Delphine with long, lean legs, her nightgown bunching up around her waist as she dips her head to give one of Delphine's nipples a mean, hard suck.

Delphine cries out—happiness, pure, pleasured happiness—and Rebecca claps a hand over her mouth and moves to the other nipple, sucking and pulling until Delphine can feel it in her belly, feel her clit jumping in response.

Rebecca nuzzles a breast, nips at it, then looks up at Delphine. "I want to fuck you," she says plainly. "But it's a bad idea."

Delphine wants to whine and kick her feet, she wants to stomp around like Veruca Salt because she wants to be fucked and she wants it *now*. "There are no bad ideas tonight," she says, trying to sound rational because she knows Rebecca likes rational. "We can just pretend we're back in the clearing still. That this is part of the ritual and we don't have a choice."

"There's always a choice," Rebecca says. "We have one now. Either we fuck, we fuck my way, and we fuck a lot—and tomorrow we wake up ashamed. Or we go to bed like responsible adults and pretend this was all a dream."

"Is this really a question?"

Another eyebrow from Rebecca.

When Rebecca doesn't answer, Delphine says impatiently, "The first choice then, please. The one with fucking."

"You have sex one time, and now you're insatiable," mutters Rebecca.

Delphine wriggles underneath her. "Yes. Can we do more sex now?"

"You're lucky you're cute," Rebecca tells her. "And that I need to fuck you so badly."

For some reason, this kindles warmth in Delphine's chest in a way that all of Auden's sweet and romantic sentiments never did. She beams up at Rebecca as if Rebecca's just recited sonnets to her.

"You think I'm cute?"

"No, I only bite the breasts of women I *don't* think are cute. Put your hands up above your head and cross them at the wrists."

Delphine does as she's told, and then smiles again. The feeling of her wrists crossed above her head is better than being handed a bouquet of flowers. She doesn't know why. Maybe it shouldn't be. Maybe she should hate anything like this after what happened to her at Audra Bishop's summer party.

But she doesn't. She loves it. It's like everything is starting to make sense now that she's found this, and now that she's here, she can't help but think *of course, of course it's this.*

Of course this is where I should have been all along.

And then Rebecca moves up to sit over Delphine's face, lifting the silk nightgown and bunching it against the taut, dark skin of her belly. "This first time is going to be fast," Rebecca says. "But I have to come now if I'm going to take my time with you later."

And then all Delphine can taste and smell and breathe is Rebecca's garden-smelling skin and the secret place between her legs, and she doesn't think anything at all but *yes, yes, yes* for a very long time.

Auden gathers the wet blankets and dark lanterns, checks anything that was ever on fire tonight or that ever even thought about being on fire, and then makes for the path. Becket's already gone ahead, murmuring something about needing to get back to the rectory and sleep a little before morning Mass. So it's Auden alone who piles what he can into his arms and leaves the slow-misting ruins behind him.

All told, it's not a pleasant walk. The blankets are sopping wet and cold as hell, and the three lanterns he managed to hook with his fingers are clanking together with an obnoxious racket.

But he barely notices. His thoughts are everywhere else.

His thoughts are back in that tiny shower stall, crammed in with Proserpina's tiny, curvy body and Saint's sculpted one. His thoughts are on the swollen silk of Poe's cunt as he plucked an orgasm from her like ripe fruit off a tree.

He's never done that before, made someone come, and in the last two hours, he did it twice. And fuck if it wasn't the best thing he's ever felt, someone coming all over his hand, someone buckling and moaning and spilling everywhere because of *him.* It's as good as spanking. As good as kissing every cut on Poe's hand and then dressing every little wound. As good as feeling St. Sebastian's lip ring against his mouth.

His thoughts are also still on the ritual, on the sex, on the fire. On the thorns. He thinks about Delphine, who's no longer his, and his heart jolts, and he thinks about Proserpina naked in the firelight and his heart jolts harder. He thinks about how he felt walking the path up to the clearing, about the strange, near-violent clarity that came to him as they moved through the ancient motions of the ceremony.

He feels different, although he can't exactly quantify *how.* He's still being ripped apart from the inside by the same thorns, but it's as if they've finally found a place to take root. A place to anchor themselves. He doesn't understand them—his needs, his hurts, the hopes he's forgotten how to name—but it feels like, for the first time, *they* understand *him.*

And that's something he didn't have before Imbolc night.

By the time he gets back inside the house, he feels resolved to one thing at least—it's time he figured things out with Proserpina. It's time he courted her, if such an old-fashioned word can be permitted. He'll go in and he'll snuggle her for the rest of the night, and when she wakes up, he'll tell her everything. About the things he wants, about what he wants with her. She told him what he'd have to do to earn her—now he'll tell her he's ready to begin.

As for Saint, he has no illusions things will change. There's too much past between them for a kiss and a hand job to make any difference now. Which is fine.

Just fine.

Saint's hurt him enough for one lifetime—although honestly, Auden can't think of a single way Saint could hurt him any more than he already has.

Wet things deposited and rain boots pulled off, Auden makes his way upstairs to Poe's bedroom, his heart easing with each step. He knows it's too soon after Delphine, but he'll figure it out. He'll do as he has done and take things slowly, he'll speak transparently, let Poe take the lead—

A low cry reaches his ears, a low cry coupled with heavy, masculine grunts, and Auden freezes.

It's coming from behind Poe's door, and even though he knows, he knows immediately, he still forces himself forward to the door and he opens it, just a crack, to witness the scene within.

St. Sebastian is braced over Poe, rutting fiercely between her legs. And she's rutting just as fiercely back—arching her back and whimpering deliciously. They're fucking.

God.

They're fucking.

And he's about to close the door, he really is, when Poe comes.

He's seen her come on someone else's hand, he's seen her come on his own—but this is different, and he can't tell if it's jealousy or shock that makes it that way, only that it does. Only that it reverberates through him with something more potent and dangerous than arousal on its own, and he can only barely fight off the fantasy of banging the door open, striding inside, and taking both of them in hand.

He's hard before the first cry even leaves her mouth; the heel of his palm is grinding against his erection before the second cry even starts.

He could do it, he knows. He could shove his way in there and—

No.

No.

He drops his hand and closes the door as quietly as he opened it, and then he turns around and slumps, his cock throbbing and his heart pounding and something hurting so pitilessly behind his ribs and up in his throat that he nearly drops down to his knees.

No, this is not his bedroom, that is not his bed. The two people inside are not *his*, although by God if they were, he'd spend every minute of every day making them know it. He'd fuck and spank and bite and tease until they were his by right, until he'd earned them. Like he was going to earn Poe, before.

Before just now.

Before he knew she wanted someone else.

Tears prick at the back of his eyes, and he feels like an idiot. Foolish for thinking lovely, perfect Poe was interested in him, as spoiled and thorny as he is, and foolish for thinking Saint didn't have the power to hurt him anymore. He rubs at his throat, his chest, his face. He tries to take a deep breath, but it seems to stop somewhere right below his collarbone, not making it down into his lungs.

He won't have the chance to earn Proserpina Markham after all.

Down the hall, Rebecca's door opens and she emerges in a silk robe, saying something over her shoulder to someone inside—presumably Delphine.

She turns to go to the bathroom and then sees Auden against the door.

"What are you doing?" she asks at the same moment a broken, telling moan echoes from out of Poe's room. Her face lengthens in sympathetic understanding, and she comes forward and loops her arm through Auden's and pulls him away, down to the very end of the hall.

"You okay?" she asks him, bending her knees to catch his eyes because he can't seem to lift his head.

"Yeah," he mumbles in a voice that means *absolutely not.*

She gives him a brisk, Quartey hug and then puts her hands on his shoulders. "It's been inevitable, Auden, they've been mooning after each other since the day she got here. You would have had to have been blind not to see it. And you've been engaged up until *last night.*"

"I know. I know. I just thought…"

He doesn't even know. He doesn't even know what he just thought.

He suddenly feels like the worst of everything, not just stupid but also selfish, and not just selfish, but also toxic. Like his father but worse because he'd known better and he'd still let this place infect him. He'd still let it sweep him away, he'd still chased after its secret ways and hidden stories as if they mattered in real life. As if they could erase all the ways he was slowly failing everyone around him.

I don't kneel for selfish men. Isn't that what Poe said to him last night?

And what could be more selfish than the craven, grasping man he is now?

But looking down into his best friend's concerned face, there is still one thing that makes sense. One thing that doesn't feel tainted or ruined or unworthy.

"I want to learn," he says abruptly.

Her eyebrows pull together. "Learn what?"

"I want to learn how to be like you."

"I'm guessing you don't mean a Ghanaian landscape architect," she says slowly.

He shakes his head. "Kink. How to do it right. How to play. How to keep everyone safe."

She searches his face, as if trying to decide how much of this is genuine and how much of this is about the couple still moaning down the hall—but whatever she sees there seems to satisfy her, because after a long minute, she finally gives him a short, businesslike nod.

"Okay then, Guest," she says. "I'll teach you."

"Thank you," he says fervently. "Thank you."

She touches his cheek, shaking her head a little. "You need it as badly as Poe and Delphine do. I'm not sure how you've gone this long, but we'll get you all fixed up, and within a week or two, all of this—" she waves back at Poe's door "—will be a distant memory."

"God. Do you promise?"

He gets the definitive Rebecca nod for an answer.

"I promise."

28

For the second day in a row, I wake up to my phone ringing.

"Hello?" I mumble, sitting up and then shielding my face against the blaze of sunlight. *The rain must be gone*, I think. *Maybe we really did bring in spring.*

"Poe," comes St. Sebastian's voice. "You need to come to the chapel. Like right now."

I yawn, stretching my shoulders and pointing my toes and feeling deep, deep parts of my body twinge with delicious soreness. I vaguely remember St. Sebastian kissing me on the lips and telling me he was going to the ruins to chop up the tree, but it was an event that immediately fell into the black hole of narcolepsy sleep.

"Are you calling from the ruins?" I ask. "Can you even get good service out there?"

"No. I'm calling from the edge of the woods. Please, Poe. Get dressed and meet me."

His voice is grim when he adds, "It's important."

Within thirty minutes, I'm at the edge of the woods, where St. Sebastian is pacing. Without a coat, predictably.

"How are you not cold?" I ask, as we start mounting the path up to the clearing.

"Been chopping wood," is the short reply.

"Why again?"

He runs his hand through his hair in a jerky movement that reminds me of Auden. "Because it needed doing. You know. If we wanted to use the chapel again."

Again.

Last night was perfect, perfect and magical and everything I'd hoped it would be, and so why should we stop? Why shouldn't we do another one?

Maybe for May Day, like Delphine had suggested. My heart tightens with excitement when I think about it.

"That was thoughtful of you," I tell him. "Thank you."

He bites his lip ring. "Please don't thank me."

"Okay?"

But he won't elaborate, and eventually I don't have enough breath to talk anyway, because he's walking so fast that I practically have to jog to keep up.

"Slow down," I puff as we reach the clearing's edge. "I'm too short to keep up with you."

He glances back at me without answering, and then keeps striding forward. I narrow my eyes at his well-defined back, deciding to be irritated no matter how good that back looks through the worn cotton of his T-shirt. I fail to see what could be so important that it's worth dragging me out of bed and then jogging across half the estate—

Oh.

Holy shit.

St. Sebastian has clearly been hard at work this morning, and the entire length of the fallen tree is now stacked in charred, even chunks off to the side of the platform, which he's left intact—presumably for future use.

Chopping all that wood is an impressive feat, but that's not what has me stunned. It's the altar itself. It's what's left of the serene, grass-covered hummock that we used just last night.

"The earth was so soft from all the rain that the tree displaced almost the entire mound," St. Sebastian says of the muddy mess. "So after I chopped up the tree, I grabbed the shovel and thought maybe I could clear some of it away, you know. Just the worst of it."

"Of course," I say, approaching the former altar. "Smart idea. Was there anything underneath the mud?"

"Yes," he says slowly.

My blood races fast and curious. "There was? Like the original church altar? Saint, that's a huge deal!"

"I found something made of stone—I think it was the church's altar. But…Poe—"

I'm to the altar now, ready to move around to where the most mud seems to have been cleared away so I can see the stone, but something in St. Sebastian's voice stops me. I turn to face him.

He's stopped a few feet behind me and he's holding something out. Something small and colorful in his hand.

"It's plastic," he says, a little hoarsely. "So it didn't—"

I take the little card out of his hand, and I'm about to ask him more questions—what it is and where near the altar he found it and why he looks so upset right now—but then I glance down, and everything in my body seems to rush up toward my head. My stomach, my heart, my blood—everything floating up and crowding my mind until I can't breathe or hear or think.

From my fingertips, a happy, healthy, and alive Adalina Kernstow Markham smiles up at me. Probably the only woman in the Kansas State Licensing Bureau's history to smile in her driver's license photo, but there you have it. She was a smiler. Every picture of her on a dig was her covered in dirt and grinning up over some piece of pottery that looked like every other piece of pottery that she'd found. She'd only been in her mid-thirties when she left us, but even by that young age she'd had smile lines around her eyes and mouth.

She used to laugh so much that strangers would compliment her on it.

I look down at her driver's license and nothing makes sense for a minute. Why is it *here*, in the chapel, why is it covered in flecks of mud?

"It was behind the altar," Saint says quietly. "My shovel caught the tip of it, and then I had to."

"Had to what?" I whisper, turning back toward the mud.

"I had to keep digging," he says. Sadly. "To see if there was more."

I take a step and then another step, but I'm not even really sure where I'm going or why I'm going—except I do know, that's the terrible truth, I do know where I'm going.

I do know why.

Saint didn't have to dig deep. Less than foot down and a foot into what used to be the hummock of the altar, I see the pearled scatter of finger bones. Higher up, the deceptively graceful curve of an orbital bone and the unmistakable beginning of the dome of a skull.

A human skull.

Human finger bones.

My mother's driver's license trembles in my hand.

"No," I say.

"The license was where maybe a coat pocket would have been," he says softly. "Poe, I'm so sorry, I'm so fucking sorry."

"*No,*" I say again, louder this time. My voice doesn't sound like my own—it's garbled and broken and so high-pitched it sounds like a child's. "*No.*"

"Poe..."

"They searched here," I tell him, my voice still wavering and thin. "They *searched* here. They didn't find her. She wasn't here, this isn't her—"

"Poe."

"It can't be her," I say, I plead, and then I'm crying, so fast and so hard that my entire body is shaking with it. "It can't be, I know it can't. She can't really be—"

I'm on my knees now, but I don't remember falling there. I'm on my knees and Saint's on his too, and he's holding me, crooning something low in my ear, soothing me like you'd soothe a wild animal. He's stroking my hair and rocking me back and forth and nothing is real, nothing can be real right now or ever, ever again.

"Shh," Saint comforts me. "Shh." And then he starts murmuring something I don't recognize at first, until suddenly I do. It's the Salve

Regina—the closing prayer of the Rosary. One of those prayers Catholic children grow up with stitched into the background noise of life, one of those prayers so ever-present that I can't even remember when I first learned it.

"Hail, holy Queen, mother of mercy," he says, "Hail, our life, our sweetness and our hope."

I know he's searching for something, anything, to help me right now, even a prayer he doesn't believe in. But it works. The familiar cadence of the words cuts through my hysteria the tiniest bit—I'm able to fill my lungs, able to feel the cold mud on my knees.

"To thee do we cry, poor, banished children of Eve," he continues, and I'm able to breathe again and again and again. I know this prayer, I've heard my parents pray it. I grew up praying it. I've heard Becket pray it.

I murmur the next part along with St. Sebastian, clutching my mother's driver's license tightly in my hand as we do. "To thee do we send up our sighs," I say. I dare a look at the bones again, at where they peek out from the wet, rich earth. "Mourning and weeping in this vale of tears."

Next to, and slightly above, the bones, I finally see the altar stone itself. Thick and gray.

I stop praying.

"Poe?" Saint asks, feeling me stiffen all over again. I don't answer, because I can't, because everything is suddenly gone from me—even the prayer, even the tears.

On the edge of the altar stone, on the side that would have faced the priest, is carved a single word in a very ancient hand. The carved letters are deep enough that most of them are still filled with mud, although Saint's scraped the stone clean enough that the word is clear and legible, a word I'd be able to read even if I'd never seen it before.

But I have seen it before.

The word is in Latin.

All along, the answers to all my questions were right here at the thorn chapel's altar. Buried and just waiting to be found. I turn my face into Saint's chest so I don't have to see that word anymore, so I don't have to see my mother's picture or my mother's orbital bone or the grass that once covered my mother's grave.

But it doesn't matter. The word is seared into my mind just like everything else.

Convivificat.

It's Only Just Begun...

Poe, Auden and Saint aren't anywhere near done with each other yet, and Thornchapel has only just started to give up its secrets...

Find out what happens next in *Feast of Sparks*, coming this June.

Add Feast of Sparks to your TBR now!

Author's Note

Thornchapel exists in a peculiar and otherworldly eddy in my brain, and therefore you will have noticed a couple of the creative liberties I have taken in order to place Thornchapel at the heart of these six characters.

Firstly, Thorncombe—along with the River Thorne and the Thorne Valley—do not exist and have no direct models, although I've pulled inspiration from the Dartmoor villages, woods, and moors I've visited, and tried to be faithful in the details, if not the structure. Thornchapel itself is the brain-baby of a few different muses: Haddon Hall in Derbyshire, Cotehele House, and Lanhydrock House (the last two are both in Cornwall) and while the chapel ruins are constructed from pure fancy, the processional stone row leading to the chapel's entrance is modeled after the Merrivale stone rows in Devon.

Secondly, I've taken some freedom around the celebrations and rites celebrated during Imbolc and St. Brigid's Day. Imbolc is not necessarily associated with handfasting, and its association with fertility is less, *ah*, obviously libidinous than Beltane's, but Thornchapel is its own little world, and therefore I've given it unique customs. Also sexier ones.

Thirdly, Poe's experience with narcolepsy is directly cast from my own, and therefore is only a very limited view of the symptoms and secondary symptoms narcoleptics live with. It's a complicated and misunderstood disease (might I add, also a *very annoying* disease), and I'm fully embracing the chance to make Poe's narcolepsy something sexy, destined and powerful, since in my own life, it's rarely these things.

Acknowledgments

Some books are too difficult for me to even trace the barest shape of my debts, but I'll try—

This book would not be here without the tireless work of Serena McDonald, Melissa Gaston, Candi Kane, and Ashley Lindemann. Not only do they keep the lights on while I disappear to work, but their patience and encouragement kept me going through the bleak winter months of grappling with the hardest book I've faced yet.

I owe a huge debt to my friends and betas—Julie Murphy, Ashley Lindemann, Nana Malone, and Vanessa Reyes—who helped me talk through this book and frame the characters and environment respectfully. I also want to thank the incredible and incredibly gifted Robin Murphy for lending me her thoughts, wisdom, and library when it came to Thornchapel's magic and ritual processes.

I'm beyond grateful for Nancy Smay and Erica Russikoff for their editing prowess and insights into story and language—and also how thoughtfully and kindly they talked me out of circles of artistic despair.

Another big debt is owed to Natalie C. Parker, Tessa Gratton, Sarah MacLean, Nana Malone, Becca Mysoor, Kennedy Ryan, Kayti McGee, Jana Aston, and Jean Siska, for encouragement, craft advice, late-night texts, or listening to me fuss along the way. Also all the Gatlinburg retreaters, ST authors, and DHI authors who form a collective of powerful, community-driven women. Thank you.

To my agent team—Rebecca Friedman, Flavia Viotti, and Meire Dias—thank you for all the time and energy you put into Sierra both at home and internationally. I couldn't do it without you!

And finally, my biggest debt is to all of you, my readers. I count myself indelibly blessed to be able to create such weird little stories and have you let me. Thank you for indulging my latest foray into the wilds of my carnal imaginings, and thank you for joining me.

Also by Sierra Simone

Thornchapel:

A Lesson in Thorns

Feast of Sparks

Harvest of Sighs

Door of Bruises

Misadventures:

Misadventures with a Professor

Misadventures of a Curvy Girl

Misadventures in Blue (Coming September 2019)

The New Camelot Trilogy:

American Queen

American Prince

American King

The Moon (Merlin's Novella)

The Priest Series:

Priest

Midnight Mass: A Priest Novella

Sinner

Co-Written with Laurelin Paige

Porn Star

Hot Cop

The Markham Hall Series:

The Awakening of Ivy Leavold

The Education of Ivy Leavold

The Punishment of Ivy Leavold

The Reclaiming of Ivy Leavold

The London Lovers:

The Seduction of Molly O'Flaherty

The Persuasion of Molly O'Flaherty

The Wedding of Molly O'Flaherty

About the Author

Sierra Simone is a USA Today bestselling former librarian who spent too much time reading romance novels at the information desk. She lives with her husband and family in Kansas City.

Sign up for her newsletter to be notified of releases, books going on sale, events, and other news!

www.thesierrasimone.com
thesierrasimone@gmail.com